Praise for *In Sho*

"A bestselling food writer tries his hand at fiction. . . . The rarely seen but quite enjoyable novella form serves this maiden effort well."

—*Kirkus Reviews*

". . . with echoes of James Salter, . . . [these novellas] are deep in their exploration of the characters' divided hearts."

—*Publisher's Weekly*

"Ruhlman dispels the notion that novellas don't allow for a well-developed narrative. *In Short Measures* is rich, textured, and carefully constructed not only for surprises, but also with a powerful love of language and description throughout."

—*Washington Independent Review of Books*

"Fans of Michael Ruhlman's nonfiction and new readers alike will marvel, as I did, at his fictional debut. Ruhlman writes with intelligence and grace about the things that matter: love and loss and redemption. This is a literary achievement of the first order."

—Ann Hood, award-winning and bestselling author of *The Knitting Circle*

"*In Short Measures* is a propulsively well-written trio of novellas linked by a sense of loss and an inquiry into the impossible past. Ruhlman's voice is poetic and visceral, and his characters feel both familiar and strange in the way of the best fiction. This is a richly layered book, full of surprises and pleasures."

—Kate Christensen, author of *The Great Man*, winner of the PEN/Faulkner Award for Fiction

"In his fictional debut, Michael Ruhlman gives us three intriguing novellas about loss, regret, and the passage of time: how we lose each other and ourselves, and what we do when we reach the outer limits of the commitments we've made."

—Lily King, bestselling and award-winning author of *Euphoria*

"The three novellas in *In Short Measures* take on the joys and sorrows of romance, especially middle-aged nostalgia for the lost, seemingly perfect loves of the past. 'We can't hold feelings for this long, can we?' one character wonders. Yes, Michael Ruhlman answers, we can, and just look what it does to us."

—Stewart O'Nan, author of *West of Sunset*

IN SHORT MEASURES

MEASURES

THREE NOVELLAS

MICHAEL RUHLMAN

Skyhorse Publishing

Visit our website at www.skyhorsepublishing.com.

10 9 8 7 6 5 4 3 2 1

Library of Congress Cataloging-in-Publication Data is available on file.

Cover design by Laura Klynstra

Paperback ISBN: 978-1-5107-1709-1
Ebook ISBN: 978-1-5107-0063-5

Printed in the United States of America

In memory of Reynolds Price
and for
Laura Yorke and Mary Brinkmeyer

Table of Contents

In Short Measures

PART I

One

He appeared again, in the archway one hundred feet away. Just his shadowed silhouette, his form, was visible from that distance, but I knew who he was with the suddenness of a blow to the back of my head.

It's the ordinary lives that are the best, and given what was about to happen because of him, I'm even more certain of this than ever. As most of us lead ordinary lives, I figure it works out right. I count myself a lucky woman to know it.

I've always accepted I wasn't put in this world for any greater purpose than daily constancy to the people around me—my family, my friends, the people I work beside. I have a job to do well each day and a small house and home in a place that matters to me. I cook for family and friends at least three times a week. When I'm greedy for more, I ask God to maintain my power to see this Carolina landscape, to inhale the birch and pine forests I came of age in, to feel the red clay between my toes, to taste the barbecue and fried okra and sweet iced tea native to my place. I've kept my girlish figure without trying, thank you—maybe my one point of pride. Sleep comes easily and my dreams are rarely troubled.

We all have an age we're dealt at birth, an age we hit when we are most ourselves. In men it's more obvious. Anyone who's half awake has encountered thirty-year-old men who are sixty in their souls and will only truly feel at home when their actual age aligns with their spiritual age. The regrettable fact is the majority of men are seventeen at heart and spend their whole adult lives trying to deny it, making themselves and the families they've created miserable. Women tend to hide (or ignore) their spiritual age and present to the world what they think the world wants to see, forever in doubt, and thinking a new haircut or handbag will change who they are so that they can be at ease, which they rarely seem to be, for any long stretch at least.

I was born aged forty-five, have dressed all my life with the same tasteful conservative style as I do today—now that I am actually forty-five—and really for the first time feeling in sync with who I am and where and what I've come to. At life's halfway mark more or less, I'm happy in my daily toil as a curator of collections in Duke University's Rare Book and Manuscript Library, grateful for my brother and sister and their children, and lucky for the few friends I have, content even in that I'm single, relying on the odd flings to make sure the old pleasures remain available and viable. There was a time for me when sex was one of the most reliable sources of unalloyed pleasure I knew, but that's faded. Age, I guess. Today sex has become kind of like cleaning out the fridge—a bit of a hassle but it feels really good once you're done.

Again: good work, good family, good friends, in a place I love. I've seen enough of people to know that this is the best of all possible worlds, and that those called upon by God or Darwin to greatness, whether in the arts, or statesmanship, or any kind of public life, and certainly the very wealthy or very famous, more often than not are unhappy. Certainly the *desire* for any of it—money, fame, power—is a sentence to spiritual purgatory.

But I once suspected I had an actual *purpose*, and I write now with a renewed sense of it: to be there for Em, to watch him and give him whatever he needed, and now may need still. Loving him was a hard side effect of my need to fill him, to tell him it was okay, to let him know that his recklessness and narcissism were necessary for what he aimed to accomplish, were part of the fuel of his ambition, and that his genuine love of the world was his own gift to those who loved him, no matter who he'd burn through in his own hurtle through life.

There, like that, I was utterly and absolutely content the afternoon of May 18, 2010, a warm day, four months ago, in a smooth navy dress, straight brown hair just long enough to keep in a neat ponytail, frameless spectacles befitting my bookish self. There I was, standing in Duke's main quad when he reappeared, descending the steps of the archway where I'd first seen him twenty-five years earlier. There I was, and then I wasn't.

*

One of the qualities that set Em apart, I would come to know after a few short years of obsessive watching long ago, was the fact that he seemed to be both thirteen *and* seventy, and these opposing forces—unmanageable passions and intensity paired with wisdom (or what seemed like it; how would I have known wisdom at age twenty?), barefooted, swami-like calm, understanding, and humor in the face of a world that was fun, kind, absurd at best, but also terrible, even murderous. That was the boy I knew. Aware, and accepting, of it all.

When did I know I loved him? You probably won't buy this, and fine if you don't, but I felt I'd already *been* loving him since before I laid eyes on him. Is that kind of thing possible? I know just enough of this world to answer yes, it is. This story is further proof. A world this cruel and wonderful is bound by mysteries we cannot fathom but are obliged to try, anyone with a brain and heart anyhow. What was it that Nabokov wrote, was it in *Speak, Memory* or *Pale Fire* or an interview? I cherish the Southern people of letters, our Faulkners and Weltys, the Great Man we were to celebrate on this day. But the words of the rootless Russian genius are the ones at the center of my own heart. It was an interview—I found my paperback, *Strong Opinions*—and the words I'm writing down here were in response to a question: "Do you believe in a Divine Being?"

Nabokov's response: "To be quite candid—and what I am going to say now is something I never said before, and I hope it provokes a salutary little chill—I know more than I can express in words, and the little I can express would not have been expressed, had I not known more."

That's exactly how I feel about love—that the world is mysterious, that the heart knows depths that cannot be put into words or actions, and that we are obliged to search and try at least to understand, knowing full well that, were we to be successful in that search, it would be only to deepen the mystery, which would demand deeper quests. Forever. That really is the only proof of success in understanding this world, to have deepened, or in some way enhanced, the mystery. This is why I believe that it was possible to have already been in love with Em the moment I saw him, my body primed just for him, a few days before he began his freshman year at Duke University. Is there a reason why? If there is, I can't say it. I just know it.

Saw him? Beheld him, more like. He appeared within the archway to the main quad, his strawberry blond hair aglow in the late-afternoon sun streaming in through the willow oaks, a blue T-shirt, torn at the shoulder, faded jeans, and bare feet. He led a small pack of fellow freshmen who looked their age, but the only way I knew Em to be a freshman was that they were all headed to a freshman orientation I was helping to run. He was far older inside, plain to see. (The thirteen-year-old part wouldn't come out for another thirty-six hours.)

I remember it today as if it had just happened because it's simply one of those *moments*. You don't forget. This boy seemed literally to glow, while his classmates remained muted, as if they were on the other side of an unwashed window while he alone stood in front of it to catch the sun. His laugh was the first note of his voice I was given, and then a sentence: "Where's the fun in that?" Easy and self-confident, smiling, but he took no notice of the three juniors on the bench outside our dorm as he passed. We were there on their behalf, volunteers to be mentors to the incoming class, Freshman Advisory Counselors, FACs, we were called. My best friend Amanda, Amanda's best friend Sterly, and me, and it took a few minutes for Amanda's words—"Dog in *heat*, dog in *heat!*"—to register and then, turning to her, one moment more to realize she was referring to *me*. And Sterly said, "Grimsley, your face just turned red as a sunset."

I put my elbow hard into Amanda's side and said, "*Y'all.*" I couldn't think of anything more. The boy had wiped my brain clean. "Come on, we're gonna be late."

*

I was seven when Daddy got a teaching job here and we moved from Hampton Park Terrace in Charleston, north to Durham. While I don't recollect much from my youth, I did hang on to the thick South Carolina accent of my mother—proudly, I should add—as well as a perpetual hunger for tidewater shrimp and grits for breakfast anytime I'm up before 6 a.m.

I'm not naturally a sneak, but that day long ago I did find out the boy's name and quickly made sure he was on the list of freshmen I'd be assigned to that afternoon in the Duke Gardens. It was easy because he had a name he himself thought slightly preposterous. We'd gathered into our groups on the big lawn there and I called his name as if I didn't know who'd respond: "Emerson Randall?" He smiled self-consciously and said, "Just call me Em, please."

"Why? Emerson's an interesting name," I said.

He looked at his bare feet and said, "Maybe if I were a nineteenth-century Chicago banker."

"Well, at least you weren't saddled with a name like mine."

"Which is?"

"*Grimsley.*"

He looked up from his feet at me then and smiled, our eyes locked for that first indelible time, and the glow came on again, as if by a self-controlled inner rheostat. I thought for a moment he loved me too, or would soon, or at least *could*, but I'd quickly see that he turned that inner light on for just about anyone who caught his attention. He smiled his natural and easy smile, all full of big white teeth straight out of a Pepsodent commercial, fixed his speckled, hazel-gold eyes on me, and asked, "What kind of a name is that?"

"Family name, a long line of South Carolina Grimsleys, by way of Kentucky."

"Grimsley what?"

"Feller."

Didn't think it possible but his smile got even bigger until it segued into an easy laugh. "Grimsley Feller," he said. He held out his hand. "Grimsley Feller." The grin dimming not one watt.

I only hoped he didn't notice how my jugular throbbed. This Yankee *boy*, not yet eighteen I'd learn, was completely at ease five hundred miles from his lower-middle-class suburban Chicago home—something of a hardscrabble family, as it turned out; he was here on a scholarship—in a sea of strangers at a big new university. And here he had me, two years his senior and unaccustomed to strong emotion, straining for composure.

And twenty-five years later, *twenty-five years*, as if planned by God, punishment for my contented complacency, I happened to be in Duke's main quad, smoothing my navy dress, feeling every bit the middle-aged woman I was, having left the Bryan Center, turned to my right and there, in the archway, he appeared again.

Two

I watched Emerson descend the steps and kept on watching until I became self-conscious, then turned so he'd see only my back if he looked my way. I took a slug from the water bottle I carried. I'd seen enough and did not need an encounter just then. Too stunned. I felt like a storm-blown tree partly uprooted, bent but standing, roots exposed. But of course, he'd been Daniel Blackmore's prize student, or one of them, and had returned to pay his respects on this day of the memorial. I hadn't known he'd be here, hadn't thought of him in years. Not that I didn't feel a part of him was deep down inside me ever since that first vision of him twenty years ago. What are we humans, we animals? How can it be that he remained inside me? Seven or eight years, at least, not a speck of him passed through my mind. Then there he was, and my soul shook. God saying to me again, *behold*. And what did it mean that my first emotion was anger? Diamond-hard and multifaceted, every-faceted, my whole life, anger. *What had I done?*

*

It's the end of summer now and I can finally bring myself to record these events in the early evening coolness, knowing fully and accepting the thrilling consequences of that day, the heavy August heat having finally abated. I can only now bear to think it all through and to write it down.

I saw Em, turned, closed my eyes, sucked down water, and caught my breath. My heart beat so hard I actually put my hand to my chest as if I could slow it. He passed, and I watched him till he turned left toward the Duke Chapel and was out of sight.

Would he have recognized me, would he have known who I was, that boy who shared my dorm room bed more times than I can count before sailing off into his future? Probably not.

How many different ways women can be angry. We circle a spot and our anger strikes its target from any of 360 degrees. Men are mad in a straight line. Simple but effective. We are elusive and unpredictable.

But why *anger*? He had never done me harm, intended or accidental. He'd never done anything but make me laugh, tell me stories, adore my body and please every inch of it. I had a really good body back then. All girl, smooth clear skin, perfect proportions, nothing big and nothing small, just right and intended for guys. A girlfriend kissed me once, out of nowhere, a hard, teeth-clicking kiss, and I kissed back—just from curiosity and, I admit, partly from the surprise of a new experience, kissing a face with such harmless skin. But as for feeling, there was none, and I never accepted or offered a kiss to any other woman. I was glad for her kiss—what was her name, a wild one, nicknamed White Chocolate, can't remember her actual name . . . I grow old. I was glad because it told me plain and clear, I was vigorously and irrevocably hetero, doomed to the sharkskin faces and urgent hard-ons of guys. And given my pleasing twenty-year-old body, I knew what most boys wanted. I just assumed that's what Em was after when he first scratched on my screened window, clinging like a cat to the tree branch. What they all wanted.

One degree of anger, in that moment and in my dry old soul, was a presumption that he wouldn't recognize me. Had I not turned and he'd cast his speckled eyes on me—that his gaze would just pass over me like a ray of sun, pushing through moving cloud cover, passing over a rock on a hillside. Sylvester with the magic pebble—read that to my nieces and nephews a thousand times—me, the rock. He'd remember me, once he knew, I was sure of that, we did share many pleasures, or I was pretty sure—no telling what life does to a person or what a person does to him- or herself. We'd stopped corresponding shortly after he graduated, so I knew only what I'd read about him, and that was years ago. So I'd have been surprised if he didn't remember me, but would he have recognized me on sight?

A couple years ago, I'd gone to my twenty-fifth high school reunion. What a wreck some of the guys had become. You ever doubt life can be hard as bad weather on some people, go to that high school reunion. The women fare worse, but the guys, they either don't damn change but for a general thickening and roughening, or they're just plain different people, fat and bald with yellow teeth and old man breath. When I read a few "Hello, my name is" stickers, I clapped my hand to my mouth as if in happy surprise, but I really just wanted to keep my jaw from hitting the floor in astonishment.

Anger degree number two: Emerson hadn't changed. Yes, thickened very slightly, uniformly, but no belly, trim as a young man, hair graying but just a little, still strawberry blond, and the same easy light gait, no hurry, wondering at it all.

But unlike in my first vision, he was not smiling. His eyes were bright and he still seemed to shine, but there wasn't a trace of a smile. He walked tentatively. If anything, he looked lost, as if he couldn't remember where he was or why he was here or where he was headed.

Three

I sat in the very back row, so far back the people at the podium were barely recognizable. Duke's president, one of Blackmore's English Department colleagues, herself an eminent poet, and two well-regarded novelists who had been students of Blackmore's in the 1960s and 1970s all spoke. Em had been one of Blackmore's prized students in the 1980s, one of about a dozen in Blackmore's menagerie over the course of nearly fifty years of teaching. I'd wondered if Em had been asked to speak, but saw from the program, with both relief and regret, that he was not listed. I wondered if he'd been asked and declined, and then I wondered, if he had *not* been asked, was he hurt? I knew from faculty gossip back then—my father regaled us with hilarious and appalling stories of internecine faculty battles—that there had been much *Sturm und Drang* over Blackmore's behind-the-scenes machinations to give Emerson the honor of valedictory speaker at the 1985 graduation, passing over Maegan Sayer, president of the student body heading to Oxford on a Rhodes scholarship. (She'd fulfill her promise by becoming our state's attorney general by her early forties and was elected just last term to the US House of Representatives.) The scholarship had been an issue as well, as Blackmore himself had earned one in 1955 and had labored on behalf of Emerson's application.

Em had told me after the fact that he didn't want it, that he had applied only at Blackmore's insistence, and at the time he did anything that Blackmore insisted upon. I believed him. Em wasn't the sour-grapes sort, and I don't think he wanted more study, only the attention and the honor of it. By his senior year, he was fairly wild and needed to get out of school, clearly ready to burst into his own in the adult world of Manhattan.

What had Emerson done upon leaving Duke? He'd spent one bad year working in Manhattan, that I knew, but after, I'm not altogether sure. Bits and pieces of hearsay were mainly what I got at reunions and in my work for the university. I kept my ear to the ground from here, via the alumni department. I knew that Em struggled in New York, as one was supposed to do, but when Blackmore's agent was unable to place Em's novel, Em segued seamlessly into journalism and used his charisma and charm to smooth-talk his way into numerous celebrity lairs for *Vanity Fair* profiles, making contacts he would parlay into even greater success in the entertainment industry. And it was in this respect that I'd last read about him—must have been seven years ago—in *Entertainment Weekly*. I wouldn't be caught purchasing this magazine, but I do confess to paging through it given the opportunity. If I'm going to actually wait for a dentist to drill my teeth, I'll indulge in some mental sugar while I do.

Em had been nominated for a TV award for his work on some new crime drama, can't remember the name (my tastes run more toward the English drawing room—filmed versions of Jane Austen novels, *Upstairs, Downstairs*). I remember being genuinely glad for him. He was photographed with his wife, Collista Meriwether, a Los Angeles fine art photographer from a moneyed family. (I Googled her that day, the left side of my mouth drool-slicked and sagging from the Novocain.) He looked in the photo very much as he had today, and his wife looked like your average Los Angeles socialite—blond, ravishingly good looking, and slim from who knows how many egg-white omelets.

I never learned if he actually won the Emmy.

This was *not* the last time he'd entered my mind—rather the most recent knowledge I'd had of him. A few weeks before today's memorial, I'd read some letters he'd written (not to me), but I'd glanced at them only briefly, read one completely, and felt little—mild curiosity if anything, some regret, perhaps, *for him*. I didn't linger on the letters. The truth of the matter is that for four years while Em was a student here, he occupied me continuously, but time mercifully let me forget him, and neither those few traces in the arc of his life I've noted, nor the more personal letters I'd found, unearthed the old feelings. And yet his physical presence on this day, the particular mix of carbon atoms and water and DNA that composed his singular body, seemed literally to transform me as he walked past me, engaging that long-unused gear that had twenty-five years earlier altered my course.

*

The memorial ended with words read by the man himself. He had a rich baritone, and was famed for his readings around here, but the words had in fact been recorded at my mother's funeral service, five years earlier. Blackmore had spoken and concluded with a reading from one of his own favorite poems by Ben Jonson. It was touching then because it showed me how close my mother and he had been.

It is not growing like a tree
In bulk, doth make men better be,
Or standing long an oak, three hundred year,
To fall a log at last, dry, bald, and sere:
A lily of a day
Is fairer far in May,
Although it fall and die that night;
It was the plant and flower of light.
In small proportions we just beauties see;
And in short measures life may perfect be.

Blackmore had enunciated the word "small," drew it out smoothly, deeply, for special attention. I remembered it from five years ago because it was so touching, but now it was simply sad, the smallness of us all, ultimately—our mortality, Daddy many years ago, my mom dead of lung cancer, Blackmore of . . . I was going to say simple old age, but let's just call it what it is: The

Inevitable. And soon, me. Life's single certainty. It's the happiest story there is, it's said: "The grandfather dies, the father dies, the son dies." But still.

Organ music filled Duke Chapel after the poem to bring the memorial to an end, and my eyes were dry. I'd known Professor Blackmore ever since we moved here. My father was his exact contemporary; the young author, though, was a star on the campus by the time we arrived. Blackmore had arrived at Duke fairly needy from his home state of Virginia, the site of so many of his novels and stories. But he and I weren't close. He was a prolific philanderer in his early days, occasionally with students, or so I heard; he always treated me like Daddy's little girl, kind but aloof. I never took a class from him—too intimidating for me at the time. He reserved most of his heart and mind for his writing students, those who shared his love of the great Western texts.

Not grieving, only thoughtful and sad, I was clear-headed enough to consider my options as the crowd filed out. Near the door, I could bolt for the library, where I had actual work to do for this occasion (a collection of Blackmore's work and honors—first editions, medals, letters—had been organized by me and my colleague, Don Glassman, in the Rare Book and Manuscript Library, in the small room off the entrance of Perkins Library, the Mary Duke Biddle Rare Book Room). Or I could wait for Em to exit, catch him then.

Which brought up another fraught decision. Call out to him? Place myself where he'd see me and pray he recognized me? The latter terrified me, of course. For if he failed to recognize me, then I'd clearly have meant even less to him than I'd thought, and I couldn't bear this devastation. And if this were so, I don't believe I could forgive him, or forgive my pathetic self. Truly, he was so important to me those years ago that were he to fail to know my face, my eyes, then I'd deluded myself. I don't care how many layers of time we'd built up between the selves we were then and are now.

I could already feel my blood getting hot just thinking, and so, blinded by rising anger, I never saw him coming. He appeared before me out of the crowd like a shark rising to the surface, every bit as surprising, beautiful, and dangerous. To me at least. And I'm sure I took a breath but I don't recall because I was paralyzed, struck so dumb for so many long, blank moments that he was the one who had to speak.

"Grimsley," he said. And then he said, "It's *me*. Em." I still said nothing, only stared into those intensely familiar gold-speckled eyes. "Emerson."

And then we embraced and I swear to God a physical *hunger* for him opened up inside me wide as a cavern, that gear I mentioned turned—and a hundred others with it. I felt I still knew every muscle and curve of his body as my arms wrapped around his back, face pressed into a white shirt that smelled of fresh starch. He actually had to pull me by my rib cage off him, gently but insistently.

But it was clearly not to be rid of me, for he held on to my ribs, and beheld me, his eyes brightening, a smile alighting. But only momentarily, for the brightness dimmed and the smile melted away. His jaw trembled, his eyes filled. He said, "Please excuse me." And like that he was gone, dove straight into the departing crowd and was quickly out of sight.

And so was I. After five stunned, frozen-like-a-statue, what-just-happened seconds, I departed the chapel, pausing at the steps as the crowd parted around me. His slender but strong fingers still seemingly impressed on my ribs, I took a good, long breath. I smoothed my navy dress. I tightened my ponytail as tightly as I could, pushed my glasses high on the bridge of my nose, and headed down the steps and over to the adjacent library.

It would be a day like any other.

I and my days are as constant as the sun. I rise, I arc through my work, see a friend, call my sister, cook for myself or myself and a friend, and read till I dip below the horizon. Sometimes I'm hazy; sometimes I feel radiant. I arc low in winter and high in summer but every day I am there, like the day before. And this day would be no different. I determined it would be . . .

Except for the not-routine exhibit and reception people were now streaming toward—one I'd helped to build—consisting of a small narrative in letters, manuscripts, books, photo albums, and videos of the novelist and poet we'd just said goodbye to.

The mentor of my ex-lover.

Instead of checking in on the Rare Books room (where we'd moved couches and tables around to set up the exhibit) to make sure all was well as I normally would have, I entered the first doors to the library beneath the tower and took the marble steps to my office on the second floor. I sat at my desk. I straightened papers so that all edges were aligned in the three to-do piles I'd created before leaving for the ceremony (not knowing that I'd feel like a different person on returning now). I had no pressing matters since the exhibit was done, a full month's work excavating the history of a protean man of letters who lived to age eighty-seven—two hundred boxes of archives.

It was then that I'd sought out a cache of Emerson's letters in Blackmore's files. My colleague and friend, Don, was the main curator of this particular collection, but I'd been the one to sift through Blackmore's correspondence from the last two decades of his life. True to his egotistical nature, perhaps planning his legacy since his solitary childhood, he'd saved copies of his own letters, at least those he thought might be of use to his archivists. That sounds mean, so let me just say that I'm truly glad he did, if only for the first letter he saved from 1992, which begins thus:

Durham, 10 Jan 92
Dear Em,

Your long good letter came yesterday; tomorrow noon, my classes begin so herewith a not-too-long-considered answer.

I was not a fan of Blackmore's work—I'd read three novels (of the forty or so novels, essays, memoirs, and volumes of poetry he'd published during his career)—but his letter touched me to the point that I hunted down a folder on which Don, in his elegant script, had penciled the words "CORRESPONDENCE, EMERSON RANDALL, 1990–2009." The folder, in the "CORRESPONDENCE To" box, contained forty or so letters and notes, and a few postcards from Europe from Em to Professor Blackmore. The first of the letters were from New York—the college graduate giddy from the excitement of the big city—then a few from Los Angeles—a torrid romance with the woman who would be his wife (I skimmed)—but the one I was looking for was dated January 5, 1992. I needed to know what had elicited such words to a young writer, my long-ago friend, from the old master. There is a moratorium of twenty years on all but a selection of Blackmore's papers according to his will and estate, but I have access to them all.

Emerson addressed his mentor as Professor Blackmore, as he would deferentially throughout their correspondence. After a deceptively light, but relatively hopeful description of being newly wed and the absurd nature of traffic in Los Angeles, he gets to the point that required Blackmore's immediate response:

I have just discarded 102 pages of what was to be my second attempt at a novel and now that the despair has subsided, I feel strong enough to ask for your counsel. How on earth to proceed? Since age eleven I've written stories, have always known that I intended to earn my living as writer, as a novelist I had always presumed, because, well, that's what any serious writer has done for the past few centuries.

We all know it's hard and wanting is not enough, as countless have tried and failed before me. In class, you lined the path with signs reading "Stay Out," "Beware of Dog," "No Trespassing" for anyone poking through the underbrush toward serious fiction. In your essay "To a Young Writer," you begin succinctly: "If you can stop, you probably should."

Well, I can.

For all these years I have felt compelled by the pressure of my life to write stories and I've come to what I fear is an either/or moment. Continue my attempts at fiction or follow the lure of the entertainment industry that has tugged at me since my arrival here two years ago.

I know that I must write. The compulsion I mentioned above is very much physical as well as intellectual. Given this fact, I'm asking you for your hard advice. You always told our class, "If you really want to know what I think, ask, but don't ask unless you really want to know." I didn't then because I thought I knew, or was arrogant enough to think it shouldn't and didn't matter what you thought, but now I'm asking. You actively helped me a few years ago by making the introduction to Lee, as wonderful an agent as any young writer could hope for. You encouraged me after reading the first thirty pages of the story I've recently discarded. Now, knowing what you do of me and my work, I'm asking for your frank assessment. Financially, we're fine, but I don't know how long I can comfortably lean on Collista, much as she supports my aims. Her family is very generous but the well is far from bottomless; we live just within our means as it is, and if we have children, as we both hope, I will need gainful employ. But mostly, I do not want to be that poor soul who lies to himself. I fear terribly that script- and screenwriting, where there are actual money-making opportunities for me, will burn too much of the muscle required for writing the fiction I aspire to. That is, I don't know that I can do both.

If you want to say to this twenty-four-year-old writer, "If you can stop, you probably should," then I will. But if you think that I have words in me that may be of use to another living soul, that, given my innate compulsion to tell stories, that it is a matter of time and work, of running in place a while longer, then I'll take that course.

Please know I feel terrible putting this on you, but I need guidance as I never have before. If you don't feel comfortable responding, I will not ask again, and will remain forever grateful for all that you've given me—truly, only my own father has given me more or shown me such uncommon generosity, asking nothing in return. For everything, thank you.

Ever yours,
Emerson

So you can see why I felt a little regret for Em, knowing of course that he never did publish a novel, though I couldn't know if he'd *written* a second. He may well have, given Blackmore's response, a response that warmed me and gave me a sense of why my mother and Emerson felt such affection for and devotion to a man I perceived only as famous and cold.

"I understand your frustrations, right down in my marrow," Blackmore wrote back. *"When I left Duke at age 22 and headed to cold dark Oxford, I worked in*

resounding silence for three long years." The letter is five typed pages, worthy of publication, and I'll leave the letter-to-a-young-writer-ly stuff contained therein for the bound volume twenty years hence should our culture want it (I hope it *does*) and get right to the conclusion that so moved me—his answer to the young writer in question.

However fortunate you've been till now, you've almost surely had your big primal encounters. Whether they're yet available for exhumation and working, neither of us can know till you've dug deeper and longer.

One word of caution. I urged you to stay in Durham, or return to your home, if you intended to write. New York, long mythologized as the place to go if you would be a writer, is in fact the worst place for a young writer, as you found, filled as it is with so many wonderful and terrible distractions. You chose a place where you can work, but remember that no writer of serious fiction flourished in Hollywood. From Fitzgerald and Faulkner to someone like Charles Jackson— that you don't know the name is its own instruction—to Richard Yates, their time where you now make your life was time wasted, did actual damage to their bodies and minds, the instruments of their art.

But I can see you've built the hardest muscles a young writer must have for the work: the management of your time, the discipline to sit down and write, daily, and then to find some non-poisonous way to spend the remaining hours of your day. I'm referring, of course, to alcohol and other substances that so many American writers fall prey to. If you don't believe me, check the liquor bill of any full-time successful writer of your Anglo ilk. From the sound of it, though, and as your marriage suggests, you've avoided this trap as well.

Therefore, I can tell you that it is, now, a matter of time, work, love, the dingy but ultimately sterling heroism of daily constancy in an effort to watch the world, see it (the rarest of skills), then comprehend some useable pattern and record it memorably for others. The rest of life needs much the same devotion; writing's no biologic sport, no terribly special skill.

So on, hard as it is, and blessings on it. And thanks for the gratitude you gravely and credibly proffer. What you, in particular you, are doing now is something I'm proud of, deeply respectful of, on a daily basis. So the welcome words are received most gladly, my friend—in this New Year and for many more, I beg. Love to Collista,

  and your worthy self

                                                    from
                                                Daniel

I smiled at the professor's lovely words—the last three lines of the otherwise typed letter written in perfect fountain-pen cursive—and was warmed also to see confirmed Blackmore's gratitude for Emerson's deep devotion to him, which I well remember. But this Blackmore letter wouldn't be pertinent to the exhibit we were creating, so I had returned it to the box and continued my sifting. Emerson's words had kindled no feeling for my long-ago love, no visceral stirrings. Cold words on old paper. Not a hint of what his physical being could do—which was to boil my blood.

*

After straightening the papers at my desk, I aligned three very sharp pencils beside the papers. I looked for comfort to the photos standing on the right quadrant of my desk, photos of my younger brother and sister and their families, so solid and contented. My dad and mom. And at the far right, the biggest of the frames, Mom alone and at her best, with her big brunette feminist hair; she was teaching women's studies at the time of the photograph. She left Duke after Dad died in 1996 to become executive director of the AIDS Task Force here because she wanted—I know it sounds cheesy, but here it is—*to give back* to the community. She told me she'd spent enough time shut up in books and teaching mainly privileged kids she no longer knew what, or what for. This was when AIDS was still a killer disease, a death sentence, and not the horrible chronic illness that it has become, and which she dealt with, primarily in the poor African American communities of the Raleigh–Durham–Chapel Hill triangle. It was exhausting on body and soul, but I know she was prouder of that unseen work than anything she'd ever done.

My mom, Elizabeth Bowden (she kept her name, unheard of when she married in 1960), was second to none in the goodness and brains department. I held the photograph and whispered so softly no one could have heard my voice: "Where are you now, Mom? I need you. I need you now like I needed you then."

Before I could begin to cry, Don's head appeared around the doorjamb. When he saw I was at my desk, he entered and leaned against the wall, hands thrust into his pockets. He was handsome in a scholarly way, not librarian-y but preppy. Salt-and-pepper hair, stylish glasses, natty tweed jacket—you'd have guessed he was an editor at a big-time New York publishing house. He was a curator like me, but he also helped develop collections, which I did not do. Don was sweet and a dear friend, five years my senior. We'd had sex once. The benefits way. I made that clear at the outset. It was fine and all, completely comfortable, but I didn't want an inner-office affair because those invariably end either badly or in marriage and I didn't want either, then or now.

"Really nice choices for the exhibit," he said.

"Well it's not as if you didn't do most of it!"

"Yeah, but you got the cool stuff. Where did you find that interview with Dick Cavett? I didn't know that even existed."

"Dante helped me find it. And he also knew how to get a digital version we could run on our equipment."

Dante was a thirty-two-year-old assistant curator, of Italian descent as his name implied and his looks confirmed: the kind of deep brown eyes where you can scarcely see the pupils. Skin that looked tan in February. Long, dark, thick, glossy hair. Now *he* was someone I was seriously sexually attracted to, though he desired exactly nothing of me. More than a decade between us, and I didn't want to embarrass him or me. He made no overtures, so I let the lust—that's all there was, he wasn't my type in any other way, the always-texting-type youngster—I let my lust smolder and die out.

"He's down there now, just so you know," Don said, and I didn't know if this was a soft jab—reproach for not being in the room myself—or if he really did mean to assure me all was well. Could he sense me trembling inside? As he develops collections, he's not my boss but he is one rung higher on the ladder of what is a very bureaucratic, hierarchical department. At least one of us always had to be in the room, with all that valuable archival stuff out. You'd be amazed by what people will steal—it's appalling.

"We still on for the movie tonight?" Don asked.

I'd forgotten. We had a date.

"You know, I'm not really feeling up to it tonight. Can we make it a rain check?"

I expected he'd smile and say sure, as he and I had both done in our long years as colleagues. But a look of consternation came over him, even discouragement. So much so that it surprised me. He looked like a little boy for a few seconds. But he rallied and said, "Of course." Then, "Everything all right?"

I looked around at the objects on my desk, for no reason other than to avoid Don's eyes. "I'm just not feeling myself today."

"Are you ill?"

"No, I don't feel ill, I just feel . . . I don't know . . . not myself." And now I had to look at Don, because he left the wall and came over to my desk and planted his butt right on the edge of it next to me—which would have been perfectly fine and always welcome . . . *on any other day*. Mine was a large desk, but we were still close. I pushed my chair out a little and swiveled so that I faced him directly.

Now he looked away. "Well, it was kind of yourself that I was hoping to talk about tonight."

"Me?"

He turned back to me and looked into my eyes to drop the bomb. "Well, us."

I said nothing, and he waited for me to absorb the fact that something was coming.

"Grimsley, I've been thinking about this a lot. A lot. We're getting old. We're going to die. And I don't want to die alone."

He paused to see if I wanted to say something. I didn't.

"I know we both love each other as friends. I'd like it to be more than that. I'd like us to be partners in that love so that maybe it would grow."

"Holy Jesus," I said and took a moment to swallow. "Is this a *proposal?*"

He waited long enough for my heart to get up to a hundred twenty beats before saying, "No. Yes. No." He looked toward the window. "It's an *idea* is what it is. And it's a serious one. I'd like us to share our lives."

"Look, you know I'll cook you dinner most any night of the week. Often have!"

"Yes, many lovely dinners, every single one, every one without exception, I've enjoyed immensely. And exactly why I'm asking you to consider my proposal—the enjoyment of a meal shared with you. If I needed a cook, I'd hire one. And no it's not *that* either—I know what you're thinking."

I wasn't, he was ahead of me here, but now that I *was* thinking about it, I very much didn't want to be.

"Though I hope you'd acknowledge that we are compatible *that* way as well."

I stood immediately, so abruptly that Don stood, too, and we faced each other. "Dear friend," I said. I must have closed my eyes and shaken my head. I simply had no words. "Don." I breathed hard. "This is just something . . . I can't even begin to—"

Rude or not, I didn't know what else to do but leave. Walked out on him, mid-sentence. My own mid-sentence. I heard him mutter, or moan, "Oh God," when I was out the door. Poor man, he must have felt humiliated; I'm so sorry for that. But I couldn't think about him at that moment. I couldn't.

Where could I be alone? I wasn't allowed to leave. Trish Davitt, the head of my department, my boss, wouldn't allow this—a real stickler for details and time clocks (read, *bitch*, but you didn't hear it from me). The stacks. No one would be in the stacks today. I could be alone there. I all but ran down the steps, into 103 Perkins, strode behind the desk—a new girl, didn't even remember her name, was manning the desk but probably tooling around on the Internet since no one was working or researching here today. I went two stacks in to the very back, where excess Blackmore archives had been shelved (ones we wanted to show but didn't have room for) so that if, on the off chance Trish appeared—and she was precisely the sort of person who had a knack for appearing exactly when you least wanted to see her, such as now—I could at least pretend I was looking for something related to the exhibit.

I leaned my head against a shelf. I wanted my mind to go blank for a while, hoping three minutes of blackness might reboot the system.

"Grims? Hey, man, you all right?"

Dante had found me. I'd dropped to one knee, arms crossed over that knee, head down. Kind of like you see football players do when Coach says a pregame "Clear eyes, full hearts" and all that.

He was squatting to my level and I looked up blankly.

"Seriously, you all right?"

"I just, I just got dizzy for minute." I stood.

He touched my throat, my jugular to be precise, then touched my forehead. He used to be pre-med and he knew I knew this, so it wasn't odd or forward.

"Really, Dante, I'm fine."

"Okay."

And then we stood, and we stared at each other for an inordinate time—he was really good looking. I finally had to say, "I assume you came here for something?"

"Oh right!" he said and grinned. "Trish asked me to find some chapbook of poems Blackmore published in the 1950s. Damn, I knew I was going to forget the name." He actually scratched his head, digging his fingers into that gorgeous floppy black hair—there must be a reason we do this, scratch our head to think. Finally, squinting, he said, "Something about a lily."

"Weren't you at the service? Weren't you paying attention?" Unembarrassed, he shrugged his Gen-X shoulders. "It's called *Lily of a Day, 1956*," I said, relieved to have a work issue to solve, though solved too quickly. I turned to the top shelf where it would be. He moved next to me to help me look. He wasn't pre-med anymore, but he still had that Type A

I-can-find-it-before-you-can!-win! mentality. Our hands touched as we each reached the thin volume simultaneously. Tie! He was a gentleman and let me remove it. I handed it to him.

He smiled warmly, a little longer than was necessary, I thought. Then he said, "Thanks, you're awesome," and departed.

I now knew where I had to go—not to be alone but rather to be around strangers. The Mary Duke Biddle Rare Book Room and the exhibit. I had to focus on work. That I could do. I power-walked down the hall on Dante's heels.

The room was crowded with strangers, thank goodness. I loved working the room at these things. People always asked a lot of questions and I knew the answers; I all but dared people to stump me.

Don had returned, glanced at me, and then looked quickly back to whomever he was speaking to.

What we curators do is stroll, and look, stroll and look, in the altogether too-quiet hush of the room. I stopped at a couple bent right angle over a photo album.

It was a young couple, local—judging from the man's accent as he whispered to his companion. They hovered, arms behind their backs, intensely interested in little Danny Blackmore in short-legged overalls pulling a wooden wagon, with dog Spot in the back, along a dusty backwoods path; there he is in the back row, fifth grade; there he is, the dashing Lothario, arriving for his freshman year at Duke, dressed in a khaki suit and narrow tie.

The man looked to me and said, "Can we turn the pages?"

"I'd be happy to turn them for you," I said, and did. You never know, he could have been eating a brownie at the reception down the hall.

The Mary Duke Biddle Rare Book Room was outfitted like a Victorian living room, heavy on the maroon and brown damask, with formal sitting chairs, coffee tables, and side tables, lit a dim yellow by several lamps and sconces. On the tables, and in a couple of glass cases, were manuscripts of first drafts, journals, and letters to and from people as diverse as Vivien Leigh, W. H. Auden, and Nelson Mandela; citations and medals—he'd won seemingly everything available, save for an Eagle Scout Badge and the Nobel Prize, which probably irked him, since one of his friends and contemporaries, Toni Morrison, had got it. I once heard him say, "The Nobel Prize is a great honor, of course, but I'm told it steals *a year of your life* just to handle the flood of correspondence and invitations." He had an ego the size of Texas; he'd have bathed happily in such a theft. Blackmore was an obsessive keeper of photo albums, as any self-respecting narcissist is, and we had a couple of these set out on which people doted.

I bent to turn another page for the local couple, but nearly tore the page out of the book when I felt two hands on my waist. Two hundred twenty volts would have yielded a milder result.

Em stood back, now a big grin on his face, which turned quickly embarrassed.

"Wound tight!" he said at normal volume in what was a library-quiet room.

I must have given him my how-dare-you, or hands-off bitchy look because he was clearly taken aback. And I, I was just not myself.

"That's not a Grimsley I ever knew!" he said, his smile returning.

I turned back to the couple I'd been helping and excused myself.

"You snuck up on me," I whispered. And yes, I definitely caught Don pinching his chin as he stared at us.

"Sorry, didn't mean to," Emerson said. "I was glad to see you. I didn't know if I'd lost my chance."

"Your chance at what?"

"To see you. To talk. I'd like to know who you've become."

"I'm just me, I'm afraid," I said, trying my best to sound casual. "Only more so."

"When do your duties here end?"

I checked my watch. "We start rustling folks out in about thirty minutes."

"I'll be at the reception. Will you find me there? Do you have time to talk?"

*

I could scarcely believe how little changed he was at forty-three. His skin remained smooth, the whites of his eyes bright, and apparently every strand of hair he'd ever grown remained glossy and fixed to his scalp. And he was, as ever, completely at ease with himself.

When I found him in the reception off the main lobby talking to some beautiful woman, probably one of his actress friends from LA, he turned and he, well, he *beamed* at me. He completely undid me. He hugged me again, an easy hug that was so natural it calmed me, strangely, and I felt like myself for the first time since seeing him. Sort of.

"Let's go," he said. He bid his beautiful friend farewell and actually took me by the arm to stroll us through the lobby and out into the lovely spring air.

We sat on the stone bench immediately outside the front doors of Perkins.

Emerson removed his jacket and laid it across the bench beside him. He leaned back on the support of his arms, hands on the edge of the bench, long legs extended forward, ankles crossed, black wing-tipped shoes highly polished. I sat like a prim old maid beside him, as if to hold off the bizarre events of this day, hands in my lap, knees locked together, and my short dress feeling several sizes too tight in the hips.

"Apologies," he said, "for the abrupt departure in the chapel. I honestly don't know what happened. I ran around to the side of the chapel, sat on the steps, and cried. Hard. Just bawled."

"No need to apologize. We all have to grieve."

He sat forward abruptly. "Hm." He put his elbows on his knees and stared at his own hands as he wrung them. "Is that what it was?"

"You hadn't grieved, obviously. He was an important man in your life, one of the most important men in your life. You've lost something really big, you needed to let yourself grieve."

"I wonder, Grimsley. That's the thing. I didn't feel any grief, not coming out here, not during the ceremony, not big grief. He was very old. Daniel Blackmore lived a long and happy life, well into his eighties, died peacefully from what I heard. If it was grief, I need to know what I was grieving for."

I felt my insides unwinding, returning to something like myself. Em put me at ease, as he had managed to do on so many emotional occasions when we were students. What a pleasure and surprise. We'd always loved talking to one another but it was as though no time had passed.

I said, "If not grief, then what?"

He looked at me hard, as if the answer were in my eyes, then he turned and said, "Shame?"

"What have you done you wouldn't have anyone know?"

"Is that the definition of shame?"

"You're here this one day—I'm guessing—and flying out tomorrow?"

"Yes."

"So here I am." I held my arms out wide, proof. "Use me. I'm your confessor. Unburden yourself to a friend who still cares about you but is unconnected to whatever life you've made. Tomorrow, you'll be gone, and we're not likely to see each other again."

This was all true, but the last part of it quaked me not a little—the truth of it, the finality, our mortality. There was little reason he'd have to return to North Carolina. This *was* the last I'd ever see him.

So here's what I did. I wasn't myself, as I've been saying. I took his shoulder, the far one, and pulled it toward me so he was facing me. I put my nose to his neck and breathed in. I smelled his hair. I licked the skin of his neck, just above the collar. And I pulled away.

And I had to laugh. "You should see your face!"

"What did you just *do*?"

I had to talk, no time to think my way out of this one.

"I can smell and taste shame."

He looked at me dubiously. "What did you discover?"

Here I told the truth. "That you're still you. You haven't changed one iota in all this time." I paused. "And I know you had *no* shame back then!"

He snorted lightly, smiled a little, but was still bothered, I could tell. Me, my blood was thumping in my neck.

If you've ever returned to a special place from your youth, what you notice first is the smell, how smell more than anything launches you back in time. It's not the sight of an object, a remembered rock, or tree, or a cornice or an old settee, not the sound of a church bell or a dinner gong. It's the *smell* of a place that registers deep in your animal psyche. I visited Charleston shortly after Daddy died, found my old home, knocked and asked to visit. Nice married couple, versions of my parents, pre-kids. I remembered the house from my seven-year-old perspective. How small the rooms seemed now. The shape of the upstairs hallway and the curve of the banister. I remembered but I did not *feel* them. Decades of other people's lives had been lived out in them, thousands of meals cooked, and so the house did not smell the same.

But I ventured out to the garage and it was here—where the smell of gasoline and motor oil and cut grass mingled permanently—that a shiver ran down my spine and I became that seven-year-old girl. I was her again, found her again deep inside me. Which is why, I later understood, I'd returned. I was searching for that girl, I loved that girl, missed her and simply wanted to be with her for a few minutes before surfacing to the present.

And that is what had happened just then, when whatever it is that makes up a man's scent entered my brain: I was my twenty-year-old self, just for that moment and, God, did it feel good. I didn't need to taste his skin, the way I'd needed to smell it—I'd just wanted to, and it was right there, clean, no cologne, just soft savory skin. I love skin. And that cavern of hunger I'd felt in the chapel when we'd hugged, it yawned even wider, a big black mouth of physical *want*.

"So tell me about yourself," I said, knowing if I didn't change the subject I was a goner, that life as I knew it would end and I was too afraid of what the new one might be—it certainly couldn't be good. "You've got a wife I know."

"I don't wear a ring, how do you know?"

"Google knows all. What I never looked for were children. We both know you're fertile."

"I couldn't bet on that now, but yes, two children—a son just seventeen, a junior but already hoping for East Coast Ivy. Daughter will be fifteen next month and I can tell you I am already not looking forward to entrusting her to the Los Angeles freeways."

"She won't be the first teenaged girl to live into old age in LA and won't be the last. She'll be fine."

"I'm sure you're right. Laws are much stricter now, and education much better. I shudder anytime I recall my own recklessness at that age."

"So where are they?"

"All home now, why?"

"No, *pictures*. I want to see them. Surely you carry pictures."

"Of course," he said. He reached into his pocket, retrieved his iPhone.

I tried to at least look interested, but physical beauty was never something that held my interest. His impeccable wife, his gorgeous children, miraculously behaved, beloved and brilliant, no doubt. What I more noticed though was Em's face as he showed them to me. The way he lingered just a moment extra on his wife after he showed her to me. He said, "Collista," that was all, and his finger should have swiped the image away, but it didn't. It remained, one, two, three moments longer and I could see he was admiring her, was unable to take his eyes off her, had to will his finger to bring on the next image, and he could do so only because the next photo was one he obviously cherished more, his daughter, Alexandra, and then his son, Peter. Each image seemed hard for him to let go of until the fourth one, a family picture, all four of them lit by low golden light, a blue sky and vineyards behind them—"last summer, visiting friends in Napa"—almost a parody of the perfect family. He seemed to see this or sense my response because he put the phone away abruptly, before I'd had a chance to view it thoroughly.

"Tell me you're all as perfect as you look," I said.

"Don't be mean."

"The contrary. I've known only a few truly happy families, least of all one as beautiful as yours."

"Collista and I have had our issues," he said, looking away. "All marriages do, and we've weathered them."

"No infidelities?"

Em snapped his gaze back on me hard, clearly wondering what I was up to, and I retreated.

"I'm sorry. That's none of my business. I apologize."

"No actual infidelities, no, not on my part and none on hers that I'm aware of. I doubt we could weather that." I don't know if it was his anger or my hunger but something was humming between us, like actual vibrations, which rose to a crescendo then faded, and he turned. "For seventeen years we've been anchored by the kids. Nothing more important to either of us. True, good anchors in stormy weather they always were. Even when they start making storms of their own. And these distract a couple from one another." He leaned back again, extended his legs. "You?"

"Me? You mean kids? No."

"I see no ring either?"

"One offered and refused, fifteen years ago," I said.

"Why?"

"He loved me too much. Visiting poet."

"Anyone I'd know?"

"Not unless you read literary quarterlies. We'd have been a good couple, and I felt that I might grow to love him, but it was too unbalanced. His affection was so much more intense than mine for him, I knew it couldn't last. Mine could, not his."

"You were and are as constant as the sun."

Yes, indeed, this was when the line had been returned to me—I am. When he said it, I smiled at his game. We'd seen the Zeffirelli version of the star-crossed lovers together, in Chapel Hill, and used to quote from it, that fall and winter, long ago.

" 'Therefore, love moderately,'" I played along. " 'Long love doth so.' Yes, my poet was the gunpowder *and* the fire to light it with. I didn't want to stand on the sidelines of his passion."

"Regrets?"

"About turning him down? No."

"Any regrets at all?"

I paused. My life had been so routine for so long, I rarely asked myself about my choices. But here I did and I answered plainly since I was asking him to be so honest.

"I'd have liked to have had a child. I'd have liked to have been a mom."

This, I was relieved to see, seemed to hurt him, so I continued with the truth rather than to let it lie there, meanly. "Not *that* child, or that kind of mom. Me, a college senior, can you imagine? We did the right thing. *I* did the right thing." He put his hand on my knee, smiled at me. I touched his hand, just smoothed the back of it. It felt good and natural to do so.

"It doesn't make me sad," I continued. "Life is what it is. I've been an orphan now five years. Father died of pancreatic cancer at age sixty, ten years before Mother. I mourned her five years ago this month, in our dear Duke Chapel on a day very much like today. As far as offspring goes, I'm alone as a tree stump. But I have a brother and sister who are raising families nearby, I have this university, which is very much family to me, and I have five close friends I can rely on absolutely, and as long as I live here, on this land, I know who I am."

"That makes me happy, Grimsley," he said. "You do seem content." He touched me again, rested a hand on my exposed knee with a fondness so benign it deflated me. "I always, always felt so good when I was with you. You always put me so at ease. I'm sure I never said that, or thanked you."

I looked away. He took his hand off my knee.

He said, "I have two hours till I need to be at the dinner. Walk with me? I want to see the place again."

*

Places built to be great don't change, and Duke University is like that, though it looks older than it actually is. This West Campus—designed by a black architect I'm proud to say, from a state that did so much damage to African Americans for so many hundreds of years—was constructed during the early part of the twentieth century, but its Gothic style evokes the old eastern Ivy League schools. The chapel where we'd just been hadn't been completed until 1935. East Campus, a mile to the east, was built first, starting in the 1890s, in a neo-Georgian style that I much prefer to the dark and heavy stone of West Campus. East Campus brings to mind the light and innovation of a Thomas Jefferson, with its great lawn extending hundreds of yards to the domed Pantheon of Baldwin Auditorium, whereas West Campus carries the heavy weight of Western Literature and Law and Medicine. Or so it feels to me.

But on a spring day such as today, with the campus cleared of the bulk of its students after last week's commencement, a warm breeze and afternoon light falling softly here and there through the full spring leaves onto the walkways, with Em beside me, it was lightness and ease, as if the campus could at last breathe.

"Anywhere in particular you want to go?" I asked. "The gardens?"

"No, I always found the gardens kind of stuffy."

"You liked the woods better."

"As did you," he said, leaning his shoulder into mine, dipping down slightly to do so. "Though it is in the gardens where we met," he said, looking at me as we strolled.

"Is it?"

"Of course it is! Don't you remember?"

I paused long enough to consider, then lied. "It's kind of fuzzy."

"Freshman orientation. Come on, Grimsley. You were my FAC."

"I know *that*."

"I remember you, just as you were. You were hot."

"I was *not*," I said, bumping him back with my shoulder, trying not to smile. "I was plain as wood."

"I saw through that in two seconds," he said. He took two more strides. "You're still hot, I hope you know, and in exactly the same way."

We were walking the perimeter within West Campus, clockwise past languages and the psych building, past social sciences, where Em had taken so many of his English courses. We had crossed over the roadways where the East–West shuttle bus picks up and unloads, to the other side, the long connected rows of Gothic residences, buildings whose arches lead into a variety of smaller quadrangles. I did my best to ignore what he said, having no idea why he would say it. Though he was always straightforward like that. Guileless. The boy I met and knew here was utterly lacking in cunning. He hid nothing. And you could feel it on you as a genuine warmth. His natural optimism and faith in his fellow creatures was so complete he seemed, to some, simple-minded. Many of the smarter girls complained that he was dim, but I figured they resented his being so good looking and smart, supremely confident and outgoing *and* a sensitive writer–type. But how could he have lasted in Manhattan and made a success of himself in Los Angeles without a little inner Machiavelli? Maybe his was ultimately a cunning so deep and well hidden I never saw it and was fooled the whole time, even after he'd left me.

I stopped and turned to him. "Did you ever love me?"

He stared at me seriously and calmly, and I knew then that there truly was no cunning in him, because there was no need whatsoever. He would say the truth because it was the truth—straight at you like a knife.

"Grimsley, if I'd loved you, I'd never have left you. Or I'd have made you come with me."

He said it with a smile as easy and light as though he'd just told me how pretty I look in a dress. What felt like an old-lady's dress by this point.

"You do remember that, don't you?"

"What?"

"Please tell me our last weeks together are not so far away or meaningless that you've forgotten—that month we lived together before I headed to LA?"

"How could I forget that?" I said.

Indeed, it was one of the best months of my life, one of the most truly carefree, happy months of my whole life, but, as it was followed by blackness, I really hadn't thought much of it since. And so the details were unfocused—Em was always the one with the incredible memory, cursed with it, I suppose—only the emotion of ease, of summer afternoon, followed by a wintery cold snap driven in from the north, that's what I retained.

"Grimsley, if I'd loved you, I'd never have let you go," he repeated.

33

And then he reached for my hand. He held my hand, turned me gently, and we walked, just like that, hand in hand. We entered into Few Quad. I could scarcely believe it, walking hand in hand as we had many times on these same fieldstone paths.

He took a deep breath, exhaled heavily. I could feel him smiling at me, but I looked around at the lovely day to avoid his eyes.

"You see?" he said, drawing my eyes to his.

"See what?"

"This feels so good. I've been down for so long, frustrated with work, a difficult daughter, Collista and I are too often annoyed with each other about meaningless issues. It's been so long since I've felt . . . at ease." He took in a breath that was the meaning of the word: he inspired. "You were always such a . . . comfort. As you are this very moment. It's as though nothing has changed, how can that be?"

"Why should anything have changed?"

"Because it's been more than twenty years since I last saw you! People change. We've had different lives. We've become different people from who we were."

"How do you know that?" I asked. "You don't know me. You know nothing of my life now. Now look at the evidence of your feelings. In my experience, people change only if they're forced to. And most people aren't forced. They cloak themselves in layers of time that dry and toughen around them. That you feel as you do, immediately at ease with a friend you haven't seen in all these years, tells me you haven't changed, and that I haven't changed."

He stopped me from walking, not letting go of my hand, and said, "Tell me that's a good thing."

"You don't need me to tell you that."

"I think I do."

"Then yes," I said, "it's a good thing."

I kissed him on the mouth.

Just once, just to close the last little distance between us. It wasn't a peck, nor a probing kiss, just a good one-two-three *smooch* on the lips. The fullness and softness there, this remained too, and returned to me on contact, the tactile memory of those lips. They hadn't changed either. They felt exactly the same.

Was he shocked? Not from the looks of it. He'd neither participated in the kiss nor pulled back from it. He gave me the easiest smile he had. I held his gaze; I hoped I was smiling in exactly the same way he was.

I suddenly felt my whole self slipping away from me. It was as though I'd stood up suddenly and all the blood left my head and I couldn't see. I think I blacked out, because when I regained my senses, he was gone.

I turned, and he was moving toward the magnolia right outside the back entrance to my old dorm.

"Hey, Grimsley," he called, "remember this old tree?"

*

I hate clichés as much anyone. But it's true! Damn me if it isn't true! *As if it were yesterday* . . . But it's not the cliché that's bad, is it? What's so grave about them is how they turn sadness and pain into Muzak. *Stop, you are so beautiful*, I thought as I watched him move toward the magnolia.

For truly, yes, I did remember that tree. The night after I met Em in the gardens, that beautiful boy climbed this very tree before me now to scratch on my window screen and wake me. And it now seems to have been moments ago, a tesseract, a wrinkle in time touching this spot to that one. How unbearably sad it is, "as if it were yesterday." Well it was yesterday, and what have we done in the meantime? Where did our lives go? What have I *done*?

He'd let his jacket drop on the dry grass like a careless boy and swung from a branch, back and forth, back and forth, building momentum, then leapt so that he arced to his feet. He let out an "oof!" when he landed and then pressed his hand to the small of his back.

"All right?" I asked.

"Barely. I can't believe I did that. Terrible back. Too many hours, too many years hunched over a keyboard."

"I was going to ask you to show me how you got all the way up there but I guess I'd better not."

"A repeat performance is not in the cards, I'm afraid."

"A pity."

We stood side by side to regard the modest but sturdy old tree. I wondered if he was reminiscing; he studied it so hard. Then I looked, too, and thought about it.

My room had been the first window, second floor beside the small tower that contained the stairway, four flights in all, from below ground level up to a third floor, which held a few long, narrow rooms, dormers poking up from the slate roofs.

"Gosh, you gave me a scare that night."

"Did I?" he asked, smiling at me.

"I thought you'd died."

"Died and gone to heaven," he said, smiling the same bright smile he'd shown me that night.

Untitled

"Grimsley."

Slowly the girl, a junior in college, surfaced to consciousness from the hum of a stick being dragged against her window screen.

"Hey, Grimsley!"

She felt disoriented, afraid something terrible had happened.

"It's me, Emerson. Remember?"

It took her several moments before she realized where she was, safe in her own room. Gradually what appeared to be an apparition just out of reach solidified into the boy she'd been with most of the evening, he and his two roommates.

"What are you doing?"

"Talking to you!"

"You're drunk."

"But oh so happily!" He tried to crawl toward her window, but the branch wasn't long enough.

"Be careful, you're going to fall."

"Won't fall. Already climbed up twice. Wouldn't make it up a third time."

"Why twice?"

"Climbed up the first time, couldn't reach the window, couldn't wake you, sleep of the dead. So I had to go back down and find a stick to reach your window screen. You left the party—I couldn't find you, where did you go?"

One of the fraternities had had an early welcome for some of the freshmen, same old red plastic cups fighting for the keg's tap. The girl, the FAC, had brought her charges there and stayed as long as she could bear.

"It was one a.m. I went here and went to bed. What time is it?"

"Still night," he said.

"What do you want?"

"To kiss you."

"What?"

"You are so beautiful."

"Didn't know you were that drunk."

She was flattered, nonetheless. She was not by any stretch beautiful, with a broad nose, heavy eyebrows, and the plainest of brown hair. It was what it was, she was used to it, and anyway, it kept her from doting on herself in the mirror.

"Can I come in?"

"Now how do you reckon on doing that?"

Not only was he as far out on the branch as he could get without its bending and dropping him off, but the dorm room windows were too narrow to slide through easily even if the lead glass frame opened fully—they opened outward like a door when you cranked the handle—and the screen hadn't been in the way.

"It was one of those cross-that-bridge-when-I-come-to-it situations," he said. "Hadn't given it much thought."

"Why didn't you just use the stairs like a mortal?"

The girl's eyes had adjusted, and there was enough light to see that a look of genuine perplexity came over him.

"You can do that?"

"I'm beginning to think you're retarded."

"This is a girls' dorm. I thought there would be some kind of matron sentry at the entrance, protecting the damsels."

"This isn't 1950."

"You mean I could walk right in?"

"Yes, so if you need to talk, climb down and come up, room 201."

"That seems altogether too easy. Where's the fun—"

And with that, Emerson tipped over the edge of the branch as fast as if he'd been on a log in water—he just rolled right off. She heard branches, followed by a sickening thud. She called his name, first out of shock, then again in worry. By standing on her mattress, she could attain an angle to see the ground below her window, enough of it to see the boy's legs spread and unmoving. He'd landed on his back.

"Emerson!" she called again. Nothing, no movement or sound. She wore only a short cotton nightshirt, the evenings still being so warm and humid. She hurried to find something to put on in the dark. She still hadn't unpacked completely but found her jeans in a clump in the closet. She put them on with increasing panic that he was badly hurt.

She flung open the door to the always lighted hallway and hustled in bare feet to the stairway, down a single flight, and out the heavy door, looking for the spot, but he was nowhere. Was she dreaming this? No, she saw the blue T-shirt, pale in the night's light, floating toward the archway, slowly, delicately.

"Emerson, hey!" she stage-whispered. He stopped at the archway, put his hand out on it, propping himself up. She flew to him, recognizing he was hurt.

He spoke haltingly, struggling even to moan. "Wind. Just." He rasped in another gulp of air. "Getting. My breath."

"You could be hurt."

"I'm." He continued to struggle. "Dandy."

"Come to my room. I need to see in the light that you're all right. People die from falls lower than that."

"If I can walk I'm okay."

"You can walk up to my room so I can look at you. At least give you some aspirin. You're going to need it."

He surely would. He was walking so gingerly she took his arm and put it over her shoulder, led him to the door. She was right to do this; he truly could have injured something, internal bleeding, concussion. The alcohol would dull dangerous pain. He grunted, taking the first step, squinting in the harsh hall light when she got him inside.

"I definitely did something. Ribs."

He walked more easily and breathed calmly by the time they got to her door. They entered and she seated him at her desk, turning just the desk lamp on.

"Well that's one way to sober up," he said.

"Let me get you some water." The bathroom was down the hall; when she returned with a glass of tap water, his head was back and his eyes were closed.

"Here, drink."

He opened his eyes, took the glass along with three aspirin. She watched him down the whole pint.

"That was good."

She clawed her fingers through his hair, looked into his eyes, which were a little glassy and dazed. "Who am I, what's my name?"

He squinted, "Nancy Reagan."

"I'm serious. I need to know you're not hurt. Tell me your home phone number."

"Only if you're calling to ask me for a date."

"Please just say it," she implored.

He recited a number and said, "I'm okay, Grimsley. Ribs hurt."

"Let me see."

He stood, but winced when he moved to take off his shirt, so she took hold of the hem and pulled it up and over his arms. She examined his left side, gently stroked the abrasion, just pink, no blood, a bruise beginning.

"I hit a branch on the way down."

"Likely saved you. You could have broken your neck."

"But I didn't."

She'd taken her hand off his skin, but he'd reached for her hand and returned it to his side. It was then that what she saw registered in a new way—the tautness of his skin, the firm chest.

"It wasn't exactly elegant, but it worked."

"What worked?"

"I am where I intended to be." And he put his hand on her where hers was on him. They held each other's gaze, and with an ease that in retrospect she would find disconcerting, he leaned down and kissed her.

She lowered her gaze. She couldn't calm her breathing. She grew self-conscious. Her nipples were practically poking holes through her old cotton nightshirt. His hand accepted their beckon, cupping one, and she drew a deep breath. She kept a hand on his waist and put the other on his chest. They kissed again. He seemed so at ease, and this put her at ease. He broke from the kiss, and slowly, slowly enough for her to object if she'd wanted—but she did not want to—he lifted her cotton shirt over her and let it fall to the floor. He stared unashamedly at her torso and said, "Oh," in a way that was almost musical. He fell to his knees, kissing her flesh, unfastening her jeans, tugging them loose but not down, kissed her just above the line where her underpants would have been had she been wearing them. And he stood, lingering on each perfect breast for pleasing moments and then to her neck and back to her mouth as she tugged his belt free.

And when it was undone, she drew the pants down, helping each foot out, then working her way up, taking in with her eyes his entire form, which was as ready for sex as any seventeen-year-old boy could be. They kissed.

She would look back on this moment, grateful that she had so quickly given in because never again would she feel so at home with another body, feel that her contours fit his contours in so perfect and natural a way that they might have been carved from the same block of soapstone. And so would the sensual contours of their sex that first time seem as inevitable and unstoppable as the tide. Their fertile, healthy bodies so hungry for one another there was no thought or medita-tion in any of their actions, only hot, hungry feasting till the end.

And they squeezed together in her narrow bed, she against the wall, he so near the edge he kept one leg on the floor for support, both panting from exertion and soaked in the humid night. He said, "Ooooooh!" And he grinned. "Oooooh, my ribs!"

And she laughed and kissed him. She scooted down the sheets and caressed his side where a sickeningly bad bruise had emerged, and she kissed it and kissed it again, willing it to heal.

When she inched back up, she could see he was falling into sleep, allowing her to regard this beautiful boy and his perfect form, his strong chest, a light coat of gold fur making a T across his chest and down his flat belly, his still full but beached cock, his long slender legs. She must have stared for five minutes before nestling into him. Shouldn't we get some warning when we wake, *she thought giddily,* some small divine preparation that the person who you are this morning will not be who you are the next, that your life will pivot today?

Grimsley slept so lightly, so happily, that the first birds woke her. And she stroked her new and perfect lover, until he couldn't possibly sleep. "Grimsley," he mumbled, "what are you doing?"

She said nothing. She moved his hips to the center of the bed, mounted him and worked alone, happily until his obvious conclusion, a single thrust and smile. His eyes opened, regarded her; she, pleased and proud to be watched this way in the lovely dawn light, the cool air.

"Oh my God, thank you," he said.

She lifted herself off him, lay beside him, completely and absolutely content, listening to the sweet calming birdsong.

"Grimsley," he said. She nestled closer, but didn't speak. "I think I'm really going to like college."

She put a knuckle gently into his ribs, but the pain left quickly and he laughed.

Four

W hat I can't figure out," he said matter-of-factly, "is how in the hell I was able to reach your window."

I looked back at him, squinting to fathom the male mind. Here I was recalling a whole big night and all Em was doing was working out an engineering issue.

"I mean, where's the branch?"

"Well, obviously the one that's now up near that dormer."

"Wow, you think?"

Maybe the smart girls were right after all.

"Hm," he said and bent to pick up his jacket.

I felt the anger rising up in me again.

"Tell me you remember the rest of that night," I said. "Tell me you weren't actually drunker than you seemed."

I faced him full on and he faced me directly now, because of my tone.

We stood on the grass an arm's length apart. He lifted his right hand, as if a Bible were under the other, and I did think he meant to swear, but his hand was cupped. Was it in reference to that night, his touch, cupping my young breast? I don't know. Did my forty-five-year-old chest heave out toward that hand as I inhaled with anticipation? I'm afraid it did. But he did not reach out. He made a fist instead and held it to his heart, or maybe just his chest. I do have a tendency to overread a situation.

"I remember every moment," he said.

I honestly didn't know if this was a lie, and he could see this on my hard face.

"Grimsley, how could I forget?! You still look the same, you still *smell* the same, my God. My second night on this campus. How could I possibly forget?" He grinned and gave me a friendly squeeze on the shoulder.

I could have slapped him.

"Hey," he said. "You're the one who didn't recognize me. In the chapel? Don't get mad at *me*."

I walked away, seething. He really thought that I didn't recognize him. *And it didn't bother him*—not in the least.

I headed toward the archway to leave the quad.

I heard the quick rasp of his wingtips on the stone, jogging up behind me. I expected he'd grab my elbow and turn me toward him. I had an instant fantasy that that's what he'd do, that he'd turn me around, stare at me, and kiss me, all Gothic-romance-novel-like. He'd kiss me.

He slowed beside me instead and said, "If I owe you an apology for anything I've said today, or anything I ever did in the past, say so now."

I kept walking.

"Hey," he said. "*You* kissed *me* back there. If you'll recall. What's going on here? What do you expect?"

I kept walking only because I didn't know what else to do. I've always believed that when you don't know where you are or what you're doing, you should at least try to make some sort of progress till you know where you are.

"So, what?" he called out. "You're just going to keep walking? Nice seein' ya?"

I stopped. He was right, of course. I was out of hand and we both knew it. What was I thinking? I stopped, turned. I waited for him to walk to me.

"I think," I said, "that I want to be that girl I was when we were together. Which is not possible." I looked down. "That's unfair of me."

"That's not what you claimed a few minutes ago."

"You always did have a strange effect on me. *That* hasn't changed. I should never have kissed you. I'm sorry."

He smiled and I knew the nuance of this one, and my heart lifted a little, a wounded bird making a few tentative flaps to right itself. He had enjoyed it, was glad that I had kissed him. I could see it. A glimmer of ego. He'd been flattered by the kiss. A weakness.

"Grimsley, I'm thoroughly and devotedly married. I couldn't and wouldn't do anything that would jeopardize something I care so much about."

"And I wouldn't let you. I will do nothing more. Again, I'm sorry."

And this time, he came to me. He hugged me. A friendly hug. At first anyway, a chest hug. He is tall, more than six feet, and I am not short but nor am I tall. My nose pressed against the collar and knot of his tie. I got nothing of his scent but cloth. But he smelled my hair (I could hear the deep nasal inhalation) and for a moment our bodies, surely independently of our minds, his mind anyway, simply moved to where there had always been a perfect fit. Our pelvises and upper thighs connected. He released me before any stirrings could happen down there in those stylish slacks of his, before I could know if there would have been any had I worked to maintain the embrace.

*

I eventually brought him to the bench where I'd been sitting with Amanda and Sterly when I first saw him. I had gotten him a cup of coffee at the Bryan Center because he said he was tired and still on Los Angeles time, hadn't slept well. We'd walked slowly and easily. He was inquisitive despite his fatigue, asking about my work, my social life, my love life (sex life, I guess I should say, since I've loved only one person, as I now acknowl-edged). Then I asked about his and he quieted down considerably and changed the subject to what I actually did all day, which is about as inter-esting as watching someone else not catch any fish on a still lake.

I live in the books I read, and I thrill in watching this university come to life every fall, the peculiar interactions among my bookish col-leagues. Mary, my younger sister, lives in Raleigh, I told him, and I engage in her life, help her with my two nephews (ages ten and twelve now and all joy for me). I let her vent about her well-meaning but lumpish husband, who works for IBM in the Research Triangle but I don't know exactly what it is he does, though he's tried to explain it to me at least three times. My youngest sibling, David, is the communications director for the Department of Medicine at UNC Chapel Hill and is a saint. This always makes for an exciting March and a healthy Blue Devils/Tar Heels rivalry as the NCAA basketball season concludes. He has two daughters, ages five and seven, angels so far, but destined to be more complicated than the boys. This is plain to see already though David and Stephanie, his wife, a peach, have no clue what's headed their way. I help them out when they need to get out of Dodge and have a solo weekend (usually Vegas, Lord knows why).

And here I am, Grimsley, the only odd name in the bunch—my parents had to use me to figure out that straightforward Christian names were the way to go.

"Don't say that," Em said. "Your name attracted me to you, as I recall."

"Not my body?"

"Well, that, yes, of course. But as I remember it, I was attracted first to the sound of your voice. It's faded a bit though. Not the contralto lilt but the accent."

"Yeah, not as geechie as it used to be. All things fade, and it was really my mom's voice. Once I lost her, I didn't want any unnecessary reminders."

Just as I was beginning to feel self-conscious at becoming emotional on this point, I felt his hand on my shoulder. He pulled me close in comfort.

"I'm sorry, Grims. Truly. My dad died three years ago. No one can prepare you for it, and it doesn't go away."

"I remember you were close with your dad."

"Something of a moral compass for me. The most important man on Earth."

*

So, really, by the time we'd strolled the long concrete walkways to and from the Bryan Center to emerge again into the main quad, all leafy and old, he with some high-test coffee and I with iced tea, I'd pretty much told him all the main points so that there wasn't anything in between he couldn't infer. My life is simple, as I said, and I like to think, as many have noted, that there's genius in simplicity. But now I knew that we shared at least one new thing we didn't before: the loss of a vital force in our lives.

"How's your time?" I asked.

Em looked at his watch. "I've been invited to a small dinner at 5:30, so I have an hour or so, then a reception at Washington Duke Inn. You? Do you need to be back at work?"

"No, I'm done for the day. I'd been planning to see a movie with a friend, but—"

"Boyfriend?"

"Male and a friend, yes. Let's sit," I said, nodding to the bench where I'd been sitting that late summer day, just before classes were to begin, in the fall of 1985.

He stared at the bench. These were big, broad, solid affairs, twelve feet long, elevated, comfortable to sit in, with tall backs, and a beam to push your feet against. Not really a bench so much as a place to congregate, lounge, study, gossip. They were scattered throughout the campus, totems in front of fraternities painted with Greek insignia, plain ones in front of dorms. And the longer he looked, not taking a seat, the older he seemed to become. It was almost as though I were watching him age before my eyes, as though the man I'd been seeing was the boy I knew then and, just now, as he gazed upon this bench, the years blew over him like a breeze, and I watched his once smooth skin coarsen and sag, his golden hair dull, and the whites of his eyes take on the yellow-gray cast of old newspaper. Was it me, or was he actually changing? Aging before my eyes. More likely my eyes, fogged as if waking from dreamy sleep, were simply clearing.

"Interesting choice of benches," he said, stepping up onto the platform and deflating into it as though defeated. He slid down to make room for me and I sat.

I couldn't believe he knew that this was the bench where I'd first seen him. He couldn't possibly have remembered. When he'd passed me that day, he literally hadn't known I existed. So this could not be what he was referring to. What then?

"I don't understand," I said.

He looked at me, partly glad, partly disappointed. "Well, then I feel better."

"Did something I don't remember happen here?"

"It's where I broke things off between us."

"Is it?"

Now I had to race back in my memory, for I did of course remember exactly what he'd said, the words he'd used: "*I* asked *her*." They don't seem like much, but they were a dagger at the time. I'd thought it had been in my room, after sex—that's where it happens in my head (clearly that's unconscious resentment on my part). And then I'm in the bathroom down the hall from my room retching into a sink.

"It seems a little more than coincidental, don't you think?"

"What?"

"Directing us to the sight of our first . . . coupling. And then to the place where we broke up. Are you trying to tell me something?"

"Such as?"

"Are you being mean?"

I truly was surprised by this. If there was any meanness, it was completely unconscious. Mean was the last thing I intended to be to him.

Untitled

She saw him approach through the very same archway, though by now his posture and gait were familiar, and always a welcome sight. It was early April, and the willow oaks that lined the quad had their new leaves. The air was finally warm enough for shirts only, but the ground was too cool for bare feet, Em's preferred footwear. He had on his ragged Top Siders held together with duct tape, jeans, and a white button-down shirt. One of the many things she liked about him—his indifference to clothes and style.

He was likely coming from his friend David's room, a fellow apprentice writer and his closest male friend and drinking buddy, who had pledged the Beta fraternity. Like her, Emerson had little interests in groups and so had avoided joining a fraternity, though he did enjoy their parties.

She checked her watch, registered the time (four p.m.), the date (Tuesday), recollected her roommate Amanda's schedule—chem lab from three to six. Emerson lived, like many freshmen, in a dorm room with two other roommates, so they rarely went there. Amanda had an off-campus boyfriend, so evenings she often stayed there. This left them with a happily empty dorm room and wonderful, carefree sex and talk and more sex.

The girl closed her Complete Pelican Shakespeare *(presently Lear).*

"Hey," she said.

He smiled and sat beside her on the bench, but he looked out.

"Have you decided on a topic yet?"

"Topic?"

"Familial infidelity in King Lear*? Animal metaphors in* Othello*?"*

"Ah, the Shakespeare paper."

When this second semester of his freshman year had begun, they'd both enrolled in Professor Porter's Shakespeare 201, a senior-level class Emerson had talked his way into, as freshmen were discouraged from that level.

"No, not yet."

"You'd better get on it," she said. Even the word "on" had two syllables when she said it—ooh-wn—and he smiled at her when he heard it—ooh-wn. "You know Professor Porter will be gunnin' for you in particular."

"I'll be all right."

It was evident that Shakespeare was not on his mind, but that something was, and her first emotion was concern for him.

"Grimsley." He said it with such weight and finality that her concern immediately turned to herself, her turning stomach.

"Yes," she said cautiously.

"David is bringing me to the Beta formal next week. He's convinced his 'brothers' that I should be encouraged to join their ranks."

"I thought David knew you better."

"Evidently not, but he's a sweetheart and has insisted."

She paused, still waiting for whatever was to drop. "And?"

"I'll be attending with Ashley Bennett, a Tri-Delt. Do you know her?"

She did indeed, a stunner from the Upper East Side of Manhattan, a junior like her. "I don't think I do," she said. And then she exhaled, feeling relieved at what she knew would be easy and happily said. She even chuckled a little. "You. You know I'm not the jealous type. You can go. If someone asks you to something you want to go to, I'm not going stop you." She gave his shoulder a nudge.

He turned and looked her in the eye and said, "I asked her."

She knew she'd responded physically in some way because he winced.

He said, "I'm sorry."

"I think I understand," Grimsley said. She waited a few moments more. Perhaps a lifeline would appear. When he offered no more, she knew she did understand, and she stood and left the bench. She climbed the flight of stairs to her dorm room. She placed her big book on her desk. She leaned on her desk, breathing unevenly. She headed back down the hall to the bathroom, thinking she would splash water on her face. Instead she looked at her reflection—hateful to her in its plainness—stared down into the sink, gripped either side, and retched clear, viscous fluid that clung to the dry drain.

Five

Wow, I thought, looking from the bench to my old friend in his middle-aged blazer, holding a cup of coffee. How long buried the actual memory had been, unearthed now intact.

"Ah, yes," I said. "You're right." I took a deep breath. "It hurt pretty bad at the time."

"But not for long, yes?"

"That I can't say. I don't have a good memory for pain." I'd become a terrible liar today!

The truth of it: I was shattered for many weeks. I, of course, saw him in class each Tuesday and Thursday, and this was fine—good, even, as it gave me a reason to be near him and a chance for us to at least small-talk on neutral ground. And I could watch and admire him without feeling self-conscious, as he was often a lively presence and liked being the center of attention. It was after one of these classes that he'd first given me a short story and asked if I'd read it. How could I say no, or ignore my quickened heart that he wanted my opinion? It got to be almost regular—he set himself the task of writing a story a week on top of his schoolwork.

It was when I saw him outside that class that it was bad, when he was with someone else. During those first couple weeks apart, before he asked me to read that first story, which allowed me to stay intimately connected with him, he knew I hurt and so never sought me out in a let's-just-be-friends kind of condescension. When I was headed down the ugly concrete walkway to the Bryan Center, the relatively new social, arts, and commerce center of the university, and he was leaving it, heading my way with his arm around a girl, he'd remove his arm when he saw me. That spring he gravitated toward the East Coast neo-hippie types, long skirts and bangles. As we'd pass, he'd say, "Hi, Grimsley," gravely, not with false cheer or ease.

I'd be able to muster a straight-faced, "Hey," clutching books to my chest.

We both kept walking and I'm sure he didn't look back, though I wouldn't know. It was all I could do to make it through those doors into the carpeted, air-conditioned center and find a banister to lean on until it went away. It felt like stomach flu. I'd close my eyes till the nausea passed and ultimately try to focus on my class work, my savior that spring. I could dive into books and forget about him for hours.

"Well it didn't last long," he said.

"I'm sorry, what?" I asked, shaking my head to clear it.

"I meant that it wasn't long before we were enjoying the best parts of ourselves," he clarified. "On occasion at least."

"Which parts," I asked, "the sex or the stories?"

Just thinking about that time a quarter century ago brought back the stomach churning, but his comment pulled me out of it—moving on to what was a happier period after the pain of the break—and it became clear that I hadn't necessarily lost him completely, that there was hope, a hope I guess you could say I hung on to for four more years.

"Both," he said. "I hope you don't remember either with regret."

"No, I can say truthfully. That one day, that one sentence, that was the worst of it. Unhappy dagger."

"That's not the line."

"But that's how it went."

"I'm sorry."

"I don't doubt it."

I retrieved my buzzing cell phone. I sighed, looked at Em. "It's my sister."

"Take it."

"Hey, Mare-bear," I said, turning from Em. My sister has a knack for calling at the exact worst moment.

I hung up and turned to Em. "I've got to go pick up my sister's dog from the kennel. Long story."

Em nodded.

I turned away and said, "Fuck."

"Is it that bad?"

"I just *hate* that both my brother and sister think of me as lonely old Grimsley who, unmarried and childless, has nothing but time time time on her hands and is happy to do any and all errands for them."

"So say no."

"I can't."

"Why?"

"*Because.* They're right!" I smiled. I stalled a little, then said what I was thinking: "I'm not ready to say goodbye. I haven't heard a thing about you, what you're doing. Mr. Big-Time LA writer."

He smiled self-consciously. After a moment he said, "How long an errand is it?"

"Half hour each way."

"If I come with you, can you get me to the restaurant—I think it's called the Grocery—by five-thirty?"

"That's a great place, and yes, five-thirty we can do."

"I'm not ready either, and I'd kind of like to take you up on your offer."

"Offer?"

"To hear a confession of mine."

"Well, come on then!"

And then he grinned at me, and I knew why, the way I pronounced "on"—ooh-wn. It just came out like that. He was bringing out my mom's geechie accent from way back.

*

And so it was on this hour-long errand down to Raleigh and back that I heard how my old friend was. He hadn't won that Emmy. In fact, that show had been the only one that had ever made it to the screen. He'd moved out of magazine journalism when he'd sold a script for a bundle of money, though it was never made. The money was too good to pass up, even though it was usually just that—money—with nothing to show for it but the things it bought. He became a highly regarded script doctor, noted for his ability to elevate and condense dialogue. So he was often paid during a movie's production to come fix a script.

"A couple years ago," he told me, "Jeff Bridges walked off a set and refused to do another minute's work until they brought me in to get the dialogue right."

"You are kidding me!" I said. "*Jeff Bridges*?"

"Yep," he said, slapping his knee in a way I knew to be proud and ironic. "Great guy, by the way."

"What movie?"

"*Men Who Stare at Goats.*"

"Never saw it."

"Consider yourself lucky."

We were cruising west on I-40 toward the doggy-daycare center where my sister boarded her boxer-shepherd mix, McGee, which she couldn't get to because of a doctor appointment/soccer game conflict, and Eric, her husband, was traveling. Em kept his window rolled down and his hair was whipping around his face.

He raised his voice to be heard. "You see *The Blind Side*?"

"Loooved it."

"That Sandra Bullock speech about family and watching each other's back to get Michael to play hard and use his strength?"

"Sure."

"That was mine."

"Get *out*!" A quick glance and I saw he was staring out the window at the pine trees whizzing by. "That is so cool. So if I Google it, will you come up?"

"Nope, that kind of work goes uncredited. Screen Writers Guild has all kinds of rules about who gets credit for what."

"Does that bother you?"

"Nah, pay is too good to complain."

"But you don't like to do it, sounds like."

"I'd rather be writing my own stuff."

"Why aren't you?"

"Money."

"I thought you married into a wealthy family."

"Why did you think that?"

"I thought I read it somewhere."

"Well, a lot can be mishandled in a generation. I mean, there is some money in trusts, we live really well, the kids' schools are taken care of. Collista is accustomed to a certain style, and I still have to work. And I *want* and *like* to work."

"I can hear a 'but' in there."

He turned to me. "For the past five years, I've been pitching television ideas and writing pilots, getting paid a shitload for stuff I know—even while I'm working on it—stuff I *know* will never make it off the written page. I find myself sometimes *dreading* that I'll get a call from my agent saying a network has ordered a pilot."

I said nothing.

He said, "It's a living."

I still knew him. I knew what he'd been. And knew—I could hear it in his voice and see it in his face—what he felt inside.

"Have you tried returning to fiction?"

He grunted.

"But you're still telling stories, what you always wanted to do, what I always thought you did best. Just in a different form."

Silence.

"What was it Professor Blackmore told your class? This would have been your senior year—I remember because I was working at the library by then. You opened the book right there and read it to me. Something about how stories were fundamental to our . . . our *species*. I remember that. You were checking out one of Blackmore's books and you read it to me right there, like you were on fire."

Em stared straight ahead. I waited for the light at the end of the exit ramp to change, staring at his Romanesque profile.

"The need to tell and hear stories," Em said, quoting words all but literally etched into his mind, "is essential to the species *Homo sapiens*—second in necessity apparently after nourishment and before love and shelter."

"So does this have anything to do with the shame you spoke about earlier?"

He didn't answer. Neither of us spoke after that until he asked, "Where are we going?"

"Canine Castle," I told him.

Untitled

She hadn't been roused in the middle of the night since Emerson had scratched on her screen and begun the affair that had ended so abruptly eight months later for reasons she still didn't know. It was now early May, a month since he'd told her he wanted to see someone else. They had remained friends, possible only because, well, she adored him, and he was so guileless and natural. And of course the short stories, which flattered her (though they were only okay, and she was gentle in her written critiques). They mainly saw one another on Tuesdays and Thursdays during their Shakespeare seminar. She loved to listen to him spar with the professor, who finally acknowledged that Em was not out of his league amongst the few juniors and mainly seniors in this upper-level class. Grimsley herself struggled to keep up, but she was glad she'd taken the class. The sight of him still charged her—happily, not sadly, and she didn't think this happiness strange. She did not feel heartsick.

They had just finished reading Hamlet *(finals were this coming week). Oh, how Emerson loathed Hamlet. Hamlet the character. He'd had the respect of the class since his bawdy reading aloud of* Othello *(he could have been an actor if he'd wanted), but* Hamlet *left him cold, so when Professor Porter caught him drifting, he called Em out. There were about twenty students, a standard classroom, rows of individual desks, facing Porter's large wooden desk, Porter pacing back and forth in front of a green blackboard. He was a hulking man, six-four and built like a defensive lineman. He had bushy hair and rosy cheeks above a full salt-and-pepper beard, a hearty fellow in all ways, which made the sickly looking lips all the more out of place. Porter mainly talked and questioned, didn't use the board at all, but throughout class he flipped a piece of chalk as he paced and occasionally took a drag from it. Nicorette had yet to make it to the United States and Porter was doing his best to quit smoking.*

The class erupted in nervous laughter when Emerson explained that he was sick of reading about "a pussy."

"Would you rephrase, please?"

"Okay, wimp."

"You're speaking about one of the most famous characters in literature."

Without referring to the text, Emerson said sarcastically, "Ohhh, 'how weary, stale, flat and unprofitable are all the uses of the world!' So get on with it. Character is about action. Character is action. Here is an entire play devoted to a main character who fails to do anything on purpose. It drives me bananas."

"Until he kills Polonius."

"He even fucked that up! He thought it was the king! His first action was an accident."

Grimsley was the first to laugh—he always made her laugh—and the class followed. But not Em, who was overly serious at this point.

"Your language, please." Porter paused. "Isn't inaction a kind of action, Mr. Randall?"

Older teachers still used student surnames.

"No. Action is action. Romeo and Juliet risking all to marry and enjoy a night in the sack, that's defining action and drives the plot forward."

"But Hamlet is debating murder. Have you ever tried to imagine how difficult it would actually be for a good human being to kill someone, a family member no less?"

Emerson responded, "It was apparently pretty easy for the king."

"But that, we surmise, is because of the type of man the king is. And he's no Hamlet."

"Exactly!" Emerson said, slapping his hand on his desk. "We know who the king is through his actions. Here is a whole play devoted to a character's inaction and the horrible, and stupid, consequences."

"Shit or get off the pot, is what you'd like to say to Hamlet," Porter said.

"Thank you."

Porter turned his back to Emerson, took a drag from the damp chalk, and said, "Youth to itself rebels, though none else near." He turned to the class and said, "Page nine-sixty-six, act five, scene one, Ophelia has drowned. Suicide, yes?"

The sound of twenty hands riffling pages, Emerson's included. Professor Porter could always reengage him.

"That's an action, no?"

"Ah!" Emerson said. Now it was just him and the prof, and we were the audience, which is how I think he liked it. "From inaction to death. That's how it goes for most, is it?" He turned a few more pages. "I'm with Yorick. At least he made people laugh while he was alive."

"Soon, you, too, will be with poor Yorick," said Professor Porter.

"Not sooner than you, I hope!" Em shot back with a sly but friendly grin. He knew Porter was the scholar and not him.

Porter smiled, removing the chalk from his lips. "I hope so, too, Mr. Randall."

*

Grimsley let him in because he still made her tingle on sight. Because he was a writer, and she liked writers. And because she knew that even though he'd left her, he was still sweet, was and always would be the kind of guy who would leave a bundle of daisies on his girlfriend's bed on a gloomy February day, Valentine's Day (melted her heart). He thought about that kind of thing. He was special. She had felt herself lucky then, when she'd found those flowers, and she felt herself lucky now.

He went immediately for her, held her, put his nose to her neck and breathed deeply.

"I miss you," he said.

She knew that he missed her body.

"You've stopped giving me stories."

"I got tired of hearing whom they were derivative of."

"They haven't all *been derivative."*

He was still smelling and kissing her neck.

"That 'If I want to read Salinger, I'll read Salinger,' remark was kind of harsh."

"I hope it did the trick," she said.

He force-walked her to the bed and they crashed down on it. They rolled. His hand went for her crotch but she gripped his wrist.

"No."

"Oh, God, please. I'm so hungry." He put her hand on his crotch.

59

"Begging for a mercy fuck?" she asked, giving him a squeeze.

He sat up immediately and faced her. *"No, there's sex to be had all over this campus tonight. I want you. I miss you."*

He seemed genuine.

"Do you think you could love me?" she asked.

He thought long about this. She wasn't sure if he was considering a lie or trying to figure out the answer himself until she heard his response.

"No—I don't want to love anybody right now. But I really, really like you. And I want to know you forever."

That seemed like the truth. So she rolled on her side, propped her head on her hand, rubbed his crotch. *"Oh, my,"* she said. Then, *"Tell me a story."*

Em groaned. *"Oh, please. Grimsley."*

She was enjoying this. She could tell how aching he was for release.

"Can it be really short?" he asked.

"The shorter the better. Tell me the shortest story you can."

Em settled a little, thinking. He faced her, head likewise propped on his hand, a mirror image.

"Baby shoes for sale. Never worn."

"I've heard it. Attributed to Hemingway. I want a story from you. And besides, that's not a story. A story is where something happens."

"The king kills himself," he said.

"Still not a story."

He smiled and said, *"The king killed himself, and the queen died of grief."*

She smiled. She grabbed hold of his belt, said, *"That'll do,"* and kissed him.

*

That was their first time after the breakup and last time before school ended. If anyone had better sex on campus, she wanted to know who and how.

A month later, she wrote to Emerson in Chicago where he had a summer job in the factory where his father worked (conveyor belts, she never bothered to find out what kind) to tell him of the pregnancy. She'd forgotten to put her diaphragm in, she said, so surprised by the visit. They'd gotten lucky their first time (but after *that she'd always taken precautions). She was sorry. She was writing to let him know she'd gotten the confirmation only hours earlier and did he have anything he wanted to say?*

He phoned immediately; they discussed the situation. He asked her if she wanted him to come down to be with her. She said she hadn't decided yet what she was going to do. She could all but feel his stomach turn in the silence on the other end of the line.

"Well, do you have anything you want to say?" she asked. "It's not mine alone, you know."

"You're certain it's mine."

"Yes."

And here she felt he committed the single act of selfishness she'd experienced. She never felt their relationship was selfish, that the sex they'd continue to have without commitment was selfishness. She never did anything she didn't want to do. But here, she felt he thought only of himself.

"Jesus, Grimsley, you're not thinking of having this baby."

"As I said, I haven't decided what I'm going to do. These are the first words I've spoken aloud to anyone in the few days I've known."

"You can't have this baby."

"Well that's not a fact."

"Think what it would mean for you. Would you leave school? How would you take care of the baby. I beg of you—"

When he didn't say more, she said, "I wouldn't ask you to do anything. I would make no requests. My family and I will take care of anything and everything. I won't even tell them whose it is. Though if I did go ahead with it, I'd never shut you out. I'd welcome you in if that's what you wanted."

"I can't do it, Grimsley."

"I'm not asking you to."

"Grimsley, if you have the child, I can never see you again."

She was so hurt and shocked, she didn't speak.

He said, "This is something I don't know. Are you religious, is this a religious decision for you? We've never discussed religion, I only assumed you weren't, given our relationship."

"No, I'm not religious. Per se."

"Then why on Earth would you have a baby in the middle of your senior year of college?"

"It's why we're here, isn't it?" she said. "I mean, it's the one thing we know for sure is that we're meant to have babies. That and death. We're all going to die, and our only known purpose is to have children. Otherwise, it's the end of us, right?"

"Generally speaking, I suppose you're right, but the human race is not going to die out soon from underpopulation, and this is by no means your own single opportunity to have a baby. There will be time, once you've got a degree and have a known way of supporting a child."

She said nothing.

"I'm sorry, Grimsley, I'm amazed you would even consider having a baby."

"Well, at the moment, that's all I'm doing."

"I urge you not to go through with it. I certainly can't be a part of it and am grateful beyond words that you claim that's an option for me."

"Are you angry? You sound angry."

"I'm just upset that's all."

"Well, so am I," she said. She hung up in anger, leaving him to stare at the phone in his hand.

Ultimately it was her mom, who'd come of age in the sixties and had fought for abortion rights in the early seventies and had rejoiced only a decade earlier at the Roe v. Wade *decision, who had convinced her daughter to terminate the pregnancy. Grimsley agreed it was best and really knew from the beginning what she was going to do when she realized she'd never be able to bear telling her father. Her mother was with her every step of the way and, while the procedure went without incident, it was passing through a line of anti-abortion protesters, under her mom's powerful arm, that was the worst part of the affair.*

A few days later, she wrote to Emerson a two-sentence letter: "It's done. You don't need to worry anymore," signed only with an austere "G."

She received his letter the very day she posted her note, and he broke her heart with the kindest apology she'd encountered to date. He explained how terribly he'd been feeling when he thought back on their conversation, and said that while he stood by everything he'd said, he felt that given this, it was her decision to make and that he would support it in his heart if she followed through with it. He begged her forgiveness. He asked her to please let him know one way or another what she was going to do, so that he could sort things out in his own mind. And he said the most important words of all to her: he said summer would be over in two months, noted the date that he planned to arrive in Durham to begin his sophomore year, and wrote that "I hope I haven't broken our friendship beyond fixing with my selfish response to a situation that must be so hard for you, far harder than it is for me. Will you see me when I arrive?"

She wrote back immediately, fearing that the coldness of the letter he'd receive in a day or two would be misconstrued and that of course she'd never not *want to see him, explaining more fully her rationale and how it had all played out. And they corresponded all summer. He even sent her a story, though he confessed he was so tired from work that he wasn't writing nearly as much as he'd hoped. She wrote to tell him how much she loved the story (though with a little more enthusiasm than she actually felt). By the time he rolled into town, it was as though they hadn't been apart at all. If only because he felt completely free to ignore her.*

He called her the day he arrived (he'd bought a used car and driven down himself). After a tentative reunion on the quad, they decided to have a beer at the Hideaway, the on-campus watering hole. It turned into a delightful pitcher, several beers. It was easy and fun. They laughed. They embraced chastely on parting. They didn't see each other again for three weeks.

Six

I turned right on Broad Street, back in Durham, having accomplished our errand. He'd stayed in the car when we'd arrived at my sister's with McGee. Thinking it wasn't like him not to want to come in—he was always a gleeful snoop and a gossip when we were together, always hunting fodder for story, wouldn't dare *not* look in a medicine cabinet in the bathroom of a stranger's house—and asked him why not. It was a development McMansion, and he was pretty much right when he said, "I can already see what's inside—it'll depress me." I knew what he meant, though I suspect it wouldn't have depressed him as much as he presumed.

The worst part of the trip was the ride back to Durham. Because we didn't say anything. He just stared straight ahead and I kept trying to come up with something to ask, but each question—how's your relationship with your kids, your son and your daughter, what are you working on now?—I could foresee from the look on his face would muster only a half-hearted answer. I didn't want to do that to him, and neither of us went in much for small talk. Honestly, he was that low. And I didn't know him well enough, after all these years, didn't know how to make him feel better or at least try to buck him up.

Truly, I was so sad for him that I was ashamed of my behavior earlier. What had I been *thinking*? How awful to throw more confusion into his mind. Something was going on. Maybe there was more to it with his marriage (there always is—no one is ever honest about their marriage if things are bad). Maybe financial matters were worse than he was letting on. People say that sex and death are pretty much what everything boils down to, Eros and Thanatos, but if you don't have the money you need, that ranks pretty high. The responsibilities of being a parent, too—I wouldn't know, but judging from the fathers I'm close with, kids weigh heavily. Was he having issues with his children? He'd already shown me pictures and mentioned nothing beyond the suggestions of an argumentative marriage—but one he adored—and a difficult fifteen-year-old daughter, which is par for the course according to every parent I know.

So whatever it was, I couldn't know, and I couldn't do anything about it.

I pulled up in front of the Grocery, a restaurant run by a Durham native serving really good, locally sourced food, and looked at my watch. "Bingo, right on time."

He didn't move to leave the car.

"Food's really good here, you're going to love it."

He turned to me. I held his gaze. It looked like he wanted to say something, and desperately at that, but couldn't. As in a dream when you're fleeing something and can't move, he looked into my eyes, lips parted—nearly trembling, I thought—but saying nothing.

I put my hand on his shoulder and said, "You need to do something for *yourself*."

He smiled sadly and said, "Such as."

"*Write*."

He smiled. "You're the best, Grimsley. Always were."

If this whole day hadn't been so charged, I'd have gotten out of the car to say good-bye, give him a last hug, but I didn't want to risk it. I'd have done something, I know it. So I said, "Ditto."

He waited. He waited some more. He wanted me to act, I could see it. Now was my opportunity to take what I'd initially and immediately wanted at his first embrace in the chapel. I did nothing (sometimes inaction *is* action). He got out of the car, paused a while, let me stare at his starched shirt midriff, then leaned down through the window.

"Hey. There's another gathering of some of Blackmore's old students, assistants, colleagues at the Washington Duke. I mentioned it, eight to ten. Will you join me?"

"I'd better not," I said. Did he know what I meant? Did I? "But say hey to Professor Porter for me." I called him by his first name now, Elgin, when I saw him, retired but still around.

"Good Lord, is he still alive?"

"Alive? He wasn't *that* old when we had him. He's late seventies but in pretty decent shape. The chalk treatment worked!"

That got a smile out of Emerson, but it quickly turned sad again as he continued looking at me with that seeming urge to say something.

"You should join me then."

"I'll think about it."

He nodded and reached his hand out to me. My hand met his but he simply touched my fingertips.

"If I don't see you . . ." he said. "Well. Maybe I'll be back in town one of these days. Research for a biopic on Daniel Blackmore."

"Do you *think* we'll ever meet again?" I asked.

"I doubt it not," he said.

"Then *adieu*," I said, and was soon headed to my very lonely house, nothing but sadness in my heart. The image of that fine-looking face framed by the car's window—how pale his face had gone when I asked if we'd ever see one another again. He surely presumed we wouldn't, as did I.

Untitled

Memory is untrustworthy, but there are landmarks in most people's lives that can serve as reliable, permanent markers in a trek through one's past. For instance, she would never forget the summer she had the abortion, the August before her senior year—that was too awful to forget, though she didn't let him know how she'd actually felt about it till years later, the wretched words shouted at her by the protesters. Both recalled his third nocturnal visit to her dorm room during the fall of her senior year—as a senior she'd been able to get a single—in which they had resumed their physical relationship. They hadn't seen each other, except for that once at the Hideaway, drank a pitcher of beer between them, embraced once, and went their way. Three weeks later, he showed up at her room a little before midnight. She'd been studying. He was clearly tipsy but he hadn't been hunting sex. He had a short story he wanted her to read—the first since the one he'd sent over the summer. It was the third draft of something he'd begun in the summer, and rewritten— "figured out what it was really about," he said. He hoped to present it to Professor Blackmore for the longer narrative fiction class he'd been accepted to. (Blackmore refused to call writing "creative," arguing that fiction was not the only writing that was creative; maybe not instructions of how to put together your outdoor grill, but newspaper articles, even recipes for tomato sauce can be creative, and not even to a degree but absolutely creative.) Em's eyes were electric and his whole body seemed charged, not from the alcohol, but from excitement, from the sheer youthful energy of his work, and she found it powerfully attractive.

"What's it about?" she asked.

"It's about the accidental death of a thirteen-year-old girl and its impact on her boyfriend and both of their families. It's about the way love and death—"

"Well, gracious," she said, hearing her mom in her voice. "Don't tell me. Who else has read this?"

This halted him. He looked at her for what felt like a long time. "No one," he said, apparently baffled by the question. "Who on Earth besides you could I show this to first?"

She thought immediately of the girl she'd been seeing him with all over campus. Short and cute with very dark hair who dressed in long, hippie skirts and a lot of bangles (walk the hallways of most dorms and half the music coming out of the rooms was Grateful Dead, a band she never took to). She thought of this girl. Why not show her? Or his friend and fellow literary aspirant, David?

"I mean, who else could I trust?" he asked. "I need to know what you think before I give it to the class. David is smart but far too ruthless and articulate, damaging rather than useful. In class they're knuckle-headed hyenas. But you. You're such a good and thoughtful reader. Your criticism, it doesn't hurt, unless you think it should. Mainly you say things like 'Here's what gave me pause.' Instead of 'Here's what's wrong,' or 'The problem with this is.' And even when what you say stings, you're always right."

She felt an enormous rush of pride. Suddenly joyful, as if the story were his heart itself. And wasn't it?

She nearly knocked him off his feet. She hugged him. She drew his head down and kissed him hard. He resisted a little but maintained the embrace.

"Are you seeing anyone?" she asked.

"Off and on, nothing serious."

"Then what's the problem?"

"I'm just surprised. I didn't come here for this."

"You've earned it," she whispered, undoing the button and zipper of his jeans, giving his mind no time to override the body. She was pretty sure there wasn't a guy alive who didn't love oral sex, so even if he wasn't in the mood, they'd been together the previous year enough that she knew exactly how to get him going, and once she got him going he'd never be able to stop. He moaned when she stopped to stand and remove his shirt, so she knew he was hers and would carry them both through to their mutual satisfaction.

That time he stayed the night, and he was always welcome. They made love in the morning, which, like their very first time, was brief and quiet and for him alone. And this was fine for her. She loved every moment near him. But sometimes he waited till she slept and was gone when she woke, or sometimes he dispensed with any waiting at all and simply dressed and departed with a kiss. And this was fine, too. Whatever he needed.

The next time he showed up, it was three in the morning. He'd been drinking with his buddies. She'd been dead asleep. She opened the door a crack, squinting in the fluorescent light.

"I'm sleeping," she said and asked him if he knew what time it was (he didn't). Beer made him exuberant and playful and, if anything, overly solicitous. He'd start going Elizabethan in his language, which annoyed her vaguely, but no matter how much he drank, she never worried about his being overly aggressive.

"Where's the story?" she asked, joking. Sort of.

"What?" he asked.

"Good, then I can go back to bed."

"I've got the first draft of one, but it's not ready."

"Can I read it?" she asked, yawning.

"If I can come in," he said, grinning (this time it was plain why he was here).

"How do I know you're telling me the truth?"

"Yea, verily, Grims, I'd never lie to you."

This she believed but she said, "Let me see it, I want it here in this room." Since he wouldn't have lied, he'd be able to go to his dorm room, which was on the other side of the quad, and this would give her time to brush her teeth and prepare for sex without any unpleasant consequences afterward. He was panting a little by the time he got back, rushing, no doubt afraid she'd fall back asleep, which she had. But she'd left the door unlocked and he found her naked underneath the sheets. She noticed he'd taken the time to brush his teeth, too, which she found sweetly thoughtful, given his aroused, semi-inebriated state. Mercifully, he truly was famished for sex, finished quickly, and just as quickly, she was asleep, waking at nine in her room alone. She stretched, and the memory of the night came to her. She looked to her desk and saw, happily, his pages. She retrieved them and tucked herself back in beneath her warm comforter to read, her favorite thing to do on waking.

These pages were okay (she always enjoyed reading them, good or bad). It was very first drafty, as he said. When she recalled the sex, though, she figured he'd had about as much lasting pleasure from her as she had by the time she'd finished reading, so in a way it worked out even.

But it had been the first story he'd given her, that first time when he'd arrived with that story and she, overjoyed, had seduced him, that set the bar for all the visits that followed. It would be work-shopped in Blackmore's class, rewritten and rewritten again, but the following morning after he'd left, the draft had transported her. It was a real story, an original work that was completely his, unlike any of the writers he loved. It was the beginning of a world that she knew was unique to his psyche.

The story concerned the drowning of a thirteen-year-old girl at a community pool. The girl had been swimming with her neighbor (and, secret from the adults, her boyfriend, also thirteen), when an epileptic seizure carries her under. The boyfriend—they had only kissed, but had done much of that, and had exchanged vows of their forever-love—had gone to the concession stand to buy candy, a package of Now & Laters, her favorite. His mother, their chaperone this July day, had been reading on a lounge chair and was taken from the reading only by urgent whistles and calls to clear the pool as four lifeguards pulled the girl from the water. The neighbors, the parents of the drowned girl, had kept the epilepsy a secret. While no one could be blamed, blame and guilt are inevitable.

Both families attempted, unsuccessfully in their own way, to cope with the tragedy. Only at the end did Em reveal that the story has been narrated by the boy, from his adulthood decades later, as he details the enduring consequences for him personally (he blamed himself for not only her death, but all of the damage). Seeing the ways families damage themselves, intertwined with the powerful effects of young love cut short, made the story end with kettledrum finality; the combination of damage and love from the vantage point of the boy, young and old, created the kind of additional layering of meaning that couldn't have been common among nineteen-year-olds.

I never wanted to know the provenance of his fictional stories, preferred to keep them purely in the magical realm fiction transports me to. But here I was seriously tempted. I did not ask, though, and he did not offer.

Blackmore thought the story, "Now and Later," so good, he asked Emerson to send it to Esquire, *and he, Blackmore—at the time fifty, an accomplished and nationally recognized novelist—would call Rust Hills's attention to it, the magazine's fiction editor. Hills rejected the story because, at nearly twenty thousand* words, it was too long; but he had admired it enough to encourage Emerson to feel free to submit more work to him. Emerson published it his junior year in Duke's literary journal, which he was editing by his senior year. And the association with Hills would ultimately lead to Emerson's first nonfiction piece for the magazine and his start as a journalist.

But the power of that story, for her, reading it that Sunday morning, so undid her that she wrote him a long letter about it. A long, serious critique, mainly admiration but with questions she had, and thanking him for the best work he'd done to date.

And that was how sex went between them as well. He would arrive with a story and they would have sex. They didn't date and they rarely socialized. The stories and the intimacy they gave the friendship for the most part squelched the nausea she'd initially felt when she saw him with other girls. She had her own relationships, more sexual than romantic. But it would be years before she realized how unusual and lucky it was to be so sexually compatible with a man as she felt with Emerson. She simply enjoyed it, and never demanded anything from him other than to be the first to read his stories. Of course, he didn't always arrive with a story, but arriving with a story had become something of a secret handshake between them. The sex felt better when he had a finished story to offer her.

Only once did things end badly. It was early February of that same school year. Emerson had not only remained in bed after their love-making, which was unusual, but he furthermore slept in. Perhaps because he was nervous about the story and wanted to be there when she read it or, more to the point, nervous about her response to it.

She didn't even finish it.

"Get out," she told him.

He woke, squinted and rubbed his eyes.

She held up his pages and tore them in half. She dropped them in the wastebasket.

"Grims, that's my only typed copy."

"I want the handwritten copy as well."

"Did I write something wrong, is anything in it not true?"

"That's the problem, it's too true. I will not be written about. You will not write about me, and you will not write about us."

"But why?"

"Because it's my life. What happened last summer is mine. And it's private."

"But the story is fiction."

"No, the names have been changed. Everything in here happened."

"Is the story itself no good?"

"I didn't get far enough to tell." Her heart raced as she tried to be reasonable. "There's a difference between personal fiction and memoir veiled as fiction or taking events in my life and making them yours. You need to understand the difference."

"You can't tell me what to write," he said.

"Then this is the last we see each other." She paused. "Get out."

"Jesus, okay, I won't write about you and me, I won't write about you at all."

"Thank you."

She stood by the bed in her white terrycloth robe, arms folded.

He lifted his eyebrows and said, "Come back to bed? Could do with a little send-off."

"Get. Out."

Realizing for the first time that a woman's anger is not quickly doused, he dressed and left the room, carrying his shoes to put them on in the hallway rather than endure her heat a moment longer than he had to.

That had been the first week in February. On Valentine's Day she found daisies on her bed. She didn't see him again till after spring break. It got so close to the end of term, she wondered if she'd done something permanently wrong, or worried that she'd asked something genuinely unreasonable. Indeed, she wasn't quite sure of the reasons for her visceral response to being written about.

The night was warm and she was dressed in her favorite light blue cotton T-shirt, windows open, sheets only, comforter no longer needed. She woke at the knock. He always knocked though she rarely locked her door. She looked at her clock, glowing red in the dark. One-thirty, almost.

"Grimsley, it's me. You awake?"

She opened the door just wide enough to show one squinting eye.

"I don't have a story."

"Come on in," she said, sleepily. "I was getting worried you'd never come back."

He watched her strip her shirt off, took great pleasure in the form of her perfect body, the arch of her back, her angular shoulders and wing-like blades, and her graceful movements rolling into bed and pulling the sheet over her. She smiled at him and said, "Well, come on, then, Romeo."

"God, I missed you," he said later, by then on his back, both of them giddily spent.

Seven

What I did next is easy to say. I went to see him at the reception. *Why* I did it is considerably more complicated. What happened as a result did change my life and I can only pray it didn't damage anyone else—most of all Em—though I shudder when I think of it. I truly was interested only in his welfare at this point, speaking my mind and trying to help, though you may not believe me. I understand why you wouldn't, given my erratic behavior in the afternoon, before I saw how sad he was. It wouldn't be the first time a teller's motives for the story were questioned or the first time a narrator's reliability could, and should, be considered. Be my guest. Judge for yourself.

Know this, this I believe: in my heart, I went only to *say* what I did.

I'd gone home, heated some leftover chicken and potatoes. Watched the news. I tried to read but couldn't keep my mind on it. I felt churned and sad inside. I felt worried for my friend; he was clearly in serious doldrums, a big boat on an endless, mirror-still ocean, not a breath of wind to fill his strong sails. But I also felt something I almost never felt. I felt lonely. Alone. It had been a long time, years and years ago, when a traveling buddy headed south to Switzerland and I stayed a few extra days in a rat hole in Antwerp. Such a lovely city but I was lonely there. That, and when my mother died, but that was a bad patch so vast as to be beyond description in actual words, at least in my capacity with them, though others have tackled grief well (I read all I could at the time).

As I said, I'm one of the lucky ones. I'm part of a family I love, in the place where I've been most all my life. I have few material cravings; and only one true and modest addiction—buying first-edition hardcovers; how could I not buy Jonathan Franzen's *Freedom* the day it was published? The latest by DeLillo or Roth or Toni Morrison? I looked forward to anything David Foster Wallace published and will forever lament when I think of that anguished soul, and that I will never read a new book by him again. I take one major trip a year—this spring it's Israel, already planned, with a friend from work who's single like me (or the trip that was supposed to be; all travel being up in the air right now). I like my work and my colleagues, I'm paid well enough to afford what little I need, and will in three years finish the payments on this small house I own just a five-minute drive from Duke.

I couldn't get him off my mind. I knew, *knew*, I would never see him again. I kept picturing how ashen he went when we said good-bye. I needed our last meeting, probably ever, to be better than that. It didn't have to be good-bye forever. There were never any strings to our relationship and I wanted him to know that if he was in trouble, he had a friend in Grimsley down here in Durham. No strings, not ever.

So I waited till 9:50, arrived at the Washington Duke Inn five minutes later, hoping to catch him leaving the reception rather than going in and finding him. If I'd missed him, I could call his room, I figured.

I parked in the left lot where I always parked. I'd earlier changed into jeans and a shirt, wore my Jack Purcells, so I wasn't dressed for a reception even if I'd wanted to go in.

I didn't have to. When I entered the inn, Emerson was leaning on the check-in counter. He turned with an envelope in his hand and slipped it into the inside pocket of his jacket. He literally started when he saw me standing there.

"Grimsley," he said.

He looked nervous, so I said, "It's just your old friend Grimsley with one last thing to say and then I'll be off. Promise"

"I was going to have a drink at the bar."

"I love the bar here, but could we just walk? I'd rather be alone."

We exited through a back door to a patio where conversation and ice rattling in glasses were soft. We took the steps down to the right, passing a row of golf carts to the path surrounding the practice putting green. The air remained warm and still and sweet.

"First, I want to apologize for the way I behaved this afternoon. I feel terrible. It wasn't right. You just brought me back to those days so powerfully that . . ."

"I know, Grims—me, too. But I just couldn't possibly."

"I'm glad you couldn't possibly. That's very much you."

We strolled slowly. He looked at me then and said, "You didn't have to drive all the way here just to say that. And I hope you know no apology is necessary."

"No, that was not what I needed to say." Silence. "Two things, one angry, one sad, and since I don't want to end angry, I'll start with that."

"*Angry?*" he said. "What did I do?"

"Nothing."

"Explain, then."

Here, I stopped so that I could face him, the fine features of his face softly and clearly lit, partly from the moon, partly from the hotel's lighting, which he faced; my features would be dark from his vantage. "I was going to say disappointment, but it's anger."

"At what, please."

"That you haven't been better, that you haven't done more, done what you set out to do, done what so compelled me to you always. Telling stories."

"Ah that."

"Yes, *that.*"

"I tried, you know, but it turned out not to be my lot. And you have no right to put that on me. Life is hard, and fast. Kids arrive. The need for money bears down. We make our choices and live with them."

He turned, not wanting to face me, but strolled slowly, not fleeing and not lashing out.

"Emerson, stop." He did. I went to him, and now I stood on the other side so that he could see my face. I wanted him to see my face when I said it.

"Take. Yourself. *Seriously*." He looked puzzled. "You took yourself seriously once. Do you remember what you did?! You were the son of a factory worker in Chicago and you wrote to Terry *Sanford*, the president of Duke University; he was this state's governor before he came here and became a United States senator after. No slouch, in the smarts and influence department. You had the balls to write him a letter personally and it was so appealing he set you on a course toward that A.B. Duke scholarship."

"Me and twenty-five others."

"But you got it, and you got here. Do you remember what charisma and ambition you had? You *flew* when you were here. You were prized by one of the country's great writers. You became a great writer. You went from dirt in Chicago, to the upper echelons of Manhattan and LA. You have a beautiful wife and healthy kids and you tell me you're fucking bummed out at *life*? How *dare* you complain?"

"Sorry, Grims, I just can't accept blame for how I'm feeling. It is what it is. But if what I think you're telling me is that I need to write again, I'm grateful." Then he said, "It was hard for me when I lost my dad. He died just three months after he retired and I could never help him the way I ought to have."

"Okay, so maybe that's where the sadness I see comes from, but I don't think so. You loved your dad and he loved you and that's a damned lucky thing and it's also better that you outlived him and not the other way around."

He turned and walked. I jogged after him. "Like I said," I went on, "I don't know why or what happened, I don't know anything about your life, but somewhere along the line, you clearly stopped taking yourself seriously. What I saw today and what I heard, I know. So I'm begging you as your old friend, *and* lover, please, take yourself seriously again."

He said nothing, which was like him. He was always thoughtful, always listened. Whether in the classroom, or struggling through a personal problem, he first took in whatever information was available, listening before responding. There had been a big drug bust that involved a number of friends his senior year; he was asked to write about it for the university newspaper but didn't know where his allegiances should lie. He sought the advice of professors, me, David, and other friends, absorbing our words first before taking what he needed or knew to be useful and only then writing his opinion piece. So I knew he heard me.

We strolled again in silence.

"Okay," he said, "I'm ready for the next."

"I suspect it's related to what I just said. But I don't know you well enough anymore or what's happened in your life, but it's just what I see."

"What do you see?"

"I saw today how *sad* you are."

He flinched. "Sad? I'm not sad, I'm just, well, in a spot in my life. Collista says we're both going through our midlife crises." He put his hands deep in his pockets. He said to the sky, "This too shall pass."

"Crisis maybe, but midlife has nothing to do with it," I said. "Sad, way deep down. It's so far down, you can't even see it anymore."

He chuckled a little. "You think?"

We'd come to a division in the path, one that led back to the patio, the other I could take around the building to the parking lot. I stopped to face him.

"It's as plain as your face to me."

"So you came all this way to tell me I'm depressed?"

"No, I came all this way to let you know that your old friend is still true and here for you. Anything you need."

I was still, after all these long years, in love with him.

I took a breath. "I got so shaken with worry when you said goodbye, that this really *would* be the last time I saw you, I had to find you."

"With worry you wouldn't see me again, or worry for *me*?" He'd jumped on this without even a pause for consideration, he was wound so tight with self-consciousness. Not self-absorbed, fragile, self-hate, just clear self-consciousness about all, except for the sadness I could see. That's what I saw in his face, in the speed of his response.

"Worry for you." He didn't avert his eyes, so I kept on. "I don't expect to see you again. But it doesn't mean I can't know you. I want you to be in touch when you're back. Call the library and ask for me. Search my name on the site—it includes my email. Will you do that?"

"Well, sure." Now he looked at the pines that lined the eighteenth hole. "Of course."

"I hope I'm wrong. But I see what I see. And I just want you to know that if the sadness I think I'm seeing rises up on you as a real threat, if you need to talk, or whatever, I just want you to know I want to help."

He gripped my shoulders and said, "I'll be okay, Grims. And I'll thank you forever for what you've just said. You are a good, good friend." He gave my shoulders a parting squeeze. No embrace.

"Will you *write* to me?"

He paused but said, "You bet."

I smiled. "All right then."

I turned and walked to my car.

"Hey, Grims."

I turned full around and stood, just ten yards away. He smiled that too-familiar smile, his *old* smile, that youthful, seductive, evil-beatific smile, like he knew something you didn't want him to know, and he shook his head. "You *still* teach the torches."

A knot in my throat yanked taut at the particular Shakespeare reference, but I managed to swallow and fake a grand smile. "You're a doll," I said and turned for my car.

I was at a full-on weep by the time I turned onto Cornwallis Road— tears so plentiful I almost missed the driveway I'd been turning in to for some twenty-two years now.

Why? I wish I could say it was for him.

Eight

I certainly didn't know my own mind or soul by the time I stepped through my front door. I'd sat in my gravel drive in the dark car till the tears wore me out and I figured it was safe to go inside. It wasn't. And not because there was an intruder or a snake (I'd actually had a troublesome house snake a few years back, a big black razorback). My house proved unsafe precisely because it was empty. I'd never felt so alone or so foolish, so utterly wasteful, as I did when I saw the old jug by the fireplace.

I'd gotten it on a trip through that area of North Carolina famed for its jugs—actually referred to as Jugtown—and the quality of the clay in that land that makes them so fine; it was once a thriving industry, but is now more or less a little pocket of hippie artisans practicing this once-lively craft. Moonshining also used to be a way of life down here. Now that craft is kept alive, just barely, by tourists. I'd bought the jug as a souvenir, an old-fashioned moonshine jug with a ring holder at its narrow opening that would have had a cork in it were it to be of use. But it wasn't destined to remain a souvenir of the place I loved so. It was just an empty vessel, of no use beyond sentiment, remembrance of things fucking past, and the sentimentality of the object itself suddenly revolted me. This empty, useless vessel.

I smashed it on the brick hearth. Then, when silence flooded in again, and nothing, absolutely nothing had changed, I collapsed in a heap as if all the bones in my body simply vanished, cutting my arm on a shard of Jugtown kiln-fired clay, and I kept sobbing till there were no more tears, till I was just wept dry.

Eventually, I suppose I pushed my body up, forced it up, in my recollection of it—this was just three months ago—like a prisoner of war who's been beaten simply because he annoyed the prison camp's general, who as far as I was concerned that night was God himself, to be thrust back into my self-built cell.

I found a broom in, yes, the broom closet—even *that* I hated, I hated that I had a broom closet where I kept a broom. I remember distinctly hating myself for it. I swept up the shards of my broken jug but left them in a pile in front of the fireplace. I didn't want to cut my feet, but I was too despondent to actually care to pick it up, rid the nice little symbol I'd made for myself on my own damn floor. One sweep of the broom spread blood across the floorboards at the hearth's edge, which was when I noticed I was cut. Not badly. I put the broom back and dabbed the cut on my triceps with a paper towel.

I walked up the five steps to the third level of my little house in the woods. It's nestled into a beech forest, this house, and my back patio looks out onto a pond where all kinds of winged creatures come to play. The middle level has a small kitchen and dining/living room with the comfiest reading chair on Earth. And there's a lower-level, rec-roomish space that leads to the garage. In this room, I keep my desk and watch occasional TV on an old leather couch big enough for the occasional guy; we can watch a movie and do whatever else feels right or needed. It's also where I found that snake, so I tend to make noise when I head down there.

Tonight I hated my funky little house for the boring little nothing that it was (I, of course, being the boring little nothing, not my house and home of two decades). I took a shower, hot as I could stand it, wanting it to scald me. I combed my hair and let it leave a soothing water mark on the back of my night gown. Wondering how on Earth I would sleep, I pulled a bottle of bourbon from the cupboard, poured three fingers into a juice glass, and drank it down. I leaned heavily on the counter.

When I turned, I saw Emerson through the glass door leading from the patio back into the living room. Though I was so shaken I wasn't sure. It was dark outside and lights were on inside. I walked closer, not believing my eyes. I approached the door, unthinking. I saw my reflection super-imposed over his image, just enough light to illuminate him, but barely, enough to doubt what I saw.

*

It was him, not my imagination or a play of the light. But he didn't move when I unlocked the door and pulled it toward me. He stood, arms at his sides, without expression. Too terrified, I judged from his stone-cold stare. I'm not sure how long we stood there. Long enough for my heart to rev up to full throttle, like the first time we'd exchanged words in the Duke gardens. He just stared at me, my old friend, once twenty-one, now past forty. But even with two decades of husk enclosing his true self, I still saw the boy he'd been that first moment on the main quad. He surely saw the same in me because he was, well, *here*. But he was so clearly wrecked, inside, that I knew it was up to me to act. Thinking only of him, of easing him through why he was here, I first reached out and touched his hand, just a stroke to make sure we both knew we were actually here together in the flesh and not dreaming. I needed that at least.

"Em, you're here. I know why and you shouldn't try to deny it, so let's get it over with and figure out the consequences when we can think straight. It's already been done. You're *here*, for a reason, it's done in your head. What we're about to do is just signing the papers. You can't not do it. It's over." When he didn't move or speak, I said, "I want this, too. It will all work out."

When he stepped through the doorway, I realized how clearly upset he was. He continued to stall, so I took the back of his neck and pulled is face down to mine and that cavern of want I'd felt in the chapel all but moaned open for him. We kissed hard and long with the old familiarity, as if nothing, but *nothing*, had changed in all these years. That kiss was like opening a long-lost book of poems to your favorite one and finding your old self responding emotionally to the words exactly as you had in your passionate, poetry-loving youth, but with a freshness and perspective you'd then lacked.

I broke from the kiss, took off his tie, and said, "Take your shoes off."

Those were the last words spoken before we crossed over. I led him the five steps up to my bedroom. I was just in a nightgown, easily dispatched. He got out of most of his clothes, all but his shirt, still on but unbuttoned as he lay on the comforter, chest heaving, the deed done and the bed still as neatly made as it had been this morning.

It's important for you to know this because it's how it sometimes happens. The sex was about as fast and pleasant as a punch in the nose. He was only half there and came upon entry. It scarcely qualified as sex at all. I maybe would have laughed if it hadn't been Em, and therefore troubling, not to mention a pretty serious situation generally, what we'd just done. This certainly was no longer the boy I knew.

After I'd given him a few minutes to calm down, I said, "I hope this was just nerves and fright and not something seriously wrong with you."

"Me, too," he said.

"Can I get you anything?"

"Water. I'd really like some water."

I put on a robe, descended to the kitchen, and filled two glasses with ice and water. I gave him enough time to put his clothes back on if that's what he wanted or needed. But I did truly hope to find him still in my bed, ever my favorite place for him to be this many years later, I realize now, the one man I'd ever, and still, loved. He was in bed, hadn't wanted to bolt; his shirt was on the floor with the rest and he was under the covers, staring at the ceiling.

"Okay then," I said, "have a good long drink. Then we talk."

He sat up to drink.

"You didn't get drunk after I left, did you?" I asked.

"Thought about it. It was literally drink you out of my mind or come here. Tell me I didn't do the wrong thing."

"I think you did what you had to do."

I snuggled into him, put my head on his chest, and again the familiarity both startled and comforted me.

"I'm sorry," he said.

"For the performance? Don't be. You just did something deeply against your nature. You've been unfaithful to the person I'm guessing is your best friend. I'm the one who's sorry."

"Are you?"

I thought I was until I answered. "No. I think you had to do this. I've never met your wife. I guess I'll be worried and sorry if I've been part of some damage that turns out to be permanent, which maybe I have been. I guess my question to you is, do you wish you'd never seen me today?"

"Yes, I truly do wish I'd never seen you."

We were quiet for a while. I shouldn't have asked if I didn't want to know the truth.

"Should *I* be sorry?" I asked.

"No. This was my doing, my responsibility."

More silence. "When was the last time you had sex?" I asked.

"More than a month ago, and it wasn't pleasant. We've been fighting a lot. The intimacy is hard. And my equipment hasn't been operating the way it used to. I'm getting old."

"They have little blue pills for that now, have you heard?"

"Yeah, well, if there were some kind of actual desire I felt coming from Collista, I kept hoping I wouldn't need it. Maybe you're right, it's been going on for a while."

"Either of you taking anything for depression? That can take down the libido from three hundred yards."

"I didn't know I was depressed till you told me tonight, remember?"

I paused. "Has my body changed?"

"Your body, what little of it I caught sight of just now, remains one of the most perfect I've ever beheld."

"It isn't anymore."

"Like you said earlier, we don't change fundamentally. Yours is not only a beautiful body, it's the most generous I've ever known."

We were quiet then. I snuggled into him after that sweet thought (he may have dozed for a little) and let what happened cool off. But then my flesh got hungry again, my hands, my breasts, my legs, my belly—it all just wanted to merge with him. And before long, his body answered back. And he was right; he didn't need those pills at all.

He was so surprised he threw off the covers and stared at his own engorged cock, a lovely pink flag pole, *throbbing*. "My God, I haven't felt that in years."

I took hold of it, smiled and said, "Me neither."

He sigh-moaned from the pleasure I'd begun giving and, well, I will only reveal that during the next ninety minutes I was returned more completely to the young woman I once was than I ever had been and surely ever would be.

*

Emerson said a sweet but definitive good-bye the following morning. I called work and told them I wouldn't be in till noon. Trish didn't ask why, likely too surprised since I'd never missed a day in twenty years, except for once when my sister went into labor at a very inconvenient 4 a.m. with my youngest nephew. My love—for I knew he was that and had always been and would be forever—departed for a 10 a.m. flight, after a final and customary and lovely early morning pleasure for him. He showered and dressed. I delayed work because I wanted to enjoy this uncommon spring morning, with hot coffee and birdsong. As I sat on my back patio staring out at my pond, the heron arrived, which I took to be a good omen, a blessing somehow.

After the second sex . . . remember how I said a woman can be mad from 360 degrees? Well, the best of us can fuck that way, too, and I took Em through most of them. After the second sex, the really good, protracted, amazing sex that night—we both liked it athletic—we were too keyed up to sleep. I poured us both a bourbon. He asked if I had a cigarette, and I did, in the freezer, for just such occasions; this is Durham, after all, tobacco central. We sat out on my back patio in the cool, still air. It was then he told me more about what I'd already sensed.

After Duke, when we let our connection go, he was productive, he said, but terribly alcoholic. Not sick alcoholic, but he hated being poor in the city, and said he was pretty much either drunk or getting over a hangover from the day he got there till the day he got a sweet assignment for *Vanity Fair*, then recently resuscitated, profiling a young new actress named Julia Roberts. He said he was surprised I hadn't remembered this because we'd talked about it when he'd left New York and stayed with me before heading to Los Angeles. I told him that was more than twenty years ago, and my mind wasn't what it used to be. But anyway, this led to more stories, more connections, a healthier life in Los Angeles, meeting and marrying Collista, kids, and eventually big money writing movie scripts and the television shows he now said he had little respect for.

After a second drink, I thought his infidelity began to weigh on his mind when he grew quiet, but he said, "Grimsley, I don't feel bad about what happened, and I don't want you to. I'd have guessed I'd feel terrible, but I honestly don't. What we just did was so good and so right, how could I? But I'm not going to tell Collista. In fact, it's somehow made me want to commit more to her, to repair what damage I've done to her and to us, and I hope she'll want to do the same. Does that make any sense? I'm thanking you for that, and for this, what's happened, and I hope you understand."

He looked down, took a deep breath. "I hope you don't think I'm an asshole who used you."

I laughed.

"Thank you for laughing," he said, still looking down.

"I know what I'm doing," I said, "who I am, and who you are. We're still the same people, and we still have the same relationship we always did. Great sex and no strings, and I'm good with it if you are. I'm true to my word, old friend. I'm here if you need me, but you have your life and I have mine, and I truly *am* happy. Never more so thanks to what just happened, I know. You probably just saved me, coming here. I'm exactly where I want to be. I will be sad when you go, but no worries about my showing up on your doorstep with a surprise." (Not true, as it would turn out, but it wouldn't matter by then, not the way I'd have thought, had I known then what I know now, anyway.) "I loved what we shared years ago, and I loved our renewed glimpse of what we had just now. And God knows my body's still hungry for you as it ever was. Don't think you're being selfish. I am so happy and satisfied by what just happened in there. For me, it's truly a 'more that I give, more that I have' situation. Our bodies are just *good* together. I don't know what it means. But that sex just now was deeply good for me and I hope somehow good for you, or at least I hope it causes no harm."

"Grimsley, I've had a number of lovers, good and bad, for love and for need, but I can honestly say, I have never had better sex than I have *always* had with you."

"Same here."

"For some twenty years, I've thought about the sex we used to have, like the sex we just had—and I swear, I didn't think I was actually capable of it anymore, or feeling it like that—I've thought about our long-ago sex so, so many times, maybe in my mind I've never left you, that part of you."

"Maybe," I said. "But I'm going to be sad about it, since I now know I'm still in love with you and it's not likely we're going to see each other again."

He didn't respond to that one. Our cigarettes were long gone and we'd drunk even the melted ice so our glasses were dry. "Time for sleep? What time's your flight?"

"Grimsley, I think I can say this now and truly mean it. I do love you, and did. I love you, my old, old friend."

"I love you, too. I always have. But it's a different love, and we'd never work that way, so I'm going to try to understand that and try not to be sad." I stood. I didn't need any more talk or love. I pulled him up by his hand and held it as we went to my bedroom and slept a good and easy sleep.

So. Wordless sex at dawn like old times, a shower for him while I made coffee, and a good kiss good-bye. He did want to make it clear that this *would* be the last time we'd see each other. He hoped I was okay with it. I told him yes, that I was rooted here and happy and truly grateful to be returned, briefly, to the girl I was by his still-magnificent body and gorgeous face and the smell of his skin. To know that we don't really fundamentally change.

I reiterated my request that he remain in touch by email or letter or phone.

I know he arrived safely in Los Angeles, because he emailed when he got there:

Dear Grims,

Can't thank you enough for helping me see clearly again. But especially for you. I finally see you for what you were years ago and are still, an actual angel.

If I write a story worthy of your eyes, I'll send it along. I just may put my mind to it.

Yours,
Emerson

I wrote back:

I hope you do! And I meant what I said, dear friend. You know how to reach me.
G

Those literally have been the last words we've exchanged, and now I need to decide whether I'm obligated to say more.

Nine

I began this story in early August, with lightened duties at the library, to try to understand what happened that day in May that would change my life.

In July, Maggie, my primary care physician, looked over my blood work from my summer physical and said, "Well, I can tell you one thing for sure: the reason you've stopped having your period is not menopause." Then she looked at me hard and said, "You, girl, are *pregnant*." She closed the manila folder and said, "You're also old for pregnancy. So we've got some talking to do."

I nearly tipped over in my chair.

Maggie, who's my age, went on to say she'd seen this only once, a friend of hers, not a patient, spontaneous pregnancy at age forty-five. The situation was fraught enough, she said, that if I wanted to proceed, she recommended I also see a high-risk pregnancy specialist, someone who would do something called a CVS, an invasive but reliable test to examine actual chromosomes, and could also perform specialized ultrasound examinations for spinal, heart, and stomach abnormalities.

If I intended to keep it, she said. Given the risks for the baby and me—my age, the difficulty of raising a child at my age, single no less—she recommended I at least consider termination.

It took two minutes, at least, for the shock to wear off, but it felt like ten silent hours of time—me alone—the shock of it—how I'd never even given a thought that I'd be able to conceive. Not a single thought of it. But when the news sank in, I decided immediately to accept it as the gift that it was—its very unlikelihood a sign in itself—and, provided it and I could be healthy, there was not an ounce of doubt about what I intended to do this time around. Now, at the end of August on a day very much like the one I described earlier, two days before the beginning of the term, when I first beheld Emerson twenty-five years ago, I conclude this memoir. I imagine my son as an adult and I pray to be alive to see him off to college. I hope he's every bit as beautiful as Em was, and as beautiful as the young men strolling the Duke walkways past me now as I type these words, beneath the magnificent willow oaks that line the main quads.

Yes, I know it's a boy from all the tests. I waited thirteen weeks to give him any chance to end himself if that's what needed to happen, telling myself every day not to hope too much, to assume the worst, that at my age my eggs were more likely than not to be defective. But he stayed. I've had all the tests that are available at Duke Medical Center and more are on the way, but yesterday, fifteen weeks from the day of conception, Maggie looked over all the reports from the specialists and said, "All systems are go, Grimsley. You're *having* this baby boy. Hope you're ready."

"I'm ready for whatever comes," I told her, with what I know was the biggest grin of my life. I was ready, was and am. My son already feels like a breathing creature I can love for all time. I know for certain he will be the second man I'll want and be meant to love.

*

Of course, the question of whether to tell Emerson about my situation has been the main thing on my mind since I found out, and I've been back and forth on it, worse than Hamlet.

I haven't told anyone yet, although my colleagues will pretty quickly know something's up when I forgo our regular occasional night out at Magnolia Grill. I have maybe four cigarettes a year so, that's not a problem, and I will miss that soothing glass of wine when I pick up a book at the end of the day to read. Maggie asked me if I had any concerns about social issues—*it's not common for a single woman your age to be pregnant*, she told me, *there will be talk, you'll probably get more attention than you want*. She said, "You haven't offered who the father is, so I'm guessing that's going to remain unknown for the time being."

"Yes," I said.

"Well, that will *really* stir things up in this little university community."

"So let people talk. They're so damned bored with their own lives, they'll have a ball with this one."

"I don't know, it's kind of conservative down here if you haven't noticed."

"Anyone who judges me harshly for what I choose to do with my own body can sit on a corncob."

Maggie chuckled. "I'm glad I know you, Grimsley."

"Feeling's mutual."

She put me on a wagonload of vitamins, told me how much and what kind of exercise I needed to do, daily, to prepare my body for this, and the exercise has become a form of meditation, transcendental even, a religion, caring for my body with a devotion I'd rarely given anything other than reading. I didn't think of my uterus as some delicate wine glass that had to be handled with care. I thought of my whole body, this carrier of a new life, the way an athlete must think about hers. I was preparing for one big important performance, and if that went well, I'd have some strenuous years ahead. I'd seen those shadowy lidded eyes on my brother and sister after long periods of sleeplessness. I'd seen the relief on their faces when I stayed at their home so that they could get away from the kids for two nights— you'd think it was New Year's Eve, they'd be so giddy! Mary told me she and Jim didn't have an actual adult conversation for eight years after their first boy, Connor, was born. That wasn't going to be an issue for this old maid.

But Emerson. This was a question.

I started, I think, no fewer than twenty emails to him over the summer. I tried another ten on a legal pad with a ballpoint pen, and I could scarcely get through more than a few lines, whether from "Well, old friend, life throws us some wingding curveballs, have you noticed?!" to "I'll just come right out and say it since I don't know any other way."

Problem was, I didn't know if he'd *want* to know. I didn't know enough about his life to predict the consequences of the news. Last thing I wanted was to hurt him or his family.

But I also didn't want to deprive him of his part in the situation, if this time he wanted a part. And say the marriage didn't actually work and he or Collista called it quits? Then he truly might want to know. Wouldn't he? Maybe not. I hear parenting is hard even for youngsters, so maybe this would be one too many anchors that would keep him from doing what he needed to do for the second half of his life.

Ultimately, whatever the consequence for him, whatever he'd think about it or want to say, it wasn't going to change what I intended to do, which was to bring this baby into the world, best I could, whether Emerson wanted me to or not.

So, in trying to figure out a way to tell him, I just started telling myself this story, who I am and how it happened, and once I started I realized that I wasn't writing my way to an understanding of that day and night, or to an answer as to whether or how to tell Emerson the news. I was writing this for the boy inside me, so that he would know how he came to be. I figured it was a good enough story to tell, and one he'd need to know. This record will be here for him when he's ready for it.

I love my dear boy, already I do, and not just the idea of him. I love the living cells of him in my flesh, half mine, half Em's. I want my son to know that Em was the one man I ever loved, that he was a good and a smart man who honored me in every possible way; he was always kind and good to me, and his parting gift to me was this precious new life. Maybe that was the reason for all of it from the very start. Who knows—the world is full of mystery and wonder and, yes, shame. Whether or not I decide in the end to tell Em, I will know in my heart that I did what I thought best, and I hope our son will understand.

And I now know. Just this very second! The weight has lifted! Thank you, keyboard and computer! Thank you, Act of Writing itself. Thank you, *story.*

I will not tell him.

It's clear. At least not till our son is born whole and breathing, a viable little man, and provided he doesn't kill his mother in the process. Odds are better than they used to be in these parts, but it can happen, and I am nearly a half century old. I figure if that happens, then whoever raises the baby—my sister or brother, or their kids—they'll know about this document and give it to him when they feel he's ready. Perhaps he'll want to hunt down his father—I'm guessing that he will. I hope he will keep in mind the physician's credo: first do no harm.

So, that's that. Hamlet should have been a writer; it would have taken longer, but everyone wouldn't have had to kill each other!

My due date is the first week of February 2011. I can hardly wait.

Part II

One

I arrived in Los Angeles in the early evening on November 5, twenty-six weeks, three days into my pregnancy. I'd fixated so much on my pregnancy, and keeping the growing life inside me healthy, that length of pregnancy was how I measured all time. The longer I went, the more I stressed about it. I was terrified of waking in the middle of the night and giving birth prematurely, or worse, having a *stillbirth* (how can two words so sweet in themselves, terrify me with their awfulness when combined?). I felt as though this life inside me *was* my life and if I lost it I would die myself. This is probably wrong, not literally true but emotionally true, as my therapist would insist I acknowledge. Yes, got one of those, too—a therapist— never would have believed it myself given how skeptical I am of psycho mumbo jumbo, but I did, to deal with all this, and I'm glad for her, good old-fashioned Germanic Ericsonian; she's regularly telling me, "Grimsley, we can control our actions, but we can't control our emotions. We try to manage them, but we can't turn them on and off like a light switch. It's okay to *feel* as you do." Yet I did feel it almost literally, as if this little man inside me was my actual life, this beating heart, my heart, the elbow or heel that's pressed on me from within, my own soul wanting to be unleashed. With two months to go, I prayed to God Almighty. *Laus deo.*

*

I was so rattled just to be in a rent-a-car at LAX trying to type my destination into the GPS machine I'd also rented that I couldn't figure out why it was taking me so long to type in the name of my hotel. I typed with the speed of a chimp, thinking it was my addled brain. And I was addled, because it wasn't till I'd finally got the zip code and half the name of the hotel in that I realized that the keypad was in alphabetical order, with A in the upper left and Z down in the lower right. (Never realized how programmed the brain can get for the qwerty keyboard system.) Once I realized it was the keypad and not my brain that slowed me, I calmed a bit. And lordy, that GPS thing, what a godsend. How on Earth would I have found the Standard without it, light fading fast as I drove up La Cienega Boulevard. "In 200 feet, turn right onto Sunset Boulevard." A woman's voice but definitively mechanical; I've heard guys actually have fantasy relationships with their GPS's voice. No danger here. "Turn right onto Sunset Boulevard." Thank you, GPS.

A valet parked for me and I had a carry-on packed for a two-night stay with a redeye home Sunday evening.

All seemed normal outside. But goodness, I felt like it was 1983 and I was on mushrooms. One of the grad students I work with, who's from here, told me I should stay at the Standard. It was like a party, not a hotel lobby, music was thumping away, there was a woman in what looked like a giant fish tank reading an iPad, and scantily clad, yes *scantily*—I'm not kidding—in a glass case behind the very gay check-in guy. My room had a bean bag chair! All of it disorienting for a Durham girl.

I stepped out onto the small balcony overlooking an impossibly blue pool around which throngs drank and smoked to the music. Happily the place had a decent retro diner, where I devoured a burger at the counter. Then, three hours ahead of LA time (and about three decades behind it), I slept fast and hard, despite the music and crowd noise, my nerves and disorientation having exhausted me and given way to deep blackness.

Part of my exhaustion was also the nature of the errand, not a happy one. This trip to the West Coast was entirely unexpected. Frankly, I wasn't completely sure I knew why I was here. I wasn't obligated to be here, but I felt I did *need* to be. But I slept because the big sadness had simply not hit yet, as I was sure it was bound to, and did, surprisingly—the literal knowledge yes, but the visceral sadness was two days away.

*

The diner was open twenty-four hours, so I could get some tea and food when I gave up trying to sleep at 4:30 the morning of the service. Google maps told me the Beverly Hills Presbyterian Church was just a few miles down the road, and I was assured that the notorious traffic in L.A. would not be an issue.

I had some orange juice and hot mild decaf tea, served to me by a sleepy young man with a handlebar mustache.

So. The sadness.

Em died on Halloween in a car accident on a road I knew only from a weird movie a decade old. Mulholland Drive. I'd put him on Google Alerts just to keep track of his doings, but there hadn't been any news of him whatsoever. Like I said, I intended to keep the news of my pregnancy out of his life—at least until the little man arrived, and more likely forever—but I wanted to know what he was up to. Recognizing this, and combined with our one last wonderful night together, well, I can't say I wasn't sad after he'd gone irrevocably, returned to his family in Los Angeles. What did I do that morning after he left and I'd had my quiet coffee looking out over my pond? I swept up the broken jug and dumped it in the kitchen trash bin, put on practical work clothes, and headed to Perkins Library. I treated it like a kind of death, because in my mind that's the way it had to be. I had to keep my word and accept that I'd never see him again; for the second time in my life, I had to let him sail off to LA. And I did have my life and family here, older now, and we have only so long on the surface of earth—talk about small proportions, one life relative to all of nature—so I was okay riding this small life out, knowing I'd been luckier than most. Having had a true and genuine love that had been wonderfully confirmed twenty-five years later. That, in addition to what I've already confessed at the beginning: gratitude for my life so far.

Yes, I wanted to hear from him, be there for him, tell him to write, *write for your life*, encourage and inspire him as I once did and always could. Even from a distance I knew I could do it. I did it when he first moved to New York to become a "real" writer.

I had, until recently, forgotten when our correspondence actually ended. Honestly, I couldn't have told you. I'd thought it had been gradual rather than traumatic. And he did say that last night we were together that he'd send me pages if he wrote anything he deemed worthy. Sadly he hadn't. Sent me the pages, that is.

But as I was saying, truthfully, I felt nothing but gratitude for what I'd had by midlife and accepted the day Emerson left that this was my lot, the family I had and the work I loved in the place that was my home. Until Maggie dropped the bomb, and the whole game changed, and I spent most of the summer writing my way toward an understanding of what had happened and what to do in terms of telling or not telling Emerson. And by then I had six months before the next big decision might have to be made—I'd take it as it comes.

As I'm taking this latest development. I returned from work and checked my email and there it was. "Google Alerts" in the subject field, and without even clicking to open the email itself, I could read the news from the *Los Angeles Times*: EMERSON RANDALL, WRITER AND PRODUCER FOR FILM AND TELEVISION, 44, KILLED IN AUTOMOBILE ACCIDENT.

Details were slim, but there was a suggestion that, pending a coroner's report, alcohol had been involved. And indeed the second, and only other, Google Alert I received was in my mail the next evening (after a day of normal work that I recall only for its flatness, a day without any texture or color or emotion at all), a follow-up story and complete obit. When he'd driven off the road and hit a tree dead center, his blood alcohol level was more than three times the legal limit. The article included details of when and where the service would be held. I immediately checked flights, but I did not purchase a ticket right away. I waited two full days before I felt sure that my initial instinct was right. Again, I didn't know why I was actually going. I only knew I had to go. So on Thursday after work, when that sense had not abated, I booked the flight to LAX via Charlotte. To give myself time to absorb it all and perhaps take in a little bit of the city that Em had made his home, a place to which I'd never been, I delayed my departure till the end of the day Sunday, departing at 11 p.m., which would allow me to arrive at work on time Monday, though it would be a difficult shift, I knew. And I knew if I wanted to catch a morning flight out once Saturday was done, or felt too tired, I could rebook a Sunday morning flight. As it turned out, I'm glad I kept that Sunday clear.

The cloudless day was pleasantly cool, uncommonly, or so I was told by Mr. Handlebar Moustache, who had a look at my destination on my iPad and assured me ten minutes tops on a Saturday morning.

*

It took seven minutes, and I had a good half hour to kill before I could even go in, but at least I got a parking spot. The service was at eleven so I kind of loitered nervously up and down the street beneath the lovely banyan trees growing along this quiet stretch of Rodeo Drive. The church was lovely, a Spanish Mission–style building with a tower, a front gable, and a gabled entryway with barrel-tiled roofing. After I watched five couples enter the church, all elderly, I allowed myself in and sat in the second to last pew on the right. I liked the dark, woody feel of the place, uncomfortable pews, kind of Arts and Craftsy, décor-wise. Anyhow, it was neither a showy venue, nor a New-Agey one. I knew Emerson didn't believe in a Christian god—we'd talked about this—or at least he didn't back then, but maybe he'd had a change of heart. I kind of hoped so, given he either knew he was wrong (I prayed for his life everlasting) or perhaps he was right and most of the world is wrong and there really is "nothing but blackness" waiting for us, as one of Em's writer-heroes, Richard Yates, put it somewhere.

I was grateful that the church filled up. And yes, I had to keep myself from ogling. Because there was Sandra Bullock herself—sunglasses, hat, and stylish black dress. Julia Roberts, too, looking kind of old, actually. And George Clooney—every bit as good looking in person as he is on screen I was a little annoyed to discover. No Jeff Bridges, unless I missed him. But mostly it was common folk, or as common as they get in these parts.

The minister said a few words of scripture, but kept it to a minimum. Said a few cursory words about Emerson and losing one's life so early, before leaving the podium where four people spoke. A Marc Somebody who had his own production company (according to the single-page program) talked about Emerson's invaluable work in the film industry and made public not just his admiration for Em's work but his regret that while "we" all knew his impact on film industry, few outside the industry recognized it. Happily, Marc Somebody said, Emerson was exactly the kind of person "not to give a shit." This got an appreciative chuckle from the crowd, but not from the minister.

The next man to take the podium said he was a fellow writer and I racked my brain for where I'd seen him before, thinking I'd met him, until it dawned on me that he'd been clutching an Oscar the one time I'd been sucked into watching the Academy Awards on TV a few years ago, though I didn't recognize the name on the program. He talked about Emerson's impact on television writing, noting that the shows he'd written for or produced had been seen by many tens of millions of people. He also noted how few people would attach Emerson's face or name to a given show or movie and that, to his credit, in an industry and city of elbow-to-elbow egos, Em didn't have one, at least not that you could know about. In a business where greed and backstabbing were simply part of life as usual, Emerson was the very soul of generosity and loyalty.

To Collista in the front row, he said, "Em was the personification of loyalty and truth." To Alex and Peter, beside Collista, this writer, who might have been Em's twin brother, he said, "It will be many decades till you realize the depths of this, but you couldn't have made up a better father"—the writer choked up here—"that even in a fatherhood cut way too short, you were beyond lucky. He lives on in you. He lives on in me and a thousand others and I will miss him every day I'm alive."

I've always been a sucker for grief; watching others grieve has always hit me hard. There are no words for it; grief requires years to convey. But that honest choking up I saw brought the real sadness bubbling up from the depths in me, and a tear did career off the side of my nose.

I felt enormously grateful that Em's mother spoke next. I had never met her, and I don't think Emerson and she were close, but who knows. He always kept his personal history in the deep background department. I don't know why—I thought his rise from the lower middle classes with zero familial financial support had, well, he'd made it to a funeral like this, hadn't he? Famous, smart people speaking of their indebtedness.

Mrs. Randall, gripping Kleenex, spoke about his "indomitable spirit," even as a youth, how bright he was. Not smart, she said, though he was that, we all knew. He was like an actual light. "In a house that saw more than its share of darkness, he was my beacon," she said.

A few more tears and I had to get out my own Kleenex and try and blow my nose as noiselessly as possible.

And last, Collista spoke. She is a beauty, with abundant, shoulder-length hair, light brown, but with highlights that could very well be natural, given all the sunshine here. I could just make out the backs of the children's heads from where I sat. The girl, Alex, blonde, and the boy, Peter, had Emerson's strawberry blond exactly. I liked Collista on the spot. There was something, I don't know, *stately* about her—in her heart she was older. Elegant on the inside as well as out. Something that would be confirmed when I shook her hand at the receiving line after the service. Something I hadn't been planning on. Hell, I wasn't planning anything at this point; what could I do other than take things moment by moment?

Collista spoke about Emerson the family man, to complete the picture of work, friendship, and family; they truly were the triangle that described his life. I honestly didn't know if there was a hypotenuse; I guessed it was family, the longest and most important side, but if all sides were equal, that makes for an unworkable structure in life juggling all three in equal measures; the golden ratio, as I see it, is what we should work toward. My life had been, until Emerson stepped in. Or rather till I threw myself under his self-powered steam engine. At any rate, they truly were the three pillars of his life, of most lives I guess, unless you're the president of the United States or Elizabeth Taylor. Then I guess you're not even human.

"He worked so hard for us," she said. One of the speakers had used the word *loyalty*, and I didn't think twice about the veracity of it. But when Collista said, "And he was so true, to me and to us," looking down at her kids, her mother-in-law, her own mother and father (I presumed), the other two older folks in the front right pew. "From the beginning," she said, and looking up to the audience, "always true." Did the baby kick me or did it just feel that way from guilt?

I didn't hear any more, my mind blanked, until the minister noted there would be a reception at the Randall house immediately following the service "for friends and family." I tucked the program and my soggy Kleenex in my purse and waited in a slow-moving procession to depart the church. I was back-and-forthing on whether to attend the reception. I wanted to go, wanted desperately to see the life he'd decided to make here, the house he'd lived in. I felt it would help me with the loss and help me better know who my baby's father had become. Or was I simply being a horrible voyeur *and* making an unthinkable trespass to get what I felt I needed? Also, I didn't really want to have to confront Collista; that wasn't desired or necessary, but could probably be avoided if the gathering were large. I was just starting to wonder why the line was moving so slowly, taking forever to get out of here, when I approached the front door. I was in a receiving line. I'd noticed many bolting for the side door; I'd been standing in line with those who were offering personal condolences here.

If I bolted it would look weird. A hundred jumbled thoughts prevented my acting, and the line continued to move as I did nothing. *Keep your composure, Grimsley! Take a breath.*

I had a few moments to consider, a few handshakes and hugs away, and I got okay about it, because I knew that Em had been true to her in his heart. But just how true? I could only guess it was far more true than she would ever be able to know without knowing the rest.

Also I realized I'd be able to shake the hand of my son's grandmother, first in the receiving line, to have at least touched her flesh. I would also get to see up close Em's son and daughter—my son's half brother and sister—next in line. I would do this, and not attend the reception, much as I wanted to see the kind of house and life he and Collista had created. Since I was doing this, taking more seemed wrong, almost selfish. The service itself showed me the life he'd made out here.

His mother stood beneath the barrel-tiled gable of the exit, gray old-lady hair, plainly dressed and lightly scented with cheap perfume, and was so red-eyed and confused from grief I said only my name, then, "Emerson was a dear friend I knew at Duke. I'm sorry."

"Thank you for being here, those were good years for him, some of the best. I'm glad you were a happy part." She didn't give any indication that she recognized my name, that Emerson had mentioned me—which is one good thing about uncommon names: people don't forget them. But I did feel, or catch in the corner of my eye, Collista glance at me when I said Duke, just briefly. She snagged on that word, her glance at me definitive. Next in line was his seventeen-year-old son, Peter, who was shaking hands with his right and clutching a handkerchief in his left to dab his leaking eyes and nose. I said nothing, mouthed "I'm sorry," and moved on to Alex, the daughter who was a beautiful young lady a little too stylishly dressed for this occasion. She was dry-eyed and stone-faced. Could she have been—bored? That's what her expression said. Presumably bulwark, keeping in the grief.

I got a good look at her as I waited to shake Collista's hand because a bony, weepy woman was sobbing on Collista's shoulder and Collista was doing her best to console the underfed creature.

And then, Jesus God, a new possibility hit me, and I got a major adrenaline rush and started breathing hard: *what if he had told her?* I knew he said he wasn't going to tell her, but he also said he was going to try to repair their marriage. What if it had been part of their therapy, or if Emerson confessed out of guilt?

Freed from the wet embrace, Collista turned to me. I paused, trying to contain my nerves, long enough to tell if I'd set off an interior bomb in

The Wife. No. Not that she let on. I said only, "I was a close friend of Em's when he was at Duke."

Collista, hair long and straight, falling naturally over the straps of her black dress, was completely composed, steely even. "Are you Grimsley?"

"Yes, ma'am."

She asked pointedly, "You don't live here, do you?"

"I live in Durham."

"You've come a long way."

"Twenty-five years ago, your husband meant a very great deal to me. I've followed his career, but from a distance. I'm very sad to be here, and sadder still for your loss but am glad I came. To share the grief with people who knew and loved him."

Her eyes were bright blue and she was beautiful, but up close the dryness of her skin, the crow's eyes, the lines of life creased her face. She had been a genuine beauty once, clearly, but she was my age or a little older, and mortal like the rest of us. She looked me dead straight in the eye, no emotion, only seriousness, uncommonly composed given the situation. "Will you come to the reception, please?"

"I'd be grateful to be there."

What else could I have said? What should I have said? "If you're sure" or "If I'm welcome" or "I've come all this way, but really, I can't"? Also, it seemed almost as if it hadn't been a question but rather a command. She'd turned her attention to the couple beside me, waiting.

Well, okay then, I'd been given my answer.

*

I plugged the Brentwood address into my GPS and drove until the mechanical voice said, "In five hundred yards arrive destination": a lovely and large suburban house, lots of trees and shrubbery, a detached garage, connected to the house by a portico. I parked in the street. I took the fieldstone front walk, passed beneath a hedgerow archway, and followed a stream of strangers through the open front door into a spacious foyer.

The house was lovely and well appointed. It might have been waspy given its classical Georgian design, but instead it felt rustic—hardwood floors, distressed rather than polished furniture, wrought-iron sconces and chandeliers. The kitchen was immediately to the left, a large spacious one with a breakfast area decked out with laptops and iPads. Here a small catering crew prepared food at a large central island, and at the far end Peter was surrounded by five friends, four guys and one girl, talking quietly. I didn't and wouldn't see Alex. A woman in a black vest stood behind a bar in the foyer, offering wine and beer, soft drinks and sparkling water, which I requested. The living room was elegant without being showy. A large modernist painting hung over the mantle—it looked like a Francis Bacon, whom I'd studied in art history at Duke—this would have been interesting, but the signature was an artist I'd never heard of.

French doors along the back wall of the living room opened out onto a patio; to the right a swimming pool where those who'd arrived were already congregating, moths to flame, LA natives to blue pools of water; to the left was a wooden structure built around a large outdoor fireplace, crackling away, and beside it a wood-burning pizza oven, comfy-looking furniture for lounging, and a wet bar. All of it shaded by an enormous sycamore taller than the house. Not knowing anyone, I wandered more, through the dining room, a table laden with canapés. I circled back through the foyer, saw framed photos of formal occasions of the family—in front of a Christmas tree, gathered on a dune on a beach, the standard family images that don't really tell you anything. A stairway leading up held lovely, artful, formal black-and-white photographs of the children at varying ages signed "CM" and dated—Collista's work surely.

I passed again through the living room, at the back of which was a closed door. I turned the handle slowly, not knowing if it was meant to be private, or who knows—maybe I'd find a couple copulating. One can hope for something startling behind a closed door in an unfamiliar house, no? That actually happened in an Anne Tyler novel I'd read and loved ages ago, an older couple have sex at someone's funeral reception and are caught. So

I paused to listen if I detected movement. When I didn't, I peeked in, then entered what was clearly Em's office.

White woodworking, floor-to-ceiling bookshelves, a lot of books, but also shelves lined with half-inch-thick volumes, inexpensively bound and titles written by hand on the spines in thick black marker—scripts, I guessed, because there was *The Blind Side* among the two dozen or so lining a top shelf. Some more I recognized, most I didn't.

I could see all this from where I stood in front of a large wooden desk, which faced the door I'd come through. I walked around the desk to where Emerson would have sat, a leather desk chair, a large iMac, stacks of papers, legal pads and scripts, books, Post-It notes with to-do items—the desk of a man who was still alive, from the looks of it, the desk of a man who had finished a hectic day and had simply stood up when called for dinner, fully intending to return.

"I haven't been able to touch it except to read what he'd been working on."

The voice made me jump and take a breath, feeling immediately guilty for the intrusion. Collista stood in the doorway.

"I'm sorry, the door was closed. I shouldn't be in here." I came out from behind the desk. The room, the wood paneling and dark carpet bright with sunlight now, two maroon club chairs on either side of a table stacked with books, more French doors that opened onto a side patio.

"No, I'd closed the door because it's a mess. I haven't been able to move anything, I'm afraid."

"I understand."

"Grimsley, again, yes?"

"Grimsley Feller, yes."

"He mentioned you."

And when she said this, I swear she gave my entire body a once over. I'd started to show, of course. And my figure was pronounced by overall weight gain encouraged by Maggie. Long a physical sloth most invigorated by a four-hour stretch of reading than of cycling or hiking, I was in better physical shape than I'd been since well, Emerson—but still I was eating all I could. So with my clothes off, my pregnancy was definitively evident, but I'd bought a dark loose-fitting dress for this day, so the particular curves weren't distinct and, having scrutinized myself, and the way the smock hung, for an hour this morning in my room from every angle, knew that it was entirely possible to presume only that I was simply a bit of a porker. You had to see the newly deep arch of my back, not apparent from what I was wearing and her view, to recognize that it was a pregnancy and not just a bit of a potbelly.

But look me over she did. Shamelessly, actually.

"Said he saw an old girlfriend. Your name is memorable."

"I'm afraid it is."

"He saw other friends when he was there. You're the only one who came today that I'm aware of."

"I'd like to tell you why," I said. This was a surprise! Just came out! Terrible nerves? Guilt? Would have slapped my own hand over my mouth as if to take it back, but Em's son, Peter, looking like a fine young man in his dark suit and a tie of aqua and gold, hair slightly slicked, appeared behind her and said, "Mom? The Andersons are here and asking for you."

"I'll be right there, Peter."

He departed and she returned her focus to me. She looked surprised, more open, less suspicious, as if I'd surprised her with good news. "Thank you. *Thank* you. And I'd like to hear why." Her eyes steely blue, I noticed, cool as her voice, not accusatory, but sincere, rather, and so I relaxed. A little. I suppose.

"And I also have a question," she said. She looked down then up to my eyes. "But it requires a conversation that can't happen now," she said, and her demeanor changed, warmed further. "Not today, not with all these people. I'm exhausted already and will be spent by the end of the day. How long will you be in town?"

"I leave tomorrow evening."

"Would you be able to return tomorrow, late morning?"

"Of course."

"Eleven o'clock?"

"Whatever time is convenient."

"Thank you. And I hope you'll stay and have some food. I haven't been able to eat in a week—somebody should. Also I hope you'll introduce yourself to people who knew him here. I'm sure they'd like to hear what Emerson was like when he was a young man."

"Thank you. I'll say good-bye to you now, then, in case I'm unable to find you later. This is a hard day. I am truly sorry for your loss."

"Thank you."

I extended my hand and again, she took it but looked hard at my bulge.

I honestly didn't know what was going on in Collista's mind. Had Emerson confessed the affair and she suspected and did the math? Why on Earth would she have any inkling I was pregnant with her husband's child unless he had confessed the affair? So maybe he had. Or was I just being completely paranoid? I decided to believe the latter.

Until I got in the car. Good Lord, she'd asked me to come back. *Why?* I mean, I was glad—I'd come to LA, I now knew, needing to know what happened during his last months and to glimpse the life he'd made. Now I needed to know why. But what did she need to ask me if it *wasn't* about our liaison? *Shit.*

I'd steel myself for that and try to be as honest as I felt would be useful to my love's widow, whom I cared about simply for the fact that I'd loved Emerson always, and this was the woman he'd chosen to love, to share his life with, and to bring two beautiful children into the world with, and so a part of me loved her, too. I had no feelings for her one way or another—the love I felt was a compassion for her and empathy for how bereft she must feel. I had seen how Em had clearly loved her when he showed me her photograph, how he lingered on her image with what I knew to be love and admiration and pride. I also knew what a compelling man, and father, he surely was. You saw it when he walked into a room—it was just always that way. And now he never would walk into any room at all. How does a woman live through that loss? And surely whatever difficulties they'd been having, which he'd only alluded to, were now moot because of his death, and she would reflect on only the good parts of their relationship. Perhaps regret over things said—one never knows. Perhaps they'd had a terrible fight the night he died and she felt responsible. I couldn't know.

Nor could I linger in this home and strike up conversations, let alone tell stories about the Emerson who was eighteen and his best self, the Emerson who was kind and ambitious and smart and talented, imbued with unfulfilled but certain promise, and so beautiful. You simply wanted to stop him right there, to stop time. You are so beautiful. A lily of a day. Is it beautiful because it dies young? Can true living beauty endure or must it die to be beautiful?

I had to keep my mind from cranking like this for about twenty-four hours, try not to think about anything until I knew what Collista had to say, and hear how she might answer my questions. And why did I say what I did? Did I think the truth would help? Maybe, now that it was done. I did love him, after all. I said what I did partly because I wanted to help her. If his death was a mystery to her, perhaps knowing would help. Did I simply want to unburden myself, confess and save my own soul? What was done was done. As ever, I would play it as it lies tomorrow.

First thing I did was find a shopping mall, the Grove, it was called, to buy another dress that might obscure my form. I'd brought only this one decent outfit. Beyond that I had only comfortable traveling clothes, jeans and a clean shirt for tomorrow, and it was just large enough to button around my belly but showed that I was preggers and not fat.

I've never been a shopper—get in and get out is my shopping motto— but I'd never shopped with such purpose before, and having hours to kill, I took my time. The Grove was a new outdoor mall, pleasant for walking. I found a dark brown linen dress that hung smock-like over my form—it went with my hair, which had just started to gray, and my brown eyes, and generally accentuated my plainness (a description that I don't mean in a self-deprecating way at all—once Emerson was gone for good, I'd always considered it an asset; I wasn't one to *want* to be noticed). The only thing that didn't go were the black flats; they would have to do as I wasn't about to spend more money on shoes I didn't need—I'd worn my old Jack Purcells on the plane, which go fine with the jeans but would look goofy beneath six inches of bare shin and a dress. I bought an inexpensive black brooch (in the form of a snake to remind me of home!) hoping to tie it all together, and I also bought a black ribbon to tie my hair back.

I returned to the hotel at 3 p.m., tired and intent on keeping my body on East Coast time. I read by the hotel's pool beneath an umbrella.

The Kindle app of all things. For my birthday, Don had bought me an iPad. I thought it was a joke. We work with rare books and manuscripts, *hard* copies. More than that, he knew my love of books as physical objects. When he said, "You need to be aware of the way our world, our particular reading world, is changing. And that boy you're carrying is more likely than not to be carrying not only his novels but his Psych 101 textbook on it as well, if not his *Grey's Anatomy* and *OED*."

(Well before I'd begun to show, I told Don the news. He was the only non-family member I'd told about the pregnancy and the only person I'd confided the whole story to. He'd known Emerson had been a student here, recognized the uncommon first name, from the Blackmore letters. Don is an archivist, and therefore a very discreet secret keeper; I knew I could trust him: the back story of my days at Duke with Em, the unexpected tryst on the night he, Don, had surprised me with his question. I owed him that much, I figured. It also helped me just to talk it out. He's such a dear man, all concern for me—after the shock, followed by his confession that he'd been hanging on to the hope that I might one day reconsider his offer and how this pretty much did him in. I asked his forgiveness and he gave me a sweet, chaste hug and then took me to Magnolia Grill, long considered the best in the city, for dinner, where we continued to talk.)

I resisted the iPad for a week, leaving it on the kitchen table, and passing it the way one passes a rabid skunk. But Don had already downloaded my favorite novels, *Lolita* and *The Great Gatsby*, to ensure that I'd give the electronic reader a whirl. I reread those books on a regular basis.

Within the hour I'd finished—devoured, more like—Ann Patchett's *State of Wonder*. Patchett was already one of my favorites, but when I read the plot on the jacket in Duke's Gotham bookstore, a medical story

(I was obsessed with medicine now), woman doctors, and a hunt for an older doctor who'd disappeared in the Amazon searching for a drug to extend women's fertility? Sold!

It was over all too quickly there by the pool at the Standard, and I had nothing else loaded.

I wasn't in the mood for the Russian genius, and *Gatsby* . . . I could not bear, and doubt that I'd ever read it again, period.

How Emerson had idolized Fitzgerald. Dangerously so. I remember Blackmore and me discussing this his senior year (I was working for Duke by then and he knew of our friendship, knew Emerson always gave me first drafts before they reached his eyes). Blackmore told me, as a warning he knew I'd pass on to Emerson, that while Fitzgerald did indeed write great novels, and some prose unequaled in beauty, still, there could not be a worse model for an aspiring writer: a "sentimental, insecure drunk." I remember the words exactly because Blackmore spoke like this, "who'd ruined the instrument of his talent by age forty and was dead on the darkest night of the year four years later."

Remembering Blackmore's words gave me pause, there by the blue pool and overlooking the Hollywood where Fitzgerald had died, that Emerson had died at the same age but had not published a single novel. He had written for film and television very successfully, though, I say in sad defense, something Fitzgerald had tried but failed at. It was probably Hollywood that killed him. "Poor bastard."

I'd read *The Great Gatsby* in high school, but it failed to move me. It was nicely done, but I didn't get how that slim book remained one of the great American novels *and* a commercial bestseller (though out of print when he died, alas). I saw not a single appealing character. Nick I picture as a flabby pale cipher, Tom an ass, Daisy a twit, Jordan a stuck-up bitch who cheats. At least Gatsby had ambition for something, but for what? For Daisy, after only one or two dates? I just didn't buy any of it.

Until Emerson read it aloud to me, one long lovely spring morning and afternoon, near the end of his senior year.

Yes, read it aloud, the whole thing in one go, ending at dusk. He had it open on one of those lovely mornings when I woke to find him still in my bed. He would soon be lying on the Plaza fountain in Manhattan dreaming of Gatsby, stone drunk and not working, but his reading of it to me that long Sunday afternoon was one of the best literary experiences—one of the best days, *period*—of my life.

"How, how can you not like this?!" he said, forcing me awake.

I rolled off his chest onto my back, blinking. "I never said I didn't like it, I like it." Then I yawned and stretched. "I just never saw what the fuss was about."

And then he read the first sentence—"In my younger and more vulnerable years my father gave me some advice that I've been turning over in my mind ever since"—and it was like someone turned on the music behind the words. I said nothing. I knew Emerson would keep reading because I knew he liked the sound of his own voice, rich and clear, subtly theatrical when he desired. I just listened until he finished the last sentence of the first chapter: "When I looked once more for Gatsby he had vanished, and I was alone again in the unquiet darkness."

He closed the book. He stared at the ceiling.

I said, "Okay."

"O-*kay*?" He shook his head in disappointed wonder.

"Okay, as in, okay, I'm listening," I said.

He brightened like a child just given permission to ride the roller coaster one more time.

"On one condition," I said. "You let me pee, and you get us both coffee."

He was a senior, I worked at the East Campus library and lived a block away at the corner of Onslow and Green, in a house I rented with my forever pals Sterly and Amanda. It was a ramshackle bungalow with a lovely front porch. I slept in a downstairs room right off the porch, so when Emerson came calling, as he often did, it was less hazardous than it had been four years earlier. He really did come in through the window on this occasion. He was most welcome. I hadn't seen him in a few months, and maybe that's why he stayed rather than bolt like the backdoor man he often was—he missed me, I'm guessing all these years later.

One of the best literary experiences of my life, honestly. I lay propped in bed with coffee, and he alternately paced or sat at my desk. During longer prose sections, he paced, waving his right index finger like a wand conducting the orchestra of Fitzgerald's prose. During dialogue, he sat, and gave just enough tonal change in the voices that I could distinguish between Nick and Tom and Gatsby, Daisy and Jordan, but not so much that he sounded affected. Listening to him read this way, conveying his own personal love of the language directly to me, that was what was thrilling. Like I was mainlining his love for the language.

After concluding chapter three, he closed the book.

I said, "No."

He grinned wide. "What are you doing today?"

"Listening to you finish this story, I hope."

"Really?"

"Are you kidding me? This is a *pleasure*."

"Fix us some eggs, would you?"

I had a can of corned beef hash, which he loved with an egg on top and tons of pepper and hot sauce.

After breakfast, he read chapters four through seven on our porch with more hot coffee, me on the swing, him perched on the rail, leaning against a post (he was always perching, he liked to perch in odd places—in stairwells, on stone walls, thinking, pondering, often crouched as if ready to spring). He occasionally stood to pace the porch and keep the orchestra on its toes as it were. The occasional dog walker lingered to listen, but no one whom we knew came or went, and so we were undisturbed through chapter seven, the day and night of the car accident.

By then we needed a break. He took a quick shower and, hair unbrushed and dripping, he was out the door, promising to be back before I was out of the shower (he knew I liked to take my time).

When I appeared, towel wrapped around me, combing out my hair, he showed me what he'd got. Biscuits and mustard and ham and some good cheese and two bottles of cold wine. "We're having a picnic, on the lawn behind the art building. I'll finish there."

I found a quilt and we strolled the block to the back edge of East Campus, and there he finished. So go read that book now, if you haven't already, so you know what I'm trying to convey. Some of the most beautiful sentences ever composed, uttered by the most beautiful boy I'd ever seen. Also know now how desperately I long to be borne back into *that* past, that singular day.

Light was fading by the time he finished—"borne back ceaselessly into the past"—one bottle of wine gone, and we sat and ate the biscuits and ham and cheese in the dusk, having brought some votive candles in the wrinkled paper bag, and we finished the wine. I don't recall what we talked about—story, writing, craft, he liked to talk about craft and other writers' lives. I do remember a few things that followed. We returned and he actually stayed. I think it was the only time we spent two consecutive nights together after he broke up with me his freshman year. I remember that we fell asleep watching *Casablanca* in my bed. And I remember, oh how I remember, that only when he was asleep, well before the usual suspects could be rounded up, how only then did it dawn on me that, for the past four years, I'd found a bunch of daisies on my bed every Valentine's Day. That first rainy February when we were actually dating, and every year that he was in Durham since, and one year after that. I should have known then, that day, what they meant, but I didn't, and so I wasn't sad when they stopped coming, because by then he was gone. Maybe I should've been, maybe I should've realized it for the death that it actually was. I didn't know at the time what I know now, what I realized only in thinking about that day he read *The Great Gatsby* to me—why the *daisies*! He did love me.

When I woke the next morning, after that long Sunday reading *The Great Gatsby*, and most of *Casablanca*, he was gone, and I didn't see him for three weeks, a week before graduation.

*

Anyway. That's the reason, seated at the pool at the Standard, twenty-two years later, I could not reread *The Great Gatsby*. Even though there it was on my iPad.

Now, here's the other cool part about these new devices. I had just been in the Amazon jungle—in the Patchett novel, no pun intended—and had liked being there, so I thought of the best jungle story there was, one of my favorites, *Heart of Darkness*. When I searched for it, I was able to download it for free and start reading in seconds, without even leaving my chair. I took a moment to be properly amazed and page through it a little ways, then dug in.

Midway through—it's a novella, a one-sitting read—I ate another burger in the diner, followed by a vanilla malt, then I headed to my room, finished it, and turned out my light.

It was only when I woke, 4:30 again, that I realized a maybe meaningful coincidence. *Heart of Darkness* is a tale-within-a-tale deal: Marlow, the narrator telling the story of the corruption of Kurtz, the darkness at the heart of men's souls and all, a little gimmicky now but it works in the time Conrad was writing. The account ends with Marlow traveling back to Europe, the civilized world, to tell the Intended, the woman who was to be Kurtz's wife, of Kurtz's death. And he tells this colossal lie. Kurtz's last words, famously (especially after Coppola's *Apocalypse Now*), were "The horror, the horror." But instead, Marlow lies and tells the elegant white European woman in her well-appointed apartment, far from the jungle, he tells her that the last word Kurtz uttered was her name. Otherwise, he reasons, it would have been too dark altogether. Appropriate for the time Conrad was writing in, as I said, but now? I don't think so. It dawned on me, lying awake that morning in the actual, not symbolic, darkness, that I was on a similar errand. I had no idea what Collista was going to ask me or what she wanted to discuss regarding her dead husband, but I told myself that whatever she threw at me, I was going to tell the truth. Not about the baby. That would be too much, but rather the affair, and why, and maybe try to understand or convince her of the rightness of it, rather than the wrongness, how it had confirmed his love for her, as it surely had, since he had not contacted me, our connection severed, both of us keeping our word. Maybe I was just deluded. Could my own thoughts even be trusted?

Two

Dressed as described, uncommonly nervous, I lifted the tarnished brass knocker and gave three solid raps. I waited at least a minute, maybe longer because I was starting to think it rude since I'd arrived at just two minutes after eleven. Collista opened the door, wearing a blue Oxford cloth shirt hanging untucked over skinny-girl jeans, bare feet, hair brushed but not done up. I saw in her eyes the reason for the delay: she'd been crying and hadn't completely composed herself.

"Hi, Grimsley, come in, please forgive me."

I remember following her into the kitchen where she got me ice water—my mouth was so dry from nerves, my tongue had to peel away from the palate when I spoke—poured herself black coffee, and led us to the living room. We did not remain in the easy kitchen or sit outside, though the day was warm and perfect. This was to be a formal conversation.

She led me to an upholstered chair, waved palm up to it, for me to sit. She sat at the edge of the couch, directly across from me, set her coffee on the coffee table that separated us. She set a coaster at the far edge from her, beside an orchid, for my water, but I hung on to the glass like a buoy.

She didn't look at me, exhaled brusquely. "This has all happened so quickly. I'm still not myself."

"I'm not sure you ever will be."

She looked at me, startled.

"What I mean to say is that I know that Emerson loved you. When I saw him last spring he showed me your picture and it was clear from the way he looked at it. I can see from your grief you loved him, deeply. He was the father of your beautiful children. The old you went with him. It's a life-changing loss and you need to work your way to who you're going to be next, find your next best self, for your children and for yourself."

I said this partly because I knew it to be true when you lose a partner of those many years—my mom had been that close to me—but I was also, selfishly, trying to circumvent any direct questions about his May visit.

"Wow," she said. "I'm going to have to think about that one." She took a sip of coffee, set it back down, then looked dead hard into my eyes and said, "Why I've asked you here."

"I do admit to being anxious about this. What do you need to know from me?" Well, there it was, hadn't thought, just spoke and opened myself right up, and she fired truly.

"What happened last spring? What happened at Duke?"

I felt completely paralyzed in a way I've never felt before. Don't play dumb, my instincts told me, and don't delay, out with it. "What do you mean?" I asked. Okay, dumb, delay.

"*Something* happened on that trip, and I need to know what it was."

Delay, Grimsley! Give yourself some time; this is a minefield for her.

I hadn't heard the footsteps descending the wooden stairs or the approach of the young man who'd appeared in the entryway to the living room. When I saw that Collista's eyes had gone from mine to his, I turned. It was Peter, dressed in a white T-shirt and faded jeans, his strawberry blond hair, not slicked back and formal like yesterday, but soft, unbrushed and askew from sleep.

"You okay, Mom?" he asked.

"Yes, Peter, thanks."

I heard him but did not watch him leave because I'd turned away. I'd set my glass down, tried to stand, to remove myself, but my legs failed, and I curled over myself, just crumpled like an aluminum can back down into the chair, gave in finally to the tears that had yet to come—till now, till the vision of that boy who was so clearly Emerson's son, in looks and voice and stature, returned me to my first sight of Emerson himself more powerfully than when I'd seen him last spring. Peter *was* that image of the young Emerson, so beautiful, and it felled me, obliterated me, and I lost it right there in that chair. At first quietly, just silently convulsing, bent over myself, face hidden. Until I just couldn't contain the grief and started sobbing loudly, sobbing like a goddamn girl. Worse than that bony creature who'd preceded me in line the day before at the church. Heaving, loud sobs. Self-conscious enough to hear Collista leave the room abruptly, aware enough to hear Peter's quiet voice—"Who is she, Mom, is she all right?"—so clearly reminiscent of Emerson's voice and care. My sobs redoubled and redoubled again if that was possible. Collista returned with a box of tissues.

"Go on," she said. "I've been doing it all week. It feels better when it's over."

And so I did. I kept crying because the one person I'd ever loved was dead and yet there he was. There he was, *right there*, he was that beautiful boy I'd loved, now grown and gone. Gone, *gone*.

I took her at her word and cried for so long she likely got bored waiting for it to end. But end it did, ten or twenty tissues later, in my lap, at my feet. The crying stopped and I gathered up the teary, snotty balls.

Collista said, "There's a bathroom to the left of the front door."

I went as directed, disposed of the Kleenex, splashed cold water on my face, dried it with some paper towels lying in an elegant silver box. Took a deep breath, looked at myself, and knew what I had to do.

Call me Marlow!

Before I sat, I said to Collista, who was back in her seat, legs curled beneath her, cradling her coffee and staring off, "Thanks for giving me the go-ahead. You're right, I feel better, or emptier anyway." I sat, back straight, knees together, prim and ready.

She turned her cool eyes on me and said, "Well, that tells me you loved him."

"I did, yes. I wouldn't have needed to be here otherwise."

Her legs uncurled, she planted her feet on the rug, set her mug down. "I need to know what happened at Duke."

I got it over with fast and clean: "Nothing. Nothing happened at Duke. If you're referring to him and me."

I could see from the way her face, her whole being, eased—that he hadn't told her *and* that I'd been right to lie.

"We talked a lot," I said.

Then with sudden tension and renewed energy she said, "But I need to know what happened. Because *something* happened."

I said nothing. She waited me out, staring. I asked, "What makes you think something happened?"

"Because when he got back from that trip, he was different. He'd changed."

"In what way?"

"It was like . . ." she said, and looked off for a long time. She returned her gaze, friendly now, not a foe. "It was like he was the man I married. That young. Twenty-seven. He was *euphoric*. At first I thought he was being overly solicitous because he had done something wrong. He told me about seeing you and how renewing it had felt. He told me he'd had a powerful response to the ceremony celebrating Professor Blackmore. And the euphoria didn't go away. He charmed me all over again, loved me in a way I couldn't doubt. Which is why I believe you." She snorted and said, "We even started having sex again, regularly, amazing, wonderful, loving sex. In July, on our anniversary, our eighteenth, we did one of those vow renewal things. I didn't need it; he's always been the sentimental one and wanted to, so we did. Invited our closest friends and recommitted ourselves in their presence, and then we ate an amazing meal and drank all night long, the last of them leaving when the birds started chirping again. Like the kids we'd once been.

"We paid for it, the next day, or that day rather. But it was worth it."

She paused again.

"So, Grimsley, that's why I wanted to know. *What happened?* Because whatever it was, it didn't last." Her breathing grew noticeably heavy. "And now. He's gone. And I need to know . . . why."

"I was kind of hoping to find that out myself. That's mainly why I came out here, having briefly reconnected with him last spring after twenty years. What happened between the accident and when I saw him? Because he seemed hopeful when we said goodbye."

"And that's how he returned. So why?"

"Why," I said. "Well, from our conversation in May, I sensed he was depressed, that life was heavy on him. He'd confessed that you two had been having issues but he didn't say what, and I didn't ask."

"It's true, yes," she said, looking away.

"He also told me he'd lost his father not too long ago."

"Yes, that hit him hard," she said, then squinted at me. "You know, the moment he came back he told me something that I can't stop thinking about. He said after the ceremony, he cried. He said he'd seen an old friend, you, and then suddenly the urge to cry came on so strong that, well, he said, he ran around back and bawled his head off. He was sentimental to his core and easy to cry. I don't know how many times he saw *It's a Wonderful Life*, but every time Harry Bailey raises his glass and calls his brother George the richest man in town, Emerson's face is smeared with tears. But he didn't weep from sadness that I ever saw, he wasn't a crier in that sense. So I said what seemed obvious to me. I said, 'You've recently lost your father. Now you've lost the second most important man in your life, so of course you responded that way.' He didn't say anything, he just hugged me hard and told me how much he loved me. In a way that felt desperate." She paused. "Was it you? And did he mention it to you?"

"The crying jag? Yes, he did."

"Did he explain it?"

"He seemed kind of baffled by it."

"What did he say?"

"He said he thought it was shame, but couldn't, or didn't, explain why."

Collista turned away for a moment but that was all the answer I got on this point. She looked back to me.

"Once the slide began," she said, "I thought it was grief, that he had yet to properly grieve his father and his mentor."

"And I said something along those lines, too. So, are you saying you no longer feel this way?"

She looked at me hard, really hard, cold and mean, like a child. *Weird.* She said, "No," and slurped her coffee. I didn't like the silence so I babbled just to fill it.

"From what I've seen, and forgive me for this, but I think it's harmful for us to believe that marriage is natural, let alone easy, so that when marriages go sour, there's shame all over everyone. Eighteen years is a long time."

"Twenty we've been together in all."

"That's a long time, and marriages have to evolve or die. But as I said, I could see that he loved you, and his children, and his family as a whole. So, frankly, I wasn't worried about that part of his life. Not from what I saw."

"What did you see then?"

"His work. His work was killing him. *That* I could see."

"That's interesting, because that's when the slide began. He worked very hard. Even among his writing colleagues he was admired for the quantity of work he got done, never missed a deadline."

"But there was part of his soul that needed to generate a certain type of writing that he hadn't done in many years," I interrupted, "and this is what I urged him to pursue. This is what we talked about.

"When we were friends at Duke, and I should note that we dated during most of his freshman year until he broke things off. And we never dated again." This was true, this was a fact I could offer. "When we were friends at Duke, throughout his time there, even after we'd broken up, I was his first reader. He gave me stories to read and we'd talk about them. It seemed he was most alive, most himself when he was excited about a story he was working on.

"He used to quote Blackmore, who noted that story is fundamental to our species, that we *have* to tell stories, that its importance in our lives is second only to food and water. And I believe this. No one lives in silence. We're telling each other stories now, you and I. I came out to learn the story of what happened to my dear old friend. Our brains tell ourselves stories when we sleep, and we know from studies that people who are prevented from dreaming, they go crazy. Life is no longer viable. We're a story-telling creature, and Em needed it so bad he made it his career. I just told him during the several hours we spent together that he should carve out a part of his time for writing what he cared about. I asked him to send me pages if he did."

"Did he?" she asked. Her voice had become frosty now, almost angry, and for no reason I could figure.

"Did he send me pages? No, why?"

"Because he did start writing. He got up early and spent two hours daily.'"

"Wish he had sent them. I'd have happily read them."

Collista leaned forward, took a big sip of coffee, set the mug down, curled her legs back under her, clasped her fingers in her lap, apparently growing more comfortable, but when I look back on it now, I'm wondering if it was calculated to put me at ease.

"So how did you guys meet?" she asked.

"I was a junior and assigned to his group of incoming freshmen."

"I guess I mean how did you start dating?"

I paused, thinking back to the day. "He pursued me."

"Oh?"

"It was actually kind of a funny story. I lived on the second floor of my dorm and his second night on campus he climbed a tree—"

I stopped immediately. While Collista didn't actually move, her whole body tensed, and not just tensed, but rather looked like she'd been paralyzed by a current of electricity. I only noticed that the knuckles of her tanned, clasped fingers turned vivid white.

"I'm sorry," I said, "this is more than you need to know."

"Did you ever see him after that time at Duke last May? Please be honest."

"The honest answer is no."

She stared me down.

"Check his cell phone records, I have a 919 area code. I had zero contact whatsoever, by email or phone, let alone in person. I haven't left Durham since spring break last March."

"I believe you, but I had to ask."

"Why?"

"Let me tell you what happened. It's brief. I've already mentioned our renewed relationship and his writing. Well, the writing didn't seem to last. He took on a project, a pilot for HBO. It's a lot of money. Basically we can make our entire nut in the fall on a single project, and the rest is gravy. This has been how it's worked out here for a while. And it's been fine because, well, nothing ever came of them.

"Except this time," she continued. "The show was picked up for production and he was obligated to write the first ten shows, and also be the show runner. At first, he was elated. We celebrated. Because finally he was going to have his own show, 'created by,' and if it was a success, really, really good money. But now that I think back on it that was kind of the beginning of the slide. So there could be something to what you've just said. It didn't help that Peter was clearly distancing himself, as all teenagers must—Em adored Peter, and missed the young Peter terribly. And I thought this was part of his depression—a third man sustaining him in his life leaving him. Our daughter, Alex, well, she's sixteen and wants to have as little to do with us as possible but in a much more cynical way that never really bothered him; he admired her independence, while I think he felt Peter's a sad betrayal. I thought that contributed to it as well, because he loves them, desperately, but they are working at becoming who they will be without us.

"Our spats resumed but not badly, petty arguments. He told me he loved me every day. But the drinking got worse. So much so that I started keeping track. He told me he needed it to sleep. He'd get so wired from working that it was the only way to relax, that and two Valium every night. Well it got to the point where he was drinking, gosh, it must have been nearly a pint of bourbon a day, or night rather. He never drank during working hours.

"One morning I saw that his car was not in the garage next to mine but was in the driveway, partially blocking mine, carelessly parked. And so I asked him if he'd gone out last night after I'd gone to bed. He said he had, that he needed the fresh air, to clear his head, listen to music loud and drive. This is part of why I wanted you here, Grimsley. It occurred to me that he could be having an affair, that's where he was going. After a whole summertime of love-making, that too became less frequent. He assured me he wasn't drunk and that he'd been safe. It happened a few more times, that I was aware of, the music, old music, college music, Talking Heads, Grateful Dead, Neil Young, it would wake me up when he returned because he always listened to the end of the song in the driveway. He was obviously drunk when he'd stagger into the bedroom. And I could see how hungover he was the next day—so I guess an affair was physically unlikely. But he always got the work done, so what could I do? I couldn't force him not to. He wasn't a violent drunk, his personality didn't change. He was meeting all his deadlines, helping out with the kids, driving or picking up our daughter when I couldn't, making dinners.

"And then, well, then early on the morning after Halloween, last Monday, before dawn, I got the call."

When she was done, she wasn't looking at me. She hadn't really been looking at me at all. I think she was just retelling the story that had been playing in her mind since the day of the accident, hoping to understand. I didn't know whether to be angry at Emerson, at what sounded like pure selfishness—and, like I said, he was a world-class narcissist—and that kind of irresponsible behavior by a husband and father is just that, selfishness. But the sadness was bigger—I was just plain sad for all the loss, for everyone's loss. Sad won out. Sad for his wife, sad for his kids, sad for me, sad for everything he left behind, sad for all that he'd never do.

She reached for Kleenex, dabbed her eyes with it, and blew her nose. The sight of her tears brought some to me. I took a deep breath, exhaled.

"He loved you," I said.

"He may have loved you," she said

"I know for a fact that's not true." No turning back from the first lie.

"How would you know?" she asked.

"Because I asked him."

"What?"

"When we saw each other at Duke. I asked him. I *had* loved him, had been *in love*, he broke my heart, and I asked him if he had ever loved me. And he said—I remember it exactly, because he was customarily straight-forward—he said, 'If I'd have loved you, I'd never have let you go.' He said it with a smile. He wouldn't have lied."

"That sounds like him, but I think you may be wrong. I think he may have been wrong. I think he may have cared about you more than you knew, or that even he knew."

Oh, God. I knew what it was then. I knew exactly what it was and why she said this. I covered my mouth, sat erect with this new information.

Collista watched me. She knew I knew, and so she spoke. "I'd like to send you what he was working on when he died."

"Okay," I said. "I'll be grateful to read it. Is there anything I need to know in advance?"

"No. Is there anything *I* need to know before you go?"

"Only my reassurance that we didn't see each other after that day, had no communication whatever, if that's what you're looking to find." If she'd read about our affair in a fictionalized form, it was important she know this at least was the truth.

"I'm looking to find an answer as to why my best friend and husband killed himself."

"You're not saying he did it on purpose, I hope."

"It doesn't matter—he did it to himself, whether intentionally or not, he did it. Drove fast and drunk dead center into a tree, shiny new BMW convertible, bought with the new influx of cash. And I mean dead center, as if aiming."

"What about seatbelt, airbags?"

"Seatbelt was engaged but behind him, had always been like that. He hated having to put it on for a two-second drive to the Brentwood Plaza, so he just left it like that. The airbags weren't enough. He was going too fast. The entire car was crushed. They had to cut the car to get him out. So you can see why I might have reason to believe—"

She began to tremble. I sat beside her.

"I don't know what more to say," was all I could offer.

"Well, if you have any insights after you read the pages—there aren't many—I hope you'll write to me. I need to know and am afraid I never will."

"I promise."

She turned to look at me, eyes now empty of suspicion, anger, even sadness, strangely empty. "I printed them out and read them and destroyed them, so I'll have to email it to you. Do you have a card?"

"Actually, I don't. But it's my first name dot last name at Duke dot e-d-u."

She stood, "In my state I'll never remember." She stood. "It's still on his computer. Come."

I followed her through the door I'd entered yesterday.

She engaged his computer, clicked the mail icon, clicked NEW. She wasn't even seated, just resting her left arm on the chair back—this would be quick.

When an empty new email popped up, she said, "Could you spell it please?"

I did and when I got to the M, my full email appeared, grimsley.feller@duke.edu.

Her eyes darted to mine. "Looks like there *was* some contact."

My heart raced, thinking back, but I couldn't remember anything. "There wasn't."

"There must have been."

"You can check," I said.

She did. Which was pretty cold-blooded, now that I think about it. Or perhaps she was just responding to everything now like a tortured animal.

She typed my name into the search field. Two emails appeared, the one he'd written on the day of his return, and my response. When she'd finished reading both, she simply said, "I'm sorry." Then she clicked the REPLY button, attached a document called "Untitled." She typed the first letters of her name in the cc field—"So you can reach me if you have a reason to"—and hit SEND.

"A little forewarning," Collista said, "You're going to get a little shock when you see his name in your inbox. At least I did when I sent something to myself from this computer. Like he was alive and sending me something."

"Thanks for the warning."

"Thanks for coming here. It couldn't have been pleasant."

"I came only to grieve and to know what happened to my friend. If I'd had something to hide, I wouldn't have come. I hope you believe that." Lie upon lie. (Why did I offer?)

She looked me over as she had yesterday, looked at my dress but really wasn't looking at my dress.

"One last question," she said. "I can't get it out of my head. Are you *pregnant?*"

Straight at me like a fist. It required a street-fight-fast aggressive response, which came to me as though I did improv professionally: "I hope you're embarrassed when I tell you no."

Her eyes rose to meet mine. "Well, when you read what's in your mail, you won't wonder why I asked you here."

*

I'd never seen Venice Beach; it wasn't far and my flight wasn't till late. I figured a beach would be a good place to sit and think. That was wrong. As I drove down and down, the sun went away. The closer I got to the beach, the cloudier it got until the sky was a flat mat of depressing gray. The air was damp and cool. From hot and sunny to cold and damp. And that was just the air, that didn't include the freak show that ran the entire length of the sandy, asphalt path—freaks and homeless, skateboarders, a three-legged dog, shop after shop of chintz and shitty carnival food.

I removed my shoes and walked to the water's edge. I was mainly alone there. There wasn't much surf, and it just kept getting colder the closer I got to the water.

I sat to think. I checked my email—yep, there it was. Collista had been right about the shock, just for a moment, his name in big bold black letters. I didn't open it. Instead, her parting words when she showed me to the door sounded off in my head:

"You have my email if you need to reach me, if you have any information to convey. If all that you've said is true, I don't hold you responsible.

I want you to know that. But nor is this an invitation to be friends. Our connection ends here unless you have something you think can help me. I'm doing this for me, not you."

I didn't even say good-bye because there didn't seem to be anything good happening just then other than my getting the hell away from her anger and sadness so that I could think.

Hold me responsible? My stomach turned, and by the time I was buckled into my car, I thought I was going to be sick. I took a slug of bottled water, warm by now, started the car, and pulled quickly away. When I was out of sight, I pulled over and rested my head on the steering wheel. What was I going to do for ten hours before my flight? I plugged Venice Beach into the GPS.

The gloomy beach and this particular swath of misfit humanity weren't doing anything but enhancing my disorientation. I walked north till beach access ended, then just walked along the decrepit streets, passing funky little houses set in crumbling concrete. Eventually I turned left, hoping that farther from the beach was better than closer, which was sort of true. I came upon a semi-decent street with boutiquey shops and restaurants. I walked into a darkish bar called Hal's. I wasn't hungry but knew I should eat. I would have rather had a drink and a cigarette, but I had another burger instead. I'd had three meals in LA, each one a burger. I forced it down with multiple glasses of sparkling water.

It took me about an hour to find my car, but I finally did, and the airport was minutes away. Soon I found myself in an ordinary airport concourse, teaming with America. It wasn't Venice Beach, but everyone looked fat and ugly to me. I bought a biography of John Cheever, whom I hadn't read in ages, and about whom I knew little, available as a thick paperback—that would easily last me. And I was in the mood for a real story, not make-believe, something true and grounding. A book. Something solid.

Three

My connecting flight from Charlotte to the Raleigh-Durham International Airport was on time and I was back at home by 8:30 on Monday morning. I started coffee, then stood for a long time beneath the hot water of the shower—just stood and let it soothe me. I rubbed my growing belly, which was smooth and tight. This too was comforting, moving my palm in a circle over my little Buddha. I tried to think about what I'd have to do at work, what chores needed to be done, what I'd need to buy at the grocery store today. Did my sister need me for something? I couldn't remember. What day was it? Monday. No, surely I'd planned to keep the day empty because I knew I'd be tired and a little disoriented. I hadn't planned on how much. Surely it was partly how the daylight in California had altered my body and mind, no matter how brief it had been, and no matter how I'd tried to keep on North Carolina time. You just can't trick your body that way. Also, I hadn't slept well on the plane.

That and what I read before I landed at the Raleigh-Durham airport.

It was only after the plane was definitively in the air above California that I had determined to read the document. But stupid me forgot to download the document so that it was actually in my device. I hadn't realized that I'd needed an Internet connection to actually download the document contained in the email. So I tried not to think what might be in it. I presumed it was about me and Emerson, but I didn't know what, or how much. Had he written an account of our affair, and was that why it was "secret"? I dreaded seeing that—God I hoped it wasn't that—and feared that Collista had to read an account of that night and realized from my presence that it hadn't been fiction. But there was nothing I could do but read my new book and try to sleep. I half-slept, as best I could in the uncomfortable seat, the twenty-something seated in the center seat beside me hogging the armrest with her blubbery arm and listening to music loud enough for me to hear, but not really hear what it was, so that it only sounded like mosquitos perpetually threatening. And she didn't turn off the TV monitor in front of her, so its flickering images of old sitcoms and *Entertainment Tonight* kept vying for my attention. So I was groggy on arrival in Charlotte. I hurried to the gate for my flight to Durham, which was already boarding, but I had enough time to click on the email, then tap the untitled document and see it engage.

The first line was "*Heather.*"

But with the second line—"*Slowly the girl, a junior in college, surfaced to consciousness from the hum of a stick being dragged against her window screen*"—I knew I'd been right. I had to stick my phone in my pocket to board, to find an overhead bin for my bag, to take my seat. I reopened it and skimmed. He'd called himself Scott, and me Heather, but that was all that he'd changed. The flight attendant announced that the doors were shut and was scolded into turning off my "device."

The Charlotte to Raleigh flight is so short they don't even bother with a beverage service. So as soon as I was allowed, I turned my phone back on and skimmed as best as possible on the little screen of my iPhone.

They were vignettes mainly. I'd catch on details I remembered. *He* certainly remembered. How did he know that I was so upset when he broke up with me that I retched in the sink? I must have told him. Did I remember it, did I even do it? It sounds right, it reads true. I hadn't thought about it much, what I did, actually; I recalled only the sharpness and immediacy of the pain, and I felt utterly bereft. He was the one, when he visited last May, who remembered that I'd taken him to that bench where he broke up with me, not I. He always said, memory's a funny thing. There were events he wrote about that I remembered and some I did not—he was allowing some fictional license, I could see. But not with one, a big one

I'd buried deep—the last time we'd seen each other, 1991, a year after he'd graduated. How could I have pushed that time down into the bottom of my memory? I put a rock on the earth to keep it from coming back up in my thoughts, watching him smile sweetly at me, wave and start that U-Haul down Onslow Street for the last time, bound for Los Angeles.

But the plane began its descent and I scrolled fast to the last paragraph. It ended there, more or less, with that last visit in 1991. I couldn't know if it worked as a sustained story, I hadn't read it for that. And I couldn't know how he would have ended it had he lived or what he would have done with it.

I couldn't know if there'd be a next chapter or part that began, "In May, 2010, Scott Stevenson, having returned to his alma mater to say farewell to his mentor, appeared at Heather's back door, and she led him in."

I stepped out of the shower, chafed my hair as dry as I could get it with a towel, brushed it out. I regarded my naked torso, swept my palm top to bottom straight over my belly. No denying it here in the mirror, even though my ass has gotten a little fat, boobs too, hanging a little heavy. My legs were solid, and my arms were sexy (I thought). I wonder if Collista knew. She couldn't have known for certain since I flat out denied it. Em obviously hadn't confessed the affair, nor had he written about it, so I knew, logically, that I didn't need to concern myself with whether she knew or even suspected that I carried her husband's child.

So I guess it makes that last line of hers especially chilling. *Responsible for what?*

I broiled some cheddar cheese on bread while I drank coffee. I was dead tired, but the kind of tired that's so deep you know you can't sleep. So I was glad for work. I ate the toasted cheese as I drove so I wouldn't be too late. The day was dry, overcast, unseasonably warm, could have been fifty degrees, and the campus was throbbing with students heading into their last weeks of classes before the winter break.

Don was manning the desk when I arrived.

There are a couple of worktables and computers in the front of this room, 103 Perkins. It's a long, narrow space with offices to the left and archival stacks through the door to the right. The room was cut in half by a glass divider where the actual research area was located. Don and I took turns at the desk when assistant curators weren't on it, signing people in and checking people out. No food or drink, no bags of any kind are allowed. We give people a lock and a locker for their belongings. We have to pass all material through a glass window once they're inside, and when they leave we're required to check all their materials to ensure no one's absconding with anything we've given them.

When we're at the desk, we're the gatekeepers.

I caricatured hurrying because I wanted him to know I knew I'd made him late for his meeting with Trish; he was already gathering up his stuff before I reached the desk.

"Sorry," I said.

"I told her I'd be late when I got your text, thanks." He took hold of my left hand and asked, "You all right?"

Don was the single person who knew the specifics of my errand.

"Yes, I'm glad I went."

"We'll talk later then. You must be exhausted."

"I'll make it." I took a seat at the desk. "Anything unforeseen on the agenda today?"

"Not really. That woman at the end"—he pointed to a woman with red hair at the farthest table, a folder open and a large narrow box filled with more before her—"is doing some work on Styron and was looking for her own correspondence with him from 1967 up through 1979." He lifted his eyebrows, quizzically.

Tired as I was, I was still on my game: "Years between *Nat Turner* and *Sophie's Choice.*"

"Well done."

"Anyone I should know?"

"No, academic only, I think. I've been through all but the last year of his general correspondence, looking for her letterhead, if you could handle that for her when she asks. Also a guy from New York will be here later to work with the *Rulah: Jungle Goddess* comics series."

"They've been ordered?"

"In the back waiting."

Most of our archives are held in a warehouse off campus and have to be ordered. Our library has one of the biggest comic book collections in the country, if you happen to be into that kind of thing.

*

Of course, one of the emotions jostling against my insides was the hurt for Em, and then for Collista, to realize that during those final months with his family, renewing his vows with Collista, having loving sex, feeling *young* again—he was spending a powerful part of his day with me.

Is that what Collista meant when she said the word *responsible*? That he was having an affair in his head? Or that what I suggested he do was unsustainable? That the *thought* of me alone could not sustain him. Nor could story. I'll give her that much—she said what she did because she wanted me to feel that I'd somehow been complicit.

And now how could I not consider this? What if he had not come to Duke that day? Good God, *had* I caused his death?

No. He knew where I was. He could have come back to me anytime for whatever life I gave him. Or maybe not, maybe he could do neither— "like a man to double business bound" in the play he once so despised, he could only stand in pause, considering both, paralyzed. Perhaps *this* was untenable.

Untitled

She leapt into his arms—that's what he remembers, looking back. How could he have left that leaping body so thoughtlessly? He'd parked the U-Haul in front of her house. Stepped out of it, stretched his arms and back, having driven eight hours from Manhattan. He heard the screen door smack shut, and by the time he was on the sidewalk, she had lofted herself at him like some kind of flying squirrel and had wrapped her legs around his waist and arms around his neck, 120 pounds of girl wrapped around 180 pounds of guy.

He laughed, always music to her ears, from the very beginning. He turned 360 degrees, hugging back, before setting her down. He held her shoulders and looked at her.

"Oh, man, you're a welcome sight."

She grinned, taking him in with her eyes.

She sighed a long, relieving exhalation, shook her head, and held out her arms. "Welcome back, stranger!"

They hugged again and he smelled her hair, and she knew from the hug how glad he was to be here.

"God, I love the sound of your voice."

"And I love that you're finally here, safe."

They released each other.

She said, "But you smell of cigarettes and car B.O. First thing you're getting close to is a bar of Lifebuoy in my shower. You have clean clothes?"

He chuckled at her, said he did, and retrieved a duffel from the passenger seat. An empty can of Diet Coke clattered onto the street and he tossed it back in. He hoisted the duffel over his shoulder. She took his left hand in her right and led him up the walk. "I mean, no offense or anything. You know I love your smell when you're gamey from living, but right now you're just plain smelly."

He laughed again, so happy to be where he was, feeling so right.

"Grims, a good hot shower and change of clothes are exactly what I need."

"You hungry? What can I make you to eat? I have some fried chicken I can reheat."

"Anything with substance. Eight hours of Marlboro Lights, Diet Cokes, and I-95 has left me pretty empty."

"Since when did you start smoking?"

"New York. Does things to you."

He stopped on the porch. He stared at the swing. He remembered it so well, that one afternoon more than a year ago reading Gatsby, a college senior about to graduate, one of their last days and nights before he packed his bags and headed where aspiring writers felt all but required to go. He then turned to look at the street, to look at the house, taking it all in.

"Grimsley," he said. "Thank you. I feel so lucky to be here. I feel like I got out of Hell Town in the nick of time. I was all but killing myself."

"And I feel lucky to have you here."

"Are you sure it's okay, a month? My new lease doesn't start till July first."

"Of course. You can stay forever if you want!"

She said it lightly, but he knew she meant it, and he tried not to think about that. He said, "You're a lifesaver."

"Come on, let's get you cleaned up."

*

While he showered, she put fried chicken in the toaster oven and leftover mashed potatoes in a covered bowl to microwave.

Sterly was still at work, and Grimsley had moved into Amanda's room upstairs after Amanda got a job offer in Charlotte. She and Sterly had both gotten raises and could afford the rent, though Sterly spent most of her time with her fiancé. Grimsley waited on her bed as long as she could after the water stopped. When he was taking too damn long, she slipped into the steamy, shampoo-scented air. His hair was slicked back, and he was just finishing shaving. She saw that he hadn't changed— narrow waist, swimmer's shoulders, a body she just couldn't keep her hands off of.

She wrapped her arms around his chest, pressed her cheek to his warm smooth back, smelled his skin.

"Yep," she said. "Still the same old sexpot!"

He chuckled, got the last spots on his chin and neck. He hit the drain knob to let the water out. Holding her gaze in the mirror, he said, "You were only a sexpot with me."

"True."

"Lucky me!" he said.

Somehow the towel wrapped around his waist slid to his feet while he, still facing the mirror, washed the remaining shaving cream from his face; her hands worked their way down the front of his body. He sighed, turned to face her.

"Grims?"

"Uh-oh."

"No uh-oh. It's just that I feel toxic from New York City. I'm too frazzled right now."

"I understand," she said and hugged him, her face against the chest for which she just then realized she'd been longing for a full year. She looked up at him. He smiled and leaned down to kiss her. Ah, those lips.

When the two parted, she said, "Welcome to Spa Feller. We'll get you detoxed. Posthaste."

He smiled—she'd picked up that archaic verbiage from him long ago. He gave her a long hug. "You're the best."

Again, she sensed something difficult coming at her, so she addressed it rather than ignored it. She hadn't seen her old friend in a year and here he was.

"You didn't pick up any bugs in the city I hope."

"No."

"AIDS is running like an actual plague through New York, moving into the hetero world, I hear."

"Precisely why I took precautions. But frankly, Grims, I didn't have a single meaningful relationship there. This whole past year I've been three things: working, drinking, and getting over a hangover, often all at once."

"That's not good."

"No, it's not, but it goes a long way in terms of explaining why I am so lucky to be where I am right now. I honestly feel lucky to have made it out alive."

They kissed again and she said, "Let me get you that food you need."

*

It was Friday, late afternoon. She'd taken the day off from work to clean the house and prepare for his arrival and enjoy a three-day weekend. There was enough chicken and mashed potatoes and she also boiled some frozen peas. They shared a bottle of cold white wine at the table in the center of the kitchen. He told her New York stories.

"Here's one," he said. "This embodies the whole of my New York experience and it didn't even happen to me. A coworker, Frances, sweet girl my age, she and a friend were walking home from an East Village bar at 4 a.m."

"I heard that city never sleeps."

"They were all coked up, they'd see daylight before they slept. Except for they almost didn't do either. Guy walks straight up to them on First Avenue and puts the gun straight in Frances's friend's face. She thought they were both goners. The friend instinctively stepped to her right off the curb and out of the line of fire. Immediately someone started screaming, not Frances or her friend, just this wild crazy screaming. The mugger got spooked and ran away. Frances's friend had stepped off the curb and onto the face of a homeless woman sleeping in the street! True story.

"So right there, Grimsley, it's all there—the violence, the drinking and drugging, the homeless people. I swear, a month ago I walked right over a home-less person lying in the middle of Park Avenue South, coulda been dead. It was two blocks later that I realized, I just walked over a homeless person and didn't give it a thought. Not a thought. That was the moment I knew I had to get out of there."

She reached across the table and held his hand.

Emerson had two thousand dollars saved (cash, he noted, though he had credit card debt), and an assignment for Vanity Fair in Los Angeles, where he'd secured an apartment in West Hollywood. He looked at her hand and then at the face he'd seen for the first time nearly six years earlier. It was June. He could have gone home and lived there for the month, but he was glad he'd chosen to return to Durham, that Grimsley was still here for him. He told her this with his eyes then, and she smiled back. They didn't need to talk. She was always there for him, she was always such a comfort to be near, and he felt lucky.

"Let's take a walk around East Campus," he said.

They bumped into Sterly on the front porch, returning from work. Sterly was tall and lanky with big curly hair and a blazing smile. A native of Durham, she had that accent Emerson had grown so familiar with when he'd been a student.

They hugged, even though they had never been great friends. She was protective of Grimsley and resentful of what she considered his overly casual relationship with her best friend. She never saw the best moments, only the conflicted ones when Grimsley, confused by her own emotions, needed to talk.

"I hear you're bunking here for a few weeks."

"I hope that's okay," he said.

"Our house is your house," she said and seemed to mean it. She looked to Grimsley and said, "And Bo is off on a guys' golf weekend at Hilton Head, so you'll be seeing me."

"I'll have three to cook for instead of two!" Grimsley said.

He loved that she loved to cook.

*

They walked slowly through the warm evening air, all around the campus, sparsely populated now that school was out, catching up. But also giving in to easy, long silences. She noticed how deeply he was inhaling. He was taking it all in. He loved the air of this place, she could tell. They walked until dusk and headed home.

When she'd locked the front door, he asked, "You wouldn't happen to have any whiskey by any chance, would you?"

"Actually, no, we're not big drinkers, me and Sterl. Not like we were in school anyhow!"

Emerson looked at his watch. She knew he was calculating whether an ABC store would be open where he could purchase some.

"Hey," she said, "I thought you needed to detox. If you can have that whiskey, then I presume you can do other things as well?"

She grabbed him by the belt and tugged him to her. They kissed. She hummed and said, "That food and walk have you sufficiently relaxed? My body seriously misses yours."

He kissed her again—yes.

*

When he woke, she was gone from the bed. He lay awake listening to the birds and smelling the cool morning air, leafy Durham in June. The day was already bright. He smelled bacon cooking. He went downstairs in his boxers and a T-shirt, scratching his head and back and yawning.

"Look who's up," Grimsley said. Sterly took her plate to the sink and said, "Well, you really are making yourself at home."

"Think of me as your little brother."

She thought about it, smiled back, and said, "I'm going shopping, you want to add anything to the list?"

"Nope," Grimsley said. "I'm good."

"Em?"

"No, but thanks."

When he was seated and drinking coffee, and Grimsley had begun to scramble eggs for him, he said, "Okay, you were right. Sex is better than drinking."

"You're just realizing that now?"

"You don't understand. I feel great. I feel really great. I forgot what it was like to wake up not hungover."

She brought him a plate of breakfast, but before setting it down, she put her hand in is his hair and tugged it, back and forth, with genuine concern.

They spent that whole Saturday outside, Emerson all but literally soaking in the air and trees and water that he hadn't had in a full year, a year defined by concrete and heat and stink, a little less human every day.

Grimsley had found an old rock quarry her senior year and, now that school was out, no one would be there. When they arrived, noon sun directly overhead, Grimsley stripped naked and went to the edge of the rock. He'd have undressed himself but he was staring at her back and narrow hips and ass and calves in genuine aesthetic, asexual admiration. She had not changed. She turned, shaded her eyes from the sun—ah, those perfect breasts in the open sunlight. "Well, come on!" Ooh-wn. He loved that. "I gotta show you where to jump." He stripped too and joined her at the rock's edge. The heat of the sun felt good on his whole body.

She pointed to the left. "See that rock there? That's the only one you got to worry about." And with that, she leapt and screamed. She bobbed to the surface, shook her head. "Well?"

"It's a long jump!"

"Chicken!"

She saw him take a deep breath and she quickly shouted, "Hold on to your balls!"

And down he plunged into the cool green water. He emerged coughing.

She said, "You gotta blow out through your nose."

When he'd finished coughing, he said, "I'm glad you gave me that first bit of advice when you did, though. Water up the nose I can handle."

"I saw a guy not do it and then he had to float on his back moaning sick for twenty minutes before he had the strength to climb back up."

She put her head down, showed that perfect white ass, lifted her legs gymnast straight, and sank out of sight like a stone, emerging twenty seconds later ten yards away.

"There's a cold spot about ten feet down, feels soooo good," she said, smiling. She smiled all day long.

They stayed through the afternoon, sunning on towels in the grass and swimming till trees blocked the sun. They were joined only once for an hour by another couple, who said hi, took off their clothes, and jumped and splashed and sunned but kept to themselves.

Lying back down in the sun, he said, "I miss living around hippies."

"You don't have to miss them," she said.

They showered upon returning home and Emerson took her out for an early dinner at a her favorite place for barbecue, and afterward they fell quickly into their old routine.

By Sunday, they'd had what felt like a vacation of a weekend. Grimsley roasted a chicken for the three of them. Later, when Grimsley and Em were eating ice cream in bed and watching The Maltese Falcon, *Sterly knocked and poked her head in.*

"You are *going to work tomorrow, yes?"*

"Yes, why?"

"Because I am too, and I need a good night's sleep."

"Yes, Mom," Grimsley said.

Sterly had closed the door, but the latch didn't catch so the door swung partly open. "I guess she heard us," Grimsley said.

"Were we that loud?" he asked.

Sterly's head popped back in. "Yes," she said. "Which would be fine"—pronounced faahn—"if you were sprinters and not long-distance runners." With that, she closed the door so that it stayed shut.

They laughed quietly. Grimsley set the last of the ice cream on her bedside table and snuggled into Emerson, returning her focus to Bogey and Mary Astor.

*

And on Monday the routine began. He'd lay awake while the girls used the bathroom and readied for work, kept clear of their rituals till Grimsley came upstairs to kiss him goodbye.

"So, what are you going to do all day?"

"I don't know. Read, write."

"Sounds like heaven."

He smiled sleepily in agreement, and for a moment something she'd said skipped lightly through his mind. Two days earlier, they'd unpacked his U-Haul to return it before heading to the quarry. A television, stereo, and speakers went into the spare downstairs room. A trunk of clothes up to her room. Furniture, a table and four chairs, coffee table, a futon and its frame, boxes of books, boxes of bric-a-brac, and one very heavy sofa that she had trouble helping him carry—all this went into the garage.

He'd said, when he'd pulled the empty truck's door down with a clatter, "The thought of filling this thing back up less than a month from now is not something I'm looking forward to."

She'd responded, "You don't have to, you know."

He paused, then grinned in thanks, but did not respond beyond that.

He thought of this until her second good-bye kiss brought him back. "I'll be home at six. Remember, no smoking inside!"

"Absolutely, already cut way back."

"And could you stop by the store? Grocery list is on the fridge."

"You bet."

She kissed him a third time, just because, and was gone, and he lay back feeling lucky.

That morning he picked up working on a short story he'd begun in New York and wrote till noon. He jogged a mile, which would become three by the following week. He hacked so badly after that first awful run, he resolved to stop smoking altogether by the end of the week, and did. He kept to his writing routine even on Saturdays, resolving to finish the story before he left. After his daily run, he'd shower, have a sandwich, and spend the rest of the day reading and doing errands Grimsley needed done. She walked to work, so he had her car. But mostly he stayed home. She made a fine meal every evening and they'd share most of a bottle of wine—but that was all, a serious change from his time in New York. Sterly was rarely there. In the evening, they sometimes went to a movie or to hear a local band and once went to a Durham Bulls game. But more often than not, they sat on the porch swing to enjoy the cool of evening after increasingly warm days. He usually read aloud to her. He loved to read aloud, and she loved the sound of his voice as much as he did hers, though for different reasons. His voice became musical to her when he read. Over the course of a week, he'd read the whole of A Moveable Feast. He'd often choose poetry he liked— especially Shakespeare sonnets or John Donne—followed by gloomy Yates and Raymond Carver stories till she couldn't bear them any longer and she made him change to P. G. Wodehouse, which she could listen to over and over. They had sex almost every night, with undiminishing pleasure.

And in the morning it would begin again.

It was a genuine summer idyll he'd never—never—know again, but, unable to know this, he did not see it for what it was.

At the beginning of the week of his planned departure, after steaks on the grill, grilled asparagus, cool potato salad, and cold red wine (it was getting too hot to want to use the stove), they had an extra glass of wine and sat on the porch swing, inhaling the rich, heavy air.

"So," she said, "when are you going to let me read the pages you're working on?"

He'd reached the point where he'd write in the morning and type the morning's work in the afternoon, slowly, one careful sentence at a time, revising as he went.

"I'm vowing to finish before I leave. So, before I leave, I hope. Or as a parting story. I'll want your critique as soon as I reach LA."

He looked at her but she didn't look at him. He loved the straight line of her nose, the straight brown hair always tightly bound with a hair tie into a short ponytail.

She was plain, as she always referred to herself, and it was precisely this plainness that was her beauty, rather than the traditional elements most people considered traits of beauty: full lips, high cheekbones, the air-brushed faces of models.

"Don't ask me," she said, not looking at him.

"How do you know what I'm about to say?"

"I've felt it all week."

"Okay, I'll make it formal. Come with me to LA."

Now she turned to him. "I can't just quit my job and move to some strange city."

"Sure you can."

"You've never once said 'I love you.'"

"Neither have you."

"Because I know you couldn't say it back." She paused, waiting for him to prove her wrong. "Em, I do love you. I love you. I loved you the moment I saw you. The moment."

He could only hold her hand.

"I would marry you right now, you know," she said. "We'd be good together. Look at us. Look at you."

"Then come with me."

She looked away, she took a deep breath, exhaled and said, "No. Because eventually you will fall in love with someone and where will that leave me?"

They both stared out into the street.

"This is my home, Emerson. I can't leave it. I can't leave my mom and her dogs or my work or this land. I won't be me anymore. But you, you're rootless, and a writer and can live anywhere." She gripped his hand, and he looked into her eyes. "This is a good place. You could be really good here. You could get a job at Duke, keep writing. We could be really good together forever."

"Academia would suffocate me."

"How do you know?"

He turned from her insistent gaze and stared out at the street, and she could see, with a fevered aching in her whole body, he was already packing his truck in his mind. And there was nothing she could do about it. He had ambition. And what can one do with Ambition in Durham? She could see it. He was putting the ambition on now, in his mind, cloaking himself in it to save himself from the choice she'd put before him.

They slept still but close that night, her head on his comfortable chest, but not a word or kiss, and when he woke, she had left for work.

*

He thought about this conversation twice. Just twice. Both times with a sickness in his stomach. Once, at the end of that week, as he turned left onto Broad Street and headed toward the highway in a rented truck, everything he owned inside it; but excitement about the journey and the life he was heading into concealed the dread. And then he recalled this moment again, twenty years later, on the other side of the country, in the very place where he'd all but exactly lived out his intended life.

But how could he have known? We can't know the future; we can only know the past. Does that young man in the U-Haul envision his older self? Yes, but it is a grand self. He doesn't envision simply an older version of his current self, wrapped in the trappings he himself has woven, leaving that original living core to struggle ceaselessly against the woven forgery. He certainly doesn't envision a middle-aged man, alone and weeping at the edge of a church in a place where he was his best self, acknowledging the impossibility of returning to the self he once was in order to change the future. And even if he could return, would he do anything differently?

Not likely. What was, was inevitable. Orpheus forever turns to look at Eurydice, sending her back to the underworld, ensuring that he will be forever without her. It is Juliet's only option upon waking to find her love dead—to join him in death because living would be a worse kind of separation.

Why did parting with what one cherishes most seem so inevitable, so unstoppable? Nothing changes, not in ancient myth, not in the story of our days. Only the backdrop changes, only the clothes and the scenery change.

He would forever pull onto I-85, June 28, 1991, open a Diet Coke, light a cigarette, and head west into the future he chose—the end.

Four

That's all he wrote. Like I said, Em was the one for remembering things. Yes, it all came back vividly with the reading. It was exactly as he wrote it.

When Em had left for good, I fell into a depression so deep it took Mom and Sterly a month to drag me up out of the grave and into the light, and then another six months of steady work and life to admit to myself that my one love did not love me, that he was gone and would not return. And now that he was truly gone, returned to me for one night and now gone from this world forever, I had to truly and finally give him up to that great beyond.

I'd returned from Los Angeles on a Monday, having read the innocu-ous-seeming concluding sentence, assured myself he hadn't written of our recent affair, showered, and gone to work. And I worked the rest of that week before I had the weekend to read. And during one clear-headed empty Saturday morning, I read the entirety of what he'd written before he died.

I think he knew he couldn't send it to me. And not because long ago I'd told him not to write about me or us. I think that when he'd finished, had gotten it out of his system and onto the page, there wasn't anything more to say; he tried to return to the life he'd created and the shame of it, the reason for the tears at Duke's Chapel, the inexorable decay inside—or life with me gone absolutely?—became too great to live with.

I wasn't angry that he'd written about me, of course. But this may well have been because the point was moot. The first time he'd tried to put our story on paper, I'd been livid with anger without knowing why. We never talked about it and I was not reflective at the time. But now that I look back on that morning, I think something registered deep in my heart, a certainty that if he were to write about me or us, it would be the end of us, or the end of me, rather. I believed that he could literally write me out of his life. And that once he did, I would cease to be. It turned out to be the other way around. Why?

I now couldn't help thinking, in the weeks leading up to Christmas, if I were, in fact, responsible, as Collista had implied, that I'd *caused* his death. Did he wish that that day back in May had never happened? Would he still be here today?

I, unlike Em, do believe in "God," capital G, and have since age seven, shortly before Daddy moved us to Durham. The quotation marks are important because it's not a Biblical, mean-old-man God, not a Christian or Muslim God I believe in. And it's not a Buddhist thing—don't get me started on them with all their endless talk of suffering. I personally believe that we need to take all the happiness we can get, since life is so hard, and that we really should take each day as it comes, leave tomorrow for tomorrow, as Christ said (a great teacher, who surely had a main line of communication with that G word). I don't believe we're born sinners needing saving, and we certainly shouldn't be our own personal guilt factories, which so many people seem to be. Whether or not there's a heaven, or if our souls are immortal, it's no concern of mine presently. I'll find out when the time comes.

It was late summer 1974, when I got what I've come to believe was a gift, something I've been searching for ever since and have been unable to receive. I was seven and alone. My brother and sister were younger by two and four years and I spent most of my days in solitude, long hours by myself, always happily, and I think the solitude was a critical feature of the gift. It didn't happen by chancing on a hidden forest glade, or at the edge the Grand Canyon or anything. It was just our normal backyard, out by the garage, a summer weeknight, same smells of summer and garages in the warm South Carolina dusk. A moon had risen and I looked at it and looked at it, and it was so clear and beautiful, I soon found myself laughing. I looked all around me at the silhouettes of the leaves, the shape of the back of my house, the attic gable, the trees and blue air and the warm black-topped drive against my bare feet, and I laughed. Because I suddenly understood that everything was connected, *everything*, all of nature, the driveway at my feet, the worms in the dirt, and the moon and my parents and the bats that had come out—it was all somehow simply a manifestation of one great thing, a spinning inevitable harmony, and I was filled with a kind of joy I'd never felt before and never would again. It was simply so uncontainable I couldn't stop laughing. It was like an interior aurora borealis, waves of light, joy, washing over my entire being.

I've thought about this a lot because, well, that too is simply one of those moments you never forget, like the moment I first saw Em, when you're given a gift so big it changes your life. (I see Em now as a gift, not the dagger he so often felt to me when I was a young woman; indeed, I, the unlikely cause, or at least a part of, of his early departure kind of makes me the dagger in the end—who'd have thought, twenty-five years back on that bench in Duke's main quad?) Whatever it was, the source of this joy, the harmony of all things, was inside me, and I was an inevitable part of it, but I also recognized that it came from *outside* me. I know this now because I simply didn't have the intellect or the spirit to generate it myself, make it up, that is—it was just so huge, so endlessly vast my brain couldn't have fabricated it. I know it came from outside also because it went away, forever. I never wanted it to end, but I could feel it subsiding, and I tried to maintain it, tried to keep laughing, but it fell slowly away, and I could no more stop its leaving than I could stop day turning into night; it receded, gradually but inevitably, as the aurora borealis leaves the sky. As of course it had to. No one could live full-time with that kind of joy—the body couldn't sustain it, you'd never get anything done (kind of like being in the first throes of love). So, when I'd laughed and smiled until I couldn't anymore and the gift was played out, all gone, I walked up our back deck and into the dining room. Mom was finishing up the dishes at the kitchen sink, Daddy was in his study where he always was, my brother and sister were lying in front of the TV in the den. I went to my room and sat on the edge of my bed, just sat there, feeling so peaceful and good and lucky and happy, so so happy.

I never could have put it into these words at the time, and I was too young to realize what it was, but I *was* old enough to know how unusual it was. I tried to put myself in situations where it might visit me again, but it never did. And only years later did I understand it to be the biggest gift anyone could get. To be granted an understanding that we were and are everything, even the horrors of the world, dictators and war and viruses—it's all a good and great harmony issuing from a single source.

This conviction lives at the back of my mind always, there but out of daily sight. A single source—it's the most anyone can know, and I suppose that if you've never experienced it, you'll be skeptical of what I'm saying, as you should be, unless you've spoken to anyone halfway intelligent who has experienced something similar. But those people who have, they usually keep quiet about it, as I always have. Because it's impossible to put into words completely. I've never tried before till now. And now I do so with hopes of answering the question, what had I done to my old love? And what did it mean that he'd done himself in? Because he surely had.

The daisies were proof of that.

February 14, six weeks ago. I was breast-feeding when the doorbell rang. I put my newborn son in the crib and left him there, wailing and red in the face. I opened the door and there stood a man in a clean jacket with a logo I didn't read holding a big bouquet of daisies.

The sight of them was so shocking I didn't do anything, just stared at the guy with my mouth open. He was trying to give them to me. Again—it felt like an actual blow to the head. I knew immediately who they were from, and for long moments I thought that it meant Em was alive, literally alive, had faked his own death to return to me.

"I can set 'em down here, if you want," the man said. "But I do have to get moving. Busy day, you know?"

I took them from him and thanked him and closed the door.

There was no note. So just to be sure, I called the florist to ask who sent them. The owner, a woman, told me it was anonymous. I pressed, and she said she honestly didn't know. She explained that this was common on Valentine's Day, a lot of requests for anonymous deliveries.

"Mistresses," she said. "Secret loves. Every year, and thank goodness for it!" The woman cackled hoarsely, coughed, then said, "I can honestly say I don't know the name of the person who ordered these—cash, by mail, says here."

"Says where?"

"In our register, our book where we keep a record of orders."

"Can you tell me when the order was placed?"

"Let's see," she said. I waited. She said, "Hm." I heard pages shuffling. "Oh, right."

"Oh right, what?"

"I do remember this now. Anonymous requests are common. But what is uncommon, especially where men are concerned, is thinking ahead. I took this order myself, October 20. Four whole *months* ago."

I thanked her. I clipped the stems and put the daisies in a vase with water and brought them to the bedroom where my baby, who had been born two weeks earlier, remained wailing. I fixed his greedy mouth to my breast and lay back on pillows against the headboard, staring at the flowers and trying to figure it out, tears quietly rolling off my cheeks and onto my chest and my nursing boy, the only christening he'd get, tears of love and sorrow.

*

I still haven't figured it out, even after all these pages—what they truly meant. In college, he'd given me daisies each of the four years he was there, and he remembered to send them to me during his year in New York, the sweetheart, the last I'd gotten till now. I'd always received them in the spirit with which I thought they were given. I presumed they were meant to say, "You're important to me." Even after the Gatsby revelation. I wasn't Daisy and he didn't love me, for if he had, wouldn't he have stayed?

And I had to accept these as the same. He had to assume I'd never read the pages he'd been working on before he died. And I think the October order wasn't just because he was thinking about me a lot, but rather because he knew then he was a goner. He knew whatever was inside him was unsustainable once he'd left me in his mind for good. I was his muse, I knew, had always known, and liked being just that. That's what I'm guessing.

I wonder if I could have changed that. By letting him know that his final gift to me was a new life. But if I'd changed it, it wouldn't have been his final gift, would it? Would he have come back, stayed in our life somehow? I know now, too late, what those daisies said—that he did love me and had never stopped. But you can't change another person's destiny, and I will not blame myself.

I honestly don't know what to make of it all, but I did lean back on that old memory of what happened to me out by the garage, that big message I got about the connectedness of all things. If there's proof that it's the truth, it's simply that life begets life. Nor is it neutral, either, this force: life *wants* more of itself. For the good. And that's what this baby is, proof of it, these long years later, maybe willed on that day when I first saw my only love.

For Randall M. Feller, On or After Your Eighteenth Birthday

You were born as predicted on February 1, 2011, after a labor that felt like it was going to *kill* me until they used a knife to get you out. And there you were, healthy. Seven pounds, six ounces, twenty digits, a strong spine, and a beating heart, all four chambers intact. I named you then, on sight, with just a middle initial, only that. I don't know what name you'll make for yourself or what I'll call you. I mainly call you Little Man now, what you are.

Spring has come early and so I can sit outside by my pond while you feed. I can set you on a blanket in the grass in the soft April sun when you've gorged yourself to sleep and I can think and write.

I originally began these pages I'm giving you here to try to understand two big unknowns. First, what your father's visit and my getting pregnant with you meant, and what I should *do*. I picked up these pages again, shortly after a trip to Los Angeles to attend your father's memorial, to say goodbye to him and get a glimpse of where he'd chosen to make his adult life and who he'd done it with and who *else* he made (good people, I have every reason to believe; go search for your half-siblings if you wish, but, as bears repeating, do no harm). I finished the last of the pages about a month after your birth and it occurred to me, staring at the empty vase where I'd kept the daisies long after they'd died and had started to stink—forcing me to throw them out and accept that they were to be my last—that, unlike flowers and people, words and stories are things that *don't* die, and that these pages might be of use to you when you're an adult. All fatherless boys want to know their father's story, and this was the part of it I knew and could give to you.

And I've very much worked to make it a *story—restoring our proper names*. It's still the best way to get at the difficult *whys* of life—sorry. Also, it was the only way that I've been able to marry your father, however sadly, to intertwine our stories as we had so often intertwined our bodies.

If I haven't made it to age sixty-five to give this to you in person, there are a couple of things you should know. The original pages your father wrote, along with a lot of other stuff, is archived at Duke's library and they're not open to the public until you say so, if you wish, because I don't know if he would have wanted them available in their unfinished state. But I've made them open to you if you want to read them.

Also, by the time you're nineteen or so, the twenty-year moratorium Professor Blackmore put on his papers will be up and they'll be open to the public. You'll find letters from your father there in Blackmore's general correspondence, and I suspect it will be the best way to get to know who your father was beyond this record I'm leaving you. We wrote actual letters back then, printed on paper, folded and slipped into a stamped envelope, delivered by human hand. I'm sure you'll hear your father's voice in those letters, get a good sense of the man he was, or young man (I haven't had the heart or stomach to read them); he really was a fine writer, your father, and I loved him with my entire being.

And if you turn out to be a writer, which I hope you don't, for the record, but if you do, make copies of your good email, and print out the good ones you receive and file them, will you? This is Mom the archivist talking. We've lost who knows how much useful information about our lives thanks to electronic communication, half our stories now gone, deleted with the invention of each new device that makes sending them easier than before. How are we going to know who we are if we don't remember who we *were*, if we don't remember our own stories?

When I say I hope you don't become a writer like your father, I should add this: *do* be an author of something. Not a book or a script, necessarily, but a company, a building, a school, an organization that does good work, an invention of any kind. Make something of your own. You may end up being a part of something bigger for your work, like I am, working for this university. But at some point, make something out of yourself. I made *you*! I hope to be worthy of you as long as you need me, and I hope you are worthy of me when you no longer do need me. (The Fellers as a clan haven't had a great record of longevity, but who can say now that we've learned to cut back on the smoking and butter-soaked grits?) Neither of your grandfathers made it to seventy, so take care of yourself.

If I don't make it to sixty-five, you won't even be out of college. But I'll have plenty of time to tell you in person about what it's like to lose your mother. That's a whole other story I'm intimate with, when I sense you're ready.

That's all, Little Man. But please know this: Your father wanted to be extraordinary, and he was in many, many ways. But those ways did not make him happy (except when he was with me—smiley face icon, can't bring myself to type it, but I do say this with humor). Life is not always easy, so it's important to enjoy as much as you can, as often as you can. Above all, try not to hurt anyone—everyone struggles. Please take my words to heart, especially when times are tough. Especially when you've hurt someone without meaning to.

Strive to be extraordinary if you wish, but don't expect happiness in return. I'd rather you just have a good time. Find work you care about and be the best at it you can be. Cherish the friends you make along the way. It *is* the ordinary lives that are the best, and love is the most valuable essence in this world, love in all its forms—my love for Em, my love for you, the love your father gave to me, the love that created you. Embrace it all.

Strong Conspirators

One

Karen Markstrom floated in and out of fevered consciousness though her eyes remained open and fixed on her husband, who stared out the bedroom window at the spot where the accident had happened.

In the dim blue light, streetlights reflecting off the pristine snow, Frank appeared to be his former self, the boy she'd met, twenty-one years old, all radiance and promise. The light cast his angular chin and sharp nose in dramatic relief against the dark master bathroom and hid what few wrinkles had worked their way into his forty-five-year-old complexion. He'd kept his athletic physique. His blue eyes nearly glowed in this light.

Those blue eyes, so vivid even in her mind, now, twenty-four years later. "Who . . . *are* you?" he had said, without the least self-consciousness. All she'd done was to enter the kitchen late in the evening as the party waned, and he had zeroed his gaze on her like sun through a magnifying glass. He had walked to her, leaving whomever he'd been talking to, and said, "I'm Frank." She had been struck dumb by his looks and confidence, and when she failed to respond, he grinned wide and easily, took her arm, and led her outside to the pool.

"How did I fail to see you?" he had asked her.

"I don't know what you mean," she had said.

"Have you been here long?"

"No, I just got here. I was going to get a beer."

"Have mine," he said, handing her the bottle. "I just opened it. I'll get another."

"Can we share it?" she asked, and with that, his smile increased a thousand watts. Had he realized she didn't want to risk his returning to the party and getting waylaid? Already she didn't want to lose him.

There by the side of the pool, grinning until both their jaws ached, they learned that each had recently graduated, he with a BA from Brown, she with an MFA from Rhode Island School of Design, that he could talk about Joyce and Hemingway as easily as he could Van Gogh and Ruskin. That he even knew who Ruskin was! None of her non-painter friends knew Ruskin, or cared. He was a writer *and* had been a starter on Brown's varsity lacrosse team no less. He had that athlete's glow of health and strength and strong white teeth and confidence and could match her conversation. By dawn, all who'd remained in the summerhouse slept but for them, and he led her, out of dawn's gray light, away from the pool and upstairs to a spare room and made love to her. She woke to his face, in clear morning light, staring at her, stroking her hair, in what was not simply a new day but rather a transformed world.

And there this same boy stood twenty-four years later in the blue light. She wanted to hold him there, to fix him forever in that spot where he'd once been: *you are so beautiful*, she thought.

A chill ran through her, and the sweat on her forehead felt cooling though she also felt hot beneath the sheets. Those eyes that had looked into hers as he reached for her hand, fifteen years ago, and said, "Okay, I'm ready. I think." They hadn't talked about a baby in weeks but she knew exactly what he meant and her heart seemed to expand to fill her entire chest.

"I'm sorry it's taken so long," he'd said. "It's the biggest decision, but I know it's what you want, and so I want it, too." Those eyes, for which she was so grateful. Those eyes from which she saw tears falling onto her shoulder a year later as she held their son, Nicholas, just moments old. They cried from joy. As they would cry from grief when his father breathed his last in a hospice bed three years ago now. She could comfort her beloved with her tears, because she'd loved his father, too, and she could help him make the slow return to their new old life, one without his cherished dad in the midwestern suburb where Frank had grown up.

So real were these memories that she could scarcely distinguish what was in her mind from what she saw, the boy Frank she'd fallen in love with on sight twenty-four years ago, the new father, or the fatherless middle-aged man on his steady march through a blessed life. *Stay that boy*, she thought.

Karen lifted her head from the pillow, now coming awake, watching him. And he, hearing her stir, slowly, dream-slow, turned to look at her. And as he did, he seemed to Karen to age from twenty-one to an old man, a man fifteen years beyond his forty-five in the time it took him to turn from the window to her. A horrifying sight, one that shocked her into consciousness, where the events of what had happened on this night lived, and a nausea in her womb spread up through her gut and into her throat. Frank, saying nothing, turned back to the snow outside as a plow rumbled down their street like a galloping beast.

"I had to do it," she said. "It wasn't a choice."

He turned back to her but said nothing.

"Hold me," she said.

He got back under the sheets. His skin on hers felt cold from the bedroom air. He pushed matted hair off her forehead and he blew on her forehead to cool her.

He said, "Try to close your eyes, my love."

*

They both had breathed heavily from stress when Officer Williams and Silent Curt arrived, followed by the Emergency Medical Service vehicle, ambulance, and six other squad cars, which lit up their suburban street and the continuing blizzard and drifting snow like the Christmastime that it was, the plan already set in motion.

She had done it with very little thought, with animal quickness.

"*I was driving.*"

It's in the police report.

What isn't in the report was how she'd blurted it. It came out like a pop, a single multisyllabic word. A gush. Not tentatively, not quietly, but emphatically. *Unnecessarily emphatically?* she worried.

Karen had thrown on her boots and winter coat and rushed outside. She found Frank crouched over the woman trying to shield her from the snow that collected on her face and caught in her red lashes. Her face flashed on and off from the car's hazard lights, as if communicating with him. As if she were alive and asking for help, while the snow worked to bury her. She looked so unharmed to Karen as to be alive but sinking. Karen recognized the woman but had never met her and did not know her name. Frank and Karen had often seen her walking their street and several other curving streets of this old suburb, lined with handsome, well-maintained colonials and tall sycamores and oaks. The woman was a walker, always very deep in thought. She was easily six feet, lean, with muscled legs and hiking boots in summer, in winter a heavy parka from which her abundant, vividly red hair poured, so red Karen always wondered if it were dyed. Karen had assumed during the fifteen years they'd lived on this street that this was the woman's form of meditation or relaxation, that had to be the reason, since she was out at all times of day, in all kinds of weather, never looking up at passing dog-walkers or anyone who raised a hand in greeting.

Frank stood, stepped away from the body and the car.

Karen, clutching her shoulders, watched him. She said, "You're swaying." And then, "Oh my God, you're drunk."

He didn't respond except to curl his lips inward so that they vanished and to look at her. They locked gazes, one, two, three, and he looked away and then down.

Headlights appeared at the top of the hill, blue and reds flashing, no siren, coming on fast. Karen and Frank huddled in the plowed apron of their driveway, already blanketing up with fresh snow. Large fluffy flakes blew sideways through the archways cast from streetlights overhead. Everything silence and black-and-white, but for the flashing yellow hazards and now the colorful lights of the squad car.

Karen felt his arm pull her into him strongly and decisively. He had on the blazer he'd worn to work that day, a warm tweed going a little frayed at the cuffs.

He would surely be tested on the spot, she knew; therefore, his fate would depend largely on that of the woman lying half under the car, who was, at best, unconscious. He had been drunk and at the wheel. A fact— she knew. Not stupid drunk, not driving-with-one-eye-shut drunk—Frank wasn't a heavy drinker. But she had to assume, given the office party followed by the annual holiday dinner with the boys, the way he had swayed and not denied it, that he was over the limit for the next hour or so. No matter the blizzard, no matter how unexpected the neighbor's presence at the edge of the apron of their drive, no matter the icy road. No matter that he may well have hit the woman given the conditions had he been completely sober and actually been able to *see* her in the darkness. No matter that he'd taken not the four-wheel-drive Jeep, but rather their little, light, harmless-seeming Honda Civic four-door with the not-so-good-in-snow tires.

This was her fault. She was to have been driving. It had been her responsibility to pick up their son from the party.

But none of this mattered. She had to presume he was over the limit.

They both stood in the snow, shivering, holding each other, praying for the woman to be all right, waiting.

Karen had not even been *in* the car. She had been cleaning the kitchen and watching *The Daily Show with Jon Stewart*, at 11:30 p.m., startled by Frank as he hustled fourteen-year-old Nick into the kitchen. She hadn't seen any headlights roll up the drive and light up the garage, in view from her vantage point at the window above the kitchen sink. And it was quickly clear from his expression, from his jarring movements, all was not right, even before he said, "I've hit someone. I've called 911." And ran back out.

Karen first went to Nick, tall and slim like his father, with shaggy brown hair. She cupped his ears, looked up into his eyes—clearly he was unharmed—blue eyes like his dad's, unblinking and wide, lost, pleading. She said, "Go to your room and stay there." Then she'd gotten her coat, slipped on snow boots, and hurried out to find her husband crouched over the woman. "Oh my God," she said. "When did you call?"

"When I made the turn into the drive," he told her, standing. "The car just kept going forward, sort of sideways. I didn't even see her. It just went thud. I thought it must be a deer. I got out of the car. I called the second I saw her. I just wanted to get Nick inside. I don't know what to do."

That was when Karen said, "You're swaying." And "Oh my God, you're drunk." And when she saw his facial response, the curled lips, the way he turned his head and looked downward, she said, "Jesus," looking away herself.

The squad car slid to a snow-crunching halt in the center of the street, and the officer bolted the car and ran to the unconscious woman, not giving Frank or Karen a glance.

*

The night had *not* been routine. Normally, a Friday was like any weeknight for them, except for the fact that now they were often either alone, or Nick would have a friend downstairs playing video games and spending the night, leaving them to dine *à deux*, watch the news as they cleaned up, then watch a movie or some saved-up episodes of *Mad Men*. Frank loved that show and she had wondered why.

"It's just that it's not normally the case," she said. "Real doctors cringe at shows like *Grey's Anatomy*. Lawyers can't stand law procedurals, too many completely unlikely things happen for them to suspend belief past the opening credits."

"I don't know," Frank said. "It's basically true. And it's far back enough in time that what isn't factually accurate is accurate to the era it evokes, my dad's era. Maybe that's it. When there was so much promise in advertising, so much creativity, and so much hope *in* that creativity, a kind of naiveté about the creative process, about writing."

She'd then give him a kiss and he'd reached for the remote. Soon it would be time for bed, and Saturday would be the day to get the errands done. She did groceries, laundry, cleaned the house and drove Nick to his guitar lesson, to a friend's, while Frank went to the hardware store for a new radiator release valve, picked up dry cleaning, paid bills, and did office work, timing radio spots, working on headlines. Et cetera.

But this Friday, the day before Christmas Eve, was not routine. Frank had had that office party he needed to stay for, then his annual pre-Christmas dinner with the boys, his old pals from high school, all of whom Karen liked. And there was the party Nick was attending.

The private girls' school where Karen taught art had had a half-day to begin the two-week break, concluding with a "multicultural" holiday celebration, a spurious conceit, she felt, as it was still filled with "Good King Wenceslas" and "Away in a Manger" sung by the choir, and really—who were they trying to kid? *It's Christmas*, she thought, it's a Christian holiday, and no amount of Hanukkah and Kwanzaa was going to hide this, any more than changing "before Christ" to "before the common era" in the history texts changed the fact that it was still Christ who marked the before and after. Her own conflicted beliefs aside, the hypocrisy of the directors of the school never ceased to astonish her, but at least it gave her something to occupy her mind during the mediocre but earnest pageant.

And she was as relieved as even the most beleaguered student to have this lovely long break from school that was strangely exhausting, given that all she did was paint and draw along with her students for six of the nine periods in a normal day. She guessed it was a result of the pressure of all that female adolescence in one building, like an actual atmospheric pounds-per-square-inch increase when she walked into a classroom filled with thirteen-year-old girls. When she was at last in her Grand Jeep Cherokee pulling out of the school parking lot to pick up Nick at his school nearby, she felt that same kind of exhilarated relief and fatigue of having crawled out of the ocean and onto the dive boat after an extended dive. She and Frank hadn't been diving in years, not since before she'd had Nick, but the feeling of being on the boat remained familiar. They should plan a vacation around diving, she thought, get Nick certified, renew their own certifications.

Late in the day, while Nick showered and prepared for the party, Karen had had some leftover spaghetti with meat sauce, a juice glass half full of red wine, standing at the kitchen island and leafing through a Restoration Hardware catalogue. On a normal Friday, she'd have been cooking something for either the two of them or the three of them, on the table at seven, the house redolent of beef stew or a roasting chicken. But on this Friday, she'd had a small bite early and set both the bowl and glass in the otherwise clean sink. She had thoughtlessly splashed some water in the bowl when Nick had appeared ready to leave for the party, a fifteen-minute car ride away. Later she would wonder whether, if she had rinsed the bowl and fork and glass and put them into the dishwasher, would that have been enough to change what was to come?

She'd gotten back from dropping Nick to see Frank's car in the drive. She looked at her watch, frowned—he was supposed to be at the restaurant.

Frank swallowed a long drink of tap water and set his glass in the sink next to Karen's dishes, just as Karen's keys went *clink* on the granite kitchen island. "I got out of the party early. I wanted a quick shower before going out, now I'm late," he explained. Then he stared at her bowl long enough so that she would see him staring at it—or so it seemed to her (and she knew him, knew all his tics)—before filling it to the brim with water, stopping the water slowly so that every bit of interior touched water, which bulged higher than the rim. Some tomato sauce, a few fragments of pasta, and some broiled-on cheese were now dried to the bowl's sides.

"Karen why don't you simply fill the bowl up to the top with water to make it easier to clean?"

"How about a 'Hello, I love you, dear'?"

This was the first conversation they'd had today, as she'd had an early meeting on this last day of school before the holidays, and he and Nick had risen as usual at seven as she was heading out the door. She'd changed out of her school attire and wore a loose cotton sweater and old jeans, weekend clothes. She leaned on the island to remove her brown leather boots. They had a two-inch heel and she left them where they lay, which she knew would annoy Frank. Reduced now to her five feet six inches, she stared at him stone-faced. Her hair was a camouflage of bright blond and brown-blond now, already streaking with gray, but it remained abundant, and fell in long, loose curls every which way, past her shoulders, bangs swooping over light brown eyebrows and deep brown eyes.

He continued to stare at the bowl, shook his head, then turned to her. "Hello, dear. I do. Love you." He went to her, held her slim waist, and leaned down to kiss her. "Why do I have to be such a nitpicker? How can you stand me?"

"Because you're aware of it, maybe."

"You know what I'm also aware of? How wonderful you are. I didn't mean to be an ass. Thank you for doing the driving tonight."

She stood on her toes to kiss him and said, "You're welcome."

She lifted her boots from the side of the island to put them away. Frank went back to the dish and scrubbed at it as she removed her long down coat and hung it on a hook by the back door. When the cheese wouldn't come off, he said, "I mean, does it even cross your mind that a soaked dish is a breeze to clean, takes seconds, whereas this will take—"

"So let it *soak*. Jesus."

"That's not the point," he said, following her as she tried to leave the kitchen. "It's the thinking about it."

"Do you *really* want to get into this now? *Really*? Do you hear me bugging you to at least have the courtesy to check your pockets before you put them in the laundry basket? No. I still have to check to make sure we don't get melted ChapStick all over everything."

"You're right!" he'd said, abruptly and loudly. "I'm anal about the kitchen. And thank you for the driving tonight, I am truly grateful. I don't know what's wrong with me today."

He went back to her, held her again and gave her another kiss, which she grudgingly accepted.

How petty it had all been. Had their lives become so routine and innocuous that the only matters that aroused emotion were housework? Did it even matter anymore? No, except she would always wonder if even something as little as failing to clean her bowl might have contributed to the tragic timing of tonight. Had the sink been cleaned, he'd have gone out a minute earlier, everything might have happened a minute earlier, and he'd have pulled into the drive before the woman with the red hair passed their driveway.

The question was moot, but she couldn't stop herself from dwelling on such matters in the days ahead.

*

"You haven't left," he said.

"Just getting on my coat," she said.

She had one arm through one sleeve of her winter coat, her cell phone in the other pressed to her ear. It was 10:35. She was leaving early to pick Nick up due to the snow.

"I'm leaving the restaurant now," Frank said. "I can pick Nick up."

"Really?" Her heart lifted. She was so warm and secure in the house, and the predicted blizzard had been on schedule. When she sighed and went for her coat, she had wanted nothing more than to make a cup of chamomile tea and watch television while it snowed outside.

"Yep," said Frank.

"Are you *sure*?" she said. She meant it but she also wanted him to sense how much she would love it if she didn't have to go out in this weather. Nick was at a holiday open house four miles away at his friend Oliver's, son of their friends Len and Melissa Thompson. They'd been invited to this party as well but didn't plan to go. Frank had his annual dinner with his high school pals, and while Karen did enjoy these parties, she didn't like to go without Frank. They told the Thompsons they'd stop by if they could. When they'd been planning their week the previous Sunday, she'd offered to do the driving on this night. This way he wouldn't feel obligated to leave his friends if they hadn't finished dinner by the time Nick needed to be picked up. This seemed obvious—she had no plans of her own, and who could predict how long the dinner would go on? And, of course, news of the coming blizzard—which yesterday had closed O'Hare for several hours, and was now no doubt making traffic at Cleveland's airport dreadful—had been days away and not yet news.

As it turned out, the timing *was* perfect. Frank explained that he could arrive at the Thompsons' at the appointed hour.

"Yes, I'm sure," he said. She noted a tone of genuine willingness, even eagerness to do so.

"Are you okay to drive?"

He said, "Fine, sweetie. Believe me, you don't want to be out in this. I'm in the car, it's heating up. I'm already out, no need for you to go out, too. It's not a problem. By the time I get the car brushed off, it'll be warm."

"I think I should get him."

"Karen, I'm already *in* the car. It'll take you ten minutes to get the snow off the Jeep, and the car will be freezing."

She took a moment to glance out the window; yes, the Jeep was covered, six inches at least.

"Besides, I owe you," he said. "I was an ass. What a crank I'm becoming."

"You're my crank," she said.

"Forever, if you'll have me."

"Always."

The were both silent. Karen suddenly had the urge to remain on the line, even in silence, the way they used to when one of them was in some distant hotel room, having exhausted conversation but not wanting to be alone.

At last Frank said, "If I don't get going I'm going to be late."

"Drive *carefully*."

"Roads this bad I don't have a choice."

"It's not you I'm worried about, it's other drivers. It's a big holiday party night. Keep your distance."

"I'll be careful."

*

Once the headlights and the flashing red and blue lights appeared silently at the top of the hill and the car began its curving descent, it took only moments for Karen to make up her mind. They huddled cold in their driveway's apron, Frank's arm around her, her cheek and hand pressed against his chest. She said, "Everything happened exactly as it did except you and I were also at the party," she said.

"What? What are you talking about?"

"We were both at the party."

Officer Williams had been the first to arrive, coming to a halt in the middle of the street beside the Honda, which had stopped in the snowbank above the curb and nearly perpendicular to it. Williams did not step out of his car slowly as policemen typically did, as if they controlled time. Officer Williams was well over six feet and his heavy winter police jacket made him seem powerfully built. He bolted from the car, ignoring the shivering couple who had tried to approach him with an explanation. He ran in heavy black boots to the side of the car where the woman lay unconscious, half under the rear of the car. He felt for a pulse. He pulled a radio from his belt and it scratched to life. "This is Officer Williams, what's the ETA on the—" and he stopped when the lights of the EMS vehicle appeared in the opposite direction from which he'd come. "They're here, thanks." A woman's voice rogered that, and Williams stood as two men leapt out of the truck, each carrying a box of medical equipment.

"I'm not hopeful," Williams said, stepping away.

You'd have thought it *was* a holiday party, suddenly, what with all the flashing lights everywhere. Karen's stomach rolled as the last of six squad cars appeared. She felt dizzy from fear. The sounds of police radios, the lights, the cars, the silhouettes of neighbors in suddenly lighted windows, the incessant snow and Officer Williams's definitive bark: "Secure the area!" Karen heard other words but didn't comprehend sentences. "Punctured" and "aorta" and "bleed out." It was as if she and Frank were invisible, all activity focused on the unconscious woman in the snow, and the composed but desperate (judging from the speed with which they were tearing packages open) maneuverings of the emergency medical technicians.

Once the EMTs were taking care of "the victim," Officer Williams approached Frank and Karen and asked, "Can you tell me what happened?"

Each looked to the other, his blue eyes to her brown, and each back to the officer in one brief, fluid movement. Before Frank could begin, Karen said, "I was driving." She and Frank were both taking deep, involuntary breaths. "We were pulling into the driveway," she said. "I made the turn but the car just kept going forward. I missed the driveway and felt a thud." Frank stood frozen, did not move or respond or even blink, and stared at the Honda.

Officer Williams looked toward the vehicle, one tire up over where the curb would be.

Officer Williams said, "You've been drinking."

Frank snapped to attention at this. He locked eyes with Officer Williams.

"I can smell it on you," Williams said.

"Yes, Officer." And then he completed the lie. "That's why my wife was driving. We were on our way home from a party. It's not her fault, we didn't even see the woman, the car just floated into her."

Karen inhaled deeply.

"You live here?" he asked.

Frank and Karen answered yes in perfect unison, and Frank added, "We were pulling into our driveway."

"Can I see your identification?"

Frank reached for his wallet.

Karen stood still.

Officer Williams took Frank's driver's license. He looked at Karen.

"My purse is inside the house."

Officer Williams paused and asked, "Why is it inside the house?"

"I didn't bring it with me to the party." This could have been true. She often didn't carry a purse to parties if Frank was driving. "I wasn't planning to drive. My husband always drives. Should I go get it?"

"It can wait," the officer said.

The victim had been loaded onto a gurney in the snow. The activity had ceased and the two men who had been kneeling in the snow were no longer working. Frank let out a relieved sigh as if to say, *Thank God, they've got her stabilized.* Officer Williams looked down. Karen's stomach rolled again as one of the men, frizzy red hair and beard, a wool cap, called, "Officer?" Williams looked up. The man with the frizzy hair looked at his watch. "I couldn't even intubate. I've gotta call it."

"Okay."

"Oh, dear *God.*" Karen began to cry. Frank looked to her, not completely understanding.

"Eleven fifty-five," he said to his colleague. Officer Williams wrote this down and the EMT, who looked like a child to Frank, worked on a clipboard, wiping snow from it regularly, the paper so cold the snow didn't melt on it.

Officer Williams looked at them both and, with a note of genuine comfort, said, "I'm pretty sure she died shortly after impact. She had a heartbeat but almost no pulse in her neck. By the time they got to her she had no blood pressure. Zero. She didn't likely suffer. First shock, then nothing. I've spoken with survivors. They remember little."

Other officers were with the emergency medical crew. An ambulance had arrived. A young officer, still in his twenties, approached and told Officer Williams, "She had a wallet, keys, ID, all there. Lived around the block. Okay to let these guys go?"

Officer Williams nodded. "But keep the street blocked." He shook his head at the snow. That done, it seemed he could assess the situation. He looked up the street and down as if an answer had to be there, either end blocked off by a police car, lights flashing. He walked to the car. He looked at the corner that had struck the victim. He circled the car. He looked at the snow. Then he followed a line along the snow and up the driveway. Tracks, mostly obscured by the falling snow. Officer Williams looked at Frank and Karen. Karen was crying almost too quietly to hear.

Officer Williams took his time circling the car, making prints of his own, looking up the driveway. He wiped snow off his face as though it were weariness. He continued to write on the clipboard as he circled the car with his flashlight. He opened all four doors, peering in.

The ambulance had parked parallel to the emergency medical truck. The EMTs slid the gurney into the ambulance. When the doors were closed, the siren returned as the truck moved into gear. Soon after, the EMS truck departed. And then there was complete silence. A dark night, snow coming down hard.

Officer Williams returned to Frank and Karen, and put what seemed to be a sympathetic hand on Karen's back, but it was a preamble to a request. "Ma'am, I'd like to ask you to move the car now. Just pull it into the driveway, just past the sidewalk. Leave it here rather than in back. I'd just like it off the street now." The house sat back on a deep lot with a long driveway. She nodded like a child who has been physically punished, choking back more tears, nodding vigorously. She absentmindedly felt the pockets of her puffy winter coat. She looked up at Frank, fear all but stopping her heart. She thought, *Please don't have them in your pocket.*

Frank, eyes locked hard on hers, said evenly, "They're probably still in the car, darling."

She shook her head, sucked breath in through her snotty nose, and said, "Of course."

Officer Williams watched her walk to the car. Williams didn't take his eyes off Karen. She moved slowly as if half asleep. She adjusted the seat to reach the pedals, which is what she always did after he'd been driving the car they shared. This was the least expensive car they could find and they requested no extras whatsoever to save money, no button on the car key to pop the trunk, no electric seat adjusters, nothing. Frank had insisted. Frank was six feet, she five-six. She reached below the seat for the lever, pulled up, and the seat ratcheted several inches forward, one loud crank— and exactly as she realized her error, she heard Frank all but shout, "We didn't see the woman!"

Frank continued pleading to keep Williams's gaze. "We didn't see a thing, even when we were sliding sideways."

Williams didn't respond, only turned back to see the car backing slowly off the curb, then watch the bright reverse lights go out as Karen shifted into drive and pulled into the driveway. She parked and exited the vehicle.

She'd stopped crying and was stone-faced now, really only now beginning to realize all that had happened and what it might mean.

Williams said, "Ma'am, I'll need the registration."

She leaned back in, retrieved the envelope with the necessary papers. Thanks to Frank's fastidiousness, all was easily at hand. Had it been her car alone, she'd have had to rummage through Lube Stop receipts and hair ties and bank deposit slips to find it.

She shuffled through the mounting snow, handed Williams the registration and insurance.

"Curt?" he called. The older officer with a thick black moustache, shiny bald on top, wearing a dark overcoat approached. "You can send the rest on." Two squad cars had escorted the ambulance, and two more blocked either end of the street. Officer Williams's vehicle remained in the middle of the street, lights still flashing like a carnival, and an unmarked car, Curt's presumably, was just opposite where Frank's car had mounted the curb.

Karen had adjusted the seat. She had adjusted the seat to reach the pedals, as if she were simply headed to the post office. What had she been thinking? *Did Williams see it?* He had to have heard the crank sound it made, but had it registered? Or had Frank distracted him in time?

Williams glanced at the insurance card and handed it back. He began to write and then said, "Do you mind if I finish this inside? It's hard to write with this snow coming down." When she paused he said, "I'll need to see your ID before we go down, regardless."

"What?" she said, snapping alert. "Down? Am I being arrested?"

"Not yet. We need to go to the ER. I'll need a full tox screen."

"Tox screen?"

"A full blood test. If you have any impairing substances, the DA will need to know. If you're clean, then . . . well, one step at a time."

Frank exhaled brusquely. Karen hardened. "Let's go, then," she said.

Before heading up the drive, Williams said, "Curt, breathalyze"—he looked at his clipboard—"Mr. Markstrom."

Karen snapped around. "Why? He wasn't driving."

He looked at her hard. "Just covering all bases, ma'am, excuse me. If he's very drunk, it could become part of the trial."

"*Trial?* This was an accident!" Frank said, with an urgency bordering on desperation.

Startled by the volume, Silent Curt stiffened and Williams said, "I'll need to ask you to calm down, sir."

Frank snorted.

"You're allowed to refuse," Williams told him, "but that's not usually wise. And since you weren't driving—you *weren't* driving, correct?"

Karen didn't waste a second: "For Christ's sake, I already told you I was driving."

"Then you should consent." He looked at Karen. She stared him back down, then turned and led Officer Williams up the drive to the open back door. "I'll go get my things."

Williams followed her, but he stopped at the car in the driveway. Karen turned back to look. He opened the front door and stared inside, as though sure a missing object could be found on the floor or in the crack between the seat and seat back. Karen could see it in his expression—something was bothering Williams, but he couldn't place it. The loud ratcheting of her adjusting the seat. He closed the door and followed Karen, up the drive.

Karen, slipped the key into the lock and turned it, though she knew it was open. Inside she grabbed her purse, which was still on the stool at the kitchen island. Williams took a seat at the kitchen table without asking, wiped the paper on the clipboard clean, and carried on writing. His heavy-soled boots were dirty, so that when the fresh snow on them melted from within the treads, gray pools formed around his feet. She nearly asked him if he *minded.* But she didn't want to slow down any of this. She set her driver's license on the table. He lifted it, held it at arm's length, looked at Karen and then set his hand down on the table so that he could copy the information from the license.

When he'd finished with it, he handed it back to her and said, "Try not to drive without your license."

Did he know, she wondered? Was that tone he'd used ironic, suspicious? Why would he say such a thing? As if that was what mattered. A woman had been killed.

But he continued: "I don't think you made the wrong decision. Your husband out there smells like all kinds of liquor." He continued to write. "I think you chose to leave the party at the wrong time, is what I think. Five minutes either way, I'd be in a warm squad car, you'd be in bed, and—" and he stopped short of reiterating the worst of it. Instead he finished with: "Just another minute and I'll be done."

Feeling heat move through her, she unzipped her puffy black winter coat and leaned against the counter beside the stove, facing Officer Williams's back. He turned and gave her a once-over and then turned back and resumed writing. "Don't worry, we'll leave ASAP. The sooner I get that tox screen, the better, from my position. I can finish the report at the hospital."

Frank came to the back door, brushing snow from his jacket. His golden-brown hair was darkened and flat on his scalp from the melted snow. He stamped his feet hard on the back doormat and stepped into the kitchen. Both Williams and Karen looked at him.

"Point nine," he said to Karen. "Just over the limit."

"Still, I don't know what the issue is," Karen said to Officer Williams.

Williams answered by standing and saying, "All right, ready?"

Frank said to Karen, "I'm coming with you."

Her eyes grew large and she shook her head once, *no.* She felt Williams's gaze on her and said, "There's absolutely no reason for you to go." She hugged him, putting her face to his cheek and away from Officer Williams and whispering, "Stay out of this. Check Nick." She released him and kissed his lips.

She zipped up the long black down coat and said, "Let's go."

*

"I couldn't help but notice, Mrs. Markstrom, your clothes," Williams said, staring at Karen in the rearview mirror and through the grate as they headed to the Cleveland Clinic's emergency room. She'd never been in the back of a squad car. Officer Williams had pulled away, Silent Curt in the seat beside him, having left his car along the curb in front of their house, like a black headstone, Karen thought, as they peeled away from the scene. The power of the car made her gasp. This was no ordinary car. Like Officer Williams, this vehicle felt charged, powerful. She guessed it had to be. They had driven in silence for only about a minute before Williams made the statement.

"I'm sorry?" she said.

"I saw in the kitchen, you're wearing a sweater and jeans. But your husband is wearing a sport coat. Were you at the same party?"

"It was a casual get-together. My husband was late from work, he didn't even leave the car. Just honked, I grabbed my coat and ran out."

They rolled through the empty streets, lights flashing, pausing only to check at red lights before accelerating through intersections.

"Didn't he have an overcoat?"

"No, remember how warm it was this morning? And dry?"

"It just seems odd."

"Can I ask, am I legally required to answer these questions?"

"I haven't made an arrest, I'm not making a charge till after the tox report, so I'm not required to read Miranda. But no, you aren't. I will be asking for a full accounting of the events preceding the accident after they've drawn blood. You can refuse to speak, in which case I'll have cause to up the charges. If I do that, you can also call or request a lawyer, or you can call one now, in which case—"

"I was only curious," she interrupted. "You'll find that I'm clean. And no, this was an accident, so I don't know how paying a lawyer to sit with me will help anyone."

"Good," he said, accelerating.

He paused at an empty intersection to crawl through a red light. Karen saw the bald pate of Silent Curt turn to Williams. She heard him tap something, a notepad of some sort. Williams seemed to nod as he accelerated.

"Can you tell me where you were coming from?"

She didn't want to pause. "Shaker Heights, Len and Melissa Thomp—"

"That's fine, ma'am. I can get the names later."

She hoped she didn't throw up in the car as they accelerated and the hospital came into view. Of course they would call Len and Melissa to corroborate the story.

*

"Good news," Officer Williams said. "You're clean."

"Not news to me," Karen said. She had sat in this generic exam room for what seemed an eternity and now felt ill and exhausted. The clock on the wall read 1:30. She could scarcely believe how little time had passed.

Silent Curt followed him in, then leaned against the door, shutting it with a click.

Williams said, "I can fill out the rest of my report now, here if you want. Or we can do it back at the station. I'm calling this an accident. It seems clear that this was an accident." He turned to look at Curt, who did not look back at Williams, only stared coldly at Karen. Williams returned his gaze to her as well. "So I'm charging you with negligence. But I don't need to bring you in. You'll be sleeping at home tonight, with the agreement that you not leave town."

"I'm hardly going to *flee*," she said, giving Williams a look of mortification and confusion.

"I only said that because it's the holidays and people travel."

"Oh. No, we spend Christmas in town."

"Good." He pulled up a chair and said, "Okay. I've got to take a statement. Technically you're now under arrest. The victim did die, this is confirmed. I'll be charging you, so I now will tell you that you do have the right to remain silent and the right to a lawyer."

"That won't be necessary, I'll give you a full accounting of what happened."

"You're waiving your Miranda rights?"

"Yes, I'm aware of my rights."

"To confirm, this is a voluntary statement?"

"That's correct."

Officer Williams appeared relieved.

Karen had had a full hour to compose her thoughts and reason out the details of her story as the driver of the car.

*

Karen entered through the back door, closed and locked it.

Frank had fallen asleep with the television on, his head tilted back, his mouth slung open. The alcohol, the stress, the hour—the clock read 2:45—had allowed him to sleep. *It's a Wonderful Life* was on, as it seemed to be everywhere at this time of year. She found it unbearably pat, but Frank adored it and she loved his adoration, loved his capacity for innocent belief in this story. As far as she was concerned, Lionel Barrymore's verdict on George—"*Sentimental hogwash*"—was an apt verdict on the movie as a whole. His love of the movie reminded her, after all these years, of the love she had always felt for him.

She stared blankly at the screen, a graying Jimmy Stewart striding down a sunny, snowy Bedford Falls street, pipe in mouth and newspapers in hand, a happy man without a care on Christmas Eve day, moments before it all goes south on him, what the whole film has been leading up to. She shut off the TV and Frank awoke with a start. Not sleepily, but alert, as if having fallen asleep while on guard.

Panting, and realizing where he was, he said, "Thank God you're home." He stood and they hugged hard.

"Yes, I'm home."

They rocked slowly for a solid silent minute before releasing one another. She unzipped her coat and hung it on the hook by the back door.

"What happened?" he asked.

"I'm officially charged with negligent vehicular manslaughter."

"What's going to happen?"

"I don't know," she said.

"What can I get for you, sweetheart?"

"A very stiff vodka, please."

He set it before her at the table, refilled his water glass, and took a seat at the table.

"How's Nick?" she asked.

"Presumably asleep. But I've spoken with him."

"And?"

Frank shrugged. "I told him the truth."

"Everything?"

"Yes, everything. He was *in* the car. He turned back and saw her as I was bringing him in. He knows what happened."

"Okay. Did you tell him about *after*?"

"Yes, I told him that, too."

"How did he respond?"

"Quietly. Confused. Terrified. He understands how bad it is. I think things will be clearer in the morning. That's what I told him anyhow, that nothing more would happen tonight and we'll know more then."

He waited for her to have another gulp of her drink before saying, "Okay, what happened?"

She stared at the table, finished off the drink, went to the sink, and filled the glass with water. She sat again. She took a deep breath, said, "Okay," and recounted the events, the ride to the hospital and what was said, the taking of blood, the wait, and the report she gave, every detail of the story she had fabricated for Officer Williams and Silent Curt, which they had not simply to remember but convert in their minds to fact.

When she finished, and he'd had a minute of quiet to absorb it, he said, "But if they call Len and Melissa, we're finished."

She looked into his eyes, repeated "If," and then looked down at the table.

"You told them about Nick?" he asked.

"He was there—he's our only link to the party."

"They're going to want to talk to him."

"Yes, they said that. This was the only time Williams seemed to be mad. As if I'd withheld this information."

"What did you say?"

"The truth: 'You never asked, it's irrelevant, and I wanted to keep my son out of it.' As I'm sure he could understand. He just looked down and kept writing, saying, 'I'll need to speak with him.'"

"I told them he'd be sound asleep by now, could it wait till morning? They said yes. Or Williams did; Curt whatever-his-name-was didn't say a word, just kept giving me the stink eye. Gave me the creeps. I don't know if he was even capable of talking."

"He was. He told me in the street, 'point nine.' But that was all."

"Silent Curt. I kept thinking he knew something. I tried not to look at him." She reached for Frank's hands across the table. "Okay, so here's what happened. We were there, but the party was so big we never really saw Len or Melissa."

"*Really.*"

"It's the best I could do. And it is possible. We've been the last three years. It's huge. And you know, most of the people there are smashed. They didn't ask more about the party and I didn't offer. Big holiday open house I called it, and left it at that. Oh, except for this. What a creep. Silent Curt wrote something on a pad, had to be a question, showed it to Williams and *he* asked it. Given that I had been to a holiday party, why did my blood come back completely clean? So. I don't drink, okay?"

Frank nodded, apparently astonished by how cool she had been and was being.

"And that was it. Short report. We left the party. I insisted on driving and you sensibly agreed. I told him the car did what you said it did. That—"

He squeezed her hands hard, halting her. "Did he ask about adjusting the seat?"

"Oh, Jesus. Thank God, no."

"So you realized?"

"Yes, after the fact, after the noise it made. I thought we were done for."

"I tried to distract him. He saw it but it didn't register. I don't think it will come to him."

"There are a lot of things that won't add up in the morning."

"How did they leave it?"

"He's coming back to get statements from you and Nick."

"And then what?"

"I don't know."

Frank stood and paced around the island, rubbing his face hard with his hand. His father had done this as well. Then Frank did what she'd seen his father do many times in the two decades she'd known him. With his right hand, Frank drew two fingers down either side of his narrow nose. And then the last gesture, a strange contortion of the wrist and arm so that his palm covered the nose, and the fingers swept from one side of his jaw over his forehead to the other side. It was so uncommon that she couldn't fail to see Frank Senior in the gesture, and she knew that her husband, too, even if unconsciously, was summoning his father for help in the matter at hand.

Frank returned to his seat.

"It's not too late," he said.

"What's not too late?"

He reached across the table to hold her hands in his.

"To do the right thing."

Her stomach clenched when he said it.

"We both know what the right thing to do is," he said. "I've got to come clean."

She felt as though she were about to throw up and took a quick gulp of water.

"You can't go to jail," she said. "I won't let you."

"I might have to."

"I can't, I won't live without you."

"It won't be forever."

Tears filled her eyes and, with something close to anger, she said, "How do you know?"

Frank looked away.

"What's more Frank, I've *already* lied. I've filled a whole police report with lies."

"If I come clean and take all the blame, you will be forgiven."

"We can't know that. How do we know we won't *both* go to jail for this? I'm pretty sure what I did is equally punishable. I've lied to the police. *I* could go to jail, couldn't I? I don't know. I could and you could. We have to accept that as one possible outcome." She covered her mouth, then quickly released it. "And what if we both got put in jail—what would happen to Nick?"

Frank closed his eyes at the thought.

"Your mother's not healthy enough to take him," Karen added, as if he needed reminding. Frank, a devoted only child, was in active negotiations with his mom about moving her to assisted living, as much for her comfort and security as his piece of mind, now that she'd already taken a rib-breaking stumble in the dining room.

"He'd go over to protective services," Karen said. "Who knows where he'd wind up? Wherever it would be, even with my sister in Boston, it wouldn't be better than this home, with both his parents safe inside it. . . .

"And your *mom*," Karen said with fresh dismay. Already she cooked extra portions of nightly meals that Frank would take to Polly every other day to make sure she was eating. He'd sit with her so she had more company than the nightly news and Alex Trebek. "This will devastate her emotionally. And who will take care of her?"

"That couldn't happen. It *can't* happen. Can it?" Karen was almost talking to herself. "Since we don't know for certain, we have to accept anything as a possibility."

"No," Frank said. "If I don't come clean and we are caught, all of the above is sure to happen."

"I don't think we have a choice now. My hand was forced and now we have to play it."

"We need information," he said. "We have to find answers to these questions before we do anything."

Visibly trembling with fear and disbelief, Karen said, "This is impossible. How did this happen? It's not fair. It's not fair. This can't be happening."

Frank made the sweeping motion again across his face, as though trying to wipe everything away so that he could see clearly. Then he looked at Karen and spoke definitively: "I'll call Dan Jeffries. He'll know what to do."

"Who's Dan Jeffries?"

"Dan? He's a lawyer. You've met him at parties. We went to high school together; he was a year ahead of me. We saw him in October at the Neil Young concert."

"You want to call *that* guy? He was *tripping*."

"It was a concert."

"Isn't he an ambulance chaser?"

"He does disability and worker's comp cases. And personal injury, yes."

"Ambulance chaser," she said.

"*What pulled away from our house three hours ago?*" Frank whispered almost angrily.

That quieted her. But she said, "Can't you call Roger?"

"Roger's a tax attorney; he won't know how to handle this."

"Dan just seems a little on the sleazy side."

"He's not sleazy—he's got a wife, two kids, he's like us. He went into his dad's practice. Karen. We've both committed crimes, probably felonies. We're on his side of sleazy now. He's not the one who has broken the law."

"Can you trust him?"

"We went to high school together."

"What does that mean?"

"It means he'll help. He's smart."

"Can you trust him? I don't trust him."

"He and Grant are friends. So, by extension, I think so."

"Because you and he have a mutual friend, you can trust him?"

"Grant is my oldest friend, not just some acquaintance. The most decent guy I know. He wouldn't be pals with some sleazy ambulance chaser. Dan's a good guy." Frank paused. "And besides, right now we don't have a choice. We need to be prepared."

She stared at the ice in her glass, sickness settling into her body, like the flu.

Frank took a breath. "You should check in on Nick, make sure he's asleep."

"I know," Karen said.

*

Nick was asleep, on his side diagonally across the double bed, gangly legs hanging off one side and uncovered to reveal shins with, to her, a strange coating of fur that had arrived last summer and ankles so thick as to suggest he still had several inches to grow. His shaggy light brown hair was matted with sweat. She sat and felt his forehead—cool. She had turned off the overhead light, but there was enough light coming in from the hallway to see his soft features, so much like his father already, the nose, the eyes, uncommonly long lashes, just slightly more rounded, softer than Frank's—a young man coming into focus. Such a lovely boy.

On his bedside table she saw his phone. She never snooped around in his phone—he was a good kid and she had never felt any need whatsoever. She really did trust him, and what was his business was his. Besides, what if she came across porn sites? What does a parent do? She perpetually felt like a beginner in the parenting department, which of course most parents were until it was too late. But now she would be a different parent, and she didn't hesitate to pick up his phone. It wasn't password protected. She tapped Safari, tapped history, and saw an endless string of YouTube videos. First turning off the volume, she tapped the most recent one: a Chinese girl separating an egg by sucking up the yolk with a two-liter plastic bottle. This made her feel better somehow. Though what useful knowledge did she expect to glean? Did she expect him to be Googling legal sites? It wasn't beyond him. He was a smart kid, smarter than his B average implied. And smart enough not to already be discussing this situation on Facebook. This new possibility alarmed her, and she reviewed the entire history in the hours since he'd been home. No, nothing. She set the phone down.

Nick was in the artsy crowd at school. Last spring, he'd played Albert—rock star Conrad Birdie's manager—in the seventh and eighth grade production of *Bye Bye Birdie*. This year he had joined the writing forum. She knew he kept a journal but had never read it. Once talkative to the point of being chatty, Nick had all but shut down once he'd begun ninth grade. He never spoke at dinner unless actively brought into the conversation.

Normal, she knew. But what would become normal now?

She walked through her bedroom—Frank slept mummy-like, or so it appeared until he asked, "Asleep?"

"Yes, he is," she said. She kissed Frank's forehead. "I'm going to shower. You try to sleep."

*

It had likely been the noise of the snowplow that woke her, just enough to gaze dreamily at her husband of twenty years, who was staring down at the spot where the accident had happened. And then to come fully awake at the horrible illusion of his becoming an old man before her eyes.

He continued to stare out, streetlights through the blinds streaking him with light and shadow.

"Hold me," she said.

He took a drink of water and crawled under the covers.

"You're cold," she said. "Let me warm you."

He took her up on this, pressing his legs up and down over hers, between hers, hugging her and rubbing her back to warm his own arms. He put his face into her neck, her skin still smelling of soap from the shower.

He kissed her lips and rolled onto his back.

They lay quietly for many minutes, so desperate for sleep, for unconsciousness, that they could not come close to it.

"I had to do it," she said. "It wasn't even a choice. What had happened had happened. You could go to jail for this. Not could, you *would* have been arrested on the spot." She turned her head to look at him but remained supine. "The woman died, Frank. You would have been cuffed and put in the squad car. You would have been charged with vehicular *homicide*. You would have gone to jail. Our life together would be over. I couldn't bear it. I couldn't bear to live without you."

"Karen, I'm so sorry."

"Don't say that. I just wanted you to know that it wasn't a choice. I didn't hesitate once I saw your eyes. I became the driver, I just *was*. It's you and me, and Nick, and as long as we're together, nothing can be wrong."

He kissed her.

"I love you so, so much," she said.

He reached for her hand. He kissed her again, returned to his back and stared at the ceiling. Both were able to doze, shoulder to shoulder, hand in hand, like two dead lovers resting upon a shared sepulcher, until a 6 a.m. snowplow passed their house again, waking them both to the new darkness, soon to become cold and clear.

*

Frank got coffee going and took a shower but couldn't wait even until 7 a.m. to call Dan. Dan had been asleep. It took several moments for him to develop enough consciousness to wonder why Frank Markstrom, of all people, would be calling him at this hour. Karen sat up in bed, watching Frank pace the room silently.

"Are you still there? What *is* it?" Dan said irritably.

Frank suddenly didn't know what to say or how to say it or even if he was jeopardizing the situation. He said, "Last night there was a fatality outside our house and I need your advice."

In thirty minutes, God bless him, Dan was in Frank's foyer, Frank holding his large Starbucks while Dan removed heavy snow boots. By the time they were moving through the hall toward the dining room, Karen was descending the stairs, tying her bathrobe, frayed at the collar and belt, newsprint stains on the elbows, which had nearly worn through.

"Dan, you remember my wife, Karen?"

"Of course, we met at the Hillers' party three years ago." He looked to Karen. "Hi, Karen," he said, shaking her hand.

Dan Jeffries appeared hulking due to the slouch of his six-foot-four frame. He had dark curly hair, smooth skin, and vivid green eyes, a handsome man despite the graying whiskers of his unshaven face. He wore a red plaid flannel shirt, tight across his broad chest, sleeves rolled up, over a long-sleeved maroon undershirt, jeans, and heavy wool socks. When he shook her hand he smiled warmly at her, sympathetically.

The three sat at the dining room table, Frank at the head, Karen and Dan across from one another. Frank, showered and dressed in khakis and an old crewneck sweater, had poured coffee for himself and for Karen.

"I don't even know what I can tell you," Frank began. "Do we have any privilege here?"

"It probably depends," Dan said. "So my answer is not necessarily." He looked askance at Frank, then at Karen, then back to Frank. "Why don't we go slowly and tell me objectively what happened, who was killed and what were the circumstances. There's nothing in the paper by the way. So I know nothing."

Karen said, "We were driving home last night."

"The roads were a mess," Dan said, "I know. I was out as well."

"Our car hit a woman walking in the street. The car spun as we were turning into the driveway and ran her over. She was pronounced dead at the scene."

"Okay," Dan said, nodding. "Frank, were you driving?"

"No, it was me," Karen said quickly.

"Okay." He looked to Karen, leaned forward on his elbows, his back erect. "What were you charged with?"

"Negligent vehicular manslaughter."

"Okay, that's good."

"Good?"

"Better than aggravated, and so, better than homicide. Go on."

Karen recounted everything. Dan stopped her only once.

"Why did they breathalyze Frank?"

"The officer smelled alcohol on him."

"But he wasn't driving."

"The officer said he wanted to 'cover his bases,' why?"

"So you did it?" he asked Frank.

"I didn't see why not although I didn't want to, but, well, I was afraid to say no. Should I not have?"

"What did you blow?"

"Point nine. Does it matter?"

Dan shrugged. "It brings up a fourth amendment issue, arguably an illegal search and seizure if he didn't have cause. But go on."

When Karen had finished, Dan said, "You've called your insurance?"

"No."

"You need to report this immediately to your insurance company, auto and homeowners." Then to Karen he said, "They'll provide you a defense if there's a civil wrongful-death suit. It depends on what the police and district attorney do."

"The district attorney?"

"Yeah." Dan leaned back and swigged from his Starbucks cup. "You're going to need a couple of lawyers. One for the civil case and one for a criminal case."

"But I was charged with negligence. Is that a crime?"

"You were driving a car in unsafe conditions and you have a responsibility not to kill anyone." Dan raised his eyebrows at her. "*Clear?*" he seemed to be asking her, as if she were a dim child. "So how this plays out," he continued, "depends on the police and the DA. Now the tox screen was clear, that is very, very good. If you were over the limit or even under but close, this could move into aggravated manslaughter or even homicide, felonies, both of which carry mandatory jail time."

Karen looked to Frank.

"But if you can show them that it was negligence, that there were no contributing factors beyond the weather—it was dark, there was no reason to expect anyone to be out walking at that hour, and it seems they're already at this conclusion—then it's a *misdemeanor*."

Karen reached for Frank's hand. He looked to her. He looked to Dan and said, "I like the sound of misdemeanor."

Dan smiled, a mouth full of big white teeth. "Um, yeah, that's what you want this to be. A misdemeanor of the first degree, but still a misdemeanor. As long as you stay in that negligent category. Now, Karen, have you ever been arrested?"

"No, never."

"Were you violent, did you give them any difficulties at all?"

"No, of course not."

Dan leaned back in his chair, which creaked from his weight and folded his hands. "A nonviolent, first-time offender cooperating fully, I don't see that they're going to change the charge. So when you go to court—"

"Court?"

"Well, yeah, Karen. A woman's been killed. This will be addressed in a court of law, not in a dining room or police station. So it's important that you get a really good lawyer who can plea it down as low as possible. Hard to say at this point. A lot depends on the family. They may cooperate. They may be vengeful beyond their own civil case. Much of the if-thens are hypothetical at this point. If you're *convicted* of manslaughter, even if your lawyer can't plea it to vehicular assault, you can still avoid prison."

"Prison?" they both said.

"Yeah, it's a possibility you have to acknowledge, so, as I said, you need . . . good lawyers. But it's not necessarily going to play out that way. There's probation, there's community service. Again it depends on a lot of things. If your lawyer is good, he or she will go to the DA and say please don't press hard on this. But Karen, this is not going to come without costs."

Frank said, "But it was an accident."

Dan snapped his gaze from Karen onto Frank and said slowly, "She has an absolute duty to maintain control of her vehicle. *Okay?*"

Frank nodded contritely. Karen was glad Frank called Dan. This was not civilian Dan getting high at a concert. This was a powerful, smart man with valuable information and expertise they desperately needed now.

"Read about it," Dan continued, addressing Karen. "It's available on the Internet. Negligence. It involves duty, breach of duty, causation, and damages. I have a *duty* to operate my car in a safe manner; if I don't, that's *breach* of duty, and if I cause injury, if that breach of duty results in *damage*, then I'm *negligent*." He paused. "Okay?"

Again nods from both, like scolded children.

"So, let's look at the best scenario, which you have every right to expect. Though the family is an unknown still, right?"

"Right."

"Did you know this person?"

"No," Karen said. "We've seen her for years, often weekly, sometimes daily in the summer, and a lot in the winter. About our age, a little older maybe. We see her walking on all the streets around here all the time, in all weather."

"Okay, so the DA goes with minimal charges and your lawyer can plead it down further, so you're not going to jail and this can all go away."

Heavy exhalations from both.

"Now, civil. Your insurance will cover it to a point. I'm sure you've got normal insurance. It'll be something like three hundred thousand with a $1 million umbrella, that's your total coverage. Go over that and you have to pay the cost. I don't think a settlement is going to be over that, piercing that ceiling, but this depends on the victim—does she have family who relied on her income, what the level of her work was, things like that. It depends what kind of earning potential this person had, or if damage is all speculative. So just be aware of it." He went back and forth from Karen's eyes to Frank's. "Questions?"

Karen spoke: "First things first. Call insurance. Find representation."

"That's correct."

Frank, diminished by shame and fear, asked, "Is it possible that you could represent us?" he asked.

"It's possible. I'm normally on the plaintiff's side, but I could be a part of it. Make sure you're getting the best counsel."

Frank exhaled, held his head, staring at the table. He said, "I have a question."

"Okay."

"Another hypothetical. Let's just say that, theoretically," Frank said, now looking Dan in the eyes, "Karen hadn't been the driver." Frank glanced quickly to Karen and then back to Dan.

Karen knew she had conveyed to Frank in an instant her dismay and anger, a rigidity of posture, a tightness in the mouth—*my God, why? What are you thinking?* And when Frank turned back to Dan, she felt this to be the moment their car sped off the edge of a cliff. *Idiot.* But she could do nothing, not even reach to clutch his hand and hold him back.

"Hypothetically," Frank carried on. "What if I had been driving and then when the police arrived we switched places and Karen claimed to be the one driving?"

Dan stared at Frank with those dark green eyes. He didn't blink. When he took his gaze off Frank, he looked at his Starbucks cup. He drank from it. He looked out the dining room window to the gathering blue light.

But only for a moment, not even long enough for Frank to register regret at having asked. He turned his head back toward Frank again.

"As your friend . . ." Dan looked away, then back to Karen, then to Frank. He shook his head at nothing and snorted hard. He leaned in close to Frank, on the edge of uncomfortably close, his green eyes unblinking. "As your *friend*, I'm going to tell you, that's a crime. That's a *crime*. An *ongoing* crime. And as an officer of the court, if I have knowledge of an ongoing crime, I have a duty, one, to advise you to stop doing that crime. And two, to alert the authorities of an ongoing felony."

The power that Karen had felt moments ago emanating out of the intelligence of Dan, power that could protect them, had just reversed to a powerful sense of menace. As though Dan's actual personality had changed from bright to black, angel to serpent, as if suddenly possessed. Karen watched Frank and knew that he, too, realized he'd been a fool to go this far. Jesus, they didn't know anything about Dan. Dan was married, he had kids, but how many or their ages, Frank probably didn't even know, and she certainly didn't. They bumped into one another socially, but they didn't know a thing about this man or who he'd become, if he was good or bad, zealous or easygoing, honest or dishonest. He's an ambulance chaser, for God's sake. Karen thought, *He can now find the victim and go after us. Jesus, that's what he does.*

Frank held Dan's gaze as strongly as he could.

"I am not your lawyer and not your confessor, okay?" Dan said.

Each time Dan said okay, he waited. Dan wanted some actual acknowl-edgment that they understood every word. "If what you are telling me is true, I would have a problem." He nodded once. "So, I very much hope that this is not the case and that that was a purely hypothetical question because you are curious about the law. Because as your friend, I don't want to be in that situation."

"Is Karen's case something that you could handle for us?" Frank tried to end it there, which, in its lameness, pulled the strings tighter.

"Well, I could have been a part of it, as I said, but given certain . . . hypo-theticals, I'm going to give you the name of a very good criminal defense lawyer."

Dan looked out the window. He stretched the fingers of his left hand and made a fist, squeezing the fist tightly three times. He turned back to Frank and said, "I'm going to repeat this, Frank. I seriously hope that your hypothetical is not true. But you have not confessed anything to me."

"It was purely hypothetical," Frank said, nodding.

"Okay. Then since you're curious about matters of the law, I'm going to tell you what *would* happen.

"This situation changes from negligent manslaughter to aggravated vehicular homicide, with a mandatory prison sentence. You'd lose your license forever, which would be the least of your problems. If intoxication were involved, you would have problems with your insurance, as it moves from a negligent act to an *intentional* act. With *millions* to be gained by the victim's family and their lawyers in civil. It would, in all likelihood, obliterate you financially."

He paused for breath, the volume of his voice having risen as his thoughts pieced it all together. "Additionally, it would be a felony to have tried to avoid it in the first place. Conspiracy. It would be an obstruc-tion of justice and a perjury charge. And the wife," and here he looked at Karen, eyebrows raised, eyes unblinking, "the wife would have the same thing as well. Fraud, perjury, obstruction of justice charges. *Minimum.* These are multiple and serious felonious offenses that would put both the husband and the wife in a state prison, which are not the relatively safe incarceration facilities maintained at the federal level—I've been to the one in Lucasville and it's not pleasant—and they would likely be there for many years."

He shook his head in unrelieved, undisguised disbelief.

"So, now, here is what I'm going to say. Based on the situation, as I understand it to be, having given you some legal advice, I am *not* going to take you on as clients. While you have not made a confession, and you've given me no *evidence* of an ongoing crime, everything has been purely hypothetical, I'm informing you that we now have no attorney-client privilege, and I would recommend to you that you do not offer me any privileged information now or ever on this matter. Because if you convey to me any information, I may not be in a position to keep it a privileged situation." He looked at them both and they returned his intense and knowing glare. "Okay?"

Both Karen and Frank nodded.

"I'm going write down a name, and then I'm going to leave."

Karen rose urgently from the table to retrieve pen and paper.

Dan continued. "Just so you know, Frank, so we're clear on this. If we run into each other at the grocery store, or more likely at a party, I'm going to say, 'Nice to see you, Frank,' and I'm going to leave the room."

"Okay," Frank said. And Dan shook his head again.

Karen gave him a notepad with the word GROCERIES embossed at the top. Dan wrote down the name of a person and a law firm. He set the pen on the notepad and said, "Tell Sharon I recommended you. I hope this all goes away for you. If I can have my coat, I'll see my way out."

Karen, still standing, went to the front closet where Dan's heavy, unfamiliar canvas work coat hung on a hook. It smelled of sawdust and oil and filled the closet with the odor.

Frank remained at the head of the table, hands held flat together, index fingers pressed into his lips, and staring blankly ahead and out the window, but did not rise. The day had become bright, the sky a vivid blue. By the time Karen handed Dan his coat, Dan was staring at a framed photo on the hall table.

"Your kid?"

"Yes," Karen said. The photo had been taken last year in their living room, the holiday portrait of a happy family. "Nick, in ninth grade."

"Ours are both still in high school."

"I'd like to wish you and your family a merry Christmas."

"We're Jewish. We don't celebrate it."

"I'm sorry."

"No need to be."

"I'm . . . sorry for the presumption," she said, looking down.

Dan scrutinized her. He seemed to Karen to want to reach out and touch her, the scrutiny so warmly intense. And he did, he stroked her shoulder in a way that made her feel self-conscious about the ratty bathrobe. She looked up at him but couldn't hold his intense gaze. She felt smudged and ashamed and afraid. He held her shoulder for an uncomfortably long time. He had the power here, and she was afraid of him now. He wouldn't remove his hand until she looked at him. When she did, he smiled inscrutably at her. He put on the large jacket, zipped it up, the smell of a wood shop drifting over her. He moved to the door in the foyer that led to the vestibule and put his hand on the knob, but then released it.

He turned to face her. "A conspirator is either a strong conspirator or a weak conspirator, okay?" he said, pausing. "A weak conspirator cobbles together a story that doesn't add up and so she cannot stick to the story. A strong conspirator is one who sticks to the story, all out, one hundred percent. Plays the part, one hundred percent. Okay? One hundred percent. She *sells* the story. She sells it to the police, the family of the victim, she sells it to all parties involved, which makes it very hard for the police to break. That's a strong conspirator. Okay?"

He paused for one more moment, but she did not move, not even to nod, and then he left. She stood waiting. After about twenty seconds, he slammed the heavy door of the suburban colonial house, rattling windowsills and provoking a faint chime from touching Christmas tree ornaments in the other room.

It's Christmas Eve, she thought. How could she possibly bake cookies with Nick as she'd promised? Or dress for the annual dinner at Frank's mother's, or attend the Christmas service?

But she would.

She turned and stood in the doorway to the dining room. She stared at Frank's profile. He turned to her, a pleading apology in his watery eyes.

She didn't speak, she simply went to her phone, at the kitchen charger, and punched in the name of their long-time insurance agent, so diligent that he himself answered that Saturday morning; she explained what had happened and asked him to notify the appropriate people. The only bad news she learned was that they didn't have that umbrella coverage Dan had presumed. Given the charge, the agent said he hoped it wouldn't be an issue—theoretically, the victim's family could go after everything they had (house, savings accounts, even college savings), but this typically happened only in aggravated cases; he told her he thought they'd be safe. Karen gave him Officer Williams's name so that he could retrieve what information he needed from the police. Next she called the law office of the attorney Dan Jeffries had written down, one Sharon Talbott. It being a Saturday and Christmas Eve, the offices were closed, so no one would respond until Monday morning; but she left the time, her name, Dan's name, the charge, Officer Williams's name, and her need for immediate counsel.

As soon as she was off the phone, she poured herself a second cup of coffee and sat with Frank, who remained stunned, still as a statue at the dining room table.

"Karen, I'm so sorry. What was I *thinking*, why did I ask him that? God*dam*mit. He can hurt us now. I've got to come clean when the police get here. It's the only way to protect you."

"But Frank, you heard him. Protect me? It's done. Perjury and obstruction of justice. And you were found to be legally drunk at the scene. We'll be destroyed, Frank." She could feel her heart beating in her throat.

"It's our only hope of saving you. You did what you did on impulse, on love. And Dan now knows everything. You saw him, you saw his eyes. He could go after everything. If I come clean, he's powerless."

"No, Frank, you heard what he said. We both go to jail, our family is devastated, who knows what happens to Nick?"

"Why, why, why did I speak?"

"Frank, no, it was good. Look at me." She gripped his wrist. "It might have saved us."

Now he did look at her.

"Dan told me what to do," she said.

"What?"

"He gave me some advice and I'm going to take it."

"He gave you *advice*?"

"He was actually just making a very shrewd observation of his past experience. Lord knows in his line of work, he sees a lot." And she went on to explain what he had said about conspirators. "It was obvious what he was doing," she told Frank. She reiterated that she knew what she was going to do.

"We're in this one hundred percent now, and we have to act," she said. Karen still couldn't tell if Frank was processing this—she was always the decisive one. He weighed things; she pounced.

And then they sat in silence—Karen upright in her chair, staring forward at the wall, Frank elbows on the table, his face in his hands. A full minute of silence. Then another. Gradually, Frank grew aware of Karen's breathing. He sat back in his chair, taking a quick glance at her as he did so. She continued to stare at the wall. She breathed through her nose as her already thin lips appeared clamped shut, as if to keep something in. She snorted and said, "God," and then, "Dammit!"

He turned to look at her.

"What were you *thinking*, Frank?"

He could only exhale and stare at his lap.

"How could you?"

These questions could come only from Karen and they had no answer that wasn't sinister in its mundaneness. Now she struggled to resist tears. The shock of last night, the fatigue, the meeting with Dan, the calls to insurance and law offices moments ago left her only with how to proceed with the day, which would consist, now that there was time to think, of answering the question, How did they *get* here?

"*Why?*" she all but shouted. "How could you drive *drunk* like that? Did you even consider that you were going to pick up our *son*? That you were driving *drunk*? With our son in the car?"

Frank could only close his eyes and focus on his own breathing.

Softly and to herself: "Jesus." Again, "Why?" And again, "*Why?*"

"I thought I would be all right. I didn't want you going out."

"You thought it would be *all . . . right . . .* to *drive drunk* with our *son* in the front seat in a *blizzard?*"

"Karen," he shouted back. "Nick is not the issue here!" He leaned close to her and whispered, "I killed a woman last night. A woman is dead because of me." He leaned back in his chair and stared at the ceiling, incredulous.

"As I'm well aware, Frank. And it's not just about you. We're all in this now. And from this moment forward, I am the face of it. Never again say that."

"I killed her."

"Frank! I'm serious. Never, never, never say those words from this moment forward."

"But it's the truth, Karen. I killed her, and I'm sorry. I'm so sorry. I can't believe I'm hearing these words come out of my mouth."

She shook her head and snorted.

"Oh, Jesus, Karen, God, I'm so sorry. The poor woman, and now you, and Nick." Frank put his hands over his face, rubbed his eyes.

She snorted again but softened. She held his wrist. "Look at me, Frank. Look at me. Say it again."

Long pause. "I'm so sorry."

"I know you are, my love."

"Oh, God, thank you." He took her hand and kissed it, kept it against his lips as he said, "I'm sorry, I'm sorry."

She said, "Shhhh."

"I'm sorry."

She let him continue to say it until the words stopped meaning anything.

She waited. "Okay?" she asked.

He looked at her and exhaled as if a crying jag had played itself out, but there had been no tears.

"Okay," she continued. "You're going to say you're sorry one more time. It's going to be to Nick, and then you're done." Frank seemed to understand. "From this moment on, we are in this one hundred percent together. *I* was driving. *I* killed her. Tell me it's okay. Tell me it was an accident. Tell me it could have been anyone. At any time. That automobiles kill thousands or tens of thousands. Tell me that it was an accident. Tell me how important it is that I not blame myself. Understand? This is as bad as bad can be, Frank. We cannot falter or we will lose everything."

Karen rubbed her face, pulled her wild hair tightly back and then let it fall loose.

"Okay, we have to talk to Nick. Officer Williams will be here in an hour."

Frank said, "Nick. How is this going to affect him?"

"He'll understand."

"It goes against everything we teach him."

"The situation has changed, Frank. We are in dire circumstances. The rules no longer apply."

"But what's he going to think?"

"He's going to have to realize the world isn't as simple and black and white as it is in his video games." He looked away, and when he looked back to her, she said, "Frank, I will not let you go to prison."

Frank shook his head. After several more moments, Karen took a deep breath and said, "Okay."

*

Karen sat on the edge of Nick's bed and Frank pulled the desk chair close and sat. Karen squeezed Nick's shoulder until he came to. Then he sat up and looked at them, scared, like a cornered animal.

Karen said, "Honey, we need to tell you what the situation is." She watched him close his eyes and sigh, clearly remembering just then the situation. "I need your attention. Go use the bathroom, splash some water on your face."

Without a word, he left the bed and did as he was told. Karen and Frank looked to one another but didn't speak until Nick returned and got back under the covers, sitting against the headboard and pillows almost as if sick and waiting to be ministered to. Karen reiterated the events of the night before, pretty much as Frank had, and concluded with their intentions.

"You're asking me to lie? To the police?" Nick said.

"I'm bringing you, very reluctantly, into the adult world, honey," she said. "I'm asking you to protect us. Dad and I have created a story that we have to stick to one hundred, *one thousand* percent or we will be in very big trouble. Permanent big trouble."

Nick looked away.

"Which is why I did what I did," Karen continued, touching Nick's arm so that he would turn back to her. "I started this. I began the lie. To keep Dad out of all but certain trouble, trouble that would take him away from us for a long time. I had to do what I did to save Dad. Nick, he'd have gone to jail, a pretty ugly one, and for who knows how long, and our family could have been ruined in other ways as well." She squeezed his forearm. "And it still could. Which is why I need you to be the extraordinary actor that you are and lie on our behalf. I beg you to forgive me for having to do this. Please believe me when I say that everything I'm doing now, from the moment I realized the trouble we were in, I'm doing to save us. Sending Dad to jail will not bring that poor woman back."

Nick then snorted and rocked and turned red, and Karen didn't know if he was going to cry or pummel the pillow he now clutched to his chest.

"This is Dad's fault," Nick said, not looking at Frank.

"Nick, you can't say that, and you can't even think it."

"Well, I'm right. He told me he was driving drunk."

"He was, and he knows how wrong that was."

"So it was his fault. And you're taking the blame."

Karen looked to Frank, who leaned forward and put his face in his hands. Karen turned back to Nick and said, "No. I'm putting myself on the line on behalf of all of us."

"But if he hadn't gotten drunk, this wouldn't have happened."

"Now listen to me," Karen said, again reaching for his forearm to squeeze it, as if to indent her words into his body. "In the kid world, there are all kinds of absolutes. Lying is wrong. Smoking is bad. Period. No ifs or buts. The adult world is a lot more complicated."

Nick grimaced and looked away.

"Hey," Karen said angrily. "Here's an *if* for you. What if I had let you sleep over at Oliver's? Remember, you asked? But I didn't want you to because I knew you and Oliver would be up till dawn if you stayed the night and then you'd be wiped out on Christmas Eve. So I said no. Your dad argued on your behalf, but I made my case and he ultimately agreed. So, in this way, it's my fault."

He wrinkled his nose as if smelling something bad.

"If I'd let you sleep over, then Dad wouldn't have been driving home at eleven thirty."

Nick frowned and looked away.

"If you hadn't been ready when Dad arrived, the woman Dad hit would have been long gone by the time he got home. Remember last weekend I picked you up from Noah's, it took you twenty minutes to find your shoes? That would have changed the outcome of last night. That's how precarious, how random and unknowable events are in our world. Say you *had* lost your shoes last night, and Dad had waited twenty minutes for you to come out, and then the same awful thing had happened, would it then have been your fault for having lost your shoes?"

"Dad was driving drunk."

"Yes. He's not the first, and he's more responsible than most people most of the time, as you surely know. And, yes, the law would hold him responsible for what happened, not you for being on time, not me for disallowing a sleepover, not the woman out walking in a blizzard in the middle of the night. Dad. And he would go to prison for what he did. Do you want your dad to go to prison?"

"No." Nick wiped tears from his eyes.

"Neither do I. That's why I did what I did and I pray you understand and forgive us that we have brought you into what is for us a very dangerous situation. Will you help us? Because now *I* could go to jail for what I've done."

A look of horror came over his face. He threw his arms around her, pressed his head against her.

"Shhh, it's going to be all right if we stick to our story. Can you try to help?"

"Mom," Nick says, pulling away. "Can I get in trouble?"

"No, absolutely not. Nothing will happen to you. You are still in the kid world, you're a juvenile according to the law, and Dad and I will take all responsibility for this before we'd let anything, anything at all, happen to you. Trust me, I will not let anything happen to you. You are not in the slippery and treacherous world we're in." She paused and said, "According to the law anyway."

Long pause. "Nick, I'm asking you to grow up fast now. Because this is serious. Now, are you willing to help?"

He nodded.

"Okay, here's what I told the police, this is the official public record and you have to commit it to your brain so hard that it becomes real. Okay?" She waited and repeated, "Okay?"

Nick nodded.

"You're going to become an actor like you've never been before. Do you think you can do that?

He nodded gravely.

"Okay, here's what happened, and we're never going to utter anything other than this, because this *is* what happened. Do you understand?"

He nodded with determination.

And then Karen went through every hour of the day, hour by hour, from when she picked him up at school to when she and Frank and he left for the Thompsons.

Then she asked him to repeat the events of the day, everything from the time he arrived home from school to the moment of the accident. Then she asked him questions about his actions, at each stage. She did this three times until his third go-round was identical to the second and without hesitations or pauses.

"Okay," she said. She hugged him and said, "My brave boy." Then she stood, looked at her watch, looked at Frank.

Frank didn't stand but instead asked Nick, "Can you hang tight here till ten? That's when the police officer, Officer Williams, will be arriving." Karen looked to Frank, nodded, and said, "He should come down just as he is. Pajama pants and T-shirt, as if we'd just woken him up." She said to Nick, "Don't even brush your hair."

Frank stood, squeezed Nick's shoulder. "Okay?"

Nick looked terrified but he nodded.

"Don't worry," Karen said. "It's all right to be afraid and nervous when you talk to Officer Williams. What happened is horrible for everyone, and Officer Williams will be sympathetic to this. And as long as you stick to what happened, which we've just been through three times, there's no way Officer Williams will know anything other than what you tell him." Karen paused. "Okay?"

Nick, holding his mother's gaze, nodded. Karen and Frank both nodded back.

*

When Sharon Talbott gave them the full report the following Wednesday, Karen was relieved to see that Officer Williams had recorded how distraught she had been when he'd arrived that Saturday morning, that she had shown genuine contrition, concern for the victim and the victim's family, a desire to meet the family and to attend the services.

It had been her first question to Officer Williams, who pulled up at 10 a.m., parking on the wrong side of the street at their front walk.

"Have you reached the family?" she asked.

He said that they had, but before they got into these details, he needed to take a statement from Nick.

Officer Williams, red-eyed and looking sleep-deprived, listened to Karen explain how afraid Nick would likely be, that this was traumatic, and so Officer Williams consented to letting them sit in, provided they didn't speak.

Nick appeared, and remained, shaken throughout the questioning. Nonetheless, he performed without a hitch or stutter, always answering "I don't remember" when anything was unclear; he was fourteen, and much was unclear. It didn't take long, and Officer Williams excused Nick. Only then did he go into the details of the victim's family insofar as he was allowed. Karen pressed hard for everything—such as, were children involved?

Officer Williams explained that he couldn't give them the woman's name, but they had reached the woman's sister, who lived out of state. The victim—always "the victim," and Karen winced when he said it—apparently lived alone in an apartment in the neighborhood, did not have children, and indeed seemed to have only this sister and brother-in-law as family. They would be driving up and arriving tonight.

"Will you please, please give them my name and number and address?" she said. "If they can bear it, I need to tell them to their faces how sorry, how terribly sorry I am, how sorry—" and here she broke off, weeping at last, tears dripping through the fingers covering her face, weeping for the woman and her family and this terrible mess, exhausted and frightened, tears she did not try to restrain, tears that intensified until Frank hugged her with genuine concern. When she stopped, Frank handed her his clean, folded handkerchief. She wiped her face and blew her nose.

Officer Williams said that he would convey this, but the victim's family was under no obligation to contact her. He explained that after the sister confirmed the victim's identity, the victim's relatives would decide whether to press charges. Williams advised them to find a lawyer. "It's more than likely that opportunistic lawyers will reach out to the victim's family offering their services for a percentage," Williams noted. "Even in the case of a non-vindictive family, lawyers can be persuasive. So retain the best attorney you can find."

Officer Williams, a skeptic last night, seemed now to be on their side, in the new light of day, in their tidy living room, a festive Christmas tree lit and in front of a huge mullioned window looking out toward the street. It certainly couldn't have seemed like the home of felons. Karen had won his sympathy.

The report, he told them at the door on leaving, would go to the Cuyahoga County prosecutor's office for investigation. The lawyer they chose would know to be in touch with the prosecutor's office.

"Officer," Karen said in their foyer when he'd opened the front door to leave. He turned back. "There's nothing happy here, but I would like to thank you for your kindness and wish you and your family a . . . a peaceful Christmas."

Officer Williams touched the brim of his hat and said to Karen, "I wish you the same."

And then he left. He would call again on Monday, the day after Christmas, to tell them the date and time of the funeral service. They would see him again days later at the arraignment Friday in a courtroom at City Hall, as the arresting officer, forever an ominous reminder to her of the crimes and the mechanism that could spring disaster on them at an instant.

*

Karen knocked on Nick's door that afternoon and said she was going to try to make cookies. Did he still want to help?

Nick removed his headset and turned from his computer.

"Do you *want* me to help?" he asked.

"Not if you don't want to, sweetheart."

"I'd kind of like to just keep playing."

"Then you do that. Do whatever you need to. We're still leaving for Grandma's at six, though, all right?"

"Okay."

She did not make cookies, but she did wrap one last gift, a book of short stories Frank had asked for.

Frank had driven to his mom's at midday to fill her in on the situation and tell her not to worry. His Uncle Ed and Aunt Barb had flown in from Santa Barbara before the storm, but fortunately they were still at their hotel when Frank arrived at his mother's house. His mother appeared at first very disturbed, like an animal caught, but quieted when Frank held her hand and stroked her arm and told her not to worry, he was taking care of everything, which always calmed her. Ed and Barb would be a welcome distraction, Karen thought, from what would otherwise be a subdued Christmas for all.

Indeed, on Christmas morning, when Frank, Karen, and Nick opened gifts, the mood was mournful. Especially when, in the silence, the line from "Have Yourself a Merry Little Christmas" sounded and made Karen's stomach turn over: "From now on, our troubles will be far away. . . ." But they bore it, went through the motions of all the years past.

Karen was grateful they'd agreed to host Christmas night's dinner for the six of them because it gave her chores to focus on—picking beans, making the Yorkshire pudding batter, studding the roast with slivers of garlic. After Frank removed his mother's coat to hang in the hall closet, Karen came to greet her aging mother-in-law and received an uncommonly long hug, long enough for Karen to understand and whisper that they had a good lawyer and she mustn't worry. Throughout the evening, no one spoke of the event. Karen only wanted the holiday over.

And when it was, and they woke to a sunny Monday morning, and the situation remained utterly unchanged, all the unknowns hovering over them, and yet there were chores to be done. Domestic business didn't go away because you'd committed multiple felonies. The upcoming hurdle Tuesday morning was the most dreaded—the funeral service. Officer Williams had called, as promised, to provide the details and to say that the victim's sister wanted them to know that they were welcome to mourn with them at the First Baptist Church. He also revealed the victim's name— Sarah Childress—which hit Karen hard, the name making her a real person, not just "the victim." Karen realized they would have to perpetuate the lie to the face of the one most grievously affected by the accident, the sister, and so the routine of laundry scarcely registered as she got the first load of wash on since before the accident. Until she lifted Frank's cotton Dockers. The cuffs were chalky white from the salt, water-stained two inches up the cuff. These were the pants he'd been wearing that night. But as routine and necessity dictated, she checked the pockets because 10 percent of the time she rescued something like a pen, a utility knife, a handkerchief—and yes, a handkerchief remained in the back left pocket. It appeared to be unused and she considered not washing it. She turned it over in her hand to find that the other side was smudged. A vague impression of lips? She shook her head and squinted at the otherwise pristine, bleached cotton handkerchief.

She held it to her nose—scented, barely, but unmistakably.

Karen found Frank in front of their shared bureau and chest of drawers, tying his tie in the mirror.

She held the handkerchief out to him.

"Lipstick, Frank? *Lipstick*? Jesus."

He stared at it, seeming not to comprehend. She pushed it forward so that he would take it. He continued to stare at it as if he didn't know that it was even a handkerchief.

"What a fucking cliché," Karen said. "Where *were* you that night?"

"With Grant and the rest at dinner, as you know."

"Then whose fucking lipstick is it?"

He was so frozen with surprise that he said nothing, and she left the bedroom, pounding down the stairs and into the kitchen. Frank followed her. She stood with her hands on the sink, staring out into the barren snow-covered backyard. She didn't know where else to go. When he arrived, she retched dryly into the sink, only a thin trail of saliva issuing.

He had jammed the smeared handkerchief into his pocket and followed her downstairs. He gripped her shoulder farthest from him and pulled her to face him. She wiped her mouth with the back of her hand. "Please look at me." She did. "Here's what happened."

He took a breath and said, "I was kissed before I left the office party." Karen did not respond.

"Passive, yes."

No response from Karen.

"I was leaving the Christmas party and a relatively new account person, who was clearly tipsy, found me in my office and kissed me. That's it, end of story."

"So what's this person's name?"

Frank sighed heavily. She could see the pulse in his neck. Hers was equally quick.

"Dezaray," he said.

She lifted her eyebrows almost as if to laugh. "Seriously, Frank?"

"Seriously. Dezaray Brouley, thirty-two, native of St. Croix. I helped hire her. She had one too many glasses of punch and got a little too forward as I was leaving."

"And try as you did, she overpowered you, this Amazonian."

"No, Karen. I'm going to be completely honest here. I let her. And I liked it. And I'm sorry."

Karen felt her head jolt, her mouth hung open. She turned away and he turned her back to face him.

"Of course I liked it, goddammit, I'm not going to lie to you. I'm asking you to understand. You would have liked it, too. A beautiful thirty-two-year-old wants to kiss you? So, yes, I gave into it. I let her and I liked it. And that was the extent of it. I'm sorry. You think I'm not human?"

Karen looked away.

"Karen, it meant no more than I've just explained. I swear. The only time. Ever. With anyone. *All these years.* I swear to you."

"It could happen again."

"No, my love. Because afterward I felt like a fool, an old man and a fool. It won't happen again."

He sat her down at the breakfast table and walked her through the event completely, crumbs from his English muffin and a drop of congealed butter still on the placemat at his elbow.

"And by the time I got to the car and saw the lipstick, saw my face, I didn't feel good or excited anymore." He repeated what he'd said: "I felt foolish."

She stared coldly at him.

"Karen, I love you."

"Well, one thing's for sure, you can't leave me now. If we make it through this. And you can't be unfaithful, can you?"

"I never wanted to be. Or would be."

"I swear to God, Frank, if you leave me, I will take us both down. I did this for us. We are in this together. Forever."

"I've never wanted it any other way," he said, growing angry himself. "But not because of a *threat* of mutually assured destruction. I don't want us to rot in a prison we build around ourselves."

"Can we go now?" Nick said. He stood in the kitchen doorway, dressed, his shaggy brown hair wet from the shower.

"Go dry your hair," Karen said. "I don't want you catching cold." When he was gone, Karen looked at Frank and said softly, "God damn you." She didn't *not* believe him, but this kiss from another woman had given the anger a place to land, a hook to catch on. Now, two days after their somber Christmas, her anger seemed to hover just behind her, like a wave pushing her forward everywhere she went. For really, what was she angry at? Again she said, staring him dead in the eye, "God *damn* you." She stood abruptly and went to the hall closet for her coat.

The plan was to take Nick to Noah's house before the service. Nick would be spending the night. By now Noah's parents, indeed the whole community, was aware of the accident, had read the three-paragraph item in the Metro pages of the *Plain Dealer*, and within their social circle the news had spread like a flu. Friends and neighbors had left voicemails and emails, and two people had actually mailed letters expressing sympathy and support. Karen herself had spoken only to Anne Sutton, one of a few close girlfriends, wife of one Frank's high school pals, with whom Frank had had dinner that night.

The call was more complex since Anne and Walter had, just before Thanksgiving, announced their separation. Anne and Walter were considerably more social than she and Frank were, so the separation came with the not uncommon embarrassment and shame. And Karen wanted to confide in a friend who was hurting as well, though for different reasons. Karen, genuinely upset for her friend, had an additional motive for making a confessor of Anne. That she was so social guaranteed Anne would spread the story. Karen would say nothing of the details, letting Anne presume what she would. Because it was possible that Anne knew of Frank's dinner with Walter, and their friends. Karen simply conferred the awfulness of the situation and made it clear that she didn't want to talk about it. She wanted to know how Anne was holding up.

But it was only when Karen bumped into Stephanie Strum at the grocery store that she sensed a disturbing, morbid excitement. Stephanie was a young mom of four whom Karen spoke with once a year at the summer block party on their street and waved cordially to at such grocery store encounters as these, which invariably ended in promises to get together that vanished the moment each was out of the other's sight.

It was only when Stephanie, with a look of concern, said, "You must feel *terrible*," did Karen understand how thoroughly she disliked Stephanie. Was she digging for details? Of course this was exciting. This was news. Something had actually *happened* on their street. Karen glared at her and then left, simply abandoned her cart in the middle of the aisle and left the store. Later in the day, an email appeared in Karen's inbox from Stephanie, apologizing excessively for her thoughtlessness.

Karen immediately typed, "It's a hard time for all of us," and hit SEND.

When Nick had dried his hair and returned downstairs, Frank was waiting at the foot of the stairs. Karen sat in the driver's seat of the running car.

*

At the service, Frank and Karen heard about whose life had been taken. Sarah Childress was a single woman, aged fifty-two, who was enormously kind, who worked for the Cuyahoga County dog shelter and was devoted to her own pets, who was an avid hiker who yearly explored the canyons of Utah, Nevada, and Arizona, who loved the outdoors, and whose hobbies included photography and volunteering for the Cleveland Metroparks.

Karen and Frank had arrived for the service twenty minutes early. Karen noticed one woman engaged in conversation with the pastor— definitely the sister. Karen felt certain that the sister had already identified her, too. But to make it doubtless and to get it over with, there to the left of the closed casket, Karen said to the stranger, "It was me. I'm the one."

The woman she addressed had frosted hair, thick mascara, and unassuming lipstick. They were of equal height, but the sister was on the heavy side and about ten years older than Karen. She wore a navy polyester dress. A tall, gaunt man in a brown suit stood behind her.

"My name is Karen Markstrom, and I'm here to beg your forgiveness and to say how terribly, terribly sorry I am, a sorrow I will live with for the rest of my life."

The woman let a long silence pass between them, long enough for a well-wisher to approach from the side and then leave.

When the woman said, "It's kind of you," a thousand pounds lifted off Karen's shoulders. "My name is Shirley Klum. This is my husband, Bob."

"Oh," Karen exhaled with relief. "This is my husband, Frank." Frank nodded to each and each nodded back. "I can't tell you how grateful I am that you've let me come here today. Truly, it was a terrible accident, and I've prayed every hour that I could take back that moment in the snow."

"You pray," Mrs. Klum said.

"Yes, I pray very hard."

"Pray for my sister's good soul."

"I have and will."

"Thank you." Mrs. Klum looked at Karen hard.

"You have to believe me, I didn't even see her," Karen said.

"I know—the police told us about the weather you were having that night. My sister. . ." She trailed off.

"Do you know what she was doing out that late in a storm?"

"No, I can't rightly say, only that it doesn't surprise me. Even when we were girls, she'd be out in thunderstorms playing in mud. She didn't like to be indoors if she didn't have to."

"We were told that she didn't have children."

"That's correct. She was, well, children were never an issue, if you know what I mean."

"I see. Did she have a partner to whom I can . . . can ask forgiveness?"

"No, not presently. She'd stopped living in sin, praise the Lord. And I know the Lord will forgive her. And He is the only One who can forgive *you*." She looked away and sighed. "I don't mean to say I didn't love her. God has a plan for all of us. There wasn't a better aunt to our two boys."

"We have a son, fourteen," Karen offered.

For the first time, Mrs. Klum smiled, and her husband nodded.

"Ours are both grown," the sister said. "One's in California, the other's in the service. We haven't seen Sarah much since our youngest left five years back. Once for Momma's funeral."

"And your father?"

"Daddy? Lost him when he was not even my age. Lung cancer."

"My dad, too," Frank said.

Karen looked down.

"I'm glad Momma didn't have to be here today."

Karen sighed brusquely. "Yes."

When the organ music stopped, the pastor approached from behind the Klums.

Karen said, "I want to thank you, Mrs. Klum, for allowing us here to mourn and ask forgiveness and to have a glimpse of your sister's life."

Mrs. Klum nodded.

Karen said, "As far as practical matters go, we have full insurance, and I don't want to be crass, but insurance will cover everything—today, your hotel, and certainly beyond. However long you're staying."

"Thank you, and we do appreciate that. Bob was able to get away from the plant for a couple weeks, and I'm part-time anyway. We'll stay only long enough to take care of things here and then head back to Little Rock. We appreciate expenses being taken care of. But I want you to know we're not vindictive people. We don't want to profit from my sister's death. It's not right. Our reward is not on the surface of Earth."

Karen found herself brushing tears out of her eyes. The pastor put his fingertips to Mrs. Klum's shoulder.

Karen said, "Thank you again for allowing us to pray and to mourn with you."

Mrs. Klum nodded. "But just here, please. We've asked only her closest friends to join us at the interment."

"Yes, of course."

*

Karen slammed the driver-side door shut and wrenched the key in the ignition to start the car as though she wanted to hurt it. Frank glanced at her warily and buckled his seat belt.

As she exited the church parking lot, he said, "I'm so glad that's over. I thought that went okay, don't you? Or as okay as it could. You were perfect."

"You certainly aren't making it fucking easy," Karen said, accelerating beyond the speed limit. "It's bad enough I have to lie like a sociopath to that poor woman."

Frank pressed both feet forward as if to reach a brake pedal. He looked out the window, then turned back to her. "I've told you everything. I swear to you, it meant nothing. How can you even think . . .?"

She pursed her lips and gripped the steering wheel with her right hand at twelve o'clock, locking her arm like a fence between them.

*

Now the house was dark and quiet. Frank walked through rooms turning on lights so that the place didn't feel so empty. Karen stared into the refrigerator looking for something to eat but, seeing nothing desirable, closed it.

Frank paused before her and said, "Well, at least that's over."

Karen nodded. The cold had made his nose run, and he removed his handkerchief but saw that it was the one with the lipstick from this morning. Karen saw, too. He turned to the sink to his left, opened the cupboard below it, and tossed the cloth into the garbage. Then he faced her again.

Without warning, she hit him in the chest with her right fist. She wasn't particularly strong, but her punch was powerful enough to drive him back a step. Then she did it again, harder this time, and he shouted, "Hey!"

With her eyes squeezed shut, she pounded his chest with both her fists as hard as she could. And he took it for a few seconds but then he moved into her and enfolded her in his arms, trapping her wild fists between them, big enough to bear hug her and still her completely.

She cried a little then, the final small throes of the outburst, as she gave up resistance.

"I don't know what I'm feeling," she said.

"Shh." He paused. "You must believe me, the kiss meant nothing."

Her face was pressed against his chest and she nodded into it.

"Do you forgive me?"

"I think so."

He hugged her. "I love you so much."

She looked up into his blue eyes and asked, "Were we becoming boring to each other? Were we doomed? Are we?"

"No, sweetheart. You were and are and always will be my love and my best friend." Both felt the unsatisfying nature of the response, and so they hugged for nearly a minute more, rocking almost as though slow dancing.

Frank said he was going to heat up the leftover Chinese food and asked if she wanted any. They sat at the breakfast table eating it, not speaking until Karen said, "I am so relieved she had no kids."

"Or shattered parents," Frank said. "But still. A woman's life." He shook his head at his plate.

"Frank, you were wrong to do what you did. We both know that. But by another token, I don't know any of us who hasn't been in a similar position. And all those guys—Grant, Walter, John—they all drove that night. It doesn't excuse what you did. And with Nick, *Jesus*."

"No, it doesn't."

"She had no business being out in the middle of the road either," Karen said, rubbing her hands together to warm them. "If it had been me, it would have happened just the same. And it did. In my mind I was in the car, I did it."

"And I feel guilty about that. About what I've forced you to do, the risk I forced you to take because of my stupidity and bad luck."

"You didn't force me, Frank. And it was an accident."

They each had a few more bites, a sip of tea.

Karen looked up and waited for eye contact. "I'm sorry I said what I did about you not being able to leave me and what it implied. I didn't mean to threaten you. I was angry and frightened."

He stopped eating but stared at the pieces of chicken he was moving around among some peanuts and brown sauce. "It's true, though. There's no denying it."

"But I would never. *You* would never."

"We've seen once-happy couples do some pretty bitter things to one another."

"But not us."

"No, not us," Frank said. "But you weren't wrong: regardless of how the rest of our lives play out, in this we are locked together forever."

She reached for his hand. "I've never wanted anything else." But she released it and looked away.

"What is it, sweetheart?"

"It's not just us, though. Dan Jeffries *knows*."

Frank leaned back and sighed.

"Frank, he *knows*."

"He said we didn't give him any evidence."

"But he could now *get* evidence. He could press investigators to look harder into the case. What if a detective went back to Len and Melissa? They'd be forced to admit that they didn't actually see us at the party. That could open up our whole story. He's a friend of Grant's. Jesus. I just thought of this. Grant may know."

Karen liked Grant, perhaps best of all Frank's high school buddies, and trusted him completely. But he was a reporter for Cleveland's *Plain Dealer*, the city's main paper, his wife a photographer there. Grant asked questions for a living.

Frank said, "Grant doesn't know. The newspaper account said that you were driving. I think I even may have mentioned this to the guys. Yes! I did. I told them I had no constraints because you were picking up Nick. I even told him how generous it was of you because you actually like those things, so it's plausible we did go. And we're not talking about it and no one is going to ask us to talk about it."

"But if there's an investigation, our story is going to unravel."

She put down her fork, no longer hungry.

"We have to be smart, Karen," he said. He reached for her hand, and she looked up, her eyes brimming with fear. "Remember what Dan told you. He told you this to help not to hurt."

"But what if he changes his mind? What if he gets righteous and feels that as a duty-bound officer of the court he has to do something?"

"Sweetheart. We have no choice. One hundred percent, remember?"

*

The rest of the day seemed almost normal. Karen found comfort in folding clothes and getting the checking account up to date, as things had piled up during the lead-up to the holidays. Frank scoured the kitchen till it seemed all but unused, then straightened the living room, still littered with bits of wrapping paper, errant ribbon, an ashy hearth, and more pine needles that fell increasingly from the tree. In the evening they ate some soup with a glass of wine, some bread, watched the news they'd recorded earlier. They were even able to let *The Daily Show* divert them for another half hour.

They'd gotten some good news at the end of the day from their criminal attorney. Sharon Talbott was a tall, slender woman with broad shoulders, long, abundant auburn hair, freckles, and runner's calves. Tough but without being masculine, Karen thought. The large window of Sharon's office on the thirty-second floor looked out across downtown Cleveland toward Lake Erie and gave them the sense of competence and success. Frank and Karen had appreciated her frank demeanor, the clipped, definitive way she spoke. She had felt pretty sure that, barring anything unforeseen, Karen wouldn't do any time, especially if she could get the case moved out of county court into city. She was on good terms with the county prosecutor, said he was a reasonable guy whose office wouldn't make a case of this. He had political ambitions, she said, and this wouldn't do him any good, prosecuting someone like Karen, and could make him look bad if he lost, trying to prosecute this upstanding member of the community who already had to bear such a burden. Sharon's assistant had called to say that, indeed, the arraignment had been moved from the County Courthouse to a court at City Hall. Sharon had been good to her word, and they wouldn't see her again until Friday, the day after tomorrow, at 2 p.m.

"I'm absolutely drained," Karen said when the show was over. Frank glanced at the time, only a little after nine.

"I'm feeling the same. I'll join you."

As he undressed for bed, Karen descended the stairs in her flannel nightdress. The chilly upstairs had made her think of the bathrobe: plush, sage-colored terrycloth, a gift from Frank she'd opened on that somber, going-through-the-motions Christmas morning. So strange how life insists on going on around you no matter what. She turned on a living room lamp. She lifted the new robe out of its box and shook some green needles out of it. She put it on and hugged herself in it to enjoy its warmth and softness.

When she reached beneath the lampshade, her gaze caught on the photograph she'd taken of Frank in their first apartment. He sat shirtless at his computer, their first computer, some nineteen years earlier, a trail of cigarette smoke rising from the round glass ashtray at his left. He had been typing so intently he hadn't noticed Karen and her camera. She lifted the image, which she'd put in a silver frame, to regard the handsome young man she'd married. His long hair, tanned shoulders, so slender back then. Such lofty goals they'd had.

They'd met at a party in Rhode Island just after she'd finished grad school. She walked into a kitchen at the party of someone she didn't know, brought by a friend, and saw him leaning against the counter, a beer in one hand and grinning at her. When their glances met, she felt her heart skip, while his grin fell away, then returned even brighter. Had he seen her blush in the bright kitchen? A flush began at her chest and rose in a wave up her neck and across her cheeks so strongly she could feel the heat. He introduced himself immediately. Their conversation lasted all night by the swimming pool outside and ended in sex. That in itself was so unlike her; she'd never in her life had sex with someone she'd just met. Never. And yet it had been so swift and natural and lovely that it left her breathless and, the next day, giddy. Not a trace of regret, only the sense of amazing good fortune. She had almost not gone to the party, had tried to beg off feigning fatigue, but her friend had been insistent. If she hadn't given in, she'd likely never have met Frank. With school done, she'd planned to return home in a few days. Now it was an evening that she would carry happily in her mind forever, and one that directed the rest of her life and his.

That first summer living together was a gorgeous idyll; they never tired of the other's company and their bodies never stopped hungering, could never be fully quenched. One night at a bar, during a thunderstorm, they made out so passionately and uninhibitedly that an actual boat captain, or so he said (he was well into the Dark & Stormys), interrupted their affections and asked if he could marry them. The drunken captain had been so competent with the ceremonial language that the whole bar watched. Frank never forgot the day (it was the day before Memorial Day, easy to remember) and took Karen to dinner to celebrate their "wedding" the following year, which she thought was a hoot the first time and tired the second time—until, before dessert, he proposed, actually got down on his knee in a Manhattan restaurant, like the actor in *Moonstruck*, their favorite movie, and offered her a ring. That first summer of unbridled, passionate love was unsustainable, a summer spent on beaches and on friends' sailboats, and in bed, allowing themselves leisure after the successful completion of their degrees. In the fall they moved to New York City. He was going to become a writer, capital W, and she would paint. Karen waited tables and Frank found work as an editorial assistant at a small academic publishing house.

After eighteen months, their studio apartment on Mott Street in Little Italy had lost its romance for Karen; the bathtub in the kitchen no longer charmed her; finding that ice had formed in the kitchen sink on winter mornings depressed her; generally, the corrosive effects of penury in the crowded city ate away at her. She begged Frank to move, arguing that they'd be much better off where the cost of living was better, near not her roots in Boston (too expensive) but his, if he wished, in Cleveland, an eminently affordable place to live where he still had the support of his mom and dad and many friends.

In Cleveland, they'd gotten by on odd jobs and freelance work for several more years, but Frank's literary agent didn't have any luck selling his novel (the second he'd written), and Karen grew disenchanted with her work acquiring art for a local gallery. It became clear to her that if they were going to have children, they'd have to change. She was thirty-two and he thirty. When she approached him with the idea of actively trying to get pregnant, he resisted, even though they'd both entered into this marriage agreeing that this was part of the long-term plan. Yet how, he asked her, could they possibly have a child given their precarious finances? To which she countered: if they waited till they were financially secure, they might never have a baby. And what if she had difficulty conceiving, she added. Some couples try for years. They lived life for four months with the baby issue as the continuous current separating them, until at last, to her joy, he consented. Three months later, she was pregnant. Frank faced their situation head on, bought secondhand business clothes and hit the pavement. It didn't take long for him to land a job at an ad firm; he was charming, smart, and talented and the job market was good.

By the time Nick was born, they had health insurance and a steady, if modest, income. Two years later, they were able to put a down payment on a small house, and after ten years, once Nick was old enough that Karen too could work (teaching art to high school girls), they were able to upgrade to this more elegant brick colonial. Frank had tried to keep writing fiction, but he found he couldn't write ad copy all day and come home at night and write more, certainly not once they had Nick. Karen knew that Frank was happy and comfortable, loved her and Nick, but that part of him resented what in uncommon moments of frustration he called "this burgher's existence," with no goals or ambitions beyond being able to afford Nick's private school tuition, save for college, and meet all their monthly payments. She knew he had given up his own ambitions for her. How many novelists succeed by age thirty? Almost none. He wasn't a failure, as he sometimes thought of himself, despite his prominence in the advertising world here, his solid creative work for his firm, and exciting and nerve-racking changes underway in the new digital era. If anyone should feel the failure, it was she. But she didn't. She was content as an art teacher and mom. Frank just hadn't given his ambition enough time. He was still developing when she'd asked for a child. He gave ambition up so she could have a baby, and this fact seemed especially and painfully acute right now.

She smiled sadly at her young husband's image, set the frame down, and turned off the light.

*

Karen rolled onto her side toward him, hugging the pillow. "You can tell me that you love me and that you always will," she said.

He rolled onto his side to face her and said, "I love you and I always will." He kissed her. "Forever." He ran his hands up and down her leg. She wore nothing under her flannel gown. She knew she was lucky to have remained so smooth and firm and trim after childbirth and into her forties. He rolled onto his back.

"Mmm," she said. "Why did you stop?"

"Oh, I don't know. Didn't want to start anything I couldn't finish."

"Who says you have to finish?"

"I'm a guy. Guys have to finish. And of course, if we don't that's worse."

Karen knew the uncommon stressfulness of the week would make him even more self-conscious about performing. She noticed that he'd become erratic over the past couple of years, a slow diminishing of urgency, of frequency. Perhaps this was the reason the sex was less satisfying for her, or that since it was less satisfying for her, it made it that way for him. But then their sex life had become so routine that she knew this was part of the issue. They made love once a week, on Sunday night, and it was always the same, she always on her back, coming less and less often but urging him to carry on without her—she was fine, it was okay, she enjoyed it. She wasn't frustrated—it was what it was. They were aging. This was normal, wasn't it?

Sometimes it could be twice a week if they went out to dinner and felt romantic afterward and not tired. She remembered when they used to smoke weed in bed and then the sex was especially powerful, but that stopped with the birth of Nick; even when he was sleeping at a friend's, they feared they'd be called (as they once were when Nick awoke at a friend's, crying, and with a fever)—what if they were stoned and got that call again. So that was the end of the pot smoking. She didn't even know how one would procure it anymore.

Karen snuggled into him, massaging him through his boxers. She began to stroke, having unleashed him through the fly of his boxers, then stronger until he was fully hard, though Frank himself was unresponsive. Frozen, in fact. Had it been that long since she'd initiated sex? She had for decades simply followed his lead.

"My God," he said, "where and when did you learn to do that?"

"*Cosmo*," she said. "Does it feel good?"

"Um, *yeah*, can't you tell?" And then, "You read *Cosmo*?"

"The girls at school sometimes leave copies lying around. Subtle protests." She continued her gentle ministrations. "Do you like this? You're not moving."

"I'm paralyzed."

She clutched the shaft in her hand. She put her thumb on the tip. She smiled at him. "It's like a joystick."

He snorted. "Very much so." Then, as she began to work it, he said, with some breathlessness, "Considerably more, actually." He appeared to her as though he were flattened to the mattress as steel to a magnet.

"Oh?" she said softly.

"At this moment, it feels like the very core of my being."

"I like that," she said.

"You have *no* idea."

She stopped, held onto the shaft, squeezed hard.

He took a deep breath but was otherwise immobilized. "Sweetheart, with what you have in your hand, you could walk me out onto the roof and send me off it and I would be utterly powerless to resist."

"*Really*," she said, smiling. "Hmm, I *do* like that." She rose to her knees and removed his shorts. She resumed her grip and straddled his thighs. "I have complete power over you."

"At this moment, it is absolute."

"I did not *know* this. I think I need to appreciate this . . . power a little more." With her hand and arm, she swept her voluminous locks back over her head and descended. As soon as she had taken him into her mouth, smelled the musky-sweat scent, appealing in its animal uniqueness, the strangeness of fellating him made her realize that it had been years since she'd done it. She should do better, she thought, now happily engaged in the project, so new did it seem.

As his breathing intensified, she stopped abruptly and said, "Don't come." Then she smiled, a bit evilly, as if embracing this power for its own sake, and said, "I want the . . . *core* . . . of your being inside me."

"Absolutely," he said.

She lifted her nightgown over her head.

"Stop," he said when her arms were raised. "Stay just like that." The street-lights flooded in through the partially opened blinds. Light and shadow striped her torso, pronounced the shape of her breasts, and she looked down at them, not only substantial but perfectly shaped, round and plump with large, taut nipples pointing invitingly upward. They had always been part of her life, since they arrived in sixth grade, all through high school and college, the looking. And it rarely bothered her. But over the years, she'd become so concerned they'd eventually sag and stretch, she now corseted them in rigid bras, so much so that she no longer got those looks. They remained still so uncommonly youthful, so beautiful in this light, everything kind of bluish with just the faint blush of pink nipple and aureole.

"You are so beautiful," he said. He gripped her waist and she, tossing her gown to the floor, leaned onto her arms to kiss him, stroking his chest with her breasts. He rolled her onto her back, peeled off his shirt, entered her, and began with customary slow back and forth. She smiled and closed her eyes and tilted her head back to expose the full length of her thin pale neck. "God, your *cock* is so *hard*," she said.

He literally halted.

"Why did you stop?" she had to say in order for him to resume.

"Just surprised," he said and continued. "It's just not like you. You never."

"But you liked it, I can tell."

Now he was confused, she felt his hard-on fading, and she opened her eyes halfway and clenched his buttocks. She smiled at him and said, "*Fuck me hard.*"

And he did like it, and it did in fact work.

"Deeper," she whispered. And now, not really of her own volition, said, "Fuck me. Harder." And he did, hard until a deep orgasm spread from her cervix to her fingers and toes and nose. She clearly and loudly came, issuing guttural cries, sounds even an actress would be hard-pressed to credibly duplicate—she couldn't help it, and didn't care. They were alone in the house. She breathed heavily. And he slowed gradually and then rolled off of her.

"Oh God," she said stroking her torso with her fingertips. "I still feel like I'm coming. It's like a tide going out, so slow." Her hand wandered lazily to his body, and she felt him and said, "Oh, my God, I thought you had."

"I was too busy watching. You were so amazing."

"*You* were amazing. God, that was one of the best ever." She turned to him, smiled gamely.

Again she sensed his surprise in her unprecedented frankness. So she said, "Move over." And he did, and she rolled over and leaned on her elbows to raise her ass high. "I'm presenting."

"What?"

"Like a chimp, in the primate world, like a chimp in heat." She smiled at him and said, "You like it this way, no?"

"All guys do."

"I think I read that, too," she said. And now she worked every bit as hard, banging her small firm ass against his pelvis, until he asked without stopping, "Do you like this?"

"Of course. You feel good in me." She pushed hard back against him and harder. "We need to do it this way more."

He dismounted and stepped off the bed, pulled her to her side and entered this way, as she lay on her side, knees up, slightly parted so that she could touch herself and she smiled and moaned and said, "Now this is comfortable. You can do this all night."

But he could not, and he pushed her farther onto the bed and onto her back, climaxing in what had been their routine for so long, but now so powerfully inside her that she came a second time. He rolled off her, onto his back, both of them wet with sweat, he breathing heavily, neither speaking and both enjoying the postcoital exhaustion, the sheer spentness, the happy nothingness, just breathing and beating hearts.

"That was amazing," she said. "I have never come twice. Or maybe I just never stopped till the end."

He smiled at the ceiling, an easy, exhausted, pleased smile.

She reached for his hand. After many minutes passed, and the spentness gave way to the facts of their situation, she said, "Wow. During that whole time, I didn't think about it once. It was as if it wasn't there."

"Mmm," he said. "You're right." His breathing had slowed. "Regrettable that we can't have sex every minute of our life for the next—"

And he stopped.

"Let's not talk about it," she said to the ceiling. "I'm just going to think about your fucking me for as long as I can." And she did, drifting off thinking of the sex they'd just had—the first really good sex they'd had in a long, long time.

*

The next day, the one that followed the service for Sarah Childress, an attorney for the insurance company, Buck Heard, called to set up a meeting for the following week. Frank had taken the call and explained that he didn't think there was going to be a civil trial, given what the Klum sister said.

The attorney had chuckled with such derision that Frank was put off by the man. He was on speaker and Karen sat across from Frank at the kitchen table, and they both looked away from the phone on the table to each other.

"Look," Frank explained. "They're obviously very religious and flat-out said it would be wrong to profit from a death."

"Give 'em some time, and let's plan to meet first thing next week after the arraignment. Civil will happen after criminal, but I'll need to start preparing."

"Okay, but I'm telling—"

"Mr. Markstrom," Buck Heard broke in. "This is what I *do*."

"Yes, but—"

"Can you listen to me for a minute? The victim's family always says that or feels similarly. And religion has nothing to do with anything once money enters the picture. What happens is the personal injury lawyers invariably court them. First they explain that the insurance company pays, not actual people, so they shouldn't feel guilty about it. Once they remove guilt, they start talking cash dollars, and the idea of one million guilt-free dollars, for no upfront expenditure, no risk, is too difficult for most people to turn down." When Frank did not respond, Mr. Heard knew he had convinced Frank, and so offered, "It's not *impossible* that they won't litigate, it's just extremely rare."

This took the air out of the previous day's optimism, but Karen was able to calm Frank by convincing him that a civil suit wasn't what they were worried about, because the insurance company would pay for it—she didn't remind him that they lacked an umbrella policy. Provided the criminal hearing went as they were trying to orchestrate it, everything would be okay. She asked him to focus on tomorrow and said that they would know more tomorrow. And they did.

Sharon Talbott met them outside the courtroom as planned and led them inside, where a domestic violence hearing was underway. They sat at the back of the courtroom. Karen whispered to Sharon, "There's the woman's sister with her husband." Frank hadn't noticed as there were a scattering of people, in all manner of attire, from sweatpants to suits. Sure enough, there were Shirley and Bob Klum, seated by themselves on the other side of the room. While they waited, Officer Williams appeared along with Silent Curt, who was wearing that same black trench coat. They found seats in the second row.

When they were called, Sharon said, "This shouldn't take long."

The judge—a woman, Karen was comforted to see—named the case even before Karen and Sharon had taken their seats at the defendant's table. The judge then asked, "Is anyone from the victim's family here?"

All looked as Shirley Klum raised her hand.

"I'm sorry for your loss, ma'am," the judge said.

Shirley Klum nodded.

The judge said, "Counsel for the city is present and," she searched through some papers, tilted her head back to see through her readers. "And Officer Fred Williams?" The judge looked up.

"Here, Your Honor." Karen had turned in time to see Williams lower his hand. He did not look at her. When her eyes moved to Silent Curt, she found him staring with dead eyes at her and she quickly turned around.

"The court notes that the arresting officer is present," the judge said. Last she asked, "Karen Markstrom?"

"Here, Your Honor," she said, raising her hand. Sharon touched Karen's elbow as she stood and Karen followed.

"Mrs. Markstrom, you are charged with negligent vehicular manslaughter. How do you plead?"

"My client pleads not guilty, Your Honor."

"So noted," the judge said. "Does your client have anything she'd like to say?"

"No, Your Honor, not beyond contrition."

The judge removed her readers to look at Karen. Karen bowed her head and closed her eyes.

The judge put her readers back on, glanced at papers, and said. "I've read the report. The defendant has shown contrition. I'm setting a trial date for . . ." and she drew a finger down a scheduling book, ". . . three weeks from today, 9 a.m." She looked up. "Defendant is released on her own recognizance." The judge gave the gavel a quick thwack and turned to the next case.

Sharon turned to Karen. "See? Quick." And she moved to lead Karen out of the courtroom. "I've still got some work to do, but the worst-case scenario at this time three weeks from today is that same judge and opposing counsel will accept your no contest plea, and I don't see why they wouldn't."

Sharon looked over at the Klums, who were speaking to two men in business suits. "You've got civil representation, I trust?"

"Yes, we do," Frank said.

"They're why you need it," Sharon said.

"Lawyers?"

"Plaintiff lawyers, jackals," she said. Still looking, Sharon paused and squinted and, to herself, said, "That's odd."

Karen, hyperalert throughout, said, "What's odd?"

Frank had left his seat and met them in aisle. He hugged her and the three left the courtroom.

"What was odd?" Karen asked again.

"The attorney who recommended me to you, isn't he a personal friend of yours?"

"Yes, why?" Karen asked.

"That was his partner in there, with the others, talking to the victim's sister." The three kept walking, but Karen and Frank didn't speak. Sharon said, "Hm. Business is business, I guess. Lovely world, eh?"

They reached the front doors of City Hall, all donning coats, though the weather had warmed to the point that the parking lot was now empty of snow, its blacktop dry. Sharon said, "I'll be in touch. I'll keep pleading down as far as I can, and if all goes as I suspect, I won't need to see you until three weeks from today."

Frank and Karen thanked her, shook her hand, walked to their car, and did not speak until they were safely in their own kitchen.

*

"He wouldn't possibly do this."

"How do you know, Frank? What do you know about Dan?"

Frank paced. "I know that he's friends with Grant, and Grant wouldn't be friends with him if he were evil."

"Even if he sees a huge settlement? Even if he has potentially compromising information that could quintuple the payoff?"

"I just can't believe it." Frank took off his suit jacket and put it over the chair at the kitchen island. Loosened his tie. "Maybe Sharon was right, that this is just business. He told his partner about it and the partner simply sees it as an opportunity to get the insurance money. It's what they do. They'll get as much money out of the insurance as they can based on a no contest plea."

"Yeah, well, what if they can get more if they investigate? People do anything for money, especially those kinds of people. What if they convince the police investigators to look into it? They go back to Len and Melissa, Williams remembers that I adjusted the seat, they talk to Grant and Walter and Rob and John, all the people you were *drinking* with that night when you were supposed to be at the party!"

"They didn't arrest me, and it's all speculative. I picked you up and we went to the party."

"That's not what I told the police, Frank. What happened was the three of us went to the party together and I drove us all home in a blizzard."

Frank looked down, as much to admit she was right.

"Frank, they tested you at the scene. You were over the limit."

"It won't be admissible."

"Frank!" she shouted. "We've both lied! Admissible won't matter! Our story will not hold together. We've lied. To cover up what will now be changed to homicide and obstruction of justice."

"What do we do?" he asked.

Karen kicked off her shoes and dropped two inches. She removed her suit jacket and threw it over Frank's jacket. She went to the liquor cabinet and poured three fingers of vodka into a tumbler. She headed for the refrigerator but stopped, dispensing the notion of ice as beside the point, and took the drink in two swallows. She set the glass on the island, wiped her mouth with the back of her hand. She held the narrow end of the kitchen island with both hands, spread out to either corner, dipped down as if stretching her calf muscles, her long brown and blonde hair, with new thick streaks of gray, hiding her face. After many silent moments, she stood and raked her fingers through her hair, pulling it back. She took a deep breath, arched her back.

"We're not going to do anything."

Frank was quiet.

"As far as anyone is concerned, the current story is all that has happened and anything we do that does not jibe with that puts us at risk. There's nothing more we can do. Monday we'll know the lay of the land. Until then, we stick with the plan. We're not hiding. We have nothing to fear, we need change nothing. I am responsible for a horrible accident, and I will answer for it according to the law in three weeks. But I'm not going into hiding. In fact, we're going out tonight."

"Going out?"

"Yes. Nick, too. We'll go to Lola's."

"It'll be crowded."

"Exactly. And New Year's Day, we're going to Grant's. Call him and tell him that we changed our minds and would like to come if we're still invited."

*

Grant and Becky Alders' New Year's Day party had become every bit the annual tradition that Frank's boys' night holiday dinner and the Thompsons' open house were. Grant and Becky always made sure they got the day off at *The Plain Dealer* by working New Year's Eve; they had two kids, a senior and sophomore in high school. They had renovated a big brick house in one of the older neighborhoods, a wreck of a once-grand house that was now still ramshackle but in a lavish kind of way, with a new expanded kitchen, new baths, refinished hardwood floors.

Grant loved to cook and he worked to outdo himself; the food was reason alone to show up, even if it happened to be inconvenient or you didn't want to go. There was no better way to spend the do-nothing day that New Year's Day was, especially if you, like Frank and Karen, had no interest in college football. Grant and Becky invited forty or so friends, a little less than half declining due to holiday travel, so it was usually a perfectly sized crowd, not too intimate that you tired of the company. (The party began at one, and often the final guests were still playing pool on the third floor at eight or nine, after the Rose Bowl had concluded and Grant had created a separate distinct supper from the buffet leftovers and salad.)

Karen succeeded in convincing Frank that this was the perfect vehicle to spread their story—a brilliant device to make their story known to all their friends, a story their friends would surely repeat to friends of friends. So, as instructed, Frank emailed Grant the request to change their RSVP to an affirmative. Grant emailed back that he was glad and thought it a restorative thing to do. Frank responded with a request: would Grant mind sending out an email with the complete story to all those coming? Everyone in this gossipy social set would be dying to know what the story really was; surely rumors were already spreading. Frank didn't want any speculation whatsoever. He told Grant the story that Karen had told Anne Sutton, feeling certain no one would go to the trouble of requesting the police report; he relayed that they had attended the service of the woman, Sarah Childress, fifty-two years old, and met the sister, the only surviving family Ms. Childress had. He told Grant that the arraignment had taken place this afternoon, told him exactly what Karen was charged with, what she'd pleaded, and that a trial had been scheduled for the third week in January; Karen would plead no contest, and their attorney was 95 percent confident that if Karen received any jail time, it would be suspended.

He concluded by asking Grant to convey that they were grateful for the well wishes of friends in the midst of this tragedy, but they preferred not to talk about the accident and were offering this information simply to assuage their friends' concern. ("I.e., satisfy their morbid curiosity," Karen said, reading over Frank's shoulder as he typed.) They respectfully asked that the event stay out of conversation for the day.

*

"Frank!" Grant said on greeting them at the door, his dark hair looking especially bushy. The big mastiff called Ox pounded ecstatic figure eights around the three of them. Frank and Grant hugged. Becky, too, ever flushed and with her frizzy reddish-blond hair pulled into a ponytail, greeted them with the same natural warmth as ever.

"Karen," Grant said, earnestly. And he hugged her, two seconds longer than he normally would have. Then Becky. This continued over the next hour. The men acted as though they didn't know a single thing was amiss. The women didn't hide it so well and gave Karen long, emotive hugs. But no one said a word, and after the shock waves of the elephant's arrival, all was calm. "You know where the bar is," Grant had said. "I've got to get back to the kitchen. I'll have the food out in thirty minutes."

"Can I help?" Frank asked.

"Actually, can you chop some parsley for me? The kitchen is mobbed as usual, but no one's doing anything."

Grant had created a Southern feast: butter-poached shrimp with cheddar grits, hoppin' John, eggs he'd soft-boiled sous vide so they'd slip right out of the shells into the grits, sausage, thick-cut chewy bacon.

As Frank transferred the chopped parsley to a large ramekin, he heard, "*I know, right?!*" It was, unmistakably, the booming voice of Dan Jeffries as he handed his coat to Becky. The same heavy work coat, Frank noticed, that he'd worn a week ago. A few of the boys wore sports jackets, but most knew how casual Grant and Becky kept things.

"Jeffries is here," Frank said to Grant, just as Karen arrived in the kitchen with a glass of soda water and lime. "I've never seen him here before."

"No, he usually heads to Palm Beach with Rachel and the kids, but he claimed to have work."

"What do you mean 'claimed'?"

"He can't stand Rachel's mom. My guess is he told Rachel enough was enough and he wasn't going to put up with her society bullshit anymore or spend a week on tenterhooks worrying that the mother-in-law will get bent out of shape when one of the kids knocks over a Fabergé egg or sits in an upholstered chair in a wet bathing suit."

Grant removed a block of yellow cheddar from its plastic wrap and grated it onto a wooden cutting board.

Frank and Karen watched Dan lumber into the dining room, shaking hands in greeting and nodding and smiling, hunching down to hear and converse as he was so tall. Karen could see, with those eyes and dark curly hair and engaging and powerful disposition, why women found him attractive.

"You're friends with him," Frank said. "Good guy?"

"Yeah." Grant paused. "Definitely an acquired taste. Crazy bastard. But, yeah, a good guy. *Smart*."

"What about his work?"

"It's a living. I don't judge. He's a good family man, and Rachel is hilarious. And he's actually a really talented furniture maker. Hobbyist, but some of the stuff he builds is incredible. So, yeah, very interesting guy, never would have thought."

"What did you mean when you said 'acquired taste'?"

"Have a couple of cocktails with him and find out!" Grant grinned at Frank. "Gotta get the bacon before it burns. Could you finish this cheddar for me?" Grant turned toward the oven to remove a sheet tray of sizzling bacon.

Frank ignored the cheese and hurried to a large metal bin filled with ice and beverages over which Dan Jeffries was hunched, reading labels of various bottles. Karen, leaning quietly against the counter by the sink, watched. Frank reached down into the ice for a beer as Dan did. Frank noticed Dan's expensive-looking loafers, at odds with the Levi's and faded blue Oxford cloth shirt. Frank was quick to speak.

"Hi, Dan."

Dan twisted the top off his beer, faced Frank full on, back straight, and said with a huge and friendly grin, "Frank Markstrom! Good to see you!" Dan pointed over Frank's shoulder to someone who had caught his attention and strode off. Frank turned. There was no one else there. He watched Dan head to the living room and Frank returned to the kitchen.

When Frank caught Karen between conversations, he drew her aside and said, "What do you make of Dan being here?"

She shrugged.

"He's ignoring us," he said.

"Yes, exactly as he said he would."

Karen turned to her left when she saw Anne Sutton waiting. This first year, Grant and Becky had chosen to invite Anne rather than Walter, a decision made easier by Walter's decision to depart the city for the holidays.

Anne and Karen looked at each other. Anne said, "Helluva year, huh?"

And Karen hugged her hard. Anne had brought a date no one knew and introduced him.

*

Frank lay on the carpet staring at the football game with a few other couples, having eaten as much as he was capable of. He tried to maintain focus, which should have been easy as the second half was coming to an end with a 28-28 tie and Oregon, were they to beat Wisconsin, would get the first Rose Bowl victory for the Ducks in ninety-five years. But Karen appeared suddenly. "Frank?" she said, squatting to speak quietly to him. "I'm not feeling good—would you mind driving me home?" He didn't ask any questions. He all but leapt for the coat she held out to him. And he didn't say a word. He didn't even ask why she wanted him to drive—she always preferred to drive. After they were home, she took a long, hot shower and was in bed by eight and asleep by nine.

The following day, Karen abruptly decided to visit her father in Newton, Massachusetts, and, able to get a midday standby flight to Logan, she arrived at dusk, leaving Frank and Nick to move through the last holiday week on their own.

Two

When Frank, Nick, and Nick's friend Noah returned from the beach, Karen had just plunged four lobsters into a giant stockpot. "Hose the sand off, please," she shouted through the screened window overlooking the back deck. Nick and Noah talked so nonstop, and their conversations were to her so inane, she'd ceased to hear the content and only heard it as calming music. She knew exactly what they'd do. As Frank was using the outdoor shower, the boys would shower upstairs, put on old T-shirts and baggy shorts, and head into the woods or go look for sea glass on the beach until they got to the Watson cottage where, if they were lucky, Elizabeth Watson and her friend would be available to flirt with until she texted them to dinner.

The alarm on Karen's phone vibrated and hummed, the lobsters having been submerged for seven minutes. Using tongs, she placed each lobster in the cooler that had held their lunchtime beverages and still had a layer of ice floating on top. After the lobsters had chilled, she took each to the heavy, moated cutting board and, gripping the blade of the knife the way Chef Garreth had taught her at a cooking class last spring, she drove the blade down through the orange head of the lobster, crunching down through its face, pounding the back of the blade with the heel of her left hand through the remaining shell. She spun the lobster, flattened out its tail, and drove the knife through the back shell and tail, splitting the lobster, then rinsing the halves beneath cold water and leaving them in the sink while she halved the rest. The way she now held a knife, being able to dispatch the lobsters with such authority, gave her a sense of being a capable woman. *What else do we bring home alive to eat?* she wondered. She couldn't think of anything. Oysters maybe. She lifted the next cooked lobster, looked it in the face. *Oysters don't have eyes*, she thought. *Crack!* went the knife through the neck and head of the lobster, splitting it.

When all eight halves were back in the fridge, the pot had been dumped off the back deck, and the cutting board had been cleaned of the green lobster innards—the kitchen pristine and cooled from the evening breeze—she undressed, donned a large bath towel, and walked the planks past dune grass for a cool, nude dip from the beach one hundred yards north of their cottage. Few walkers passed at what would then be the early evening. And she could see them from either direction anyway. But she usually waited till Frank appeared, clean in his loose white shirt and faded jeans and bare feet, bearing a sand-free towel to wrap her in. But only after he made her walk nude practically the width of the beach so that he could regard her from the moment she emerged, dripping from the ocean. He enjoyed the perky bob of her breasts, nipples hard and bright pink from the cold water, her narrow hips, and the light brown, neatly trimmed V of her crotch. It was the least she could do, and she had always enjoyed the attention. He wrapped her in the big, soft beach towel. He hugged her from behind, pulled her long hair off her neck to press his mouth and nose to her to smell and taste the ocean on her tanned skin. But that was all. How cleansing these skinny-dips felt.

When she was clean and dry from the shower, she descended the stairs of the old cottage in a cotton sundress. Frank had finished the dressing for the potato salad and was now at the kitchen counter shucking peas.

She hugged his back. He set down the peas and twisted to return the hug. He stared into the brown eyes he had known for so long.

She returned the gaze and said, "Your eyes are smiling."

"Forever," he said and kissed her.

They'd been on Martha's Vineyard for the first five days of August and still had another five left of what had become a heavenly routine. She would help with the peas and at 6:30 they'd have a gin and tonic on the front porch and play a few rounds of backgammon. By seven or so, the grill would be ready, tonight for lobsters (Frank loved to finish them over coals), while she set the table and cooked the peas after summoning Nick and Noah to return for dinner. They would eat in the screened porch to the sound of the surf carried in on a breeze over Lake Tashmoo. They'd clean the kitchen and tonight would watch the news and some more TV perhaps. They'd gone into Vineyard Haven the night before, earlier in the week to Oak Bluffs, all in bed by ten, happily fatigued from the sun and ocean.

Today had been perfect, save for the unexpected wave of nausea that overcame her at the boatyard. She and Frank had begun the day with a 7 a.m. bike ride. Then they'd driven to the Black Dog and put their names in for breakfast. While Frank, Nick, and Noah waded along the beach, waiting for a table, she explored the boatyard. It was filled with planks and great curls of shavings and sawdust and strange tools and scale drawings of hulls in pencil on the floor. The nausea had come on so powerfully and fast that she had to cover her mouth and run outside behind a wood shed to retch, her sickness prolonged as she'd chosen the ditch used as the piss pot by the young boat builders. She assumed it was the early morning ride and the lack of solid food. She couldn't be pregnant, obviously. She was able to wash up in the restaurant and by the time she had finished, a table had opened up and their name had been called. The food made her feel better. Home to do some painting (she was working on an ink and watercolor portrait of the gray, cedar-shingled cottage as a thank-you gift); and Frank put in a few hours on a story he'd begun. She'd bought a lunch (and the lobsters) after breakfast so that they'd have a picnic and a snooze on the beach.

*

Karen was rocking on the porch swing looking off toward the ocean when Frank appeared with their evening cocktails.

They touched the crystal highballs—*clink*—and sipped.

She inhaled deeply. "We are so lucky."

This made him start, and when she saw his surprise, she knew what he thought she'd meant. "For the house," she said. "Lucky for this house." They sat and rocked quietly in the cool early evening air.

Frank's friend, Walter Sutton, had given him his share of the cottage. After his marriage to Anne had ended, he was allowed use of the cottage, but the new love of his life was forbidden. Walter accepted this without argument as part of his punishment for destroying his family, but he successfully lobbied to keep his allotted ten days to give to the Markstroms. No one was going to argue about that, given what poor Karen had been through, the whole family—they certainly deserved some island respite after the winter tragedy.

Lucky, though, was something that neither Karen nor Frank dared to think of in terms of the big picture. Threat would always loom. They didn't like to think of luck even in the little picture. They lived now in the moment—because truth was they had been fantastically unlucky, and it was a fact that they would always carry.

But in terms of physical consequences, having essentially gotten away with two felonies couldn't be called anything other than lucky. Karen had turned them into strong conspirators and everything, but *everything*, had worked in their favor—like a complex trip involving complicated transportations and tight flight connections, and every flight turns out to be on time, and their suitcases are the first ones to come out on the conveyor belt. It was that kind of ride—full of anxiety that it would all work, and relief when it couldn't have gone better. Once Karen committed completely to the story, she had known what to do at every step. Not least had been the unbelievable luck that whoever it was to eventually reach Len Thompson, who was likely trying to ease a brutal hangover with a stiff Bloody Mary the day after the party, had been told by Len himself that Frank, Karen, and Nick Markstrom had indeed been at the party. They didn't know why he'd said this and they didn't ask. Len and Melissa had likely been as hammered as most of their friends that night. And after all, they *had* been there, hadn't they? Karen had slipped a letter through their slot Christmas Eve day noting their presence at the party and their regret at not having had a chance to catch up. She said that she was writing to inform them of the tragedy that had ensued, and the fact that she, Karen, had been tested by police afterward and alcohol had not been involved. She was writing furthermore to make sure that while the unthinkable had in fact happened, it was being addressed as an accident, and Karen alone was being held responsible for it.

While Christmas was subdued, and the arraignment the following Friday had been nerve-racking, in retrospect, they needn't have worried. The report went from the DA's office to a lower office, which passed it on down lower. And Karen's testimony—from such an upstanding citizen and member of the community—had been taken at face value. The case had ultimately gone to trial at a low-level city court. She was sentenced to thirty days in jail, suspended in exchange for seven hundred of hours of community service and a year's driving suspension except to fulfill her work and community service commitments. Even this work seemed a kind of gift: giving art lessons to kids in juvenile detention and teaching illiterate adults to read. Work she found so rewarding, she intended to continue it after her hours had been fulfilled.

And Frank, she'd watched him throw himself into his work with such abandon and focus that he'd been promoted when his firm announced a merger with its main competitor in April. It required considerably more hours, but the raise would be enough to put toward Nick's college fund, substantially easing their financial worries.

So: Lucky.

Karen's plan had worked. She had been brilliant at every step.

*

"May we be excused?" Nick asked when the lobsters and peas and potato salad had been consumed and they were all wiping butter from their chins with paper napkins.

"Take your plates to the kitchen," Frank said.

"I got some ice cream sandwiches," Karen said. "They're in the freezer."

"Thanks for dinner, Mr. and Mrs. Markstrom," Noah said.

"You're welcome, Noah."

When the boys had left, Frank and Karen smiled at each other. They were further surprised when the boys returned to take *their* plates. "Thank you!" Frank and Karen both exclaimed. Noah was slight and had yet to grow the way Nick had; he was already filling out and stood a head taller than Noah, who looked two grades behind.

"We're going back to the Watsons', okay?" Nick asked.

"Just bring your phones so I can reach you."

"Yes, Mother," he said, mock dutifully.

When the boys were gone, Frank said, "God, those were good lobsters. I could eat another."

"I should have gotten more."

"Nooo," he said. "I'm getting fat."

"Nonsense. And we're on vacation."

"Yes, that was my excuse."

"For what?"

"I bought a pack of cigarettes."

"Frank!"

"I know, terrible."

"Vacation. Just don't bring them home."

"Promise. Join me?"

"I'll join you, but I won't smoke. I don't trust myself."

In their bohemian days, they'd both smoked. The pregnancy forced her to quit and she was glad for it, and once the baby was born, he'd quit, too. After many smoke-free years, Frank would occasionally have a cigarette at a party, but never more than a few in a given year, something he was careful about and even thought about when he'd bought this pack, given that his father had died of lung cancer three years earlier.

When they'd cleared the remains of the table—a bowl of lobster shells and emptied claws and balled up napkins, the unfinished bottle of chardonnay and the silverware—Frank reached to a top shelf in the kitchen for the cigarettes and an ashtray. She split the remaining wine between two fresh glasses. "Don't feel guilty," she said as they stepped out onto the front porch of the cottage. They sat in two wicker rockers, a wicker table between them.

"I don't," he said and took that luxurious long first drag.

"Well, you don't need to make it look so enjoyable," she said.

They sat quietly in the balmy summer breeze and stared out toward the ocean.

"We owe Walter big-time for this," he said. "I think this is the most relaxed I've been since."

"That was the plan."

"I just didn't think it was going to be possible."

"Life goes on, Frank. It has to go on."

"How are you, my love?"

"I'm fine," she said, looking away. "Tell me about the story you're working on."

"Not yet."

"Please."

"When it's ready." He smiled at her.

She stared back. His sandy hair had lightened and was thick from the salty air. He looked uncommonly healthy, almost aglow with summer.

"What?" he asked.

"Nothing," she said, smiling. "You know, Nick's getting to look just like you. A lucky young man."

"Our young man."

Karen brought her heels to the edge of the seat and hugged her knees. "Nick talked to me about it the other day."

Frank straightened in his chair, waiting.

"It was our first morning here, you were still asleep and I was making us pancakes. He must have sensed the relief of being here, away from home on an island. He asked if we were going to be all right. I said yes, and then he asked if he'd done anything wrong. I hadn't realized how much it was still on his mind—though how could it not be for all of us? I asked, 'Have you told another living soul?' He said no. And I said, 'Then no, you've been a savior.'"

"And?"

"I told him the truth. That it was something I was still working on, still trying to understand, and that I would likely be doing so for the rest of my life. As would he. And that we are bound to do this. Obligated. And that we are lucky to be doing so together and not separate, that the most important thing was our family, that we can weather anything if we stay strong together."

Frank nodded.

"And he hugged me. He's gotten so big. I was astonished at how big he's become in just these seven months, how hard he hugged me."

"He loves you."

"He loves you, too."

"You know he was angry with me," Frank said.

"When? You didn't tell me."

"The week after New Year's, when you went to visit your dad. He and I had a long talk. He had the impression that I'd made you do it. That you, we, hadn't been honest with him. I tried to tell him something along the lines of what you did. But at the time, we were still in the thick of it. I didn't know how it would end."

"But it doesn't end, does it?" she asked him.

He looked north toward the ocean and shook his head.

"I told Nick that he was the most important thing in the world to me," Karen said. "That our family was, and that I'd done what I did to *save* the family. And in this we had succeeded. And he said he knew that now."

Frank took the last drag on his cigarette and crushed it out. He turned to her and said, "You did. You *saved* us. You turned on a dime and you saved us."

He reached for her hand. She put her feet down and leaned forward to take his. They looked into each other's eyes.

He wiped away a single tear that streaked down the side of her nose and said, "Enough. We're on the other side. Let's not look back."

She nodded quickly. "Not look back." She sniffed hard.

"Tomorrow we're out on the water."

"So nice of the Watsons," she said.

Fred and Katie Watson, dear friends of Walter Sutton, noting how well the kids got along, had asked them out for a sail and lunch on their fifty-three-foot, center-cockpit yawl. It was a wooden boat, built in the 1930s and restored here on the island in Vineyard Haven Harbor, in the very boatyard she'd been exploring that morning while they waited for their name to be called at the Black Dog.

"I'm really looking forward to it," he said, and after a minute of silence and nothing but distant waves, rustling oak leaves and dune grass, he said, "I'd like to look over this morning's pages, do you mind?"

"No! Please, do. I'll clean the kitchen."

"Sure?"

"Yes. I'm so glad you're writing again."

"Promise to look at stars on the beach with me when I'm done?"

"Nothing would make me happier," she said.

*

So many stars in the sky, she thought as she pulled a single bed sheet over herself, such lovely peace. The warm, salty air . . . She lay on her back staring at the ceiling. She said goodnight when he turned out the light, and he rolled over to kiss her. He'd checked on the boys at the other end of the house (they'd gotten the room with the television and Frank and Karen had taken the smaller room with the queen-size bed and more privacy) and found them dead asleep, exhausted from all the fresh air and sea and sun.

She knew why he was telling her this.

Frank nestled into her. "Mmmm," he purred.

She had come to bed in cotton underwear and a loose white tank top. He reached beneath it, ran his hand over her soft skin, then slipped a finger beneath the waistband of her shorts.

She inhaled brusquely and held his wrist. "I can't yet, sweetheart."

Frank rolled over, exhaled brusquely. She waited for him to speak but evidently he was tired of talking about it, tired of pleading.

She held his wrist and rolled to her side to face him. "Soon, I hope, my love."

When he didn't move, she rolled to her back and they lay still, twin figures between cool white sheets.

After long moments, he said, "Of course." He kissed her cheek, then put a soft pillow over his eyes to sleep.

Karen's vision adjusted to the dark; she knew sleep would not be easy. When Frank had slipped his fingers beneath her waistband, the nausea from this morning in the boatyard spilled up through her bowels and stomach and into her chest and seemed to twist the muscles of her neck. She knew then what it had been at the boatyard, she'd placed its source. She tried to will herself to sleep, but having recognized where it had come from—what she'd tried for months to keep buried along with all the rest of the awfulness—she couldn't stop her mind from returning to it, the week after the accident. New Year's Day.

*

Grant had put the spread of food out by 2 p.m. as promised. Dan Jeffries had chosen to eat standing up in the kitchen, so Karen and Frank had eaten in the living room with three other couples they didn't see often and so had much catching up regarding everyone's kids. Karen would have liked to have had a cup of coffee and depart, but she had insisted that Frank stay for at least the first half of the Rose Bowl. Frank had more or less stopped drinking since the accident, a few sips of wine with food. But here Karen stepped in and told him, "No changes. Drinking soda water all afternoon isn't you. You always drink beer. If you don't want to drink, at least put some lemon in a lowball glass with ice water and sip that."

He followed her instructions. She was in the driver's seat in every way.

By the time dusk fell and the Rose Bowl kicked off, Karen had had just about all the small talk she could bear, and had been considering asking Frank to leave before she'd intended, when Grant, having seen off the last of those not staying for the game, found her in the foyer.

"Karen," Grant said. "How *are* you?" He gripped her shoulders and squeezed them. They hugged. She kept her face on his chest. It felt good, not having to pretend.

"Not good. Stressed. As you can imagine."

"I don't think I can."

"Thank you, Grant. No you can't, and I appreciate your realizing."

"I see you're drinking water."

"I feel better, that's all."

"I do have something nonalcoholic that might ease the stress, a little, if you want." He removed a fat spliff from his shirt pocket, raised his eyebrows.

"You know, Grant," she said with a smile. "I am going to take you up on that. That might help." Pot had always relaxed her and put her at ease, never made her paranoid or introverted, and right now she'd have lunged at anything resembling balm for her nerves.

"Come," Grant said, and led her through the cleared living room and out to a screened porch, empty but for a glass table and metal chairs. The temperatures had climbed into the high forties and all that remained of last week's snowstorm were the dark melting hills of ice built by the plows. They sat.

"Can I join you?" said a voice, startling Karen.

It was Dan.

"Absolutely," Grant said. "Anyone else out there wanting to bake?"

"They're all watching the game." Dan set a tumbler, filled to the brim with a pale liquid and ice, loudly onto the glass tabletop. "I've gotten into your tequila."

"Reposado is the good stuff," Grant said.

"That's what I found!" Dan pulled a chair raspingly out from the table and sat across from Karen. "Hi, Karen!" he said, smiling vividly at her, unblinking.

"Hi, Dan."

Dan leaned in toward Karen, ensuring she'd look at him, then swooped his head toward Grant, who sat between them at the head of the small porch table.

"You are one bad motherfucker in the kitchen, dude! Now I know why everyone keeps talking about the food! I'm not missing this again!"

"Thanks."

Dan turned to Karen, his eyes electric, his smile enormous, and said, "Am I *right*?! Karen, did you taste those shrimp! Huh? Did you?"

"I did," she said and turned to Grant, seriously, though her stomach roiled from nerves. "They were really good. Everything was delicious."

"Poached in butter!" Dan exclaimed. "What the *fuck*? Those things were better than a reach-around! Right?!"

Grant laughed at his friend, who drank noisily from his lowball, and Karen did her best to smile, but she suddenly didn't feel like getting high anymore.

"Smoke?" Grant said, removing the joint.

"Why do you think I followed you out here?!" he said, grinning at Grant and then at Karen, animated, as if to say: "We are about to have an incredibly great time together, aren't you excited, isn't this *great*?"

Karen tried to inhale only so much as to not call attention to the fact that she didn't want to get high anymore, but it was strong and she felt it quickly. And then she knew she was high when suddenly, after what had seemed thirty seconds, Grant, as though he'd been there hours, said, "I gotta put round two together."

Dan said, "Mind if we have a few more tokes?"

"Be my guests. Leave what you don't smoke here for when I'm done."

Dan winked and said, "Many thanks!"

As soon as the winter aluminum door shut, Karen pounced: "Did you know we were going to be here?"

"Sure did, got Grant's email, same as everyone else. Very interesting email!"

Again, that grin, so easy and friendly, but in such an exaggerated way, it sickened her with worry. She remained stone-faced.

"I thought we were ignoring each other."

"We were, but I wanted to get high and have none of my own." He swigged from his drink, his green eyes slightly lidded now. "And you're so ... Damn, what's the word I'm looking for?" She stared at him and watched the eyelids rise to reveal bright green irises completely surrounded by pinkish whites. He grinned and said, "*Fetching*."

She held still, watching him. "Yes?" she said. And she was no longer afraid of him. She'd calmed. She was high, but she didn't know if she were hyperalert or simply stoned and reckless. She asked herself what time it was, then looked at her watch—6 p.m., what she'd guessed.

"You're not going anywhere, I hope."

"Why do you hope?"

"Because I've always wanted to ask you. Is it true you have *perfect* breasts?"

At first she started with a blink, not at his crass delivery, just surprised. But she realized what he was referring to and instinctively hid her face with one hand. "Jesus, that was ten years ago."

"*Legendary!*" Dan shouted with glee.

Karen shook her head. This would never go away.

Not long after Frank and Karen had moved in, their neighbors (lesbians they didn't socialize with much anymore) had had a welcome-to-the-neighborhood barbecue for Frank and Karen, including a mixed social set of both couple's friends. It had started early and gone late, and Karen stumbled into a conversation by the swimming pool in which two women she didn't know were arguing over who had the better chest. Karen said a slurry, "Puh-lease," and removed her shirt. She held out her arms like a religious figure. After a stunned moment, one of the women said, "Win!" and walked off. Others nearby cut conversations short to regard Karen as she turned in place for all to see, the men astonished and delighted, their wives simply astonished. Frank had seen it, too, when the hush fell, people stopping mid-sentence to gawk. He hurried to cover Karen. She tried to push him away but was too drunk. Frank said a courteous thank you and mouthed "I'm sorry," as he bundled a topless Karen through a break in the hedge and led her across their driveway to their back door.

When she woke to a painful summer Sunday morning, Karen was dismayed that it had not been a dream, but Anne had been the first to phone Karen and say that what she had done was "fucking hilarious!" And "Good for you."

So the story had now become legend, and Karen was rumored to have the finest breasts in the city, or at least among those in their set.

"Yeah?" she said. "Well that was ten years ago and it's a judgment call anyway."

Dan grinned, then he stared at his drink, and she tilted her head, regarding him. He drank.

She said, "Want to make the call?"

He took his eyes off his tumbler and looked at her, his eyes alert, no longer lidded, grinning happily. "Not with other people around."

"Where can we go?" she asked.

*

Dan had moved with sober efficiency. They'd headed up the back stairway, out of view of a dozen or so in the den watching the game, as though toward the billiard room. But instead of taking the second staircase up, he directed Karen toward what was clearly Grant and Becky's bedroom. They went into their bathroom, remodeled into a huge bathing salon. Dan closed the door and locked it. "I'm sorry," he said, "but that was too good an offer to pass up. I'd never forgive myself."

"Okay," Karen said, leaning against a double vanity. She pointed at him and said, smiling. "No touching, okay?"

Dan only stared at her, his large chest heaving.

"Okay?"

He said nothing, but she lifted her dark sweater and the shirt below it over her head, let them fall to the carpet. She reached behind with both hands and unfastened her bra—delayed tensely by hands that had begun to tremble—and let that fall to her right on the shirt and sweater. He stood a yard away, staring at her chest the way a starved man stares at butter-poached shrimp and grits.

"Well?" Karen said, holding her palms out.

"Good Lord," Dan said and, almost not of his own volition, moved toward her. Though she said, "Whoa," once, she didn't push away the hand that clutched one breast, then the other. His hands were calloused and scratched. The squeeze was powerful, definitive, and soon she felt his heavy lips on hers, the scratch of his whiskers and his thick tongue, the faint taste of tequila.

Karen grabbed first for his crotch, then pulled his buckle toward her. She began to undo it, but he took over and she undid her own as well. She had only one leg out of her trousers before she felt herself lifted off the ground and set roughly on the vanity between the two sinks. She didn't even get a good look at his cock before it slipped abruptly, shockingly into her—she gasped, it felt huge—and she had the strange sense of watching this from outside herself, stoned, and yet still feeling the unfamiliar piston hitting new parts of her insides. He'd lifted both her thighs to pull her into him, her shoulders falling back so that she reached to support herself, knocking over and shoving tubes aside, a toothbrush and cup rattling into one sink. She heard herself grunting as if it were someone else. She looked at his face, his green eyes staring at her tits, which bounced with his thrusts, staring at her neatly shaved, demure bush, and his cock entering her and entering her again, thrusting harder and faster each time, until he looked up and their eyes locked and he shivered with a final thrust. She had enough traction with one hand to reach the other over her lifted left thigh and clutch his upper back to hold him in, to keep him inside her. Their eyes remained locked, their mouths agape. A few more concluding thrusts, the final spasms of an animal already dead, and it was done. He fell out of her, stumbling back, pants at his ankles, till his calves felt the divan situated by two windows, blinds closed, and he sat, leaning back. She had slid off the vanity and now stood leaning against it, naked but for her socks and the pants and underpants attached to her left ankle. She regarded him in full, his large dick already retreating, his satisfied smile, which seemed also friendly and warm. She did not return it. She walked to the toilet and sat down, pressed her knees together, put her elbows on her knees and looked at him. Then she pulled four squares of thick toilet paper from the roll and spread her legs, examined herself, and wiped, slowly, with delicate care.

"Here I thought you were a provincial little high school art teacher," he said, beaming contentedly. "Karen. You are one *helluva* fuck."

She ignored him, but stared at the toilet paper, folding it carefully.

Then she looked at him, remaining seated, and asked, "Do you have a good marriage?"

"I do."

"Do you love your wife?"

"I do, very much."

"Then why did you do what you just did?"

He smiled a waggish lidded smile, his electric power clearly spent. "I don't know. I'm a *baaaad* man." He watched Karen remove some more toilet paper. "The sight of your breasts," and he grinned wide now. "Like the briefcase in *Pulp Fiction!*" He chuckled.

"You heard me say no touching, didn't you?"

"You hardly resisted."

"But you heard me, correct?"

He nodded with a cautious smirk.

Still seated, she wiped herself a third time, then, still clutching the folded toilet paper, slipped her right foot into her pants, pulled the pants up her leg, then stood and fastened them.

"More to the point is why you—" and he stopped when, rather than tossing the three tightly folded wads of paper into the toilet, Karen stuffed them into the pocket of her jeans. "Ahhh," he said.

"I'm glad you value your marriage," she said, fastening her bra. She bent to pick up her sweater and shirt. "Frank and I would hate for your wife and kids to find out what you just did."

He stood, shaking his head, and pulled his jeans up, but fell back dizzily before he could fasten them.

"You didn't have to do it," he said.

"Yeah, I did." Now she was completely dressed. "One hundred percent, remember?" She looked at herself in the mirror. She found a brush and brushed out her hair. She lifted the white cup and toothbrush out of the sink, put brush in cup and set it back on the rim of the sink. She surveyed the wreckage of tipped lotions and soap bottles and hair gels, but left them. She turned to Dan and said, "I value my marriage and my family, too, more than anything in the world."

He didn't rise when she moved across the room to the door, unlocking it.

"You *are* good," he said.

"You didn't realize what I was doing?"

"I guess you could say I wasn't thinking."

"And here I thought you were so smart."

"Not as smart as you, apparently." She opened the door. He smiled a lidded, mischievous smile and said, "Hope it was worth it."

She stared at him without malice and said, "You'll make sure of that, yes?"

His smile conveyed a hint of admiration, but he said nothing. Karen departed, closing the door behind her.

*

Karen took the back steps, went to the closet for her coat and Frank's. And there she smelled it again. The canvas Carhartt work coat Dan had worn to their house just the week before. It filled the closet with the smell of cedar and sawdust and machinery oil, a smell on which it all hooked in her mind.

She went to the den where ten people were spread out on couch and floor. Empty plates were stacked on the chest that served as a coffee table. Frank was stretched out on his side on the carpet, propped on one elbow, staring at the game.

"Frank, I'm not feeling good—would you mind driving me home?"

He quickly stood, as did Becky, who asked, "Everything okay?"

"Fine," she said, "Just a little lightheaded. I need to rest."

Grant entered from the kitchen and scanned the room, perhaps looking for Dan, then to Karen said, "Leaving? I've got more food coming."

"Yes, I'm sorry, I don't feel good."

They said quick good-byes and departed. Karen handed Frank the car keys as they descended the front walk. "You mind driving?" she asked.

*

After an hour wide awake in the dark, the cottage silent but for Frank's soft snoring, Karen left the bed and took a Valium she still had from the ones her father's doctor prescribed in January. She hadn't needed them in several months, but tonight her mind hummed. She went quietly downstairs.

Fuck it, she thought. She found Frank's cigarettes. She looked in the fridge and, finding no open bottle of wine, poured herself a vodka. She sat on the front steps of the cottage to enjoy the first cigarette she'd smoked since she became pregnant with Nick.

The smell of the boatyard, the sawdust and old oily machinery—she hadn't known why she'd responded as she did, why the nausea. She had worked so fiercely to bury—even deny—the event, as though she could treat it as she'd treated the accident. But now that she knew it, recognized that it meant he was still inside her, she could no longer deny it. That smell would always bring it sickeningly to the surface. Indeed, she would never forget the feeling, inside, of being fucked by a reprehensible man who was not her husband. She wished to forget it. But she couldn't. The sex, his unstoppable urgency, had been thrilling in addition to being neces-sary—the sex itself, the strangeness of it, the danger, his animal force, her power over it and the pleasure of that power, and the guilt at the pleasure, entwined with the sex itself.

She'd risen the next morning early, knowing she needed to leave, had to clear her head and take care of her body. She booked a flight to Boston to visit her dad, who still lived in the house she grew up in, arriving by nightfall. No questions asked by her father, and Frank didn't question it. He understood her needing to get away and to be with a father she adored. She'd solidify the story of the accident with him. She felt a longing for her mom, dead twelve years from breast cancer, with an intensity unequalled since the day of the funeral. On Tuesday she saw an ob-gyn whom her father knew (he didn't ask any questions, given her state) to see if a morning after pill would work and to get checked out generally by a doctor she'd never see again. Who knew if Dan had passed something on to her, that she could pass on to Frank, who must never know about this. Never.

She began to feel at ease in the home she'd grown up in, her dad's famil-iar cooking, the smells of her childhood, healing as if from an actual rape, though she didn't consider it that—the opposite, if anything—and from the legal nightmare she couldn't know when or if she'd ever wake from. She spoke with Frank daily. And on Friday, Frank told her the news: their civil attorney, Buck Heard, had called to say that, amazingly, the Klums were accepting a six-figure offer from the insurance company to forgo a trial. Frank said that Heard chuckled at how easily they were getting off. He said that initially the Klums' attorney had alerted him that they *did* intend to litigate and would be asking for more money, more money by far, well beyond what their insurance covered. "*Millions*, with an *s*," Heard told Frank. Heard had been unnerved by the phone call, since he knew that the Markstroms had no umbrella policy.

Karen didn't respond.

Frank continued. "The way Heard described it, it was clear that this was not simply a play for substantial walking-away money."

"Walking-away money?" she asked.

"The insurance company pays the family in order for everyone to avoid an uncertain trial. But he said their attorney was an asshole—Buck's exact words were 'unscrupulous but effective and not to be fucked with any more than you'd poke a copperhead with a stick.'"

But, instead, the Klums had departed Cleveland for good, declining, as they'd originally promised, to sue Karen.

"Did you ask who was representing the Klums? Was it Dan's firm?"

"No, I don't care and don't want to know. It doesn't matter. *It's all going away.*"

"All going away," she repeated.

"You don't sound relieved," Frank said.

"Believe me, I'm relieved."

"Buck was clearly calling with not just good news, but surprisingly good news. The walking-away money is a pittance compared to what they could have gotten. For whatever reason, the Klums' attorney called and said that they didn't have a case and that the family had decided not to litigate. End of conversation. Heard said this was nothing short of bizarre, but he wasn't going to ask why, look a gift horse in the mouth."

"How's Nick?" she asked.

"Nick's fine. How are you?"

"Flying back tomorrow. Can't wait to be home."

"My love," he said. "Are you okay?"

"Of course I'm not okay."

"But this *is* good news."

"I know it is, Frank."

Karen woke up in her own bed on Sunday, and life resumed on Monday—Nick back to school, Frank back to his work, she to hers in the depths of winter, but the days were already waxing toward inevitable spring. Their new, old life.

Now, smoking her first cigarette in years, she remembered how powerful this poison was, how heady and lovely and releasing. *Who cares*, she thought? She deserved this, as did Frank. Here in the balmy August air of Martha's Vineyard, listening to the hiss of midnight wind through grass, the smell of sand and ocean, she felt free for the first time since the night of the accident. Free, in that it would not kill her with its weight. But only because she accepted that the smell of sawdust and oil would always nauseate her, she would always know that unfamiliar presence inside her, just as Sarah Childress would always be dead, and Frank would always carry the guilt of having been the instrument of her death. It's what they now lived with. This was life happening to them, and their pushing back against life, and life pushing back harder, and on. They were, in spite of everything, happy. Weren't they? She and her love, the boy she'd fallen for one random summer night by a pool, a quarter century ago, the father of her child, the man who remained by her side. They were together, as they'd vowed to be two decades ago, bound forever by their child and their love, their burgher's existence, and now also by their conspiracy, their obstruction of justice, their ongoing felony.

Would they make it? She loved none other than Frank. But she didn't know. An anger now stayed inside her along with everything else that perpetually threatened to corrupt whatever goodness remained. And how could she possibly predict the long-term effects on her son as he moved into adulthood, carrying this secret always—would it calcify or corrode? It was a law beyond her control: an equal and opposite reaction. Things fall apart. She no longer knew if they could endure it.

She had at last accepted that they had gotten away with something terrible—it was theirs, and theirs alone—and that she would carry an additional terribleness with her always, a terribleness that set what good-ness was left in dramatic relief. This blackness and light gave her the under-standing, an appreciation even, that when you commit fully, absolutely, to a single conviction—right or wrong, true or false—life pivots, doors slam shut and others open, and you are hurtled forward in directions you did not intend.

Sally Forth

PART I

Scott Murray left the throng of Chelsea Market and turned right on Ninth Avenue that languid, overcast afternoon, eager to be in his cool room at the Hotel Gansevoort where he could transcribe his notes for the current magazine story in the white noise of the air-conditioning. The teeming avenue seemed composed not of individuals but of one gray mass he longed to be apart from. He had one more set of interviews tomorrow before he could return home. He pined for home, for Martha, his love still, after all these years; and he missed his kids—sweet nine-year-old Will and Susan, age eleven but already moving toward an adolescence he wished he could keep her from. He looked forward to the solitude of his third-floor office, where he could work in peace and emerge when the smells of Martha's cooking drifted upstairs to draw him toward dinner, a glass of wine, some television, some reading, and then sleep.

Sally had seen him first, when he was midway between West Fifteenth and West Fourteenth Streets, he recalled later. She stopped, her arms out, mouth open in amazement but smiling. That's what he saw. He took an involuntary breath. Sally smiled even when she was sad because she always saw the humor in the sadness as well, which was partly why he had adored her, but here her happiness in this moment seemed unalloyed.

"*Scott?*"

"My God, Sally."

"Scott!"

There had never been a thing about her that didn't bring a smile or that failed to comfort him in some way. Even her name, Sally Forth, he loved—something of an error on the part of her immigrant parents, Russian Jews who changed their name from Fortheim, with hopes of assimilation in central New Jersey in the 1960s and unaware that *sally* was a verb as well as a name. While Sally was in college, a cartoonist gave a newspaper comic strip this name, which she laughed about when she pointed it out to Scott. That's how funny she was, she told him—someone named a comic strip after her. And here she was, arms outstretched, mouth agape. New York City so unraveled him that he did what he could to turn it off. But her, he could not turn off. She was as vivid as neon against the dull crowd.

He hadn't seen her since well before 9/11—he couldn't have placed when without thinking back. And 9/11 had been four years ago.

He'd called her immediately after the attacks to make sure she was all right because she and her husband lived downtown. She was fine, they were unscathed, staying with her parents in New Jersey, and would soon be able to move back downtown. They'd talked for an hour, and he remembered hanging up the phone, smiling and happy.

How was it that she could leave him laughing in the midst of the country's greatest tragedy? But somehow she'd always had an alignment with tragedy; an innate sense of it was one of many gears that moved her forward through the years, and this was yet another reason he loved her.

He didn't hug her immediately because of the stroller between them.

Sally said, "Yep! Enough shtupping and look what pops out!"

He smiled, and so did she.

"Awww," she said. "How are you?"

"Good, good," he crouched before the child, asked his name.

"Arthird."

"Are-third?"

"Sometimes I call him Third."

Scott tilted his head.

Sally said, "On the birth certificate it's Edward Arthur Adams the Third. Which I didn't want, but I like it now. He's the third!"

Scott put his little finger in three-year-old Arthur's hand and said, "Hi, little one."

"Hi!" the toddler answered.

Scott stood and hugged Sally and kissed her cheek, two moments longer than he needed to in order to smell her hair, grown long again, still golden though darker than it had been in college. And still the same scent, which made his heart race.

After quick explanations—she now lived in the West Village, he was working on a magazine assignment that had brought him to New York City—she said, "Do you have time? Can you walk home with me?"

"I do have time, so yes," he said.

"Excellent!" she said. "I'll make us iced tea. I'm melting! God, I hate summers here."

She had always been definitive, and he'd liked that, too. Reversing course, he pushed the stroller for her and she snaked her arm through his and pressed her head against his shoulder as though she had been doing this forever. He felt immediately conscious of the physicality, the sense of comfort and ease they'd always shared. She looked at him and he looked at her and she said, "I can't believe I ran into you!"

"New York is the city of coincidences, remember?"

"I gave you that book!" she said.

"I know."

A line from *Endless Love*. She'd made him read it because she said the sex scenes were so well done. He had agreed. But then when they were having sex, it had made him uncomfortable because he didn't know if she'd given him the book with hopes of similar sex, which he didn't think he could provide. He could have asked her. She was direct. But he didn't because he'd made it clear that he was in love with Cat, his girlfriend back at Princeton. That had been clear. That had been clear from the start, and throughout.

Sally had also pressed him to read *Tess of the d'Urbervilles*, which made him understand that so-called literature could also make for great storytelling. And she made him read *Lolita*, which was the book that solidified his desire to be a writer. And she read him Rilke and Emily Dickinson and "The Love Song of J. Alfred Prufrock" in bed because she knew he'd never read any of it on his own.

*

Sally and Edward's apartment on Greenwich near West Twelfth Street, spacious by city standards, comprised two bedrooms and a living room, with family photos Scott paused to admire: Sally and Edward's family in front of a Christmas tree, Edward in his suit and dark glasses, struggling both to smile and to contain a squirming infant version of himself. A photo of Edward in tails and Sally in wedding gown, dancing—a wedding Scott had been unable to attend, since Martha had been due with Susan that week. He didn't know that he'd have gone anyway; Sally was happy, that was all that mattered, and he was glad for her.

Her kitchen was big enough for a table with three chairs, where, having navigated the toys and crumbs of crushed Goldfish that littered the floor, he sat across from his long-ago friend drinking green tea over ice and hearing about her life as a new mom—"no more tenure-track rat race at Columbia," she'd said, "the students, what a horror show, even at the MFA level"—in New York City and her beloved banker husband.

"I've become a terrible wine snob," she said. "It's terrible. What finally having a little expendable cash can do to a wannabe poet."

"Hardly a wannabe."

"Well, one volume by a small press does not a poet make."

"You're either born one or you're not. Publishing has nothing to do with it."

She smiled at him as she had long ago.

He chalked up his disorientation that afternoon to the city, but looking back on it later that night in his hotel room, thinking of her, it was really the memory of riding a train from Brest to Paris, both of them college juniors on a year abroad. Paris, where they didn't have sex that one morning and things changed, and not long after that they were back at their different colleges for their senior year, then off into their adult lives. They rode a *lot* of trains back then. From Bristol on the west coast of England, where they went to school, to Bath; from Bristol to London (frequently); from London to Brighton on the southern coast; from London to Scotland (once). They sat between trains to smoke cigarettes and listen to Simon and Garfunkel and the wind blew her hair so that it trailed like a banner and made her eyes water so that they sparkled, and Paris was ahead of them and their whole lives were ahead of them, and now here they were: successful adults, two parents with partners they loved, sitting across from each other, drinking iced tea. Staring into each other's faces, smiles undiminished.

"The Third will stay down for at least an hour," Sally said. "Every successful relationship has a third thing—I was just reading this the other day. Edward and me and now Arthur, the third thing!"

"If you need to get things done—I remember how valuable these nap-time hours are."

"What could be more valuable than this?" she asked. And then her face—long and narrow with thick golden eyebrows, wide blue eyes, a rather large but chiseled nose he quite liked, full pale lips—suddenly became a mask of shocked recognition. And she slapped her cheeks with two hands.

"I conjured you here, to West Fourteenth Street."

He relaxed and said, "You conjured me."

"Yes!"

She vanished again and returned with a photograph. "Two days ago, cleaning out our bedroom closet, I came across some old photos, this among them. Tell me, Scott, what are the odds?"

"You never did believe in coincidences," he said, taking the photograph from her and smiling at it. A broad, sandy beach, northern France, Deauville. They were in beach chairs, sunning.

"I saw that photo and remembered how gorgeous you were," she said, resuming her seat. "And I willed you here. You're still gorgeous, by the way. You've aged well. Just so you know. You still have your hair, so you'll be keeping it."

They both leaned forward, close enough that she could reach out and rake her fingers through his hair. He continued to stare at the photo despite her touch. He knew that if he looked up, he'd want to kiss her. She'd had that effect on him from the beginning. And she was the gorgeous one, not him. That long hair lit by the sun. Those amazing breasts. Long meaty legs.

"You were so funny," he said. "You bought a yellow polka-dot bikini."

She leaned back, and he could finally look up. "When your childhood transistor radio played that *stupid* song endlessly and years later you run across a yellow polka-dot bikini in Deauville, France, how can you *not* buy it? I saw it as a personal and cultural obligation."

Scott chuckled and shook his head.

"I still have it," she said.

"Really?"

"How can you throw out a yellow polka-dot bikini?"

He laughed again.

She said, "But I don't foresee any bikinis in my future, dots or no."

"Why?" he asked. She was thinner now than she'd been. Then she'd had a fleshy voluptuousness that he loved; Manhattan had made her lean.

"Stretch marks, general aging. Sagging tits. You know."

Scott couldn't stop looking at the photograph of this girl, twenty at the time. He said, "Speaking of the latter, I was always trying to get you to take off your top, as I recall. We were in France. Women were eating topless at cafés."

"I might have but not with your friend there. What was his name?

"John, but we called him Wilhelm."

"Wilhelm! That's right. I liked him, he was funny."

"You asked him to take this photo," Scott said.

"Expressly for the purpose of using it to . . . conjure you *up!*" she said, jabbing her finger at him as she spoke. "Twenty years later."

"Is there something you needed specifically? Is that why you 'conjured' me?"

"My life is great, so no. But whyever it happened, I'm glad it did."

She reached across the table for his hand. He set the photo down to take it.

And they talked for three hours, so unconscious of the time that when little Arthur toddled into the kitchen and crawled into Sally's lap, Sally looked at the microwave clock and said, "My God, four o'clock. How did that happen? He never sleeps that long." They had spoken of nothing, of their lives. Sally had met Scott's wife once years ago, but she said she felt she knew her because Scott had written Sally ardent letters when Scott and Martha had met. "I loved your letters from the front lines of *love*," Sally said. "You always were the romantic."

"I thought *you* were."

"I was the realist, actually," she said. "Don't you remember?"

"I guess not."

Her life was perfect, she told him, except that it had taken her too long to get pregnant.

"Two miscarriages," she said. "That was a drag. I got really blue after each one."

"I remember how you got blue. You got real blue. Some weeks I could barely go near you, I remember."

"Not true, you'd bring me chamomile tea in bed."

"And it would make you cry!"

Sally laughed loudly. "I know, terrible!"

"And then you'd stay up for forty hours writing an epic poem that wasn't due for a month."

"All that morbid poetry I pressed on you, trying to be Sylvia Plath."

"You always got yourself out of it."

"Didn't have a choice. And after the pregnancies I learned to keep the blueness in its own private room," she said. "Its own private suite, in fact. Walk-in closet and everything."

"High thread counts on the sheets?" he asked.

"The best."

"Eight hundred?"

"See, that's just like you to know something like that," she said.

"I'm a journalist. A hazard of the profession is to remember things you no longer have any use for. . . . So after the miscarriages, did you stay in the room long?"

"I'd order room service. We'd have coffee, me and Blue, and when guests arrived I'd close the door behind me. Lock it from the outside."

"How was Edward with it?"

"A saint."

"Good."

"It was his mother who was the problem. Elizabeth. My mother-in-law? She started treating me differently." Scott squinted, not fully understanding. "Hard to say how, just kind of colder. Like the suit that she'd picked out for her son wasn't the one she'd thought she'd ordered from Brooks Brothers."

Sally leaned back in her chair. "But then we never really got on exactly swimmingly. I'm a Jew. They're classic WASPs, cocktail hour and everything. They name their dogs after liquor."

Scott laughed.

"When their last Lab, Brandy, died, they got a new one and called her Old Pale."

"As in VSOP?" Scott laughed. "You always make me laugh."

"Almost," she said.

She looked away, took a sip from her tea. "So. Elizabeth. Drove me crazy. Always putting her hand on my belly and saying, 'There's a bun in the oven.' Stupid phrase. And why do people think that once a woman is pregnant, they're suddenly allowed to touch her? I wasn't even showing!"

Scott looked into his glass, feeling bad; how many round bellies he'd touched without asking. He'd never thought—he used to be proud when people had pressed their palms to Martha's nine-months-pregnant belly, as if it were some special achievement that others might adore. He wondered if Martha resented it; she hadn't seemed to.

Sally said, "'Hands off, bitch!' That wasn't exactly going to help the situation."

"No," Scott said, grinning.

"So when I said, 'Hey, Betty, that bun? It came out half-baked. Not even a quarter baked, actually.'"

"You said that?"

"Yes, I was pissed. And because Edward obviously couldn't bring himself to tell his mother. They're such tightwads with the emotions. So I said it, and Edward choked on his martini, and his mother blanched. She looked at Edward and he got all formal with her about the facts. And that was that. Not another word. She only wanted to know from him whether we could try again, anything preventing that? Once they knew that there was no reason why not, it was never mentioned again."

"Not even an 'Are you okay, Sally?'"

"Nope."

"Sounds so cold," Scott said.

"I think it's just the way they are. She's actually all right, we get along okay, I guess, and she's devoted to Edward, her one and only."

"But your two miscarriages."

"Yeah, I made Edward write a letter to his parents after the second one."

"Really."

"I couldn't go through that again. So he wrote, and I slipped into my private suite and stayed quite a while. After that one."

He reached across the table to squeeze her hand and she smiled, sweet and sad, at him.

"How did you get out of the room?"

"I don't know honestly. Comes a time when you just have to, well, sally forth!" And she laughed and he laughed.

He couldn't remember laughing as much in so long.

He said, "And now you have Arthur."

"Yes, I do, my perfect little man."

When she said this, Scott felt suddenly warm inside—his smile on the outside turning up in the deep inside because his old friend was clearly so happy.

"He really is perfect," Sally said.

"Of course he is."

"No, diagnosed," Sally said. "When he was born, I asked the doctor if he was okay. I always expect the worst. But the doctor, this was the next day when our pediatrician came in to examine him, I asked if everything was okay, expecting something along the lines of 'I'm not really liking the sound of his heart murmur,' but instead the doctor locked his eyes on mine and said, 'He is *perfect*.'"

"Like the werewolf's hair," Scott said.

"Ha!" she said, "Warren Zevon, exactly!"

Another of their favorites from that time, that time when songs felt so important.

"So that *is* an official diagnosis," Scott said. "Perfection."

"Official."

As if on cue, this was when the perfect child had appeared in the kitchen and Sally had remarked on the time and lifted her perfect child into her lap.

"Hey," Sally said, reaching for a juice-filled sippy cup. "Last time we talked, forever ago, you told me you had an idea for a novel. Did you ever write it?"

"Still an idea. I may one day. Too busy making ends meet for now."

"Don't wait," she said.

"I know what you're going to say next."

"Then hear it again, dearest of old friends: 'Don't *wait*. Don't think it's morning when it's late afternoon.'"

This was from another book she'd given him way back at the University of Brighton. He knew the passage well.

*

The Hotel Gansevoort in the Meatpacking District lay a few blocks south of Chelsea Market, which housed the Food Network. Scott was in town to interview its executives and producers for the magazine *Fast Company* about the business of food as entertainment. He didn't think much of the subject, which was partly why his editor had assigned him the story. He preferred more straightforward business and environmental reporting. He'd taken a long walk after saying good-bye to Sally, feeling light and refreshed. He sat at the hotel bar with a glass of white wine, a chicken Caesar salad, and a folder of magazine and newspaper clippings. Between bites, he slogged through an article in

Gourmet magazine about the chef Emeril Lagasse; apparently the signal moment when food stepped over into entertainment was Lagasse's merging of the cooking show format with a *Tonight Show* format, complete with a band.

Scott had initially wished he hadn't taken this assignment, but with his book proposal to write about Key West—that uncommon community and the environmental issues it faced—still unsold, he'd had no choice. Now he was glad he had; he'd run into his old friend and had spent a lovely afternoon with her. Always better to get out of the house, better to say yes despite his inclination to say no, to hole up in his office. He was now very happy to have taken this assignment. He'd do an especially good job on it now; in a superstitious way that annoyed him, he felt he owed it to the story that had reunited him with his old friend, as if it had somehow been cosmically engineered. It was just good karma to do an especially attentive job here.

Scott questioned why he always ordered the chicken Caesar salad, which was never very good. He'd ordered it a hundred times and never thought to question it before. He supposed he liked that it was always pretty much the same no matter where you were. He was a creature of routine and predetermination.

Back in his room, he called Martha at home in Cleveland, after she'd have fed the kids and walked the dog.

"Quiet, Chekhov," Martha said after saying hello. Their golden Lab was a barker. "I swear, he knows it's you when you call."

"I doubt that." Scott thought the dog not very bright as dogs go, but the family did cherish the creature. "How was your day, my love?"

"You don't want to know."

True, but he said, "Of course I do."

"I spent *half* the morning trying to get our Time Warner bill down. Now *half* the channels we wanted we don't get. So they're sending someone out tomorrow. Who knows when. But I have to *be* here. Finished paying bills. Worked. Groceries. Picked up Will from camp. Then Susan. She watches too much television."

Will and Susan were both enjoying the last weeks of summer camp. Martha, a writer as well, had given up her newspaper job to have the kids and had just in the last year been picking up assignments she could write from home—for parenting magazines, health columns.

A familiar silence ensued, one they were both easy with.

"You mentioned bills. How are we?"

"The same. Fine. For now."

"Right."

"How did your day go?"

"Fine," he said.

After a long silence, he said, "I ran into Sally Forth on the street."

"Really? How is she?"

"She's great. She and Edward finally had a long-yearned-for baby."

"That's wonderful."

Silence.

"Okay," he said. "Well."

"I'm going to watch some television and go to bed," she said.

"That sounds like a good idea."

Silence.

"I'll talk to you tomorrow, then."

"I love you," she said.

"I love you, too, sweetheart."

After he hung up, he tried to read more articles in preparation for his interviews, but he couldn't concentrate. He felt tired from the day but it was too early to sleep. His mind returned to the pleasure of the afternoon. Scott thought of the smell of Sally's hair when he'd hugged her good-bye and kissed her cheek, little Arthur on her hip. So unchanged . . . He nearly swooned from the memories that the smell returned to him, and with such immediacy. He hoped she hadn't seen—she did give him a look, but an inscrutable one. She said, "Give me a call when you're back in town next time, okay?" He promised.

Scott decided to return to the bar. Perhaps a whiskey would relax him enough to focus for a little longer on the stories he needed to be up on for tomorrow's interviews.

The bar was crowded and loud with conversation. He squeezed into the single vacant seat, and it felt good not to be alone in his own head up in the hotel room. He gave up trying to read and signaled for the bartender.

"Another?"

"Yes, but a different one this time," he said.

He scanned the bottles. "Make it the Macallan," he said with what he felt was appropriate grandiosity. He'd always loved the arrogance of the "the."

He sighed deeply. Sally could right then and there be the girl she'd been in Bristol, where they'd loved to stroll the Atlantic coastline. They'd met that fall of their junior year abroad, her long hair blowing in the cool, autumn sea air.

The bartender asked Scott if he'd like another, and he looked at his glass in surprise. It was empty. He hadn't remembered even pausing to consider the flavor.

"Yes, but maybe something peaty this time."

"We have Laphroaig."

"Perfect."

On the train from London to Scotland with Sally that one time, when they'd entered into Scotland, a new ticket taker walked the aisles, conversing with the passengers and marking tickets with hole punches. A jovial, large, dark-haired man in a blue uniform and cap. When he took Sally's ticket to mark it, he spoke a full paragraph, a long collection of sentences, laughed like a man who enjoyed good food and drink, then carried on his way. Scott looked to Sally and she covered her mouth to conceal laughter and snorted hard through her nose.

"What?" Scott asked. "What did he say?"

"Scott, I have no clue! But it was English! It was the English language. And I didn't understand a word he said!" She rested back in her seat, held his hand, and said, "I am going to love Scotland, I just know it."

What a fun trip that had been—though neither of them had ever been so cold. Perhaps February wasn't the right month to venture so far north after all. Sally insisted that the best time to visit any city was off-season—that's when you could get to know a place because you met the real people.

And another thing she insisted on: they would not get a room. They would sleep in the train station if need be. They were both poor, and travel was not the time for rooms anyway. This would save money, and she loved the romance of tramping. This became an increasingly unappealing prospect as they walked shivering along dark streets. They found a bar whose windows were steamy and they hustled inside. Sally very quickly made friends with a couple their age, students at the University of Edinburgh as it turned out. These people, Scott was relieved to find, they could understand. The young man had curly dark hair and his girlfriend had very blonde, very short hair and crystal blue eyes. He had asked where Scott and Sally were staying.

"We don't have a place," Scott had said. "She wants to sleep in the train station."

"And that is what we'll do," Sally said.

"Are you mad?" the new acquaintance said.

Scott only tilted his head at Sally.

"That's nonsense. You'll stay in our room."

"No," Sally said.

"Are you serious? Thank you!" Scott said.

Sally sighed and turned away.

Scott smiled at their new friends.

The young woman said, "Sally, don't you think you'll be a wee bit cold?"

"Do you fancy whiskey?" the young man said.

"Of course!" Scott said.

"I have a bottle of the best, my favorite, anyway. Much discussed here."

And soon they were in the dorm room of these two wonderful Scots, drinking Glenmorangie. The conversation went on so long that the young man finally asked if they'd like a coffee, which seemed pleasantly contrary to Scott. When they finished the coffee, the happy couple stood and said, "Okay, then, we're off. Have a good trip."

"What?"

"You're staying here, I'll stay in her room," their new friend said.

Scott almost wept with gratitude. He tried to express this. They were utter strangers. Scott was undone by the generosity but more by the trust. The dorm room was a tiny single, and he had been wondering how they would all fit, but he hardly cared as the room was so warm and the whiskey so delicious and the coffee so soothing. Sally embraced them both and said, "You have to be the sweetest people in all of the United Kingdom."

"Cheerio," he said and the girl had said, "*Ha a guid rin.*"

Sally turned to Scott, covering her smile, then said, "I *love* Scotland."

Scott finished his Laphroaig and signaled the bartender. He asked if they had Glenmorangie, and they did.

"Do you think they'd mind if we fucked?" Sally had asked.

"Sally, I don't know if I feel comfortable with that."

"Why? I'll be on top. We won't mess up the sheets. You like me on top."

"I do! But it's been such a long day, and these sheets are so warm and cozy." What was this material—flannel? Flannel sheets, he'd never experienced this.

"Okay, you win this time." She kissed him and she turned on her side and he spooned into her warm, naked body and they fell happily asleep.

"One more Glenmorangie, please," Scott said.

But the bartender said, "Sure?"

Scott hesitated only a moment but said, "Yes, please, but then the check."

Was he already slurring? He was once an eager and ebullient drinker of all beers and wines and spirits. But no longer. He and Martha had both tapered off considerably after Susan was born. He had a cocktail on the weekend, but rarely if ever during the week. A glass of wine with dinner most nights but that was it.

The bartender poured the second Glenmorangie.

Scott lifted his whiskey and inhaled its fumes. He sipped. It wasn't as he'd remembered even the last one to be. He tasted again. It seemed to have turned. He wondered if the company had been eaten by a conglomerate and done something to cut costs. It wasn't what they'd drunk in Scotland, and it was no longer his favorite single malt.

He struggled over the check. First how much tip to leave. Then the addition. He scribbled out the first effort and rewrote what he thought was the correct number. He scratched his room number and stepped off the bar stool, composed himself, then concentrated on walking straight. He found the elevators, made it inside. He walked the long, dark corridors to his corner room, but when he reached the door he failed to stop completely and slammed into the wall.

"Sideways gravity," he said, repeating something Sally had once said when they were stumbling home from the pub, laughing, drunk on scrumpy, the West Country cider they both loved.

Inside, Scott kicked off his shoes, tossed his blazer over the desk chair, and fell facedown on the still-made bed. When his head stopped spinning, he'd undress. That wouldn't be for several hours, as it happened, and upon waking in the lighted room, it was a good ten seconds before he could place where he was.

He struggled through the morning interviews with the fog of his hangover making him slow and ineffective. The effects of the city, compounded by his headache, made him anxious to leave. He arrived at LaGuardia four hours before his flight, hoping he could catch an earlier one back to Cleveland.

*

"How was your trip, hon?" Martha said, taking his jacket to hang up and setting his carry-on by the basement, as she knew it would be filled only with laundry.

"Productive."

"Good," she said and kissed him and hugged him tightly. "I *missed* you. It gets so lonely at night once the kids are in bed."

He stared at her warm brown eyes and lovely plump cheeks and stroked her short, glossy brown hair. "It's so good to be home," he said to her and kissed her forehead. And he gave her another protracted hug, so soothing did the safety of home feel. Such *relief* had rarely overcome him this way on his return.

He looked at the kitchen clock. Ten. Will would be asleep, but Susan might still be awake.

"Can I reheat some pasta for you? Or did you eat at the airport? I saved the news so we could watch together."

"That's so sweet of you. And yes, some pasta would be perfect. I'm going to say hello to Susan."

"Careful," Martha said.

Ever since Susan had turned eleven, the whole tone of the house had changed with her new volatility. She was a straight-A student, he adored her friends, but she'd begun the years-long march toward independence from her parents. A necessity, but he missed the sweet girl who would run to him and leap into his arms when he returned after a trip.

He knocked on her door. Nothing. He knocked again.

"*What*?!" came the reply.

He entered her room.

"I just wanted to say hello, I'm home."

"Oh," she said, removing an earbud. "I thought it was Mom." She actually stood to hug him, and he was grateful. "Hi, Dad. I'm glad you're back."

He kissed her crown, she returned to her bed and her music on the iPod they'd given her for Christmas. "Don't stay up too late," he said. When he received no response, he quietly closed her door.

He peeked in on Will, so beautiful in that innocent sleep, already taking on Martha's dark good looks.

After he'd eaten and they'd watched the news, he and Martha sat in the clean kitchen talking until Martha said, "Scott."

He looked at her.

"I told you it was boring, but I'm not going to say even that if you're not going to listen."

"I'm sorry, I drifted. I'm just tired from the trip."

Martha stood abruptly and said, "I'm going to bed."

"I'll join you."

After he'd checked the doors to be sure they were locked and turned off the downstairs lights, he found Martha in her bathrobe, brushing her hair before the bathroom mirror. He squeezed her hips, kissed her neck, and slid his hand inside her robe to discover she wasn't in the customary nightgown.

"Mm," he said into her neck.

She tilted her head to offer more neck.

"Let me wash the travel off, okay?" he said.

When he'd showered, combed his hair, and brushed his teeth, he walked to the bedroom, let the towel fall to his feet, and climbed into bed.

The brevity of their lovemaking did bear noting—they'd become efficient at it after all these years—but the quietness . . . Ever since Susan was Will's age, they'd begun to make love so that they wouldn't be heard. They'd become so adept, one might not have known the two were even having sex at all, so silent and shortened the actions had become.

*

Martha fell quickly asleep but Scott lay on his back thinking of Sally—and the sex they'd had for two full semesters. How could he have known, age twenty, that this would be the best, most unencumbered, and delightful sex he would ever have? One can't know these things. But he should have known, should have seen it. By the time they'd reached Paris . . . how at ease and open she was.

And the blow jobs. Sally gave amazing blow jobs, and she knew it. Once, she'd stopped midway and looked at him. Propped on a pillow, he opened his eyes to look at her—why had she stopped?

She said, "Do you ever wonder how you stack up?"

"Stack up?"

"Yeah, size-wise. Don't all guys?"

"I suppose."

"Do you want to know?"

"Um, okay."

"You're a little bigger." But then she said, "No, you're normal. But very pretty."

"You could have stopped after the first sentence."

"Aww," Sally said, staring at it. "I've let all the air out."

Scott sighed but smiled.

"Don't worry, I can patch this up," she said, and as always she was good to her word.

Absolutely the best blow jobs in the world, Scott thought as he turned to his side, back toward Martha, and tucked into a pillow.

*

Scott had become so distracted by his brief visit with Sally that he found it hard to focus on his article. Seeing her had opened the floodgates from those happy days. He thought perhaps if he made a time line of their connections, the act would somehow allow him to close the drawer for now on Sally. The magical year abroad on the western coast of England had begun in the fall of 1983, when Scott and Sally were both twenty. They parted in Paris the following July, having spent ten solid months together.

They went their separate ways. He graduated from Princeton and she from Rutgers in 1985, both with degrees in literature. Scott secured a job at a small newspaper in St. Petersburg, Florida. He had traveled once to New York City. Having been in touch occasionally by mail after college, they met and had a good time reminiscing. Two years later, he'd introduced Martha, a fellow reporter and by then fiancée, to Sally. Scott and Martha were in New York on vacation from hot Florida. Scott arranged to have dinner with Sally in an inexpensive tavern near NYU. Martha and Sally got on well, which didn't surprise him, as you had to be seriously deficient for Sally not to find something amusing in a person. She made friends with most everyone. And Martha for her part was smart and a very good reporter.

That would have been 1989. He wouldn't see Sally again until six or seven years later. Was that it? Scott flipped the pages of a legal pad to a fresh page, past the Food Network notes, to write down the dates. Yes, it was 1996, the year he and Martha and one-year-old Susan had lived in the Hudson Valley, in Rhinebeck, to write the book on the Hudson River, which he always likened to a biography of the Hudson. He had contacted Sally, who by then had married Edward. Why didn't he drive down, she asked, even spend the night with them if he didn't mind the couch? Martha was happy to remain behind. She had no interest in bringing a baby into the city or imposing a family of three on the newlyweds.

*

It had been a good visit at first. Scott found a parking spot around the corner from Sally and Edward's one-bedroom in the financial district, but he couldn't tell if it was a legal spot. It was his first time parking in the city and even the drive in, all the way down the West Side Highway, then navigating the downtown streets at rush hour, rattled him. He must have spent twenty minutes circling, trying to make sense of the street parking signs, before giving up and deciding to risk it.

The doorman of Sally's building sent him to the eighth floor. He walked the long, beige corridor to 8H and pressed the bell. Sally opened the door and smiled at him as if he were the most hilarious sight in the world. "Scott! I can't believe it!"

"We've been planning this for a week. You were expecting me, yes?"

"But you're *here*!" She opened her arms wide and he walked into her embrace.

When they released each other he said, "You cut your hair!"

Sally wrinkled her nose and said, "Yeah. What do you think?"

"I like it," he said, one moment too late. The long ropes of blonde and golden brown hair had become a sort of professional do, cut above the shoulder.

"Don't lie, I can tell."

"I'm not lying."

"I don't like it either." She stepped into the kitchen and stirred onions in a pot. "I thought it would be more appropriate given the socializing Edward has to do as a wealth management relationship facilitator." What this was, Scott had no idea, but it sounded too boring even to ask about. "It's a lot easier to take care of, I'll say that. And it'll grow."

"Edward," she called out. "Scott's here." To Scott, she said, "He just got home from work, changing. Sort of."

"Sort of?"

"You'll see."

Edward Adams stepped into the hallway pressing the knot of a skinny black tie into his collar. He wore a hound's-tooth checked jacket, white shirt, and narrow-legged dark trousers short enough to reveal an inch of bare ankle above leather loafers.

"Edward," Scott said, "Good to finally meet you."

Edward shook his hand, gave Scott a small bow of the head, and said, "How do you do?"

"I'm well, thanks, but sorry I didn't even give you time to change."

Edward's brow furrowed, heavy eyebrows above Clark Kent glasses, and he said, "But you did."

Sally said, "The suit comes off. This is cocktail attire."

"Then I'm underdressed, forgive me." He looked at his jeans, sneakers, and a white button-down, non-iron shirt.

"Don't be silly," Edward said. "Whatever you're comfortable in. This is what I'm comfortable in." He cleared his throat and pushed his dark frames up onto the bridge of his nose. He had short, dark hair and brown eyes, and a dark brown mole above his right eyebrow. Despite the sartorial finery, or perhaps because of it, he seemed to Scott the sort who would have been picked on at school for his slight frame and odd demeanor. He didn't seem big enough to Scott to support the ebullient spirit of Sally.

Sally left the kitchen and gave Edward a kiss. "I forgot to get cheese and crackers, can you run across the street?"

"No cheese?" he asked

"I forgot!"

"Nuts?"

"Nope."

"How can we be out of nuts?"

"One of the great imponderables, Edward. How will we move forward? But forward we must."

Edward sighed and retrieved his wallet from the ledge above the kitchen counter, which opened onto the small living room/dining area.

"Scott, go with him." Sally left the kitchen to speak into his ear. "Keep him focused. He gets distracted."

"I can hear you, you know," Edward said, sounding hurt.

She flapped her hands up at the both of them, shooing them. "Both of you, go. I have cutting and chopping and stirring to do, then I can feel free to talk."

*

The grocery store was large and so brightly lit as to call attention to the scuffed and dirty floors. Edward retrieved a basket. Scott followed him to the dairy section, where Edward chose a quart of half-and-half. "Sally always forgets." Edward next found the snack aisle and put Planters cocktail peanuts and Blue Diamond smoked almonds in the basket and headed toward the cheese. Scott didn't notice a trace of distraction, only efficiency. On to the cheese, which he stood before, scanning the selection.

"I like St. André. Is that all right with you?"

Scott had never heard of St. André. "I'm sure it will be delightful."

"It is," Edward said. "It *is* delightful. Now, crackers, and that should do it."

He brought Scott to the shelves filled with crackers. "This is where I have a problem," Edward said. "She did say crackers as well as cheese, did she not?"

"She did."

"You see, I don't normally do the crackers. Crackers are Sally's purview."

"Perhaps I can help," Scott scanned perhaps twenty feet of shelf space given over to crackers and failed to help.

"The mind boggles," Edward said.

Scott paused to think. "Okay, we're in the Ritz and Triscuit section. Does Sally buy those?"

"I don't think so. I believe she bought Wheat Thins once, and she was surprised at how *small* they were." Edward lifted a box of Wheat Thins from the shelf. "She wondered if they were made by elves."

Scott said, "Made by elves *for* elves, I believe."

Edward nodded seriously, said, "That's something Sally would say," and put the box back.

"Triscuits are good," Scott said.

"They are, but she always gets something thinner and smoother."

"Perhaps this is why they make Triscuit Thin Crisps," Scott said, pointing.

Edward held out his hands. His fingers were slender, pale, and delicate. "Exactly!" he exclaimed. "How to make a decision?"

"We could just buy Cheese Nips, two in one, and put the St. André back."

Edward nodded, apparently thinking the joke was a suggestion, but pursed his lips. "Sally doesn't eat orange food."

"Why?"

"I don't know. I'm working on it."

"Carrots?"

"Nope."

"Lobster?"

"If it's out of the shell."

"How about a peach?"

"I've never seen her eat a peach. She does like the album though."

Scott chuckled. "Yes, we used to listen to that in England. I'm glad she still does."

"We've only been married a year, so perhaps I will see her eat a peach one day. I'll let you know. Do you eat peaches?"

"Too afraid," Scott said.

Edward looked at Scott, perplexed, and said, "Hm," in a way that indicated he'd have to think more on this, but that it wasn't all that uncommon. Sally would have understood and laughed. Edward slipped the basket over his arm, and walked further down the aisle. "This is hopeful," he said.

These shelves of crackers seemed much more cheese-friendly to Scott as well.

"Here we go," Edward said. "This is what my mom buys, these will work." He lifted a box of Wellington water crackers.

At the same moment, both Scott and Edward turned to an older woman in the aisle pushing a cart. She had stopped and had been watching them. "I just have to say," she said, "you two are *adorable*."

Scott and Edward stared at her for a moment, then stared at each other. The woman smiled and carried on. They watched her depart, then looked back at one another.

"Come on, darling," Scott said. "Sally told me to keep you focused."

*

Edward set the plastic bag of groceries on the counter after Sally had kissed his lips and said, "Thanks, snookums."

He said, "Everyone thought we were a gay couple."

Scott said, "*One* woman."

Sally laughed her wide-open laugh, showing her big, bright white teeth, and clapped and said, "You two would make an awesome gay couple!" She detected something in Edward's expression. "It's a compliment. And you two just met, so I love that you and my old pal look like a married couple. Should I be jealous?"

"It's not that. I think she saw me as the *wife*. I don't want to be the wife."

Sally said, "Well, Scott does have five inches and forty pounds on you." She patted Scott's belly. He had gained weight when Martha became pregnant and kept it on. "Plus, the dresser of the couple is, well, you know. You are kind of natty."

Edward continued pouting until he had made a very large martini, straight up with a twist, for himself and Scott, and poured a glass of white wine for Sally. They all relaxed and ate nuts at a small table that folded in and out to make space. Scott made a note to remember the name of the cheese. Sally said the crackers were perfect.

Sally's chicken and barley soup, along with an excellent baguette, toasted and spread with garlic butter, and a spinach salad with hard-cooked egg and red onion, were lovely as was the easy, often hilarious conversation between eccentric Edward and ebullient Sally.

But how to explain why the overnight trip ended as it had?

Scott hadn't done anything out of the ordinary. Edward had departed the table first, at nine, saying that he needed his sleep. He warned Scott that at 6 a.m., he'd be rattling about, making breakfast, but would try to be quiet. Scott stood and gave Edward an awkward hug. Then he and Sally stayed up for a couple more hours talking as easily as they always had, but now, both thirty-three, he spoke of the surprises of being a parent, of his work; she about the drudgery of academia and the happiness of being newly married.

Scott said, "I'm glad to have met Edward, and I like him."

"He likes you, too, I can tell."

"And the two of you seem really happy. The way you stroked his hand at dinner was so sweet."

Sally grinned and said, "*He's* so sweet."

It had been an enormously sweet, Sally-like gesture. While Edward had explained to Scott the details of pairing which clients with which money managers, she had reached for Edward's hand, and regarded it as she stroked the backs of his pale, slender fingers, then turned it over to stroke his palm. And Edward didn't skip a beat in the conversation, as if she did such things all the time, which she likely did.

"When you stroked his hand I noticed he wears no ring."

"Doesn't believe men should wear jewelry."

"Really?"

"He doesn't even believe in wristwatches. Those big Rolexes appall him. He carries a pocket watch."

"Sally, he just doesn't seem your type at all."

"What's my type?"

"I guess I have no idea."

She shook her head at him.

"So, what is it about him?"

"I don't know," Sally said, looking away to think, then looked back to Scott and said, "He makes me laugh!" And then she grinned at Scott—her bright, beaming, disarming smile, all those fat, white teeth and full pink lips. "And he adores me and makes me feel safe and at home."

After another hour of talking, Sally stifled a yawn and said she had to sleep. She got ready for bed, then made up Scott's bed on the couch. She gave him a long, tight hug, kissed him on the cheek, and said, "Sweet dreams. I'll make us grits and bacon tomorrow morning." Then she bounced off in her white terrycloth bathrobe, and he heard the bedroom door close softly. Scott tucked into the pillow, and the next thing he knew it was 5 a.m. and he felt like he was having a heart attack.

He got up, drank water, and tried to return to sleep but he could not. His heart raced. His breathing became quick and shallow. He felt an urgency to get back to Martha, to their small rented apartment in Rhinebeck. He dressed, folded the sheet and blanket, and wrote a note apologizing that he had to make a surprise departure. All was well, he just needed to get back upstate pronto. Thanks for all.

Once safely on the West Side Highway in the gathering light, the pressure eased. Scott tried to understand the nature of his attack. It was his new life as a parent. All these things . . . He would find his car gone—stolen or towed, irresponsibly parked. He worried about Susan, who had a cold when he drove off. He felt guilty abandoning Martha with their infant. He had work to do. The pressure in his chest seemed to ease with each mile north along the Taconic Parkway, but then the oil light went on and the engine overheated. By the time he reached a gas station, the car was smoking. He prayed it was only a lack of oil. He dreaded taking their twelve-year-old Vovlo to the mechanic because it always needed something they could scarcely afford.

*

Scott studied the dates on his legal pad. That had been the last he'd seen Sally—fall 1996—till this most recent reunion. Her form, vanishing in the white terrycloth robe. He had no contact with her for five years after that odd, abrupt departure. None. He thought of her any time a news story from Paris or London or Scotland came up. When certain songs played—"Melissa" from *Eat a Peach*, or anything by the Doors or Simon and Garfunkel—he thought of her. He thought of her once the hard cider market opened up in the United States because they'd drunk so much scrumpy in England. He thought of her whenever he saw a volume of Emily Dickinson. But these thoughts were like flashes, fire and powder, followed by pleasant smoke quickly dispersing in the breezes of his increasingly lucky life. He'd reached her by phone after 9/11 to ensure that she and Edward were fine. They'd caught each other up. And now this past trip, the chance meeting on West Fourteenth.

When they had spoken by phone four years ago, he'd been toying with an idea for a novel and had described it to her then. She had been enthusiastic about it at the time and encouraged him to write it. He almost started it, but he couldn't in good conscience spend time on a venture one had to presume would deliver little if any income. Some of his books sold well enough to earn out their advances, and Martha would bound into his office with a royalty check that had miraculously, it seemed, arrived in time to get them out of a financial pinch. But he couldn't justify writing fiction with a wife (who'd given up her work), two kids, and a mortgage on a house that, really, was more than they needed. He needed all the writing artillery available for his journalistic work.

Scott tore the legal sheet out of his pad, with the dates written in a column below her name, Sally, underscored: 1983–84, 1990, 1996, post-9/11, and now July 2005. Scott folded it, reached into a drawer for a folder, slipped the sheet in, and labeled the folder's tab "Sally." He then filed it in its own green file folder. Scott was an aggressive organizer and filer and backer-upper, having once misplaced notes for a long story for *Esquire*. He thought one more time about her, smiled at her contented life with Edward and her perfect son.

Scott was now able to focus on his article for *Fast Company* and food as an entertainment business. He hoped his book editor would buy his proposal to write about Key West and give him the money he needed to write about that uncommon place. If that didn't go through for enough money, he didn't know what he would do.

They were perpetually broke, it seemed. Living from scant book advance to the next freelance piece.

They always got by, though, and would continue to do so. With this, he thought of Sally's admonition from just three days earlier, in her kitchen, with Arthur in her lap. *Don't wait. Don't wait.* At forty-two, he was, as Sally would have put it, half-baked. When he was fully baked, he didn't want to look back and realize that he hadn't even tried to do what he had once most wanted.

So, that night, after reading to Will and saying goodnight to Susan, who was currently deep into *Harry Potter and the Goblet of Fire*, and kissing Martha, already in bed and turning pages in a book, he went downstairs.

He was a creature of routine, and she'd called out, "Not coming to bed?"

He said, "I have some writing to do."

Then he did something he rarely did: he poured himself two shots of an expensive bourbon he'd bought to have on hand for guests. Last Christmas someone had given them a silicone ice tray to make extra large, square ice cubes. He had filled it, but now they had shrunk. He used one anyway and refilled the tray so that they would be fresh tomorrow if he found that he could actually get words down tonight.

He wrote the first three hundred words of the story he had described to Sally four years earlier, a story that had been unconsciously ripening. The words came easily, as though his brain had already been writing it on its own in its own secret quarters. He had put on Mozart's *Requiem* because that was the mood of the dark love story he'd conceived. When the last of the bourbon was gone, and the water from the ice cube had melted and been consumed as well, Scott stopped writing.

For the next nine months, five nights a week when the family's schedule allowed, and when holidays or travel didn't intervene, Scott sat at his desk at 10 p.m. with a bourbon, played Mozart, and wrote until the glass was dry. He could usually draw it out for ninety minutes, by which time he'd have five hundred new words. He had so little hope for his story, and felt so guilty about spending his free time on it, that even in his own mind he referred to it as his "secret project."

He reread the Reynolds Price novel Sally had quoted from, *A Generous Man*, so that he could find the "Don't wait" passage; he'd forgotten that it was sexual in nature:

He took his hand back to his own fat crotch, cupped the fullness there. "This won't stir a warm rice pudding, not now, no more. Remember this, son. It won't cost you nothing but it cost Rooster Pomeroy most of the sweetness life can afford— don't wait, don't wait. Don't think it's morning when it's late afternoon."

The passage led him to find an old high school poetry textbook to reread Marvell's "To His Coy Mistress." This would work its way into the story he wanted to tell, he knew.

Thy beauty shall no more be found;
Nor, in thy marble vault, shall sound
My echoing song; then worms shall try
That long-preserved virginity,
And your quaint honour turn to dust,
And into ashes all my lust

Once, two weeks into his secret project, Martha, in nightgown and bathrobe, ventured to his third-floor office with its oddly shaped spaces and slanted ceilings, to ask what was he was *doing* up here. He stopped the music as though he didn't want to share even that.

"Just some personal writing," he said.

She frowned. "Is it something you can share?"

"I hope so. When, or if, I can finish it."

"Is everything okay?"

"Of course."

"Okay," she said, with a look of concern.

PART II

In 2009, Scott returned to New York to meet with his agent and his new editor. He had been with the same house and same editor for all of his nonfiction books, but that editor was unable to convince her superiors that they could successfully publish Scott's fiction. However, his agent was able to sell the short novel about love and work to a small literary publisher.

He had emailed Sally hoping he could see her and tell her the good news, but he didn't hear back from her. It had been five years since they'd shared iced tea in her kitchen. Arthur would be eight. Scott had been worried—why wouldn't she respond?—but he didn't pursue it beyond the one email.

Life had become busy. Susan, now a high school senior, was in the midst of searching for colleges, and Martha carted her to various states looking for a good fit. The previous spring the two had gone as far south as Georgia, followed by second trip to the East Coast. Scott remained home, hoping Susan would stay in state at a university they could afford. When she was away, it was up to him to tend the house and dog, get Will to and from school, make dinners. When Martha returned, he would have one trip or another that couldn't be avoided, and Martha would take over the house.

Will, at fifteen, stood nearly as tall as Scott. He was a good kid, but the duties of parenting always threw new challenges at him and Martha— most recently a drinking incident they hoped they'd taken care of properly.

Will's grades were Bs and better, his friends were good kids, so they didn't worry too much about him. And besides, the endless driving, the juggling of two cars (Susan now needed one of them), school, sports, made life uncommonly busy.

All of which was why he hadn't worked harder to stay in touch with Sally until he reflected on it much later.

It had taken Scott four years first to finish and then to revise and revise again his novel, and then sell it, and then wait eleven months for its actual publication, while continuing to write freelance articles and nonfiction books. He currently studied nitrogen, which had a complex relationship with the world in terms of explosives, the health of soil, the poisoning of rivers, and the health of one's body, and had begun the actual writing of the book, the reporting work mainly done.

Thus it would be three additional years till he (along with Martha) reconnected with Sally, summer 2012, seven years after he'd last seen her at the corner of West Fourteenth Street. He reached out by email, asking if this address still worked. It did, she responded, she'd been using it for years, and this time she included her cell phone number. He texted that he and Martha would be in town; he missed her and hoped they could reconnect.

Her response by text worried him. "Yes, I'll be in town then. Would love to see you. Have I got a story to tell you." He'd texted back immediately "Good or bad?" but she hadn't responded.

*

So much had happened in the three years since the last trip to New York when he'd reached out to her. His novel had gone virtually unreviewed—but favorably where it had been, such as in his hometown paper—and managed to sell a little more than five thousand copies, not embarrassing, but the kind of number that would make the sale of a second novel more difficult than the first. Scott didn't care. He had written it because he had wanted to, from the pressure within, from Sally's push, and he had done so without hope.

Happily, one of those five thousand copies sold had been given as a Christmas gift to a young executive at Paramount Pictures, who had passed it on to a superior, who grew interested in acquiring it. That executive subsequently moved to the Weinstein Company, working directly under Harvey Weinstein, who became interested in the project. A bidding war between Paramount and TWC ended favorably for Scott. Scott's agent warned him that the $50,000 should be considered found money and not to expect more because this happened all the time and that the movie would not likely be made (but in that event, he *would* make a considerable sum). Scott pretended to agree but secretly held his breath. He emailed his mentor, a novelist who taught at Princeton, that the rights to his novel had been sold, to which his mentor sent back a brief, dispiriting email: "That's nice, Scott. Send me an invitation to the opening." But Scott would never forget standing in his foyer, holding the nine-by-twelve envelope with his agent's return address. He had called to Martha and asked if she wanted to see something. She did. And so, a month after the movie was green-lighted, they opened the envelope and, paper-clipped to a formal statement of the option money less the agent's 15 percent, was a check for $382,500. They must have stared at if for a full minute. It seemed unreal. He still didn't quite believe it, even as he stared at the check. He'd never seen a check so large or even close to it. Lack of money had dogged them their whole married life. He and Martha were so nervous about it, they both went to the bank to deposit it. They took separate cars in case one of them got hit. They waited in line with their deposit slip and unthinkably huge check. The cashier didn't even blink. Scott took a photo of the deposit receipt before putting it into his wallet.

He and Martha treated themselves to an expensive lunch immediately after, with a pricey bottle of wine, then returned to their empty house—Susan had chosen nearby Oberlin College, Will was a junior in high school—and had the most aggressive sex they'd had in years, and only woke when Will pounded up the staircase and disappeared into his room.

Two days later, an officer of the bank called to discuss how they planned to manage the money. They hadn't really had time to think about it. But when they caught their breath, they decided to spend it on something Martha had longed for—a place of their own in New York City. She had spent virtually her whole life in the suburban Midwest and longed to get out while they could still enjoy it. Now that she was writing more, she wanted to have a place of their own in the city through which all the great writing seemed channeled. She was eager to return to her own work. And a nervous Scott acquiesced. It was 2012, and the real estate market remained depressed, so their timing was perfect. With their newfound cash as collateral, they were able to secure a mortgage on a four-hundred-square-foot studio apartment on Perry Street in the West Village. He did have to admit that it boosted the ego, to have their own small patch of Manhattan. By the time the movie based on his novel appeared, and disappeared without much of a trace, he and Martha were frequently ensconced in New York.

With Will now a senior in high school and Susan having moved into her sophomore year, he and Martha would soon be able to spend more time in the city, far from the provincial suburbs of the Midwest. Scott's income from writing (he had been paid handsomely to write the first of four versions of the screenplay of his novel) had never been better; moreover, the sheer accumulation of books now brought in royalties more steadily, money that required no work at all and that seemed like its own kind of magic. He considered returning to fiction after the nitrogen book was done.

Before he and Martha drove to New York (they were still transporting larger items to their new apartment), Scott sent Sally an email outlining all of what had happened since they'd last seen one another. He kept it subdued because if he told it with the astonished exuberance that he actually felt, it might seem like gloating. She didn't respond.

*

They met in a small park on Bleecker Street north of West Eleventh, with stone and sandy gravel and tables for al fresco eating and gathering, not unlike Parisian courtyards in which he and Sally had drunk strong, bitter coffees all those years ago.

They approached simultaneously from opposite directions on Bleecker. Sally had dressed in black, which seemed to intensify her dark blond hair, pulled into a ponytail, black Jack Purcell sneakers, black T-shirt. The tight jeans and the way she pulled her hair back enhanced her gaunt appearance, and her once fleshy arms, to Scott so voluptuous, were now taut with muscle. But, grinning, she held out her hands, palms up, in a kind of shrugging gesture—it's me! here I am!—and gave both Scott and Martha a strong hug and kiss.

The July afternoon was thinly overcast, the temperature mild and comfortable, and so they sat at an empty table.

"So how are you guys?" she said. "Some year it's been for you!"

"It has, but what's going on with you?" Scott asked. "You said you had a story."

"Anh!" she said and shooed the question away with one hand. "First you. Tell me about your place! That's exciting!"

And so they did, Scott and Martha alternately describing how they found it and what they did to it and how happy it made them. Sally grinned and seemed happy for them.

"And all this from the Hollywood money? Do you realize how rare that is?"

"Yes, completely," Scott said. "I don't know if you read the book, but—"

"Scott, silly, of course I read it." She reached across the table and squeezed his hand. "I emailed you about it, didn't I?"

"I don't think so. I'm sure I'd have remembered."

Scott had mailed the first copy he'd received to her. He had dedicated the book to Martha, because it had been his goal when he and Martha first dated and courted; he made his first unsuccessful attempts and she had stuck with him, always encouraging. He wondered if Sally had hoped for at least an acknowledgment since she truly had been the catalyst on that long-ago visit in 2005. Now he wondered if he should have a had a discussion with Martha about this, or at least figured out some way to acknowledge the person who had instigated it.

But he also was nervous that she would be embarrassed for him, because her field of expertise and her work were the great Russian writers. She taught *War and Peace* and *Crime and Punishment*, at the master's level at Columbia University—"The Lady with the Dog" and *The Cherry Orchard*, and Pushkin and Gogol, with occasional forays beyond Russia, *Jude the Obscure* and *Tess*, of course, and the Americans, Melville and Hawthorne. Scott had no illusions that he was creating great American literature at the level of his own heroes—but, yes, a good yarn, an entertainment, he thought of it, a story compelling enough to make it to Hollywood. But he worried that Sally had thought it trifling because she'd spent most of her life immersed in the great literature.

"Maybe it went into a spam folder," Scott offered.

"Maybe." Sally must have spotted a tic in his expression because she reached back over to re-squeeze his hand. "Aww. Really, I did like it. I was proud of you. And *you* should be proud of it. Honestly, Martha," she said, releasing the hand and looking to Martha. "How anyone writes is amazing to me."

"He works hard," she said.

"Both of you, no doubt," she said.

Scott said, "Are you writing?"

"Me? No."

"Okay," Scott said. "So what's the story."

"Hm, where to begin," she said. "My story or his?" She looked off, then back at Scott. "My story really begins four months ago, when I got a call from New York Presbyterian saying that Edward was in the ICU. No, let me back up to calling his office and finding out he'd been let go five weeks earlier. Then he disappeared for two days. Then I get the call that he's in the ICU at New York Presbyterian."

Slack-jawed, Scott asked, "What happened?"

"He got hit by a bus!"

"Is that a joke?"

"No!" Sally said and laughed. "He honestly got hit by a bus! It happens!" Sally slapped the table. "The M101 at Seventy-Ninth and Lex."

"How?"

"I guess if you stagger around drunk in the middle of the afternoon on the Upper East Side it can happen."

"What was he doing staggering around on the Upper East Side?"

"His story?" she asked. Martha had yet to remove a cupped hand from her mouth. "His story is that he fell in love."

"What?"

"That's right, he fell in love with somebody not me."

"He fell in love?"

"With a fucking little girl who works at Starbucks."

"What?" Scott asked.

"Ha, this is a good one," Sally said, almost delighting in the preposterous nature of her circumstances. "So I get to the hospital, and he's knocked out on drugs and a little banged up, but not terrible. Considering," and here Sally laughed again, "he'd just gotten run over by a bus!"

Neither Scott nor Martha laughed.

"Anyway," Sally continued, "I get to the hospital and find out that he's not in any danger and the nurse gives me all his stuff, his clothes in a plastic bag. And I'm sitting in the room waiting for the attending and his phone starts pinging. So of course I dig it out of the bag and look at it. And it's someone named Miranda and she's texting 'Where are you?' and 'Why won't you respond?' and 'I'm not mad at you, just tell me you're okay.' But this is part of a really long chain, so I swipe down and this tramp is texting nude selfies to him. And then she texts again, the phone vibrates in my hand."

"What did you do?"

"I texted her back."

"You're kidding."

"Fuck no, I'm not kidding."

Her vehemence, all humor gone, jolted Scott.

"I texted, 'I've been in an accident and am at New York Presbyterian in room seven-oh whatever it was.' Thirty-minutes later, this little girl with purple hair walks in and gasps when she sees me."

"You keep saying little girl. How old is she?"

"I don't know, thirties, but she's tiny is what I meant."

"What happened?"

"I looked at her, covering her face, and said, 'Don't worry, he's gonna live.' And she started crying and ran away. The coward."

"Holy shit," Scott said. "So where do things stand? Are you going to be able to work this out?"

"We tried counseling. I honestly thought when he got another job that would put things right, that with Arthur, who's only ten for God's sake, I thought we could work it out. I told him I wanted to try. He said he tried but claims he was too depressed."

"Depressed."

"Because he's still in love with her!"

"Where do things stand?"

"We're still together, for Arthur's sake. But we are history."

Scott sat back, flummoxed. Martha stared intently at Sally, unable to come up with any words.

"You wake up one morning one person," Sally said, "with a pretty clear future stretching out before you, and by the time you go to bed that night, it's as if that future was a fake backdrop that just fell down like a curtain. What looked like a Frederic Church landscape turns into a bad neighborhood in Detroit."

Scott reached across the table and held her hand and looked at Sally and she took his hand in both of hers. Martha looked away.

*

After protracted exclamations of disbelief and sorrow—really, what can one say? Sally knew this more than anyone—all agreed they needed a change of venue. It was such a fine day, they decided to walk the High Line, the old elevated train platform that had been transformed into a park. Sally said she walked it often, for solace.

As they walked south, Sally explained that, for now, she'd go back to teaching. She couldn't return to Columbia, but she'd been able to pick up adjunct work at NYU and the New School. This was mainly to get out of her own head—with Edward once again employed, money was not the issue. She could at least immerse herself in stories and poetry and the lives of students, other people. "And not dwell on myself," she said. They returned to the southern end of the High Line, at Gansevoort Street and descended. "But enough about me!" she said and laughed a low, burbling kind of laugh, not a happy laugh.

By the time they reached the last step, Sally transformed and said, "This is your new hood! How do you like it?"

"We love it," Martha said.

"We're not far from our place," Scott said, putting his arm over Martha's shoulder. "Come see it?"

"Hell, yeah. I'd have asked if you hadn't offered."

They walked the eight blocks to the apartment building on Perry Street. Scott turned the key in the front door, then the foyer door, and they took the stairs one flight up to their apartment. As he waved the women in, he realized he'd forgotten to turn off the coffee machine, and the burnt smell hung in the air. He walked to the other side of the room, past the bed, to open one of the two windows that looked down onto the street. The kitchen had just enough room for a small table and, immediately behind this, the bed, a sitting chair in the corner. Not much, but just right for them.

Sally peeled off her sneakers, walked slowly through the kitchen, and flopped into the club chair in the corner. "Nice place! You done *good*!" Martha sat cross-legged on the bed and Scott sat beside Martha against pillows. They talked about their work, their kids. And by 5:30, Sally said she had to pick up dinner and get back to Arthur.

"Actually, we have to pick up dinner, too," Scott said.

Martha said, "Weren't we supposed to meet Cat uptown for a drink?"

"I cancelled."

"Why?"

"Because I didn't want this to end abruptly. And we don't really want to hike all the way to the Upper East Side, do we? Do you mind?"

"Mind?" she said, as much to herself as to Scott and under her breath so that Sally wouldn't hear, "Like I love hanging out with your old girlfriends."

"Hey. I didn't really *want* to see her, I just felt obligated because I promised I would."

"Wait a minute," Sally said, slipping on her sneakers without having to retie them. "*The* Cat? Are you still in touch with her?"

"Sort of. Not really. I got back in touch with her after we got this place and were in the city more frequently."

"Wow, how is she?"

"Good, she said. Third marriage, this one happy, two kids. You never met her, did you?"

Sally stared at Scott as if he were dim and said, "No, never got that chance."

"Right," Scott said.

"How do you know her?" Martha asked.

"Scott left me in Paris for her."

Scott said, "You left me, remember?"

"You know what I mean. Whatever."

Martha said, "Although this is fascinating, I'm exhausted, and hungry, can we get going?"

They shopped at Chelsea Market, and when all had found what they needed for their dinners, they parted. Sally gave Martha a hug first, then Scott, and a kiss on his cheek. "Stay in touch, huh? Call me when you're back in town?"

"Of course," Scott said. "I'm so glad to be back in touch with you."

"Aw, you," she said. She pinched his cheek hard, almost shaking it.

*

That night Scott fried steaks, made a salad, and opened a bottle of red wine. He and Martha ate by candlelight, talking about their work. (Martha hadn't been interested in rehashing Sally's dire circumstances.) After, they sat on the fire escape outside their apartment and drank a small glass of grappa and watched the people stroll by. Then they dressed for bed and turned on the TV to watch *The Graduate*. When the movie was over, Scott still wasn't tired, but Martha had already fallen asleep. He poured a second grappa and tried to read. But he kept thinking about Cat. He'd stood her up. He'd ignored the several texts she'd sent. Why? Why did he feel such a need to see her in the first place?

We can't hold feelings for this long, can we? he wondered. Could he still be angry after nearly thirty years? Or did he have something to prove? The memory was still there, of course, but not the feelings, and especially not the pain. It wasn't as if there was a live wire in there with current still running through it. But then, what?

He thought back to the last time he'd seen Cat, when he'd gotten his first book contract at age thirty, twenty years ago. He'd walked from his publisher's office all the way uptown. He wanted to share the good news with her. And she'd been happy for him. But during the half-hour conversation, it became clear that her second marriage wasn't working out any better than the first. Scott left feeling bad. He'd wanted to go there, to see her in person, to tell her he had an actual book contract, but this was not really the news he wanted to share. He didn't recognize it till after and he felt ashamed. The actual reason for the visit was to say, "See, I'm not a loser. I'm going to be a writer, just as I said."

Twenty years ago, Scott thought, propped on pillows beside his sleeping wife in a Manhattan pied-à-terre he'd never in his dreams imagined having.

The previous March, he and Martha had splurged on a week at the Breakers in Palm Beach with the kids. He wondered even now about that. He knew he was hoping to see Cat. He knew her family still had a house in the north end of the island and that they belonged to the Breakers, that she had kids and would very likely be spring-breaking it with them. This had been the very place he had visited in March 1983, still ensconced in Cat's generous family. She rode horses and competed in equestrian events in the nearby village of Wellington. Mrs. Delouvrier had invited Scott to join them in Palm Beach for spring break his sophomore year at Princeton. He and Cat had flown down together, and he had fond memories of the

Breakers, the narrow island, and thought it would be a luxurious, relaxing place for the family to vacation.

Susan, a penurious college sophomore, eagerly embraced a week in Palm Beach. Will, a senior in high school and heading the following year to Ohio State, was a quiet, bookish teenager who preferred reading and writing and drawing to company. He'd had many friends in high school but seemed now to need only his one best friend, who'd gotten into Princeton. Now that they could afford it, Scott wished Will had set his sights on an Ivy League school. Princeton had served him well. It had been where he'd first laid eyes on Catherine Delouvrier, daughter of a real estate magnate in Manhattan—a privileged Upper East Side childhood she had tried to distance herself from.

He'd seen her in the quad, on an early September evening, the sun low and golden, the air summer-warm, and she spun in place while her diaphanous flowered dress rose up about her like a parachute, exposing strong, milky calves. Her hair was long and thick and black, which made her blue eyes especially bright and seductive. Her left incisor was reversed and gave her a snaggle-toothed smile, an imperfection that somehow made the rest of her beauty more authentic and natural. Even their difference in height—she just over five-feet, he six-two—hadn't deterred the initial visceral attraction and his determination to meet her.

He guessed correctly from the bangles on her wrists, the beads, the jingling ankle bracelet, and the clothes, that she'd been to the same Grateful Dead concert that he had the previous night at the Nassau Coliseum on Long Island. Maybe he was still tripping, but he felt immediately in love with her.

And when she said, "I *was* at the show. Wasn't it amazing? Can you believe opening with 'Playing in the Band' and then, oh my God, 'Crazy Fingers'?"

"Yes!" Scott said, as if she'd confirmed his love with that.

"I can get us a tape of the show," she said. "I have a friend who tapes."

"Yes," Scott said. Yes, and yes, and yes.

And they had been together all his sophomore year and her freshman year—he lived off campus and she rarely slept in her dorm room. They traveled the eastern seaboard following the Dead, both of them barely getting by in school. And when the school year came to an end, her father—an imposing figure even at five-six with a round head, abundant wavy salt-and-pepper hair, and great tufts of nose hair that Scott had to force himself to stop staring at—got him a job in the business, where Scott ran errands, helped to write brochure copy, and was even allowed to sit in on meetings on a forty-story, multi-use building going up in Midtown.

On the weekends, they'd all drive out to the house in Sag Harbor to swim and play tennis and sail a little thirty-foot sloop, a wooden boat her father had restored in his youth and kept in immaculate shape.

To a middle-class boy from suburban Illinois, the wealth was astonishing. And he'd never had more fun.

When he held her close, she craned to look up at him. And she'd smile her snaggle-toothed smile and her blue eyes would twinkle and she'd bob up and down on the toes of her small feet, like an exotic fish approaching the surface for a kiss. And he'd bend to touch his lips to hers. Blameless, with no responsibilities, nothing but fun to be had.

Until the last time she'd truly smiled at him, smiled with a sadness that showed the depth of her love for him, the afternoon of his departure. That last day in mid-August at the country house, the end of a dream. The smile was there, but it was sad because he was leaving. And not just leaving the East Coast but rather returning to the Midwest before flying to England, where he'd spend a year at the University of Bristol (a junior year abroad had long been in the plans, and he couldn't back out now). Until then, the longest they'd spent apart had been one week, over the Christmas break. He determined not to cry, which was hard when he saw a drop fall from the corner of her right eye, slip down around the nostril of her petite nose, and hang on the edge of an upper lip. He kissed her again and tasted the salty tear.

Her mother, Jean, whom Cat still called Mommy, was every bit as imposing as Mr. Delouvrier, though in the severe, matronly way of the wealthy. She had hired a driver to take Scott back to the city. And it was in this black town car that he allowed himself to weep. He wept and wept, not caring what the driver, who cast uneasy glances at him from beneath the visor of his cap, thought. He would have to wait until Thanksgiving, when Mr. Delouvrier brought his wife and daughter with him as he checked in on his London concerns. After that he would see her again when he returned at Christmas.

And he did. And they were true in their hearts to one another. And because they'd lasted these four months, he saw no reason they wouldn't last another six, through winter and spring till she could join him in Europe, a trip they'd already begun to plan. Sally rarely brought her up, and Scott didn't either. If Sally cared when he went to see Cat in London in late November, she hadn't let on. Scott kept a photo of Cat on his desk, even though Sally spent many nights there. And he figured Cat was allied with him in this way, too, in her own innocent way—that fidelity of the heart was all that mattered. He had no illusions.

He called her once a week, usually his midday, her morning, before classes, and it was always a pleasure to hear her sweet, high voice, scratchy from sleep, and her girlish laughter. Once in the spring, over the Easter break, he'd traveled to north London to spend the holiday with Andy, one of his flatmates. He'd left Andy's house after lunch on Saturday to find a phone booth at the end of the street. He'd called her and a guy answered who put her on the phone when Scott asked for her—"Sure, hey Cat . . . Cat, wake up, phone"—and she said, "Hi, Scott," but after some niceties she began weeping, and he tried to calm her and tell her everything would be okay.

When he'd hung up, he was sick to his stomach, physically ill, wondering if he'd heave on the roadside just outside the bright red phone booth. He'd been prepared for the idea of it, but the actual sound of the two voices, in bed—no. By the time he'd reached Andy's house, he'd collected himself.

He couldn't even call Sally, because *her* boyfriend was visiting for the week, and he was suddenly so grateful for middle-class Andy and his kind, British parents in their saggy jumpers offering him glasses of sherry and Andy's younger brother teaching him how to throw a cricket ball. Scott who'd been a starting pitcher on his high school baseball team, showed the brother, Keith, pronounced "Keef," how Americans pitched. Keith loved the power one could use by whipping the ball, unimpeded by the stiff overhand hook of the cricket mandate—a good metaphor for American abandon and force compared with British restraint, Scott thought. By the end of the week, he was back at the university and Sally was ever Sally and they spent all that first night back in a pub till last call, talking. He told her about the phone call and she was genuinely sympathetic; and she told him about her week, scant details before moving on. She didn't seem to have had a great week with her boyfriend—which Scott tried not to be happy about but was. Sally went with him back to his room and they made love, and he felt better, and everything returned to the way it had been. She read him Emily Dickinson that night—"Slant of light," he would never forget. "Shadows hold their breath!" she'd exclaimed. "Isn't that the best?" She seemed giddy. "But it's such a grim poem," he said. "I *know!*" she had said. And she read until he was asleep and probably well beyond. The day-in and day-out of university life carried on, as the long, cold spring finally warmed and the nights stayed bright till nine.

And before they knew it, their school year abroad was done. Sally had long known that Scott had set the rendezvous date with Cat for July 6 in Paris, which gave them two and a half weeks to meander through France on the way to the city he'd never been to. They connected with his high school buddy John, aka Wilhelm, in Calais, who met them at the ferry from Dover. They rented a car and drove through northern France, spent two lazy days on a beach in Deauville, then headed west to the summer house of a friend of John's, Philippe, on the rocky coast of Brest in the northwestern corner of France. The weather was unseasonably warm, and they spent several days sunning on the beaches. They toured sites, ate cheap delicious food and drank cheap delicious wine during long lunches, and had eau de vie with a cigarette after, and Sally and Scott would make love in their cheap room on wilted squeaky mattresses, then nap till dusk. In the evenings, more amazing food and wine and John always found some alleyway bar or club that no Americans knew about. And all too quickly it was time to head to Paris; Philippe and John headed west toward Belgium, planning to travel south through Germany, while Scott and Sally hopped a train to Paris. They had five days in Paris before Cat arrived from New York. As for Sally, she had friends who were renting a house on an island off the west coast of Greece; she had booked a flight to Athens on the day before Cat was to arrive and would travel north to Corfu.

The first days in Paris, Scott found himself deliriously happy.

On the train down, Sally had read long passages from *A Moveable Feast*, about Hemingway's early days as a writer in this city. She mapped out everywhere she wanted to go with Scott according to the book, including the Shakespeare and Company bookstore—"Imagine," she whispered shortly after they'd entered. "James Joyce and Hemingway and Gertrude Stein and Fitzgerald walked on this very floor."

Scott nodded, but he wasn't sentimental or nostalgic.

She read his face and said, "Come on, it's part of the American writer's mythology. It's important to know your culture's mythologies. Especially if you're going to be a writer."

Scott gave in because she was irresistible. They walked the Left Bank, they drank at Le Dôme and Les Deux Magots and La Closerie des Lilas and every other location she could find; she found the address where Hemingway had lived with his wife, Hadley, and wrote his first immortal stories, where he squeezed the orange rind against flames in the fire warming the cold room to watch the citrus oils flame—and then try to write one true sentence, she reminded him.

And she surprised him by taking him to a cemetery.

"A cemetery?" he'd asked.

"A must!" she said. "*Père Lachaise* is the most famous cemetery in the world. People like Oscar Wilde are buried here! And Proust! And Colette!" But her first stop was to see where Jim Morrison had been buried, the sculpture adorned with flowers and beads and a wine bottle. They often listened to the Doors, especially Sally, who would, she said, "tingle from the liberation and the darkness" of Morrison's voice. And after thinking about the singer's sad end at the age of twenty-seven, they continued to stroll the cemetery, looking at names. "And Janis Joplin," Sally said, "and Hendrix. All at age twenty-seven. And don't forget Keats!"

"Is Keats buried here?"

"No. Rome. I'm just thinking about poets, artists. He was even *younger*." Keats was another poet she'd introduced him to; "Ode on a Grecian Urn"—"Beauty is truth, truth beauty"—had been his favorite. "Keats was only twenty-*five*," she said. "I wonder if the great poets literally burn muscle in order to create. And they burn and burn until till their bodies simply don't have enough mass to sustain a life that was born so huge."

"Maybe."

"If Keats had been a teenager in the 1960s with Morrison, do you think he'd have been in a rock-and-roll band? I think he would have, and then he'd have made it to twenty-seven."

Scott smiled at her, and she laughed. "But then he wouldn't have written odes to urns and nightingales," she said. "They would have been odes to convertible Mustangs and blonde surfer babes."

"True," Scott said, and they strolled arm and arm again.

"But you write fiction. You're going to be a novelist. Fiction writers have a much longer life span, so I'm not worried about it."

She halted, gasped, and pointed at a large cement stone marker, surrounded by a low black iron fence on which a dark bust rested. "*Balzac!*" she said.

*

Sally spoke passable French, which she'd learned in high school, and so navigating the city and ordering food and asking for information was easy. Scott, having mastered the Manhattan subway system the previous summer during his real estate internship in Manhattan, loved the Paris Metro, and they scoured the city on Sally's itinerary. She meant to inspire Scott, who had showed her some of his short stories; he had been teaching himself to write.

They marveled in the mornings at the flaky rectangular croissants that had two strips of chocolate running through them. It was the most miraculous bread Scott had ever tasted. And with chocolate. They put chocolate in bread here. Sometimes they'd put it in a baguette, also a revelation.

"Sally, I want to *live* in a city where chocolate sandwiches are normal."

She hugged his arm, looked up at him, the sun in her hazel eyes as they crossed the *Pont des Invalides* over the Seine. "Then let's!"

"What?"

"We could do it! We'll find a cheap flat, and you can write and I'll get a job, and we'll live a truly bohemian life. We'd be so good together! It could be heaven."

"It could be crazy," he said.

"It could be crazy good!"

"Sally, no, crazy is not good. Crazy is crazy."

She stopped him, pressed her body against his till he was against the stone balustrade above the Seine, and kissed him long and hard on the mouth.

"Will you think about it?"

"Are you actually serious?"

"Yes," she said and twirled once, arms out and almost knocking a small Frenchman, wearing a beret no less, into the street.

"*Pardon!*" she called out, then fell back into Scott, her head on his chest. "It could be so beautiful."

"What about finishing college?"

"We can finish when we return, if that's what we want. There's no rule you can't defer for a while. Two years here, just two years, and if we don't like it, we'll have had a great, life-directing experience."

He could only smile and kiss her. He loved her exuberance and impracticality. He knew not to bring up the very obvious facts that she had a plane to Greece in two days and that he would be reuniting with Cat in three days. As *planned*. They had a *plan*. He just wanted to enjoy these last days, not upend them with the sadness of parting.

They walked the back streets of Montmartre, high above their cheap hotel room, and ate at a small café. By the time they were done, the sun was low in the sky.

"Let's get another bottle of wine and watch the sunset!" Sally said.

And so there Scott sat, on the steps of the great white domed church high above Paris, watching a red-gold sun, impossibly large, hanging above the rooftops of Paris.

Sally had made Scott go into a pipe shop earlier in the day, and she'd bought a pipe with a very long, slender, cherrywood stem and a white meerschaum bowl, as well as a tamper and a bag of cherry-scented tobacco.

"I've always wanted to smoke a pipe!" she said.

She'd sat on a bench immediately and smoked it, striking a masculine pose, knees spread wide, one arm over the bench while Scott took photographs of her.

And now she pulled it out again, filled, it, tamped it down, and lit it with a wooden match. The two shared both the tobacco and the wine.

Parisians and tourists filled the steps, also admiring the sunset, though most weren't swigging wine straight from the bottle.

Two steps below, and off to the right, sat two Asian guys, late twenties or so, one playing guitar, the other singing. Both had long, shiny black hair.

"Don't you *love* his voice?" Sally asked.

"Yeah, it's a lovely voice." He looked at her looking at him, the sun lighting the soft loops of her dark gold hair, her sparkling eyes. "What?" he asked.

"I don't know any guys our age who would use the word *lovely*. And I love that."

They kissed.

The Asian guys had begun playing Simon and Garfunkel's "The Boxer." They seemed to be playing for the pleasure of it; they had no case open with franc notes and coins in it. Scott watched them and thought, *They're doing it for the beauty of it. They are so beautiful.* Scott took a long swallow of wine. He felt giddy from it, happily drunk. Sally swayed to the music beside him. The giant sun reflecting off the rooftops of this amazing city, the giant sun setting, the wine, the travel, the people, all of mythic Paris. Scott felt at that moment that he had never been so happy in his life.

When the musicians finished the song, Sally called out, "Hey! *Merci bien!*"

They turned, and the one with the guitar smiled and said, "*De rien!*"

Sally said, "Oh, no, so much more than nothing! Everything!"

The singer smiled and said, "You speak English."

"Americans," Scott said.

The singer said, "You look like genuine Parisians. With the pipe and the wine."

Sally pointed the mouthpiece of her pipe at them and asked, "Vietnamese?"

"Laos," he said.

"Wow, Laos," she said.

"You know Laos?" he said in a flawless American accent.

"Next to Vietnam, yes."

Scott was impressed. He hadn't even *heard* of Laos.

"Yes," the two said at once, happy at the recognition.

"You're lucky to be out," she said.

"We're lucky to be in Paris!" said the guitar player, and he spread his hand out to the gold-red light shining upon the city.

The musicians stood, took the two steps up, and sat beside them. "Can we play for you?"

Sally said, "Yes!"

"What would you like?"

"Do you know more Simon and Garfunkel?"

"*Oui, bien sûr,*" said the guitarist.

Sally thought for a moment, then tilted her head and asked, "Do you know 'The Dangling Conversation'?"

The Laotians turned to one another and nodded. The guitarist strummed, tightened two strings, and then they began.

Scott didn't know this one, but from the opening line—*It's a still life watercolor of a now-late afternoon, as the sun shines through the curtain lace and shadows wash the room*—he felt it was the most beautiful song he'd ever heard. While the two young men played, Sally and Scott sat quietly, simply looking out at the setting sun, gold mixing with the red, over this gorgeous old city. Until, in the middle of it—*and you read your Emily Dickinson, and I my Robert Frost*—Sally put her lips to Scott's ear and said, "You know I love you."

"I love you, too!" Scott said, still giddy from it all, and drunk, and gave her a slightly sloppy kiss.

"*No,*" she said. "You know I'm *in* love with you."

"Sally," he said softly. He stared into her eyes. They both knew.

They listened to the song. Neither spoke.

The young men moved into Bob Dylan, "Don't Think Twice, It's All Right," then "Tangled Up in Blue," and the sun was halfway down upon the rooftops.

"The setting sun," Scott said, not meaning to speak it aloud.

After a moment, Sally said, "It rises, also, you know."

He turned to her, happy for the levity, and said, "Ha."

She said "Ha" back.

The Laotians played until true dusk set in, said *Au revoir* and *A bientôt* to Scott and Sally, and Sally said, "Well."

Scott didn't want to leave. He was too happy. But the sun wouldn't stop, he knew. She held his hand, squeezed it, and said, "Come on."

"I don't want it to end," Scott said.

She stood, tugged him up. "Come on," she said, without happiness, without anything. The dusk had muted her. "Nothing gold, and all that," she said.

She'd read him Frost as well as Dickinson, perhaps why she'd requested the song—he didn't know, as he was too giddy from the wine and the view. Reluctantly, Scott stood and, holding Sally's hand, descended the church steps and then the winding steps along the park, down, down into the seedy streets of the neighborhood called Pigalle. They'd eaten and drank so much they fell asleep almost as soon as they'd stripped and fallen onto the squeaky bed.

*

Sally and Scott woke at the same time, when the sun had risen high enough above the buildings to illuminate the brick wall their window faced, she draped over his long body.

"Good morning, you," she said.

"Good morning," he said and gave her a quick kiss.

She rubbed his chest and kissed it. Her hand descended down his naked body and felt for what was as consistent as the sun on waking. She squeezed and said, "God, I love you in the morning. It's so hard." She continued to enjoy it, to stroke. More mornings than not they made love quickly, then rested till their heartbeats slowed and then they left the bed to shower.

"Sally," he said, stilling her hand.

"Yes?"

"I don't think I should."

"Should?"

"I don't know. It's starting to get complicated."

She released him and rolled to her side, propped up on an elbow.

"What?"

"I don't know."

She stared at him staring at the ceiling.

"It's Cat, isn't it?"

He sighed heavily.

"I think I should just not today—"

"Today? *Today?*" She stared at him. She kept staring at him as he focused on cracks in the ceiling. She rolled out of bed. "I'm going to shub," she said, referring to what she'd named the small square tub with the hand-held shower head that always left the bathroom floor wet. When the door closed, he rose to use the commode in the adjacent closet and then returned to bed. When she emerged, wet and wrapped in a towel, he took her place. When he had finished bathing and had shaved, he found the room empty. A page torn from Sally's notebook lay on the bed: *Need caffeine—meet me in the café.* A café with a zinc bar adjoined their squalid hotel, and each morning they'd drink their *café Americain* and eat *pain au chocolat.* He dressed quickly and departed.

"A regular croissant?" he asked, seeing the pointed corner and crumbs on the napkin beside her coffee cup.

"They were out of the chocolate ones, goddammit." She seemed actually pissed, and un-Sally-like, and he wasn't sure what to do.

"Oh dear," is what he said, scanning the mostly empty baskets of pastries. At least a few croissants remained. "*C'est dommage,*" he said. Scott could now order his breakfast in passable French, but the frowning man behind the bar always responded in English.

He'd finished the last of his coffee more quickly than he wanted to because he sensed her impatience.

"Well?" she said, lifting her eyebrows. "Shall we . . . sally forth?"

He smiled, relieved by her breezy tone, said, "Yes!" and reached into his pocket for franc coins to set on the receipt on the bar. "Yes."

"This one you're going to love, I promise."

And off they went to the single museum she said they would go to, and even so she had to convince him that this one was worth it since he had no interest in museums.

*

They walked almost everywhere in Paris, and the forty-minute walk from the rank Quartier Pigalle had been one of the best, past the Palais Garnier and through Place Vendôme and last through the Jardin des Tuileries and across the bridge to the Left Bank and the Musée d'Orsay. He'd loved the building as much as the paintings. And their tickets included the Rodin museum, so they wandered through that before their stomachs demanded food. She had ordered a *salade aux lardons* and he a *croque madame*. Sally made them each break their yolks separately so they could watch, because it was her favorite part of eating meals topped with egg, still another new experience for Scott, eggs on top of food—on salad, on sandwiches.

"It was a train station!" Scott exclaimed. "I love that! Thank you, Sally."

"*Mais bien sûr,*" she said.

They spoke easily all the way through their meal, conversation based on the foundation of ten months of easy conversation. They each had two *eau de vies* to finish the meal and departed tipsy enough to splurge on a taxi rather than walk or take the hot Metro. Once back in their room, as had happened often throughout their days in France, they fell stuffed and light-headed onto the sway-backed mattress, sighing.

Scott felt happily drunk and rolled close to her and slipped his hand beneath her shirt to caress her breasts. He swooned. He put his nose into her neck and inhaled deeply. Then his hand went for the button of her blue jeans.

She didn't stop his hand, she simply said, "No."

"Please?"

"You *shouldn't*, remember?"

"I was wrong," he said, smiling playfully.

He kissed her and rubbed her crotch.

"Hey, I said *no*."

"Are you serious?"

"Yes, I'm fucking serious."

Scott rolled off her, startled. He'd never once heard her say *fuck*. It wasn't like her.

"I don't want to fight on our last night together," he said.

"I don't either."

"Can we hold each other then?"

"Yes," she said.

She snuggled into him, put her head on his chest. He would be asleep before a small circle of tears formed on his shirt pocket.

When he woke in the early evening, she was gone. Clothes, bag, everything but the pipe, left on the bureau. Just plain gone.

*

Scott sat up in the beach chair, scanning the bathers, the sun hot on his shoulders, his vision hazy from the saltwater and sun.

Martha lowered her paperback and said to him, "Why are you so fidgety? Why can't you relax?"

"I don't know."

"Well, as long as you're vertical, why don't you get us some drinks."

Scott put a shirt on and scanned the waves for Will. Will was seventeen, but the protective urges of parenthood didn't change. He then walked through the sand to the wooden steps that led up to the pools and the bars.

The Breakers, a towering structure in the heart of the island, was a place Scott had aspired to be able to afford, and now they could. He could recite from memory the passage from Fitzgerald's story "The Rich Boy," which began: "Palm Beach sprawled plump and opulent between the sparkling sapphire of Lake Worth, flawed here and there by house-boats at anchor, and the great turquoise bar of the Atlantic Ocean. The huge bulks of the Breakers and the Royal Poinciana rose as twin paunches from the bright level of the sand, and around them clustered the Dancing Glade, Bradley's House of Chance, and a dozen modistes and milliners with goods at triple prices from New York."

The Royal Poinciana had been an even grander hotel, the largest wooden structure in the world for a time, built in 1894 by Henry Flagler, a Rockefeller colleague who had run a railroad down to this palmy, narrow island. But the Royal Poinciana had been razed during the Depression, so Scott pretended that the Biltmore Hotel was the Royal Poinciana as he thought of that passage from Fitzgerald's story, as they'd flown over the island into Palm Beach International Airport.

And here he was, at the kind of resort where handsome young men in pink shirts and navy shorts hauled beach chairs for you to your own plot, planted an umbrella, sheathed the chairs in fitted towels, and left more fluffy white towels than a family could possibly need.

He took a circuitous route to the bar, looking. Surely the Delouvriers, and Cat in particular, kept their spring break routine after all these years. He hadn't asked her this by email. He'd simply mentioned that he would be in town. She'd written enthusiastically that she and family would indeed be in Palm Beach at some point when Scott was there. But he hadn't emailed again. He wanted to bump into her, he didn't want her to think he needed to see her. If it could be a more random encounter, that would have more of an impact. And really, he didn't need to see her, but he did *want* to see her.

She'd have a sea-blue wrap around her narrow hips and a hot-pink bikini top, he imagined. She might be wearing a large and expensive straw hat, to keep the sun off her fair skin. She loved hats. She might be getting ice creams for her boys, ages nine and twelve, she'd written. He guessed she'd scarcely changed. That if any gray had appeared in her hair, she would have colored it black. He guessed he'd notice a slight sagging in the flesh of her arms, but that she'd be otherwise unchanged. He'd seen her photograph in the Style pages of the *Times* a while back at some gathering at the Metropolitan Museum of Art, so he knew she'd kept her shape, about which she was always concerned. And he guessed the girlish laugh that never failed to melt his heart would likewise remain unchanged. She was always so much fun.

"What took so long?" Martha asked, accepting the planter's punch Scott handed to her.

"There was a wait at the bar."

Martha took a sip through the straw, then removed the wedge of pineapple from the rim of the plastic cup and dropped it into the drink. She scanned for Will, then sat back and closed her eyes in the sun.

"Did you see Susan?"

"Yes, the sun goddess is still by the pool."

Scott took a deep sip of his planter's punch and sat back in the chair, shirtless now, the sun warm and comforting on his skin. His old-man skin. He hadn't paid attention to it until Susan had remarked on his hairy shoulders. When did his barber start trimming his ear hair, he wondered. He patted his soft belly. Ten pounds he could stand to lose. Twenty pounds, if he were to be honest. Ten was a more reasonable expectation. But not on vacation.

"Wake me if I fall asleep, will you?" Martha said. "I don't want to burn."

"Yes," he said. He could never fall asleep in the sun, and today memories of Cat had returned, intensely vivid. He had loved her so. He twisted his cup into the sand beside him, lay back, closed his eyes.

*

Their final trip together had been the worst of his life. He would never forget. It didn't hurt anymore; the pain had been absorbed into his bones and had calcified. It had ended in Rome, but even when he'd returned to Princeton for his senior year, and Cat for her junior year, it hurt. The hurt faded quickly, though, as Cat made it clear that she was eager to put their relationship behind her and he had no alternative but to move on.

Even that fall, after what had happened in Rome, he'd held out hope. But Cat would remain with the guy she'd met while Scott was away all that year, a townie four years her senior (who was nice enough, Scott admitted). The voice he'd heard from all the way across the ocean. Scott knew finally to give up when he and Cat strolled the campus stone walkways, on a lovely leafy September afternoon, talking, Scott still making pathetic stabs at forgiveness and reunion.

"Why did you even come to Paris, then?" he'd asked her.

"I don't know, Scott," she said in a pleading tone, because she knew how much she'd hurt him. "We'd planned it for so long. And I felt guilty. You're such a sweetheart. I *cared* about you. And I didn't know how I was going to feel."

"Well, that's something," he said. Silence. Walking. He asked, "When *did* you know?"

"I knew the instant I saw you, once I got through customs."

"Really?" Scott said.

"Really," Cat said with genuine sadness. "I knew the second I saw you that I'd made a mistake."

"Wow," Scott said.

*

He'd taken an expensive taxi to Charles de Gaulle and managed to find the customs exit to wait. And there she emerged, her Louis Vuitton bag over her shoulder, wearing the same Deadhead skirt she'd been wearing when they met, a huge brimmed straw hat, black hair cascading down, aviator Ray Bans, two hours late. "Customs, ugh!" were her first words. But then, "Hi!" and threw her arms around him, kissed him. Those lips he'd so missed, so plump and red and soft.

"Where do we get my bags?"

307

"Bag-zuh? How many do you have?"

"Two."

"Why two?"

"One for shoes."

"Ah."

How could this be? Scott wondered from thirty years in the future, on a beach he now felt petty for aspiring to, drinking a silly rum drink. Customs must have been different back then, with 9/11 seventeen years away. But he did remember because of what he'd done, standing behind her as she scanned the conveyor for her bags. He'd squeezed her ass. Because he missed it. Because it was so petite and cute, and in the diaphanous skirt, so eminently squeezable. And he was flirting. And he used to do it. And she used to laugh and say, "Stop" but not really mean it.

But this time she jumped as if she'd been stuck with a needle. She turned and looked at him, shocked. He knew now that that had been the moment when *he* should have known.

Cat's parents had paid for an expensive room in Paris, at the Plaza Athénée. Scott had never seen such luxury, especially vivid after grimy Pigalle, which had become even more miserable for those last two solitary nights. A bottle of champagne waited for them, on ice, and there was a gigantic American-style bathroom, complete with a bidet (Cat had to explain to him what it was). On the bed were huge pillows and such luxurious sheets that he could tell from Cat's expression that his shorts and T-shirt, appropriate enough in Pigalle, were too shabby for them. She changed into a nightgown, and he immediately engaged her in what he'd longed for, but she said, "Scott, not now. I can't. All the travel. I'm jet-lagged."

And of course he said, "Of course. I understand."

But the next night was the same.

"Scott, please, I'm just not ready." She stroked his face and apologized.

They bickered at the Louvre—which she had to see—because of the crowds and the heat. They couldn't even get near the Mona Lisa. And when they sat at an outdoor table at a brasserie that had a view of the Eiffel

Tower, she said, "God, why doesn't that waiter come *here*? The service is terrible. Is he ignoring us?"

"Brasseries are like this, which is why I didn't want to sit here in the first place. Sometimes they're even slower when they suspect you're American."

Paris was so unfun for Cat (and Scott—she kept apologizing at night) that they took a train a day early to Monaco, where she so wanted to go. She spoke with her mother daily by phone and "Mommy" took care of the accommodations change. And still, he found the diminutive for her mother sweet and endearing. A child still, this one. So sweet. So petite and beautiful. By the time they'd reached Rome, though, Scott grew more vocal.

"Seriously, Cat? We cannot have sex?"

"It doesn't feel right."

"What the fuck does that mean?"

"Don't yell at me."

"I'm not yelling," he said softly.

And so it was that the following morning, as they sat in the hot sun on a terrace overlooking Rome, drinking strong coffee and pear juice—"Really, pear juice?" Scott thought—and eating the most flavorless bread Scott had ever tasted, that he'd noticed there wasn't the usual morning silence that there had been. He scanned the front page of the *International Herald Tribune*.

"Scott?"

"Yes?" he looked up from the paper to see not the clear blue eyes that he adored but rather eyes that were full of tears.

He waited. And waited.

"I'm three weeks late." She looked down and rubbed her eyes.

Memories were few from this point on. Three, in fact. First, sitting in an Italian hospital and watching the Italian nurse, a nun, no less—could that memory be right? a nun-nurse?—approach and beam at Cat, and at Scott, and to Cat she said, "*Sì! Positiva!*" Cat sat stunned, as if she couldn't translate that. The beaming nun said, "*Positiva!* You are."

And this is when Cat put her face in her hands and wept and kept them there as she bolted the hospital, with Scott right behind her.

"It'll be okay, Cat," he repeated. "Everything will be okay." All the way back to the hotel.

Memory number two, walking alone along the Tiber River while Cat called home. He told her he'd leave her so she could have some privacy, and he'd walked. He leaned on the wall overlooking the river. He removed his wallet from his front pocket. He looked through it. Saw the last of his ten-franc notes and the many thousands of lira. He remembered having the urge to throw his wallet in the water. He almost did. What did it matter? What did anything matter?

Three: returning to the room. Cat sat on the beautifully made bed, her back to him, still crying. He'd entered quietly and heard her say into the phone, "Why do you keep saying, 'Poor Scott'?" She would now have reached her beloved half-sister, Diane, seven years her senior and her confidante, whom Scott adored as well. It was the only moment he felt a small amount of comfort that whole awful trip. It lasted to this day. Scott was still grateful to Diane for saying that. Mrs. Delouvrier made the arrangements for the flight home the following day out of Rome.

*

Scott felt around beside him in the sand for his drink. He'd been thinking so long that all the ice had melted and nothing but fruit floated in the pink liquid. He drank it all down in one go, not wanting to waste the overpriced rum.

Will appeared at the foot of his beach chair. His dark curly hair dripping, chest hair matted all the way down to his flat stomach, his broad, smooth shoulders. "Dad, come back in. The waves are getting *huge*."

Scott shielded his eyes to see his son—seventeen years old, a young man with whisker stubble on cheeks and chin, hairy legs, and taut, muscular arms. Could Will possibly know how lucky he was? Scott wondered. He himself felt impossibly lucky now to be beside his wonderful wife and with his strong, healthy children.

"You *bet*," Scott said. He shook Martha's shoulder, said, "Roll over, sweetie." She did, and he covered her legs with a towel and walked into the ocean beside his son.

*

The following summer, after he and Martha had met Sally and heard the story of her broken marriage, Scott found that he had no interest whatsoever in seeing Cat. He *had* before leaving for New York. They'd exchanged emails, made the plan. But he felt so terrible for Sally and what she'd been through, he didn't think he could bear to see a perfect wealthy life on the Upper East Side. On Seventy-Fifth and Park, Jesus. He liked Cat and wanted to stay in touch—she, and her family, had been enormously important, for an admittedly brief but nevertheless powerful time in his life—but not on this day, having heard how Sally's life had been upended.

Leaving Sally to see Cat? No. He'd done that already.

Had he thought to change his plans in Rome way back then, to fly to Sally in Greece? No, he hadn't even thought it. Just wanted to get out of Europe altogether, to the security of his home and his parents; he'd been cut to the core. He wouldn't have remembered the name of the island she'd gone to, so he wouldn't have been able to find her even if he'd had the wherewithal and spontaneity and life—her kind of life—to try to find her. He didn't think of her. He pitied himself. That had been all. He wouldn't reconnect with Sally till after graduating and beginning work as a reporter. While working on a story in New York, he called a friend who'd also been with his group at the University of Bristol; she knew someone who could find Sally's contact information. But by then, when he'd reconnected with Sally in Manhattan for the first time since Paris, he had met his fellow reporter, Martha Wallace.

*

Two months after he and Martha saw Sally, he asked to meet with his editor to discuss a new book project. Really, he simply wanted to be in New York, especially in September when the city comes back to life after summer, to relish his pied-à-terre and New York City life. But he also wanted to find out how Sally was doing.

He now had Sally's email and her cell. He hadn't been in touch in the interim, but he texted her from the gate before boarding the flight to LaGuardia at 9 a.m. He delighted when he saw the dots appear on his iPhone—how he loved those dots that let you know the other person was typing. It was as if she'd been waiting for him.

Yes, I'm around, she wrote.

Yay! When?

Dinner tomorrow?

Yes!

He waited. No dots. He typed.

How are you?

Dots. He waited impatiently. Then the dots disappeared. Then reappeared. Then disappeared.

OK? he typed. When she didn't respond, he typed, *We'll talk. I'll be in touch tomorrow.*

*

He watched Sally walk toward him across the cobblestones that paved the end of Ninth Avenue, wearing a sheer black ankle-length dress. Her long dark gold hair curled down, crossing onto her shoulders and beyond, front and back; he loved her hair long like that. She still had a great body—long with full, strong hips and athletic arms.

Scott needed another charging cord for his phone, so he'd planned to get that at the Apple Store and meet her nearby. But he didn't want to stand waiting outside the store (he was chronically early) on busy Fourteenth Street and Ninth Avenue near where they'd reconnected nine years earlier. A few blocks below it, though, there was little traffic, and café tables sat out on the cobblestones at the corner of Gansevoort and Ninth. We'll walk to the restaurant together, he'd said.

"Hi, you!" she said.

He beamed at her and hugged her.

312

"Well, you *look* great," he said.

She looked down at her dress, low cut. She pressed her breasts together so that they pushed out of her black bra, as if to make them kiss. "Whaddaya think, enough décolletage?"

"Works for me," he said.

She grinned at him and smiled with sparkly eyes. She slugged him gently on the shoulder and said, "How are you?"

"Never better."

"I'm glad for you," she said. "So, where are you taking me?"

Scott put his arm over her shoulder and led her south down Greenwich Street.

"A cute little restaurant called Le Gigot."

"Aww! A French bistro! I love that place."

"You know it?"

"Of course."

"I was hoping to surprise you."

"I live here full time, remember?"

She looked at him. She looked back to the sidewalk.

He said, "Are you able to date?"

"Able, yes. Interested? No."

She pushed her shoulder into his as they walked. The evening was warm and windless.

"So, what's the news?"

"Well, Edward is finally moving out. I don't know if we're going to keep the apartment or if we'll have to leave."

"When?"

"End of this week."

"Where's he going?"

"He's moving in with *her*!"

"The barista?"

"Yes!" After a few more steps she said, "Says he loves her."

He couldn't imagine how anyone, having fallen in love with Sally, could fall out of love with her. He put his arm over her shoulder and she put her arm around his waist. They'd by now crossed over to Hudson Street. They didn't speak, just walked connected by arms until they hit Morton Street and turned left toward the restaurant. As they reached Cornelia Street they let their arms fall away.

"You," she said, "taking me to a French bistro. Did you plan that?"

"A little. But really, I just wanted some place I knew you'd like, and I know you like this food."

"Absolute favorite!" she said.

He held the door for her.

Sally ordered leeks vinaigrette and *sole meunière*, he the *brandade de morue* and steak tartare. Sally chose a hearty zinfandel and she and Scott fell into talking as if no time had passed, about his work, her classes, her wonderful Arthur, who had started seventh grade, how Arthur was handling the divorce.

"Edward adores him, of course, but Arthur's angry. He's a tough cookie, that one, he'll be a real New Yorker."

"So you're talking at least."

"Oh, yeah, we talk. We go through our motions. For Arthur. My hope is a fresh start once he moves out."

"He'll forgive him, eventually," he said.

"I know, and I want that, I really do. But enough—I came out to get away from myself for the night. How's Martha?"

"Great."

"And the two of you?"

"Never better."

"You're lucky."

"You don't need to tell me. Though we still don't see enough of each other. One of us always seems to be on the road. I thought with Will in college now, we'd be doing more things together, but we're not. I think she's felt so landlocked during all our kid years, and me on the road so often, she's making up for lost time, doing a lot of travel writing. And I'm glad for her."

By the time their plates had been cleared, Sally reached across for his hand and said, "I am so loving being with you, I don't want this to end."

"Neither do I. *Eau de vie?*" He smiled at her.

"Hell yeah! Old times, old friend."

He felt a sudden urge to kiss her. Why? To say "Thank you," to say, "I love you, old friend." To say exactly this. He just smiled.

When the drinks arrived, Scott said, "Why did you leave?"

"Where?"

"Paris."

"Oh. That. Do you really want to go *there?*"

"Kind of."

She exhaled heavily and looked away, clearly not wanting to go there. She sipped from her glass, turned back to him. "I couldn't bear it anymore. And I hate good-byes."

"But not even a note?"

"Scott, I was in love with you—*in love,* and told you so—and you were in love with someone else."

They both paused to take the smallest of sips of eau de vie.

"Whatever happened to the two of you anyway?"

"Me and Cat?" He cleared his throat. "We broke up during my senior year."

"Happens, doesn't it. Anyone after?"

"A lot of girls, a lot of sex, but no one special. Not till after I graduated and met Martha."

They were comfortable in the interstices of the conversation. But he still wanted to be back there, back then.

"Where did you go?"

"You mean in Paris?"

"Yeah, we still had one more night together."

She squinted as if trying to remember. "I'm pretty sure I just went to the airport and hung out for thirty-six hours. I was pretty blue."

"I'm sorry, Sally."

"One of the borders of my life. I crossed over it. Scott, I'm so happy to be reunited."

"Me, too. I'm here for you always. I'm a call or a text away."

She smiled softly.

When the bill was presented, Scott grabbed it. When she moved for her purse, he said, "I've got this. I want to."

The air remained warm, almost balmy. When they turned right on Hudson, she slipped her hand into his. When they reached Perry Street, she let his hand go.

"Here you are."

His place was midway down the block. They stood face to face. He didn't want to leave her and she could see this, could always see him.

"I don't want to leave you either," she said.

"I'll walk you home," he said.

She stared up at him, those hazel eyes he knew so well so long ago. Slowly, she reached to take his hand in hers. She squeezed it. She looked into his eyes, her lips parted, but her teeth clicked shut together. She waited. He waited. She said, "Or."

"Or?"

She squeezed his hand and tilted her head slightly, just a twitch, in the direction of his apartment.

Scott closed his eyes. He breathed deeply, exhaled. "Sally." He breathed again. "I *can't.*"

She looked down and said, "I know. It was just a thought."

"I just can't," he said again.

She let his hand go and turned to walk. He walked beside her, took her hand and she let him.

"Just to the High Line, okay?" she said.

"The High Line. By yourself."

"It's lovely at night. And it will probably be crowded because it's such a nice night. I love the High Line."

They walked in silence until they reached the steps up to the elevated railway-path-turned-park. They stopped and faced each other. She held his cheeks, brought his face to hers and kissed him on the lips. Neither too short nor too long, a slow count of three, just long enough for the memory of their mouths together to return to him. She stared into his eyes. "Stay in touch, you."

"Of course I will, Sally."

She smiled gently, turned, and ascended the steps in her long black dress. He watched her until she disappeared.

*

He'd had meetings all the next day and a flight home early the following morning. Work pressed in, endless emails. He coaxed Martha into taking Friday off to spend an afternoon together, a visit to the art museum, a long lunch. Sex when they returned home. A light soup dinner and a movie.

He wasn't able to email Sally until Saturday.

"Dear, dear Sally," he wrote. "Just a short email to tell you how much I loved dinner, loved being with you, loved talking with you. I know you'll make it through this patch. Call me or write any time. I know I have to return in November—I'll be in touch then and maybe you can take *me* to dinner."

He stopped to think, sighed, shook his head, then signed it simply "Yours" and clicked SEND.

He did not hear back.

When he wrote before his November visit, he did not hear back then, either.

*

The following September, Scott felt he needed to get away, and he planned to stay in the Perry Street apartment for the month. Actually he moved his flight up, owing to a new tension at home, and arrived before Labor Day, despite the city heat and smell. He moved into what he thought a good writing routine. Up at six, coffee and a poached egg on toast with the *Times*, followed by a long walk along the High Line, then back to the apartment to write. He would write until late afternoon, then read the *New Yorker* or a novel, then take another walk on the High Line. As the days passed, he found himself checking his watch more and more frequently.

He knew he was drinking too much and had made 5:30 the absolute earliest he could have the balm of a cold, strong cocktail at one of the bars along Ninth Avenue. Sometimes he'd finish the High Line early and walk the blocks between Ninth and Tenth Avenue, slowly, peering into shop windows and checking his watch, but he always had a cocktail in a public place where he could be around people.

"*Edward?*" Scott said.

Edward Adams turned on his barstool to regard Scott, and Scott knew he was not mistaken when he saw the mole above the right eyebrow. Edward pushed his Clark Kent glasses high on the bridge of his nose. "Scott Murray. Sally's friend. It's been a long time since the only time we met."

"My word," Edward said, standing. "Hello." He held out a hand.

Scott had at 5:30, this mid-September evening, chosen the Gaslight, just south of West Fourteenth Street, to have his cocktail. He came here most frequently. He liked the light crowd, the wooden bar. It comforted him.

After they'd shaken hands, Edward said, "Would you care to join me?" Scott was so surprised at chancing on Edward that he hesitated long enough for Edward to say, "I completely understand if you don't want to."

"No, no," Scott said. "I'd *like* to, actually. Thank you."

Sitting, and ordering his Manhattan—his preferred bartender, Alan, would have known the usual, but Alan was off on Wednesdays—he wondered if he should broach the topic and decided he would. "As I'm sure you can imagine, I've been wondering what happened. We only heard Sally's side. A year ago July I saw Sally. She was angry."

"And rightly so," Edward said. "Or, rather, understandably so."

Scott's cocktail arrived and the two men touched glasses. Edward's short, clipped hair had grayed considerably, but not completely, and it made him appear, in his gray seersucker suit, older than he was, but dignified.

"Can you tell me what happened?"

"I fell in love," Edward said.

"You fell in love."

"Still am."

"You're still together?"

"Mind you, it was not something I sought. My bad behavior was a result of this. I couldn't handle all that was happening. I was very unhappy. Being in love was miserable because I loved Sally so much, because she's so wonderful—difficult, but wonderful. I drank to dull the . . . the . . . the agony. Prescription pain meds. Anything I could find. But I couldn't blot it out completely, much as I tried. Until the accident. Did she tell you?"

"Yes, the bus."

"I could have *died*."

"Yes."

"Since I didn't die, that bus probably saved my life."

"Indeed."

They drank.

Scott said, "I've been trying to reach Sally, but she won't respond. I even went to her apartment but the doorman never gets an answer."

"Not surprising. She's better but quite changed."

This news so dispirited Scott—*changed* by the divorce?—that he took an extra big swallow of his Manhattan. His head spun slightly.

Then he turned to Edward and said, "Edward, please. How did it happen? How did you fall in love, in your circumstances? Were you unhappy with Sally? Was that it?"

"No, not at all, I loved and still love Sally. She could be a handful, but no, I was completely content in the marriage. The job was the issue."

"So, how does it happen?"

"*How* is easy." Edward studied Scott's face. "What I can't tell you is *why*. I imagine every case is different. Or maybe it's all the same, some chemical response. Is there something specific you'd like to know?"

Scott turned away, sipped his Manhattan, took a breath, and said to the shelf of liquor bottles, "My wife has been having an affair for a year. I found out a couple months ago."

"Oh, dear," Edward said with genuine sympathy, sympathy Scott hungered for as much as for the evening cocktail. "I'm so sorry."

Edward rubbed Scott's back and kept rubbing it until Scott turned to him. Even knowing him as little as he did, Scott knew that physical affection was not something that came easily to Edward, and this touched and comforted him.

Edward said, "It's hard business, I know."

Scott sighed. Yes. Hard business.

"How did you find out?" Edward asked.

"My wife, Martha, she told me. The wife of her . . . lover discovered the affair. The wife forced the issue. Threatened to call me herself if Martha didn't do it. She actually did call me to confirm that Martha had come clean."

"Interesting," Edward said. "If you don't mind my asking, because I'm curious about these things, how did the wife find out?"

"It's kind of funny, actually, if anything can be funny anymore. The wife was going through the mail and opened a letter from the Greenbrier resort, addressed to her and her husband. It was a note from a staff member thanking them for their uncommon generosity and hoping they'd return to the Greenbrier soon."

Edward nodded and said, "And the wife had not been to the resort."

"The resort about which my wife was writing a travel piece? No."

"Mmm," Edward said. "Where do things stand now?"

"We're working on it. We may make it. I don't know. Even if we do, it won't be the same. It's pretty damaged."

"Yes. I understand. But we move on. We have no choice."

Scott sighed.

They sipped in silence.

"So, again," Scott said, somewhat desperately. "How did it happen? For you. I'm trying to understand it all."

"That I fell in love with a performance artist ten years my junior who has purple hair and a stud in her lip?"

Scott chuckled at Edward. "Yes, that."

"It's so fascinating," Edward said. He rubbed his chin. "I saw her daily for, for forever. She works at the Starbucks across the street. Across from Chelsea Market." Edward pointed with his thumb over his shoulder. "Where I always got coffee. I found her cute, but I find a lot of women cute or beautiful. We'd banter each day, and we got to know each other through my ordering different items. I remember trying to make sense of all the odd concoctions they offer. I mean, too many choices!"

Scott smiled and said, "Do you remember the crackers?"

Edward paused, but then said, "I do remember getting crackers with you." He paused to think of it, and the slightest of grins twitched once at the corners of his mouth. "That's funny." He nodded, then turned to Scott. "She made me laugh. That was kind of it. The way she described the coffees and teas and whatnot. I almost always left laughing, happy, lighter. And then when I lost my job and was trying to figure out what to do with my life, I'd spend a lot of time in there. Because I couldn't bring myself to tell Sally I'd been let go—too humiliated, too scared—I had to go somewhere all day. They have Internet there. Sally hates Starbucks, so I knew I was safe there. And then I started drinking, more out of boredom. At the end of the day, I'd have a cocktail at Pastis, until it closed, then here. And I was in here one afternoon and in she walks."

"She being?"

"I'm sorry. Miranda. She's meeting me here soon. I can introduce you."

"Really? I'm curious to meet her."

"One afternoon I was in here and in she walked. She'd just gotten off her shift and she said, 'It's you!' The sound of her voice. It was like a melody." Edward, normally so dry, became almost dreamy, Scott thought. "Like when you hear a song you instantly love. I asked to buy her a drink, she accepted, and we sat here drinking for two hours. Laughing. I remember just laughing a lot. And then there was a long silence between us because we were kind of talked out but didn't want to leave. And I kissed her. And she kissed me back."

Edward leaned back and exhaled toward the ceiling in a way that seemed to Scott uncommonly emotional for Edward. "Scott, this is a cliché, but it was like a drug. It was as if I'd been injected with sodium pentothal or whatever it is they give you that makes you so happy that you'll tell anyone anything. It just washed over and through my whole body. I was euphoric."

"Right here? In this bar?"

"In these very seats." He paused, narrowed his eyes. "Actually those seats down there, but yes, it happened here. We were climbing all over each other, making a spectacle of ourselves, actually. But her hands in my hair. The smell of her skin. Someone actually told us to get a room. I think it was the bartender, and I believe he was serious."

"Did you?"

"No, I was expected home. I ultimately had to leave. And a good thing. Imagine if I'd been seen! Making out with this younger woman with purple hair. We have all kinds of friends in this neighborhood. I run into people I know here *all* the time, but I wasn't thinking straight. I stumbled home, euphoric. And when I woke up the next morning to shower and put on my fake suit, or rather the suit I didn't need, I couldn't stop thinking about her. I went to the Starbucks, and she wasn't working that day and I was *beside* myself. I walked all day long. Then, unable to bear it, I got horribly drunk and was mean to Sally and Arthur. I mean, we weren't great even in good times. Sally's depressions deepened. But, anyway, I was waiting for Miranda when she got to work the next day, and she saw me on the street and she literally started running, and she leapt into me and wrapped her legs around me. She's tiny. We hugged and kissed and, well, it was pretty clear what was happening. And I gave into it."

"And here you are."

"And here I am."

"Fascinating." Scott decided to have another. Edward declined. Martha had not spoken of euphoria or drugs, though she wouldn't, would she? She would and did mention boredom and loneliness.

"Edward, I need to find Sally, I need to get in touch with her. Is she okay?"

"Well, as I said, she's better but she's different."

"What do you mean, *better?*" Scott said, not hiding his irritation.

To which Edward, as if to a dim client, explained, "Well, after the . . . the *attempt*, things *changed*. There was an 'anoxic injury' in medical parlance."

"Attempt? What attempt?"

Without emotion, Edward turned away from Scott to face the bar, though he lost some of his color. To his reflection in the mirror he said, "You don't know."

"Know what?"

Edward shook his head and softly said, "I just assumed you had mutual friends, and that you'd know from one of them."

"Know what?!"

Edward turned to Scott. "Sally tried to commit suicide. *Tried*, mind you."

"When?"

"A year ago?"

Scott raced in his mind back one year. He said, "I need to know when exactly."

"I found her, so I know exactly when. It was the day after I moved out."

"How? Pills?"

"A utility knife. Sent Arthur to a friend's, said I was to be contacted to pick him up the following day as I had weekend custody. She swallowed a bottle of aspirin. Ran a warm shallow bath, water not deep enough to drown in, just warm enough to keep the blood flowing. Then she made three vertical cuts along each wrist."

Scott turned away, his heart hammering against his chest.

"It's remarkable that she lived. I wasn't supposed to go back to the apartment that day. The reason I stayed—I didn't want to stay there, but Sally had become so erratic I was worried about Arthur, I wanted to make sure Arthur was taken care of. At any rate, I'd forgotten my wedding band. I never wore the wedding band, but I was sentimental for it, nonetheless, and I did want to retrieve it from the back of the bureau we shared in the bedroom. The bathroom door was open. She'd cut her radial arteries. She wasn't conscious. I called 911. They said if I'd walked in five minutes later, she might easily have been beyond saving. The water was still warm. So she clearly *wanted* to end it. They also said if I hadn't known her blood type, she might have died. She's type AB and they were able to infuse her in the ambulance."

"How did you know her blood type? I'm not even sure I know mine. Certainly don't know my wife's."

"There were a lot of tests when we were trying to get pregnant, and it's one of the less common ones."

Scott shook his head. "I can't believe it," Scott said.

"It's a guilt I will carry on my shoulders till I die. I mean, she was bipolar, she wasn't well, but I'd clearly sent her over the edge."

"Bipolar?"

"Yes, diagnosed after we married. She battled depression. Type two bipolar, not off the rails, but severe depression alternating with severe euphoria."

"I didn't know that." As he said these words, he recognized they did not come as a surprise.

"It doesn't lessen the guilt. I still loved her, still do."

They were silent for more than a minute.

Scott sensed Edward smiling and turned to him. He *was* smiling, a sad smile. Feeling Scott's gaze, Edward said, "It's just. It was so Sally."

"What was?" Scott asked softly.

"She even gave multiple meanings to it. Or something, I don't know. But it was very Sally of her. You're a writer. I think you'll appreciate this."

"What?"

"Well, clearly she didn't want to be naked for whoever found her." Edward shook his head at his martini glass. "I mean she could have put on *anything*. She could have worn *clothes*. She could have put on one of the one-piece bathing suits she wore on vacations after she had Arthur." Edward shook his head and snorted.

"What."

"She'd put on a yellow polka-dot bikini," Edward said.

Scott took a slug of a nearly full Manhattan.

Edward lifted his eyebrows at Scott. "This requires some explanation. This wasn't an ugly joke. It was a rebuke to me."

Scott took a breath and said, "Go on."

"She'd brought that bikini on our honeymoon. And I wouldn't permit her to wear it. I mean, I couldn't *force* her not to wear it, but I put my foot down fairly hard."

"Why?" Scott asked.

"Because I was an ass. I felt it wasn't appropriate for where we were staying. We got into our first married fight. She went into one of the resort shops and bought the most heinous and expensive, frilly, gaudy one-piece suit she could find. It made her look like something in a Disney cartoon. Wore it the whole time. To piss me off. She was strong. She was not easy, but I do miss that Sally."

She was the easiest person on Earth! Scott thought. Scott turned away, faced the bar. What was he talking about?

Edward again put his hand on Scott's back.

"Bubbakins!"

Edward turned, stood, and said, "My tulip!" He kissed her on the mouth and hugged her.

Scott stood to see a sprite of a woman, five-three if that, with a purple bob and a silver stud in her lip, dressed in a black tank top, jeans, and colorful sneakers. He didn't know what to do.

Edward said, "Sugarplum, this is Scott. But we've been discussing some rather sad business."

She frowned at Edward and Edward nodded in response. "Oh, honey, don't."

Even in these brief moments, it was clear to Scott how in love they were with each other. That they already had their own shorthand language. Edward's face had noticeably flushed when he'd seen her. Edward had found his perfect match—unlikely as she was.

The sprite looked sadly at Scott. "I'm sorry," she said.

Wanting only some formality to maintain his balance, he said, "I'm Scott."

"I'm Miranda."

"I know. It's good to meet you."

*

Scott strode quickly north along the High Line, buzzing from the news that Sally could possibly be out here as much as from the two Manhattans quickly drunk. He could help her, Edward had said. And she him. Scott had told Edward that he'd been looking for Sally on the High Line because she said she walked it daily. Edward confirmed that she still had limited custody of Arthur during the week, so she walked the High Line every day to pick him up from his school in the lower West Village, and then walked back home with him. He was all but certain they took the High Line from the Gansevoort entrance to the West Twenty-Third exit. Scott asked for his bill, but Edward insisted on picking up the drinks. Scott, feeling an urgency to leave, thanked Edward, thanked him for everything. He shook Miranda's small hand and departed.

He hoped on this clement evening, on this former railway, like the Museée D'Orsay, he thought, she might be walking . . .

Alas, nothing but maddening pedestrians moving too slowly, clogging the pathways.

He headed to Le Gigot, ate a lonely salad at the bar, and returned to the apartment. He was too keyed up to read, so he watched television, first pouring his allotted three fingers of bourbon and then taking three sleeping pills.

The following day, he did his best to keep to his routine, though he found concentrating difficult. He told himself that he was just going to see his old friend, to try to help her out of wherever she was.

School, of *course*, the school hour—why hadn't he thought of this all these weeks? He imagined surprising her when she was with Arthur. He was eager to see Arthur; what would he look like now? He'd see them— "What a coincidence!"—then ask to walk home with them, and then he and Sally could talk over green iced tea just as they had ten years ago.

Scott reached the Gansevoort entrance at 3:15 and sat on the steps to wait, checking his watch frequently. At 3:40, he spotted her many blocks away. His heart raced, and now he knew why.

They approached slowly. Sally and, to her left, Arthur, who'd grown tall, with a mop of golden hair. Soon it was clear that they were not two but rather three. He kept expecting the woman on Sally's left to either pass or fall back, but as they grew closer it was clear they were together, a younger woman with fair, light-brown skin, wearing a white cardigan, unbuttoned all the way down, and a green skirt. Who could she be? Scott wondered. Arthur hardly needed a nanny at his age. From this distance, Sally looked exactly as good as she had the previous year. Absolutely unchanged, though now in jeans, sandals, and an untucked blue Oxford cloth shirt. Cuffs buttoned, he noted.

When they crossed the street to approach the steps where Scott stood, he crouched and held out his arms. Arthur made a face. The other woman remained neutral. Sally stared at him as if she didn't recognize him. But she did and said, "Scott. Hi."

"What a coincidence!" he said, hands still out, smiling.

"Yes," she said, and smiled. But it was only a half smile—that is, only one side of her smile worked. It jarred Scott to the point of speechlessness.

Sally gave him a gentle hug and said, "How have you been?"

Her voice had changed, as if the dentist had left cotton beneath her tongue.

"I've, um, been fine."

The two on either side of Sally seemed uncomfortable. When Sally failed to introduce Scott, Scott said, "Arthur, I haven't seen you since you were three. My name's Scott."

"Hey," he said and offered him a limp hand.

To the other woman he said, "I'm an old friend of Sally's."

"Anna," she said and held out her hand.

They stood there.

Sally looked to Anna and said in her new muffled voice, "The piano lesson is at four?"

"Yes."

To Scott, Sally said, "We've got to get Arthur to his piano lesson."

Arthur, arms folded, maintained a skeptical distance.

"Okay," Scott said.

As Sally began to walk and Scott moved aside to let them pass, Scott said, "Is there a time that I could come to see you? I'm in the city for a while."

"Sure," Sally said. "Email me."

"Email? I did. Many times." And texted, many times, staring at the phone for five minutes hoping dots would appear.

"Oh," she said. "I must have missed it. I'll look again."

"Good to see you," she said, with an easy and self-contented smile. And they walked up the steps to the High Line.

Scott followed, slowly, as in a dream, as if up from a grave. Anna turned to look back at Scott once when he'd reached the first landing. When he reached the High Line, he stopped and let them walk. Anna turned back once more, and when she saw Scott standing still, staring, she spoke into Sally's ear, then turned and hurried back to Scott.

"This has happened before," Anna said to Scott. "Do you know the situation?"

"Yes, I was in touch with Edward just yesterday."

"I'm a nurse. Mr. Adams hired me," Anna said.

"To look after Arthur?"

"Well, really, to look after them both. She's on medications. And she's not always reliable. But it's the effects of the blood loss. She had something of a stroke, or many small strokes, before they could get enough blood back into her. I'm sure inside she's very glad to see you. I just didn't want you to think ... Well, I just wanted you to know why she probably wasn't as you expected."

"Thank you for coming back to me. For telling me."

She stared into his eyes and said, "I'm sorry."

Scott nodded once. Anna hustled to rejoin them. Scott watched till they were obscured by pedestrians. He turned. He sat on the top step. Elbows on knees, head in hands. He rocked slowly back and forth.

*

Scott was areligious, but he believed in *something* rather than nothing, *some* force. Something incomprehensible, directly unknowable, but a force, whatever had willed the universe into being. Lucky his whole life, he naturally construed it as a benevolent force. A force that makes a man return for a ring he doesn't need, to prevent what might otherwise have happened. Now he felt otherwise. It was an amoral force, or worse. A force he now detested, and he felt an anger within him as big as the force that he wanted to annihilate.

After seeing Sally exactly where he'd expected, he knew in his soul that this force was possibly worse. But it *was* an actual force, one that willed people into being, one that crossed their paths. Had he simply been too young to see it? Sally's neon vividness was gone, as if someone had yanked out the cord. Her skin and eyes had dulled. Her smile had been cut in half. It was a shadow he saw, the mannequin version of Sally. But no, she had recognized him. Was there hope? Not right now, anyway, he realized. And not for him, either.

Scott had always sought comfort in bookshops. After seeing Sally, he had walked in an aimless fashion toward his favorite in the neighborhood, Three Lives & Company on the corner of Waverly and West Tenth, with its welcoming bright red doors.

He would read the jackets of new books, note who was blurbing whom, then read at least the first three pages of any books that caught his interest. On this day, to have thirty distinct and unique voices in his head to cover his own angry voice felt like his only option beyond doing something he'd regret. Walking the city streets forced him inside himself; when walking he needed to keep the noise and commotion that was New York out of his head. The voices of others in books could silence completely his own voice and he could lose sight of who he was and even *that* he was.

The bookshop had wood flooring, worn by the shuffling foot treads of browsers. Crown molding made the place feel casually ornate. The cashier's desk seemed more a secret warren than a space for commerce. The many walls of bookshelves, books set out on tables and other pieces of furniture from another era, old books and new, made it a warm, quirky space inhabited by the owners and their salespeople, who could make knowledgeable recommendations on books or simply chat, especially if you lived in the neighborhood. Scott had been here enough that the tall older man with graying hair shaved closely to his tanned scalp, said "Good afternoon!" with recognition. Scott didn't know his name, though he and the gentleman had talked books on a previous visit, and sales, and the fate of such lovely bookshops as this. It was a shop, he thought, not a store. A bookshop. You shopped for and found the right book here.

The shop played soft music, an eclectic though linked mix, streamed in by Pandora. And so it was that, as he set down a book of short stories by Margaret Atwood and lifted a nonfiction paperback of Elizabeth Kolbert's latest investigation of the environment, that Cat Stevens's "Tea for the Tillerman" faded out, and the sounds of a different guitar followed. And the opening lines, almost in the way that certain smells can bring you back to a specific place, and therefore time, returned him to those steps on Montmartre beneath the white domed church, the smell and sound of Paris in the 1980s, the food and the wine and the cherry-scented pipe smoke.

It's a still life watercolor
of a now-late afternoon

Why this, now? How? What kind of force sends out personal messages via song verses in bookshops? Pandora—what an appropriate name, Scott thought. The force in all its random malevolence. This was no coincidence. He should have straight-armed it, said no, and departed, instead of listening when he recognized it.

But he'd had heard the song a dozen times, at least, in the thirty years since Montmartre, and he never failed to think of Sally. Every time. As when someone mentioned Scotland, he thought of her.

And you read your Emily Dickinson
And I my Robert Frost

He for the first time listened to the lyrics, paid attention to them, in the way he might have listened to the young Sally read him Eliot or Yeats in bed, or Emily or Robert, all of which she *had*, to his great . . . what? His great *joy*, he knew only now. *That* had been joy. Joy. He'd always thought of the song as a sweet, soft, happy song, because he had been happy when he'd first heard it. So happy. Filled with joy. But it wasn't the wine or the song or the sun setting over Paris. It was her. Her all along. One of the happiest moments of his life. The steps of Montmartre, and the musicians from Laos, and "The Dangling Conversation."

> *Like a poem poorly written*
> *We are verses out of rhythm*
> *Couplets out of rhyme*
> *In syncopated time*

Now he heard the song spoken, a conversation, as if from Sally's now distant mind and voice as she used to read to him.

> *Lost in the dangling conversation . . .*
> *In the borders of our lives.*

The song faded and the Kingston Trio began "Scotch and Soda." Midway through this song, the tall man with the closely shaved head, the owner, put his hand on Scott's back and said, "Can I help?" with genuine emotion.

Scott's neck had fallen slack, and his eyes hovered over pages he couldn't see. The owner gently removed the book from his hands. Tears dotted the pages and would, if left in Scott's hands, become wet enough to ripple the paper. But the man showed clear concern for Scott and, with the regular customer still slack-necked, put his hand on the regular's back and said again, as to a neighbor, rather than a customer. "Can I help, friend?"

Scott clenched his eyes and took a deep breath. Willed the tears to stop, looked to the man, and said, "No. No you can't."

He left the bookshop, stumbled to the right of the door, and fell against the glass display window, neck arched, clenched eyes toward the sky with his new understanding, tears falling over his temples and coldly onto his ears. After a few choking sobs that were the beginning of the inevitable paroxysm he did not try to stop, Scott crouched against the wall, held his head in his hands, and sobbed.

Gone, gone.

Pedestrians paid little attention except to avoid tripping over his jutting knees. A child from another part of the country, his part, the Midwest, would have asked her mother: Why is that man crying? But this was New York, and he was just some guy weeping, and no such child passed.

Rising eventually to his full height but still supported by the book-shop's display window, he smeared the tears off his face. He removed a folded handkerchief from his back pocket and blew his nose, folded it, returned it to his pocket. He had two healthy children who were good people. He had Martha, who remained his best friend, if from nothing else then the foundation of being together for nearly three decades, no matter what secret life she had created beyond him. He would tell her he was coming home. He would convey somehow that they should let their breach scar over and try again. She had said that she wanted this. That she didn't want him to leave. He would call her and tell her he was catching the first flight home, okay?

And she, he knew, would say, "Of course, Scott, it's *our* home, all of ours." This was something, to have made something with his wife, to have created children who were good out in the world, to have written books that were still in print and read. This was important.

He walked back to the apartment. It was not yet 5 p.m.

Acknowledgments

This book is dedicated to the two people who first read the opening novella in this collection and encouraged me: Laura Yorke (my agent) and Mary Brinkmeyer (my friend). Thank you for your invaluable reads and comments. It gives me special pleasure to note that my friend Laura and I sat side by side at our graduation from Duke, in May 1985.

This book is in memory of my mentor, at Duke and beyond, Reynolds Price, who gave me the tools I needed to make my living as a writer, the only thing I ever wanted to be. It was in fact his memorial service in May 2011 that sparked the first novella. And while the character in the novel who plays my mentor's role is not nearly so generous, magnanimous, and wonderful as Reynolds himself was, some details in the novella are auto-biographical, or semi-autobiographical. In the process of working my way through the story—which began as an essay attempting to understand my relationship with him before my thoughts were hijacked by the voice of my heroine—I have used two lines from his published works, both from essays in his collection, *A Common Room:* "Letter to a Young Writer" and "A Single Meaning." Needless to say, I recommend those essays, especially to young writers. I have also quoted from a letter he once wrote to me, then a young writer who shared some similarities with the fictional young man in the story. I have always been fascinated by the interplay of fact and fiction and the fundamental nature of story to our humanity, and so I endeavor here to explain the specific uses of fact. Even a casual reader will note several thematic similarities running through all stories; I've eliminated any that were accidental. All elements of all the stories, however, should be and must be construed as fiction, which of course they are.

A number of other readers offered comments on these stories following the first reads of Laura and Mary, and I would like to thank them: Annabeth Gish, Daniel Voll and Cecilia Peck (who deserve unique thanks for reasons of which they're well aware), Annie Robbins, Rick Hawley, Ann LaGravenese, Les Jacobs, and Frank Huyler. Geoff Shapiro gave me invaluable information on the law regarding the situation the protagonists in the second story find themselves in. Finally, I owe Rob and Abby Ruhlman a debt that I will never be able to repay. I'd at least like to thank them publicly, here, for letting me cook for them and their crew at the annual Key West regatta, and leaving me alone all day with many silent hours to write these stories.

Karen Wise copy edited this book and, in doing so, helped me to make changes well beyond the catching of dangling modifiers and misspelled words. I am grateful for her thoughtful work.

Special thanks go to my editor, the fair Nicole Frail, without whose judgment I might have found myself taking long nocturnal car rides along Mulholland Drive, as well as Maha Kahlil and Sam Caggiula, and the many others at Skyhorse who have helped these stories come into being.